About the

USA Today bestselling, *RITA* nominated, and critically acclaimed author **Caitlin Crews** has written more than 130 books and counting. She has a Master's and PhD in English Literature, thinks everyone should read more category romance, and is always available to discuss her beloved alpha heroes. Just ask. She lives in the Pacific Northwest with her comic book artist husband, is always planning her next trip, and will never, ever, read all the books in her to-be-read pile. Thank goodness.

When Canadian **Dani Collins** found romance novels in high school, she wondered how one trained for such an awesome job. She wrote for over two decades without publishing, but remained inspired by the romance message that if you hang in there, you'll find a happy ending. In May of 2012, Mills & Boon Modern bought her manuscript in a two-book deal. She's since published more than forty books with Mills & Boon and is definitely living happily ever after.

Cara Lockwood has written more than thirty novels, including *I Do (But I Don't)*, which was made into a Lifetime Original Movie. She grew up near Dallas, raised by her Japanese-American Dad and Scottish/English mother. Her work has been translated into several languages. Cara lives near Chicago with her husband and five children (two by biology and three by marriage), and their eighty five-pound Goldendoodle, Theodore.

European Escapes

European Escapes:
Berlin

CAITLIN CREWS

DANI COLLINS

CARA LOCKWOOD

MILLS & BOON

First Published in Great Britain 2024
by Mills & Boon, an imprint of HarperCollins*Publishers* Ltd,
1 London Bridge Street, London, SE1 9GF

www.harpercollins.co.uk

HarperCollins*Publishers*
Macken House, 39/40 Mayor Street Upper,
Dublin 1, D01 C9W8, Ireland

European Escapes: Berlin © 2024 Harlequin Enterprises ULC.

Teach Me © 2020 Caitlin Crews
Pursued by the Desert Prince © 2017 Dani Collins
Masquerade © 2020 Cara Lockwood

ISBN: 978-0-263-32325-2

MIX
Paper | Supporting responsible forestry
FSC™ C007454
www.fsc.org

This book contains FSC™ certified paper and other controlled sources to ensure responsible forest management.

For more information visit: www.harpercollins.co.uk/green

Printed and Bound in the UK using 100% Renewable Electricity at CPI Group (UK) Ltd, Croydon, CR0 4YY

TEACH ME

CAITLIN CREWS

To Rose, in hopes you'll perform this one, too.

CHAPTER ONE

SHE WAS IN.

Finally.

Erika Vanderburg tried to breathe as elation and anticipation coursed through her in equal measure, as if in time to the deep thump of the music that wound its way around and through the crowd and seemed to rest against her clavicle. Like a heavy hand.

The notion made her warm. Maybe too warm.

Concentrate, she ordered herself.

She'd worked too hard to get in the door to waste her one chance...fluttering.

No one could simply walk into the infamous Walfreiheit Club, though many tried. The line of hopefuls stretched for acres on its once-a-month semipublic exhibition nights, like tonight. Some waited outside every night and never got in. And though Berlin was a city filled with sex clubs to suit any mood or experimental phase—or all of the above, all at once—Walfreiheit was its most exclusive.

Erika had been trying to get in the door for going on six months now. She would fly in the night before, then spend the day treating her jet lag at the Hotel Adlon Kempinski Berlin, her favorite hotel in the city. She liked to take her time selecting an outfit from the high-end shops on Friedrichstrasse before relaxing in the hotel's five-star spa. The routine was familiar now, and got her ready for a long night of waiting in line with the rest of the hopefuls outside the converted old building in East Berlin. All of them trying to look *appropriate*, whatever that meant when the place in question was an upscale bondage club. And when the opportunity to enter was entirely at the whim of whoever was at the door.

She had been reminding herself—sternly—that there was a point to all this, despite the annoyance of being denied entry month after month, when one of the terrifyingly calm and formidably solid bouncers had pointed straight at her. Erika had frozen solid.

"You," he'd said in German, then shook his head at the dark-haired woman next to Erika who surged forward. "The blonde."

Erika had been certain that he'd shake his head at her when she moved toward the door, but he didn't. He opened the rope and waved her through. It was on her to somehow…not fall apart with sheer giddiness as she was actually let in.

The Walfreiheit Club specialized in kink. Specifically BDSM, though it was whispered that definitions were kept loose to better serve the imaginations and desires of its exclusive clientele. Members played as they liked within the walls, and membership was never automatic. No amount of money could buy someone a place if the other members didn't vote them in. Unanimously. There were always stories about this or that celebrity or tycoon trying to buy his way in, only to be summarily denied, because the club did as the club liked. Always.

In the same vein, on exhibition nights, the men on the door made their selections from the vast line outside according to their fancy. Selected hopefuls were brought inside to the large, cavernous foyer where Mistress Olga waited, dressed in full fetish gear—though what was actually terrifying about her was the arch amusement she wore on her distractingly beautiful face.

Erika had not been prepared for Mistress Olga. She wasn't sure a person *could* be prepared, especially because the bouncers outside were only collecting a group of potentials for the mistress to sort through. Which she did.

With brutal precision.

The tiny yet ferocious woman reputed to be the most sought-after Domme in Berlin threw out most of the people who'd waited in that foyer with Erika at a glance. She sauntered down the line, flicking a finger to dismiss each person she didn't like. She nodded at a stunningly pretty-looking man. She studied a woman with a bowed head, then murmured an assent. By the time she'd reached Erika, she'd gotten rid of most of the people who'd been let in. And she stood there, magnificent in her spike-heeled boots that stopped midthigh, training her very cool, assessing look all over Erika until Erika rather thought she might scream. Or otherwise embarrass herself beyond repair.

She would never know how she managed to just… stand there.

"You will do," Mistress Olga pronounced, in crisp German.

Erika had been ushered into a smaller foyer, this one in all black. She and the other two selected were met by another woman, this one clearly not a Domme. Or so Erika assumed from the way she bowed her head to Mistress Olga. The three of them were made to fill out extensive paperwork, were given bright yellow wristbands that they were warned sternly not to take off, and were then treated to a long list of the club's rules and regulations.

The truth was Erika would have agreed to absolutely anything to get inside.

She'd played around with various outfits for months. How did a person broadcast the necessary submissiveness required in a place that took its sexual roles very seriously while also making sure to advertise to one specific person exactly what he'd been missing all these years? She'd fiddled with different attempts to hit that sweet spot every month. Tonight she wore a strappy little top that cupped her breasts and lifted them up, but left most of her shoulders and her midriff bare. And a tiny little skirt that flirted with the bottom curve of her ass. The only other thing she wore was a thong that peeked up over the waistband of her skirt.

It wasn't her most subtle outfit. But what was subtle about sexual escapades that started with a frank negotiation of terms, needs, expectations, desires and limits? Erika had decided to fully embrace what she was walking into.

Though that had seemed more like a power move before she was actually doing it.

"All right," she muttered to herself beneath her breath as the huge doors were opened and the three lucky selections were led through into the wall of noise and simmering dark. "You need to settle down."

The main floor of the club was big, soaring up from the open space where most of the crowd was gathered to a second-floor gallery that offered views of the action down below. And, the club submissives had told them, private playrooms. Not that a person sporting a bright yellow guest wristband would be allowed up there.

There was a bar against one wall, though that, too, was subject to strict rules. No more than two drinks for anyone who wanted to play, no exceptions, and no drinks for yellow wristbands at all. *Alcohol is a privilege of membership*, they'd been told. There were a number of small, private seating areas tucked into nooks along the dark walls, and then a wider, more open collection of sofas and tables and comfortable-looking chairs, which Erika assumed were as much for aftercare as for socializing. She'd read all about it.

There was a dance floor, and there were people out there working off their energy and anticipation—

or maybe that was just her—to the seething, brooding electronic music that filled the space. And made
everything feel edgier. Cut through with danger.

But beyond that, Erika knew thanks to the hand-
drawn map they'd been shown up front, lay the dungeon. *Here there be dungeons*, someone had written
in bold letters and they'd all laughed on cue—and
had all sounded equally nervous, to her ears.

She pulled in a breath now, then let it out in a rush.
Because she knew without a doubt that the dungeon
was where she would find him.

And she would finally be able to set her plan in
motion.

There were butterflies in her belly as she began to
make her way through the crowd, her gaze skimming
over couples in leather and latex or jeans, submissives
in various chains and collars or merely kneeling at
their dominants' feet. She took an extra moment to
admire two buff, beautiful men on the end of their
top's leash wearing bridles and jaunty tails.

She skirted the edge of the dance floor, her feet
bare against the hardwood. It felt strange to be barefoot in a club, but it was deliberate. *Submissives are
encouraged to go barefoot*, they'd been told at the
desk, where they'd surrendered their phones, wallets,
coats and bags, as well as their shoes.

Erika would have worn clown shoes if asked, and
had thought it was a silly request meant to make
the club more mysterious—but now she got it. The
wood beneath her feet felt silky and warm. It was
one more sensation to add to the mix. The heat of

so many bodies in one space. The cool prickle of air moving over the flesh she'd left uncovered. She could feel her pulse pick up as she wove her way through the crowd, carefully keeping her gaze averted from anyone she passed.

Especially if they had that particular look about them, too calm and too direct, that she knew meant they were dominants.

Erika was wearing the costume of a submissive, and she'd experimented a little with the whole power-exchange thing, but she intended to explore it further with only one very specific person. Starting tonight.

It had taken her six months to get in the door tonight, but she'd spent years working her way here, one way or another. She'd danced nearly naked beneath the desert sky one summer, then experimented in the red-light district out there in Black Rock City. That had been illuminating, if dusty, and it had spearheaded her own little journey. She'd followed her libido wherever it took her, aware that there was a restlessness in her but never sure quite how to address it. She'd tried partying. She'd tried spiritual retreats. She'd done yoga in Santa Monica and she'd surfed in Bali. She'd hiked and she'd communed and still, that restlessness had dogged her.

That had been true since she'd dropped out of university after her second year, but Erika had felt an enormous sense of relief when she'd packed up her things and left Oxford behind. She'd felt less sanguine about her choices when her officious, tight-assed older brother, Conrad—in his role as head of

the family that he'd assumed after their father had
died, which Erika felt he'd taken to a little too read-
ily and far too sternly—had cut off her financial
support.

"I'm not supporting you while you waste your
life," he'd said after he'd summoned her to his pala-
tial home in Paris.

She'd rolled her eyes. "I'm actually *getting* a life,
Conrad."

"Get it with a job, then," he'd retorted.

And could not be swayed, epic asshole that he
was.

Erika had gone right out and found herself a job in
a dive bar in New Orleans, because she was sure that
would gall her uppity brother, and she'd had every
intention of paying her own way to make her own
fun. But then her dramatic, theatrically self-involved
mother had swept in and restored Erika's access to
the family money, because the only thing Chriszette
Vanderburg feared was not having strings to pull on
to control her offspring.

At first, Erika had resisted, because she didn't
want to answer to anyone. Especially not a member
of her family. But Chriszette had implored her and
Erika had given in because Chriszette was difficult
to ignore and harder still to deny, and that was how
she'd ended up acting like a paid companion when
her mother was between torrid love affairs. And having to find new ways to ask for money without ever
being so crass and vulgar as to *ask* for it the rest of
the time.

But what she'd really missed in that time was not Conrad, who could shove his tough love up his own ass as far as Erika was concerned. She didn't care if he treated her like a walking disaster, because really, he always had. What she missed was the occasional access to Dorian.

She shuddered a little, involuntarily, as that name—*his* name—rolled through her the way it always did.

Dorian Alexander was her older brother's best friend, stretching back to their boarding school days. They had been thrown together at age eight and had been fast friends from the start. She had heard Conrad refer to Dorian as his brother.

But he was not Erika's brother.

The last time she'd seen Dorian, it had been at the family charity ball his shipping magnate grandfather threw each year in Athens. Erika had gone with her mother, who liked to order her daughter to serve as her date at such things when she didn't have a lover on hand. And yes, if she was honest, Erika had accompanied her mother to an event she could have talked her way out of for the distinct, petty pleasure of flaunting herself in front of her brother.

Conrad had been icily civil. Though Erika had seen that telltale muscle going wild in his jaw and had smugly enjoyed the satisfaction of shooting him an unmistakable middle finger simply by turning up and *not* begging him to reconsider.

Dorian had not followed Conrad's lead. He had been distinctly uncivil when Erika had chirped a greeting his way, and her stomach had knotted up with a strange heat when he'd stared at her. Unsmiling.

"Why don't you dance with me?" Erika had asked him, feeling reckless and daring. Where Conrad was infinitely disapproving and always annoyed by Erika's existence, Dorian had always been...stern. But there was something about the particular intensity of that sternness and the frank way he looked at her—at everything—that had always made Erika feel...silly.

That night she'd decided to lean into the silliness. And besides, she'd been wearing a sparkly dress that bared most of her back and hinted at her ass. Okay, more than *hinted*. She'd wondered how long he'd stay *stern* if he had his hands on her.

"I don't dance with little brats in the middle of temper tantrums," Dorian had said. Calmly.

And she'd never understood how he could do that. How he could look at her in a certain way, usually while saying obnoxious things to her, and it only made her want to giggle. Or maybe melt. Or worse, both, while the knotted heat inside her seemed to thump its way lower the longer he looked at her.

"That sounds like Conrad-sourced propaganda," she'd said, laughing.

Because she was afraid that if she didn't laugh, she'd do something far more embarrassing.

Dorian did not laugh. He was a tall, extraordinarily well built man. That had been true when he was in high school and Erika had seen him on the odd holiday he'd spent with Conrad's family instead of his own. But time clearly loved him. He looked as if he was chiseled from stone, his lean muscle honed to perfection. His dark hair was closely cropped, yet somehow gave the impression he'd only moments before run his fingers through it. His eyes were a cool coffee brown, excruciatingly intense. Powerful. His cheekbones were so high they made Erika think of arias.

And his mouth was always set in that firm line. She'd spent a lot of time staring at it over the years, so she knew its every slight quirk and the raw sensuality that seemed to brood its way out of him no matter how stern he looked at any given moment.

But the look he gave her at that ball in Athens was pitiless.

"Is it propaganda or simple truth that you flounced out of university and refused to return?" he asked coolly.

"I wouldn't call it *flouncing*."

She expected him to launch into a screed on the importance of education. Or to discuss the firsts he and Conrad had received when they'd gone up, because of course they had. She'd wanted him to, really, because surely if he was horrendously boring and too much like Conrad she'd stop feeling so *lit up* when she saw him.

Dorian was not the only person around who disliked Erika, well she knew. But he was the only one whose dislike she *felt* so keenly. And the only one whose dislike did not result in her immediate indifference.

But Dorian did not wax rhapsodic about the dubious charms of an Oxbridge degree as expected. "Your brother has far more patience with willful disobedience than I would," he'd said instead.

"I'm not sure I would consider cutting off his only sister very patient," Erika had replied, not sure why she felt flushed. With a surprising wallop of what couldn't be shame, surely. And something else she hadn't wanted to name. "But I suppose your mileage may vary."

"I don't negotiate disobedience," Dorian had said in that same quiet, intense way. His gaze was fierce and disapproving and, worse, made her shiver. "I punish it."

Erika hadn't known what had come over her then. It was part of that flush that seemed to deepen by the moment. Red and everywhere and what was *happening* to her?

She'd tilted her head to one side. "How would you punish me?"

Dorian hadn't smiled. If anything, he'd looked more forbidding. And harder, somehow, though he didn't move or shift as far as she could see. Erika had felt herself go a little weak, even as she'd felt herself get wet and needy between her legs.

Right there in a fancy dress, in a room where her mother and brother also stood.

And that restless thing in her...settled. Into a kind of expectant stillness she'd never felt before in her life.

"I generally start with a spanking," he'd said very distinctly. "And not the kind you'd think was fun,

Erika. The kind that would encourage you to change your behavior."

"Or what?" she managed to ask, though her voice was barely above a whisper.

His eyes had gleamed. And she could swear there was something like a curve to his hard mouth. "Or I would be even more disappointed with you than I already am."

And it was at that moment that a great many things about her older brother's best friend came together for Erika. With the force of a blow—or, perhaps, that spanking.

Dorian had sauntered away as if nothing had happened. As if Erika was breathing normally and wasn't the least bit overheated and reeling. The genteel crowd had swallowed up that gorgeous body of his, dressed in black tie that somehow managed to suggest that he was from another time.

Her blood had thudded inside her, making her heart feel heavy and her head light. And the sense that he'd spanked her without putting a hand on her only seemed to grow, turning into an ache. An ache that spread, then went deep.

All the whispers that followed in Dorian's wake made a different kind of sense suddenly. The very specific way certain women looked at him, as if they knew a secret about him. Erika had always thought it was simply because he was so powerful, with all that Alexander family money augmented by the tech company he'd gone and started himself after university. Apparently feeling that where there was one fortune, there might as well be two.

And when she began looking specifically for rumors about Dorian Alexander in darker, more shadowy places... Well. That was when she'd really found him. And it hadn't taken a whole lot of digging to learn that Dorian was famous for a great many things in the wider, more civilized world, but when it came to sex he was a king of a whole different sort.

In fact, they called him Master.

Her schoolgirl crush flipped inside out and turned into something far more edgy.

Particularly because, the more she thought about Dorian and spanking—and Dorian spanking her, for that matter—all her vague fantasies and all her sexual explorations seemed to spark into something new. And much, much hotter.

She'd experimented with light bondage and a few tame scenes in clubs in New York. London. Lisbon. She'd spent a particularly hot and steamy winter down under in Melbourne, playing top and bottom games with some new friends. And anytime it got to be too much, playing dominance games with tops who were never quite what she wanted, she thought of Dorian.

Master Dorian, as he was known. Master Dorian, who had used to scene quite a bit in the clubs—especially in Berlin, at the Walfreiheit—but did so less and less these days. Master Dorian, who was a legend and a favorite fantasy of pretty much every submissive she met.

Master Dorian, who had nothing to prove, had never given a submissive his collar and was the only thing Erika could take from her brother that he would miss.

He'd had no use for her as a supposedly spoiled rotten socialite, sure. But would he feel differently about her as a submissive?

It was time to find out.

She felt her pulse pick up when she saw the displays as she made her way into the dungeon. A pretty girl strapped to a table while her Domme applied all manner of wicked-looking clamps to her, murmuring encouragement as she shuddered and squirmed. In the next room, a Dom was working his submissive into a series of intricate and beautiful shibari knots, as if she was an installation piece, there with her ass in the air and her face to the floor. One scene bled into the next. Threesomes. Fireplay. Suspension. One erotic fantasy brought to life after another.

But the biggest throng of onlookers had flocked to the biggest space, toward the back, and Erika headed in that direction. Even though she felt something shiver over her, like foreboding.

Because she knew what she would see. They'd all heard the whispers out there in line, that Master Dorian was picking up his whip tonight for the first time in ages. That he was putting on a show.

But God help her, she wasn't prepared.

Dorian stood on a raised dais, facing a Saint Andrew's Cross. A woman was strapped to it, straining against her bonds, moving her head back and forth in erotic distress. That alone made Erika's belly quiver.

But Dorian took her breath away.

He looked darker and more dangerous than she remembered him, dressed in dark trousers, boots and a black T-shirt that managed to hug that remarkable chest of his like an obsessed lover. Every single one of the muscles she'd marveled at when he was clad in black tie was on display. And more, like his mouthwatering expanse of sheer abdominal fitness.

And it was hard not to appreciate his glorious corded arms as he wielded that lethal, deliciously terrifying whip.

Erika's mouth went dry. She felt her eyes go glassy, but she couldn't look away. She felt rooted to the spot as surely as if it was her up there on the cross, writhing, tears wetting her own cheeks while cuffs kept her exactly where he wanted her.

Meanwhile, Dorian made the whip dance.

He was murmuring in a low voice and the woman responded, and it took Erika some time to understand that he was telling her exactly where each strike would land. Then he waited as she writhed, moaned.

But each time she quivered. Then said distinctly, "Yes, Master Dorian. Please."

Yes, Master Dorian. Please.

The words jolted through Erika like a live wire. Like the kiss of that terrible whip, landing precisely where he said it would.

He was controlled, precise. Beautiful and terrible, like an angel. He moved like a furious dancer, a dark and mighty cloud, and Erika thought the whole crowd was as breathless and undone as she was.

And for the first time since that party in Athens, Erika thought to ask herself what in the hell she was thinking.

All her little sex games were just that. Games. But Dorian was very plainly the real thing. She'd been charging up a gentle slope and calling it a mountain, and it was only now that she understood the enormity of her error. She wanted to poke at her brother, not...this. A whip and a crowd and that hungry, greedy thing she could feel turn over inside her and bare its fangs.

She didn't want *that*. Erika felt exposed, even though she stood with everyone else, and knew no one was looking at her. Still, she felt vibrant with embarrassment and panic. Most of all she felt deeply, remarkably silly. Foolish.

The brat he'd called her, and more.

She needed to leave. Now. Before she made an even bigger fool of herself.

But she couldn't seem to tear herself away. The scene on the dais went on. The whip licked over the submissive on the stage, bringing her closer and closer to that brutally perfect end that Erika could feel all over her. Her own nipples were hard. She was much too wet. She wanted to *squirm* but she didn't dare move. Or she couldn't move.

And then, finally, he asked and was answered with a sob. But a *yes, Master Dorian, please*, all the same. Dorian shot out his arm. The whip cracked.

Then landed with merciless precision on the submissive's exposed clit.

The girl on the cross screamed, her body shaking wildly as she arched into a climax, her body like a bow against the cross. Out there in the dark of the audience, rooted to the floor and still bright red with the realization that she shouldn't have come here at all, Erika felt her own body clench and tremble, as if she was on the same slippery edge.

That was when Dorian stopped. He looked out toward the crowd and the murmurs of appreciation. He looked as if he might smile.

But then he saw her.

She felt the impact of those fierce, intense eyes. She saw the flare of recognition.

And without a single hand upon her—without anything but that outraged gaze of his—Erika felt herself catapult straight over that edge.

Hard.

CHAPTER TWO

HIS BEST FRIEND'S little sister was coming right there on the floor of his club.

That it was impossible—that she shouldn't be in the club, or dressed like that, or witness to his particular enthusiasms without his knowledge or approval—didn't change the fact that it was happening. Right there before Dorian Alexander's astonished eyes.

Her climax rolled over her, and he could see entirely too many things about little Erika Vanderburg, then, that he understood in a flash he would never be able to unsee.

Her plump, high breasts and her hard and proud nipples that poked out from behind the top she wore, begging for his mouth. Or better yet, his clamps. Her exposed abdomen, a sensuous display of softly toned female flesh that quivered with the force of her orgasm. And low on her hips, so low he could see her thong poke up above the waistband, she wore a skirt so tiny it hardly deserved the name, making him think that if she shivered *that much more* he might actually catch a glimpse of her pussy, too.

The mental image he'd carried around forever of little Erika, maybe age ten, with pigtails he wasn't sure she'd ever actually worn, went up in smoke.

His gaze shot back up to find hers. Her eyes were heavy-lidded and flooded with arousal. And something else the dominant in him was delighted to see looked a whole lot like the kind of panic that made a good scene sing.

Dorian had been reasonably aroused throughout his whipping demonstration, because he loved what a whip could do to a trembling, beautifully bound woman who let it kiss her and carry her off into bliss. He didn't understand anyone who claimed they didn't.

But looking at Erika—and that ferocious orgasm that still held her in its grip—he was suddenly as ragingly turned-on as if instead of a demonstration he'd been deep in a scene he expected to end in his own release.

That's Conrad's little sister, something in him protested, but his body didn't seem to care. His body saw only a lovely submissive, flushed and wide-eyed and panting—just the way he liked them—and all she'd been doing was watching him whip someone else.

Dorian couldn't permit himself to focus on that, so he focused instead on what he was supposed to be doing on that dais in the first place. Which was demonstrating one of his hobbies for the assembled club members and tourists here on one of the club's exhibition nights. Only a split second had passed, he was sure of it, despite the fact that to him it felt like a lifetime or two—but it was still a loss of focus.

It didn't matter how long it was. His lapse of attention galled him. He was no novice, for God's sake.

He moved over to the cross, murmuring to Angelica as he released her from her cuffs, soothing her as they both waited for her permanent dom to climb up to the dais and take charge of her aftercare. Dorian had to make himself focus the way he should have been already, because what was important here was caring for Angelica, not a bratty little sub—

Sister, he snapped at himself. Bratty little *sister*. Of his best friend. A man who was more family than friend, as a matter of fact, and who Dorian knew would be distinctly unamused at the idea that his wild-child baby sister knew a club like Walfreiheit existed. He didn't want to think about Conrad's reaction to the news that she was going around climaxing in public and, worse still, because of Dorian.

When Angelica was off the cross and in her dominant's care, Dorian's responsibilities to her were finished. He handled his equipment and packed it away, then straightened. He turned slowly, not entirely convinced that Erika hadn't been a figment of his imagination. Though why he would conjure up such a maddening little brat he spent very little time thinking about unless she was right there in front of him, he had no idea. He searched the crowd, half expecting to find no trace of her. He would find a blonde sub who reminded him of Erika instead, and the good news was, he would know exactly what to do with *her*. He would tie her up, make her scream and cry and come, and exorcise this strange demon he hadn't known lurked about inside him.

But Erika was right where he'd left her. The actual Erika Vanderburg, his best friend's little sister, in the disturbingly succulent flesh. She stood stock-still on the hardwood floor, gaping at the stage.

At him.

When their eyes met again, Dorian could feel the temperature rise, then sizzle.

He told himself it was sheer outrage.

Her eyes widened. Dorian lifted an arrogant brow in reply. It was usually sufficient to make submissive knees bend. Hers appeared to tremble, which sent a kind of shock straight through him. And even up on the dais he could see the gulp of air she took in.

He wasn't surprised when she turned around and dived through the crowd as if she actually believed she could run away from him. Here in this club that in some seasons had operated as his second home. He wasn't *surprised*, but still, the fact she was try-ing to escape him made something in him, dark and hungry…wake up.

Then focus. On her.

Intently.

He jumped down to the floor, following her through the crowd. He was aware that the people parted before him to let him through, the way they always did. He was vaguely cognizant of the usual congratulations and sultry little come-ons from the hopeful unattached submissives who followed him around in packs on nights like this, but he was focused on his quarry. He stalked her through the crowd, feeling a kick of satisfaction as she looked around wildly—then turned deeper into the dungeons rather than out toward the bar.

He followed, nodding at his friends as he passed. He was in clear pursuit of Erika, and he didn't have to say a word to explain himself. Master Dorian stalked no submissives when they all flocked to him, and here he was, going after this one.

She might as well have worn his name around her neck.

A not-unpleasant thought.

Which really should have horrified him.

It did, he assured himself. Of course it did. No matter why she'd come here.

Though the notion that she might have come tonight to play with others filled him with a hollow sort of heat that took him a moment or two to realize wasn't simply temper.

It was deeper. Richer.

He recognized his own rare possessiveness—and should have turned around right then and there.

But he didn't.

She was walking faster, very nearly running while doing her best not to look as if she was doing any such thing. Dorian followed, taking the opportunity to control his breath. To settle himself down. To make sure that he was in complete control of himself, as he always fought to be, no matter what

Erika Vanderburg was doing here or that bright fire that burned in him and seemed to spell out her name.

Erika made another mistake, cutting toward what he imagined she thought was a hallway. And it was, but Dorian knew the far door was locked on a night like this, when nonmembers roamed the premises and didn't have permission to wander all the different areas of the Walfreiheit Club as they pleased.

He slowed down, checking in with his control again and trying to separate the dominant in him from her older brother's best friend—no matter his cock's take on the matter. By the time he made it to the mouth of the narrow hall that usually functioned as a shortcut to the club's offices, Erika was already turned back around, clearly having realized there was no escape.

Then she saw him.

She jolted as if he'd used his whip on her, which, predictably, made him imagine doing exactly that— though that was a privilege she would have to earn.

No, he reminded himself. *Not her. Not Conrad's little sister.*

Dorian followed her into the hallway, casually blocking any possible exit. The hall was narrow and not exactly brightly lit—but not so dim he couldn't see that her eyes were wide. And he wasn't sure how he'd never noticed before that they were a particular shade of blue that reminded him of his grandfather's island nestled out there in the Aegean Sea.

He couldn't say he cared much for the comparison now.

He stopped when he was a foot or so away from her. He folded his arms over his chest, widened his stance and waited.

And Erika quivered. He could see the pulse in her neck, banging out exactly the sort of rhythm he liked best. She shifted her weight from foot to foot, betraying her anxiety. He had made a study of the female body in various degrees of erotic distress and he could read her easily. And still, she pulled out that careless, reckless smile of hers that she had to know always put Conrad's teeth on edge.

It reminded him, as nothing else could, what an eternal pain in the ass she was and always had been.

"Oh," she said carelessly, as if this was a chance meeting at some desperately boring society event. Some overdressed, overstuffed ball or other. "Hi, Dorian."

He knew distantly how he ought to feel about this. Unamused, certainly. Even annoyed, because this was a complication he hadn't foreseen and Dorian liked surprises only when he could control their outcome. Which was to say, he didn't like surprises. His childhood had cured him of that. He should have been thinking through how best to break the news to Conrad—and, of course, how quickly he could bundle Erika out of the club, into some decent clothes, and then dispatch her back to wherever it was she had come from. He knew that was what Conrad would have wanted.

He knew how he *should* feel, but instead, the things that beat in him were all too familiar...for very different reasons. She looked flushed and ready, her feet bare and her skin exposed, her pretty breasts thrust toward him while she fought to catch her breath. She looked like a brand-new submissive in the grip of the frenzy that often made them adorably reckless. She looked good enough to eat.

And Dorian might have found himself jaded and restless of late—wondering if it was time to stop playing and start thinking about settling down into the life his grandfather wanted for him, and wanted to see before he died—but a pretty blonde submissive with that particular hot awe in her eyes and a slight tremble to her lips…

Well. *He* wasn't dead yet.

"Try again," he suggested softly.

She shifted from foot to foot again, and it took every bit of his considerable willpower to keep his hands to himself. But Dorian was anything but newly minted. He knew very well the power in simply… waiting. Expectantly.

He studied her as he did, wondering how it was he'd never paid such close attention to Conrad's little sister before…

But even as he thought that, he knew that wasn't true. He'd certainly seen her when she'd turned up in a backless gown at his grandfather's charity ball in Athens one year, enlivening an otherwise staid and boring gala. There had been that split second when he hadn't known who she was, but he'd wrestled *that* under control. And done nothing more than chastise her a little.

He certainly hadn't let her get him hard.

The Conrad's-little-sister part, of course, had always governed his reactions to her, as well it should. He had to be ten years older than her. But when had she become this lush? With all that smooth, apparently blemish-free skin that made his mouth water as he considered how best to leave his mark—

No. She's Conrad little sister. She might as well be yours.

But that thought didn't really land. It certainly didn't impress his cock.

Because he could remember that dress much too distinctly. Erika had worn it for the precise purpose of rendering her brother apoplectic, that much was clear. Dorian remembered murmuring something soothing to his friend, likely about the established brattiness of younger sisters—not that he had any personal experience in that area. Then he'd glanced over and found his eyes drawn to the mouthwatering line of a beautiful woman's graceful back, bared entirely by a dress that flirted with the curve of her ass.

He could remember it in stark, unwavering detail. Even now, years later.

Maybe he'd seen Erika all along.

That night it had taken one second, maybe less, before he realized he was looking at precisely the dress that had his friend in fits. One second before he'd understood he was looking at Erika. He'd sternly reminded himself that Erika was ever and only a brat. Ungrateful, immature. Forever embroiled in her juvenile attempts to poke at Conrad. Pigtails. Freckles. Stuck in amber at ten years old.

That was how he knew her. It was the only way he knew her.

But now his cock was heavy, she was in his club, and he couldn't pretend he hadn't eyed her then exactly the same way he did now. Like a dessert he couldn't wait to get his teeth in.

A sweet little bite he wanted to taste. Over and over again.

Some men saw a pretty thing and wanted to lock it away in a tower somewhere. Dorian, on the other hand, wanted to mess it up. But only if she begged.

He almost had to adjust himself.

"This is *so* funny," she was saying, brazening her way through this in a way he almost had to admire. She squared her shoulders and held his gaze boldly, as if she was up to any challenge he might put to her. Which he doubted very much. "What a surprise to run into you, of all people. I'm in town for the weekend. One of my friends was talking about his favorite clubs a month or so ago and I couldn't resist checking them all out. There's one in Singapore that—"

"Do not lie to me, please." His voice sliced across hers and stopped her dead. "You're well aware I live in Berlin."

She dared to roll her eyes at him, and Dorian's brows rose in sheer astonishment. He couldn't recall the last time a submissive in this club—or anywhere else, for that matter—had presumed to treat him with such blatant disrespect. They were usually far too intimidated. He should have been furious. He was. But even so, that spark in him bloomed into a hotter, darker fire.

"It's a big city, Dorian," she declared, lifting the stubborn chin that anchored her heart-shaped face—and he really should not have been noticing things like that about her. "I had no idea that if I wanted to find you, which I didn't, all I had to do was poke my head into the nearest den of iniquity."

"No one pokes their head into Walfreiheit. You had to wait in line. You had to be dressed appropriately, yet evocatively. And then you have to make it past Mistress Olga, who has an unerring eye for posers and too-casual visitors. Would you like to try telling the truth?" Her lips parted, and he enjoyed watching her cast around for an answer. And enjoyed it even more when she didn't. "My mistake, Erika. I assumed this must be some kind of social call. That you'd come here to seek me out specifically."

"Of course not." But the pulse in her neck told him otherwise. Interesting. "Why would I? I already know that you're Team Conrad. I prefer to avoid his minions whenever possible." Again, that reckless smile. "You know how it is."

He understood she was trying to provoke him. And she was—only not in the way she likely imagined.

"How fortunate, then, that you should run into a familiar face," he said quietly. "In the midst of your heretofore unknown exploration of power exchanges in all their glory. I had no idea you were hiding a thirst for submission beneath your fluffy, spoiled exterior."

Her eyes widened further. She started to say something, but it came out as a breath instead. He liked it. Poor little submissive girl. So afraid of what she wanted.

Dorian needed to remind himself that she wasn't just another new submissive. She was Conrad's baby sister. And this couldn't happen.

But he didn't walk away.

"Well," she said nervously. "I mean, I can't say that I *wanted* to see a familiar face here. Nobody *wants* to see a familiar face when they're watching a grown man whip a naked woman until she…"

Her voice petered out. Dorian only watched her, keeping his expression just this side of a scowl until she flushed again.

"Until she came," he supplied. "And so did you." He smiled faintly when her throat worked, but no sound came forth. "If this is not a specific social call, that means you are here to play like anyone else. And I regret to inform you that you have already shown me entirely too much disrespect."

"What are you talking about? You're the one who followed me down a dark hallway to loom over me and frown dramatically. Maybe *you* should be concerned about respecting *me*."

Dorian studied her, unsmiling. "This is primarily a BDSM club and you present as a sexual submissive. Do you know what that means?"

"Of course I know what it means."

"Is that an incorrect label for you? The girls at the door are usually much better at teasing out our visitors' secret wants and needs. Surely they told you that the pink wristband you're wearing announces your preferences to all and sundry."

She scowled down at the wristband in question and tugged at it. It sat next to the yellow wristband that announced she was here only for the night, which was why she had no bright blue wristbands, one for each alcoholic beverage patrons were allowed if they wanted to participate in any play.

"I can't hear you," he prompted her. "Is that the wrong wristband?"

"This club is obsessed with labels. You know that, don't you?"

"Indeed it is. Let's be clear that you as a person can be as complicated and contradictory as you please outside these doors. In here, however, everything is boiled down to its essence. What you want. What you need. And what you are prepared to negotiate to get it."

Her rebellious chin lifted. "Plus neon wristbands."

"If you are certain a label cannot contain you, perhaps you had better ask yourself if that's the truth. Are you so terribly complex? Or are you terrified that if you took the trouble to look inside yourself you would find that at heart, where it matters, you are remarkably simple after all?"

She jerked at that as if he'd slapped her. And he wondered if she knew how dark her eyes got, telling him secrets he doubted she wanted to share.

"The only thing you know about me is who I'm related to," she threw at him, as if he'd mounted a vicious personal attack. He filed that away. "So maybe you should take the opportunity to ask yourself why you're such an egregious asshole to a person you hardly know."

Dorian smiled. "Is it clear to you that I am a dominant, Erika? And was that clear from the moment you saw me here tonight?"

"Yes," she snapped. "But I…"

"Kneel."

Dorian was in absolutely no doubt of his own power. He enjoyed playing with the wielding of it. And he might have been thrown by the sight of Erika Vanderburg dressed like a submissive wet dream, but he didn't think it was a coincidence that she was in Walfreiheit. He didn't believe she was on a club tour and had accidentally happened on him here.

Couple that with her complaints about "labels" and he had no particular reason to think that she was submissive, either.

Or more accurately, he knew she was a submissive. He could see it every time she looked at him. That longing to yield, but only to a worthy dominant force. To pit herself against his will and chase her own surrender into all the places polite society feared to tread. What he didn't know was whether or not she would allow herself to play with that need in her, or if she was the sort of person who preferred to pretend she never entertained any dark fantasies there in the privacy of her mind.

There was only one way to find out.

"What did you…?" she managed to get out while goose bumps marched down her arms and told him more truths.

"Do you need me to repeat myself?"

He watched, more fascinated than he wanted to admit, as she waged an internal battle. He could see it. Ordinarily he would have no trouble admitting he was fascinated and hard, but this was different. Because while watching a woman fight to do the very thing they both wanted—when she was as aroused by the notion as she was afraid of it—was one of life's greatest pleasures, in his experience, this was Erika.

He didn't know if she would do it.

Or what would happen if she did.

Dorian kept his expression impassive as he watched her struggle there before him. Her pretty face broadcast every last one of her emotions, making it easy to watch her cycle through defiance, longing, fear and a bright flash of straightforward need.

He didn't help her. He only waited, wondering how exactly she would handle this if she was not, in fact, as submissive as he thought she was.

"Did you say…kneel?"

She sounded almost hopeful. As if he might change his mind.

"You do not have to do anything you don't want to do, Erika," he told her, his voice low and his gaze hard. "*Safe*, *sane* and *consensual* aren't simply words we throw around for fun. But I should warn you, this is not a club where submissives balk at something as simple as kneeling to show respect. You can negotiate high protocol with whatever Dom you like, but they will all expect you to kneel. You might as well practice, don't you think?" He waited a moment while she breathed a bit too hard. "If submission is what you want."

"I just… I mean, I only…" Her eyes were slicked over with panic, but he could see the way she kept dancing from toe to toe. Dorian knew this dance. He knew that if he reached between her legs he would find her wet and hot. Better to let her dance it out. "I mean, maybe…"

"Is it our personal connection that has you so flustered?" he asked. Pitilessly. "Would you prefer I summon one of the other masters?"

She appeared to like that even less.

Which he could admit he liked a great deal more.

"I guess… I guess I thought there would be more of a buildup. This feels a lot like going from first to fourth gear in about twelve seconds, doesn't it?"

"Erika." Her name made her shiver, then still. "If this isn't what you want, I will escort you to the bar. You can have as many nonalcoholic drinks as you like, perhaps dance to the music, and feel exhilarated that you were this close to so much edgy deviance. We always expect a certain number of tourists on nights like this. There's no shame in it. But you need to tell me what you want."

"I want…"

"If you don't know how to say it, you can start the

conversation very simply." He tilted his head, indicating the ground beneath her feet. "Simply kneel."

She moved her hands to her belly, as if her stomach was knotting up. Or fluttering. Or any other of the lovely, delicious reactions she could have been having.

She shot a glance behind him, almost wistfully. But Dorian didn't move.

And in that moment, when she pulled her gaze back to his and her cheeks got even redder, Dorian had to ask himself what it was *he* wanted. Did he want her to kneel? Or did he want her to break, flip out and prove that she had come here only on one of her bratty excursions calculated to irritate Conrad more?

It was more than a little confronting that he didn't quite know the answer.

Liar, something in him whispered. *You know what you want.*

As if she heard, Erika blew out a breath.

And then, as Dorian watched, his best friend's little sister sank to her knees on the floor before him, tilted up her face and surrendered.

CHAPTER THREE

ERIKA HAD NEVER knelt before a man in her life. Not… just to kneel. And certainly not because she'd been *told* to kneel. If she'd ever been in this position before, there had been action. She'd been *doing* something. Usually something that put all the power back in her hands. Or her mouth, more likely.

This was not a blow job. This was…completely different. It was electrifying.

She couldn't breathe, and she wasn't sure that she would ever be the right temperature again. She felt much too hot, nearly feverish, though she knew she wasn't sick. It was that fire in her that seemed to burn and burn and burn, hotter and wilder the longer he looked at her so sternly. Erika was sure that her face was the color of ripe tomatoes. She was shaking, everywhere—inside and out—as if she'd done something extraordinary.

And all he did was gaze down at her, his expression uncompromising.

"Very pretty," he said after a moment.

Erika wanted to say something sarcastic. Poke

at him, maybe. Or perhaps make a joke. Anything to lighten the mood, or make the fire in her dim a little, or counter the bizarre sense of *relief* she felt that he'd complimented her, but that didn't seem to be possible. She couldn't make her mouth do what she wanted it to do.

Because the more he gazed down at her, apparently perfectly happy to stand there all night, the more she was aware of all the other parts of her body. The way her thighs felt, splayed wide beneath the short, short skirt she'd chosen to wear. The cool kiss of the floor beneath her knees and shins. Her bare toes were cool, and it felt like a notable, erotic contrast to how confined her chest and her breasts felt in the strappy top. When she'd put it on earlier, it had felt almost loose, but not now. Now she thought another deep breath would pop the straps, and expose all of her to him.

That notion should have scared her, but it didn't.

Or it didn't *completely* scare her.

She could feel her heart, beating so fast it thudded in her ears like her own personal drum. And like a thick pulse in her pussy, a staccato beat in her nipples and a riot in her chest. Everywhere else, her exposed skin felt much too warm.

Erika didn't really understand any of this. She didn't understand the reaction she'd had to Dorian with a whip in his hand. A *whip*. She didn't understand the roaring, greedy thing that had walloped her in that crowd, that had made her come and then made her run, like opposite sides of the same too-hot coin.

She'd thought that she was so edgy when she'd played around with handcuffs and a blindfold and a soft little flogger thing, but she'd been kidding herself. This was like a completely different language, and she didn't know how to speak a single word of it.

She couldn't find the words, but he'd told her to kneel and she had.

And really, Erika didn't understand why kneeling before a man didn't make her angry. Why, instead, what coursed through her felt a whole lot more like that same dark, greedy hunger that had taken her over earlier.

When Erika had always preferred her orgasms sweet and quick, spring showers to dance in rather than the crash and immensity of a sea that could eat her alive.

"I normally prefer submissives to keep their eyes lowered at first," Dorian said in that low voice of his that somehow made it sound as if what was happening between them was normal.

Because it was, she reminded herself sharply. And maybe with a touch of panic. For him, this was any old night at the club. The only difference was that she was his best friend's little sister.

Something about that fact—which she'd known full well while she'd spent all these months trying to get herself into this very position, not to mention most of her life—twisted in her differently now. It made her feel even hotter suddenly.

Erika tried to focus on what he'd said.

"Why do you want their eyes lowered?" she demanded, and she did not avert her gaze. Instead, she glared at him. "Because you hate women?"

"Because I love what it does to a woman when she surrenders herself into my hands," Dorian said. "By her choice. And your impertinence is noted. If I were you, I would rethink that glare."

That shouldn't make her thighs clench, but it did. And for a moment, she thought her pussy might take over again, catapulting her toward another climax she didn't want and couldn't make any sense of. She tried to fight it back.

And that gleam in his dark eyes made her think he knew exactly what was happening inside her. When he couldn't. Could he?

"But I can tell you're brand-new, Erika," he said then, and he had to know how riled up she was, or why else would he sound so *satisfied*? "So I will give you more leeway than I would otherwise." He tilted his head slightly to one side, that assessing look as cool as it was stirring. "And I find I quite like the way you look at me."

Whatever snarky remark she'd meant to throw at him died there in her mouth. Because she couldn't help thinking he looked more like a wolf. Poised to take the leap that would take his quarry down.

He looked as if he could pounce at any moment.

And it was hard, once again, to catch her breath.

"Let me tell you the rules," Dorian said.

"They told us at the door," she all but threw at him, filled to the brim with a kind of desperation she didn't recognize. Did she want to poke at him—or please him? "Green light is *yes*, yellow light is *I'm not sure* and red light is *stop*."

"Are you satisfied with that system as your safe word?" He studied her and he was so *thorough*. It made her ache. "Let me backtrack. Do you know what a safe word is?"

"Of course I know what a safe word is," she said. Or really snapped. Making no effort to modulate her cranky tone. "I read *Fifty Shades* like everybody else."

Dorian did not wince. Not exactly. And yet she was in no doubt that he'd come as close to rolling his eyes as she'd ever seen. "This is not the place to mention that book, if you please."

And Erika realized that she hadn't...*forgotten* she was kneeling, necessarily. It was impossible to *forget*. But it had changed into something else.

She felt quivery, the way she had before. It seemed to go straight through her, as if kneeling on the ground at Dorian's feet had plugged her into an electrical current and it kept pouring into her. Making her sizzle and burn.

But the panic was gone. She felt calmer, somehow, when surely it should have been the opposite. Surely she should have been too outraged and weirded out to stay in that position—but the longer she stayed there, exposed and vulnerable, the more she started to feel something utterly contradictory.

Safe.

"What are your hard limits?" Dorian asked in that cool way of his. But not quite clinically, she could see. There was that intensity in his gaze. The way he held hers.

It was as if she was nothing but a bright pebble closed tight in his fist.

She had no idea where that image came from. Or why she reacted to it the way she did, everywhere—from a breath that shivered out too hot to that melting, aching fever in her pussy.

"My hard limits?"

"Repeating a question is not answering it, Erika. Try again."

She thought she might be sweating. "Um. I mean..."

"I'm not familiar with those sexual practices. Enlighten me."

"There are just so many things," she said, because she had to say something. Even if it was desperate.

"Then perhaps we should narrow it down."

One of his dark brows rose, and she had the vague notion that it made him look demonic. What it did not do was detract in any way from his appeal. Maybe, she thought wildly, there really was something the matter with her. But she didn't rise from her knees. She didn't bolt again, the way some part of her wanted to do.

But only so he can catch you, a voice inside her whispered, like another bolt of electricity.

"Do you want me to tie you up?" Dorian asked, his voice somehow managing to be matter-of-fact and silky at the same time. It felt like an assault. It made her think of that whip, arcing through the air and yet landing like a kiss. She couldn't seem to stay still on her own knees. "Cuffs? Chains? And what would I do once I did tie you up? You seem to like the looks of the whip, but that's hardly for beginners. A paddle perhaps? Or maybe you'd enjoy it if I gave you that spanking you so richly deserve?"

For no reason she could think of, Erika suddenly wanted to cry. She felt emotion well inside her as if she was bruised from the inside out. She didn't know what to do with her hands, and found them lying open on her thighs, as if in supplication.

She thought she should do something about that, but she didn't.

And she didn't understand how the swelling emotion inside her could be so intimately connected with the greediness between her legs.

"I don't think…" she started faintly.

But he wasn't done. Dorian shifted position to lean against the wall before her, as if he'd never been so relaxed in all his life. She thought she might hate him.

Maybe she did hate him, but that was its own bright heat, like a lick. Right where she needed it most.

"There are so many things to choose from," he was saying in that mild tone at total odds with the stern intensity in his gaze. "Cattle prods. Ball gags. Nipple torture. Watersports. Total sensory deprivation. Pony play."

She was panting as if she was running. She still wanted to cry. And also slide her useless hands between her legs and make herself come hard enough that all these *feelings* went away. "I have a yellow bracelet on."

As if she was brandishing a rosary at him.

"That means you cannot exchange bodily fluids, Erika. It doesn't mean I can't, for example, secure a ponytail in your ass, clamp your nipples and make you ride a spanking bench until you come. After making sure your ass is a nice bright red. Does that sound like the sort of thing you had in mind when you came here? On this magical mystery tour of your newly kinky sexual appetite?"

Her head shorted out a little, as those images tumbled around inside her. She felt as if she was drowning, the parts of her body he'd mentioned tingling as if he'd already done the things he'd said he would, though he still hadn't touched her. She felt her own fingers digging into her thighs, but she was caught by the expression on his face.

A little too hard. A little too amused.

She got it, then.

He was trying to frighten her away.

And nothing that she'd felt tonight made any sense. Nothing since she'd found him on that dais, wielding that whip like a song. She'd come. Then she'd run. Now she was kneeling on the floor, staring up at him as if he could save her, when she was very much afraid that no one could. Because clearly she didn't want to be saved, or she would have left the minute she'd seen that bullwhip in his hands.

But she already knew what would happen if she

backed down. Dorian would be patronizing. He would call Conrad, who would be livid. And she would have wasted these months and accomplished nothing.

Erika couldn't quite accept that she could have gone through what she'd already gone through and get nothing out of it.

"That all sounds great," she said bravely. Mutinously. "I saw a pair of ponies on the way in. It looks…intriguing. Bridle and all."

And then, for the first time in as long as she'd known him, she watched Dorian laugh. Not smirk. Not raise those brows of his. But actually *laugh*.

It was a rich, profoundly male sound. It slid over her like chocolate, thick and dark. And the strangest sensation washed over her, centering between her legs again, and she almost thought she might come again. Just from hearing him laugh.

"I believe you'd do it," he said. And he shook his head. "That's not a compliment. If you can't articulate what you want and what you don't want, you shouldn't jump into it blindly. There are many places on this planet we can be coy about sex, but this isn't one of them."

"I'm not being coy."

"No, you're being thoughtless. Reckless. As immature as ever, and with far higher stakes than a backless gown at a charity ball we both know you wore to irritate your brother."

That was exactly why she'd worn that dress, but that wasn't the only reason she shuddered. "I'm glad you remember a dress I wore two years ago."

"I remember the controversy." The way his eyes gleamed made her stomach flip, in that peculiar mix of fear and hunger she was learning to associate with this man. "You enjoy controversy, do you not?"

"It's Conrad who enjoys controversy, since he's the one who causes it. I don't know why you can't see that, as his best friend. But that doesn't make it any less true."

"If you were here for reasons that did not involve your brother, I would handle all this insolence, Erika," he said, quietly. "But you are not, are you?"

And there was something about the very quietness that made her think of that whip again. Precise. Intense.

"I don't know what that means."

"I'm allowing you to keep your eyes raised. I'm allowing you to talk back to me, glare and conduct yourself as if this isn't a power exchange. These are gifts I could rescind at any moment."

Could he see her heart slam against her ribs? "I thought I had safe words."

"Do you feel that you need one? All we're doing is discussing terms."

"I haven't agreed to anything."

"You don't need to agree to anything to employ simple courtesy, Erika." And this time, his voice was a lash. A stark command. "When you're on your knees or otherwise involved in a scene with me, you call me sir. Or Master Dorian. And I'll expect you to address me that way every time you open your mouth."

"That's ridiculous."

But she remembered where she was. They weren't, in fact, standing on a ballroom floor in Greece in sight of her mother and disapproving brother. She had chosen to come here. She'd known what kind of club it was. That brow of his inched upward and she shook deep inside.

Even as her pussy flooded all over again.

"That's ridiculous," she said again. *"Sir."*

Because over her dead body would she call him Master anything.

"Thank you," he said, and she was certain that was an unholy amusement in his dark eyes. But his mouth remained stern, the way it always did. "It is not ridiculous. And no, I'm not on a power trip, which I'm sure is the next thing you plan to say. As insolently as possible."

"Oh, come on. Surely your whole thing is a power trip." His eyes flashed and she remembered herself. *"Sir."*

"I'm interested in power, yes," Dorian replied. "But it's not a trip. There is no power without surrender of one sort or another. A fist is only as strong as the delicate fingers that make it up."

"I don't know what that means," she said crossly. But she was thinking of a hard little stone cupped in a palm. Fingers wrapped around it, making that fist. "And I don't think any man ties up a woman if he doesn't want power over her." She saw his expression. *"Sir.* I thought that's what is hot about it."

"I do not want power over a woman," Dorian said,

very distinctly. "I want her to surrender her power to me. It's the difference between demanding that you kneel before me or waiting for you to choose to do it yourself. Do you understand?"

And she wanted to rage something back at him, but even as she opened her mouth to do it, there was that emotion welling up inside her again. Still. That bruise getting bigger, making it so much harder for her to breathe, making her eyes prickle.

She felt protected, yet she was terrified. Overwhelmed, yet so wildly turned-on it was like she didn't know her own body. And it hadn't escaped her notice that he hadn't laid so much as a finger upon her.

And sobbing on this hallway floor, she knew, was no way to do what she came here to do.

"I didn't know you were this…" she started to say without thinking.

An odd look moved over his face then, and she would have called it regret on someone else. But not Dorian.

"I am all this and a good deal more than you can comprehend," he said.

He pushed off the wall and moved closer, and it was better and worse at the same time. Sharp, impossible, until she felt heavy with longing and whatever kind of fear this was that made her head spin and her pussy wet.

He reached down, and fit his palm to her cheek, and to her horror, she felt tears well up in her eyes.

"I know why you came here, Erika. I imagine

you thought you would simply show up before me wearing as few pieces of clothing as possible, and I would fall like a stone. I imagine this is the effect you're used to having on men."

"I didn't—"

"Quiet."

And as if shushing her wasn't enough, he slid his thumb over her lips, and kept it there. Shutting her up whether she liked it or not.

And like everything else, she couldn't tell.

"My desires run a bit deeper than a hot body," he said, low and dark. "My needs require very specific outlets. I can fuck like any selfish fraternity brother you might have encountered out there, and I'll get off, but it won't truly satisfy me. So this offering of yours, while sweet, is doomed to disappoint you. You can't give me what I need, Erika." He studied her. "And even if you could, I will not be used as a tool to slap at your brother."

Erika wanted to bite him, but she couldn't seem to muster up the will to do it. Much less slap his hand away. Or really anything at all but sit there, his hand hot and strong as it curved around her face, wondering what on earth was happening to her.

Or how he'd seen through her so easily.

"I never said I wanted to use you."

"Time's up, kitten," he told her, and it wasn't until she followed his gaze down to her hands on her lap that she saw she was digging her own nails into her fists. *Ha ha*, she thought, angrily. *A kitten with claws.* "You're not here to play, which means you need to go."

"But…"

She could see from the look on his face that there would not be a second chance. She would never get back in through the doors of this club, that was certain. And she doubted it would matter if she tried to find him anywhere else. His office. His home. Whether he had her turned away by others or turned her away himself, he was done. His expression reminded her a little too strongly of the one he'd used on her all her life. Dismissive. Patronizing. Not at all the heat she'd seen before.

This was her only chance. And she might have misjudged things here, but it was only a matter of degrees, surely. The reality was that she'd watched him bring a woman to climax, and had come herself already. That alone was worth experimenting with.

She could handle him. She was sure she could.

"What if I want to play?" she asked.

"Very well."

He stepped back, taking his hand and his warmth with him, and she was afraid those tears really would spill over from behind her eyes. Would he do what he'd threatened to do? Or had that been a promise? Erika didn't know which part of it shot off the most sparks inside her. A ponytail? Or that spanking that had been haunting her since he'd first mentioned it two years ago?

Dorian's dark eyes blazed. "If you want to play, you must prove it."

"I'll do whatever you want."

His mouth curved. "Don't promise things you can't deliver."

He indicated the hallway behind him, and the club waiting for them, filled with people and music and all the kinky things Erika could imagine—plus a great many she couldn't.

"Prove how much you want this," Dorian ordered her. "Crawl, on your hands and knees, down this hallway and then out into the club proper. Keep going until I tell you to stop. You should be aware, of course, that the tiny little excuse for a skirt you're wearing will almost certainly flip up on your back as you go. Does that thong cover you well, do you think? Or will everybody who looks at you be able to see exactly how wet and eager you are? With your ripe, juicy pussy right there for everyone to see and touch and comment upon—"

And it was too much. Pony play was outlandish but what he was talking about was a humiliation she could envision all too easily, all those eyes and *him* and the *display* that was all her and yet not at all in her control…

"Stop," she managed to gasp out, while her heartbeat nearly bent her in half and that fever in her about took her head off. *"Red light."*

"Yes," Dorian said with far too much grim satisfaction. "Red light. Enough of this game, Erika. It's time to take you home."

CHAPTER FOUR

DORIAN MAINTAINED A penthouse in a quietly mon-
eyed neighborhood that seemed far too settled for a
man with his predilections. He was so kinky Erika
had imagined he would live somewhere desperately
cutting edge within walking distance of his club, but
instead his penthouse reflected the old money he
came from and the fortune or two he'd made himself.
His place sprawled across the top of a luxury building that seemed a lot like a five-star hotel, which,
once Erika thought about it—once she was capable
of thought, that was—made sense for a man like him.

Edgy, yes, but also pedigreed.

He had taken her out of the club with a swiftness
that left her off balance. But then, everything he'd
done since she'd seen him on that dais left her reeling. He'd reached down and taken her hand in that
hallway, pulling her to her feet as if she weighed less
than a euro cent coin. And as far as she could tell,
he'd been utterly unaware of the way the touch of his
hand against hers…stormed through her.

His dark eyes had swept over her, through her,

seeing everything with that same uncompromising
gaze. Seeing things Erika couldn't have articulated
if her life depended on it. But oh, could she feel it.

He'd pulled her around until she was in front of
him, then kept her there with a hand on the nape of
her neck as he guided her back to the club proper.
It was louder than before, or she was more sensitive
to the sounds. The crack of leather against flesh.
Moans and screams blending in with the pumping,
seductive music.

Erika felt drunk. Wildly intoxicated, spinning and
strange, when she was actually far more sober than
she usually was in a club. Maybe that was why she
did…nothing. She simply let him guide her, shiver-
ing a little because he was either really good at it or
she was remarkably attuned to every little press of
his strong fingers. Both, probably.

She was vaguely aware of him saying something
to someone when they left that little hallway, but
she didn't think anything of it. She didn't *think*, really. There was a riot inside her and his hand heavy
on her neck, and she was still lit up from what had
happened—and what hadn't happened—between
them. He led her through the crowds, past the bar
and into a different foyer from the cavernous one
she'd entered before. This one was all dark stone
and dim lights, and all the things she'd surrendered
earlier were waiting for her.

"Put on your shoes," Dorian ordered her in an undertone, his mouth so close to her ear that she could
feel the words.

It didn't occur to her to disobey. Or even to discuss it with him.

Everything seemed dreamlike, or feverish. Or again, so deeply intoxicating that strands seemed to wrap around each other outside time. What she remembered was not how she bent and slipped her feet into her shoes, but instead that moment when she'd glanced up in the middle of it to find Dorian staring down at her. His face had been set in the same stern lines, but an odd gleam in his eyes made her wonder what tenderness looked like on a man like him.

And more, what she could do to earn it.

His hand settled on the nape of her neck again, and that was what she remembered most of all. The heat and the heaviness. The separation between his thumb and his fingers, and the way his middle finger rested on her pulse as if he was monitoring every last beat of her heart.

She had the strangest thought, as she simply allowed him to guide her out into the Berlin night, that she'd never felt quite so safe in all her life.

Though that thought didn't make sense. Because whatever she was, it certainly wasn't *safe*. Not with Dorian.

Surely she knew that now.

There was a car ride through the sprawling city outside her window, alive and kicking no matter the hour. The brash, almost punk-rock east gave way to the plump wealth of the west, the history of Berlin—torn apart and sewn back together—rolling out before her. It wasn't until they arrived at his building, and

he led her across a too-bright lobby into an elevator
that required he release her to use his key, that she
gathered her wits about her enough to remember that
she had her own hotel room.

She realized that wasn't accidental. He'd let go of
her, ergo, she could suddenly think straight.

Erika stood across from him as the lift soared
upward, knowing she needed to open her mouth.
She needed to say something—anything—to break
this spell.

But she didn't.

She told herself it was natural. She was curi-
ous, that was all. She wanted to see how a man like
Dorian lived. Was it whips and chains in a red room?
Or a medieval dungeon in the lounge?

By that measure, the expansive apartment that appeared when the elevator doors lid soundlessly open
was a disappointment. If a person wasn't looking for
iron spikes and spanking benches, it was exquisite.

Erika followed him into the great room, blinking
as Dorian switched on lights. Then he moved farther
into the apartment, seeming to pay her absolutely no
mind as she looked around the loft-like space, with
dark wood walls and concrete floors. She hugged
herself as she stood there, taking in his aesthetic of
clean, modern pieces mixed in with the odd, sumptuous rug that would not have been out of place in
a sultan's palace. There was astonishing, confronting art on an otherwise bare wall. Across the room,
another wall was taken up with bookshelves that
somehow managed to look clean and spare despite

the tremendous number of books they held. So many books it seemed possible he actually *read them*, and wasn't using them as a design element.

She didn't know why it was so hard to imagine Dorian simply sitting down and reading in one of the deep, wide leather chairs or sofas that made up different sitting areas in the great room. He seemed too powerful to ever really be at rest. As if he had to be in constant motion, or standing over her the way he had in that hallway—or back in that ballroom in Athens, for that matter—or he would sputter out into darkness.

Erika didn't realize she was staring intently at his books, looking for clues to mysteries she wasn't sure she could name, until he walked back into the room.

And she didn't hear him come back in. She knew he was there without having to hear his foot against the floor and without having to glance over her shoulder. The hairs on the back of her neck prickled, like his hand had settled there again. She felt that now-familiar heat bloom in her all over again, coiling low in her belly and into her pussy. Only then did she look up.

Dorian stood in the opening where one room bled into the next, with massive windows all around so she could see the sparkle of Berlin out there in the dark.

"It's late," he said shortly. "I suggest you get some rest in one of the guest suites. They're all located on this floor. I'll call your brother in the morning."

He might as well have slapped her back into awareness. Or doused her in ice-cold water.

Either way, Erika's fingers curled into fists again and she suddenly felt much less fuzzy.

"Or, you know, you could also not call him."

Dorian gave the impression of sighing and shaking his head without actually moving at all. Impressive for a man doing such a terrific impression of a stone wall. "That was a statement of fact, Erika. Not an invitation to negotiate."

"All right, then." She held his gaze, even though there was that part of her, quivering and soft inside, that wanted to lean further into all those things they'd only brushed against in the club. The part of her that wished she'd crawled before him the way he'd requested she do, exposed for all to see. She fought off a telling shiver. "You go right ahead and call Conrad. I'll call your grandfather. He's always had a soft spot for me."

Dorian stared back at her. Erika felt the tension in the room surge toward an almost unbearable breaking point. But she refused to break. *She refused.*

Meanwhile, Dorian looked as arrogant as he did… astounded.

"You little shit," he said in a kind of awe that she chose to interpret as affectionate. Or close enough. "Are you threatening to *tattle* on me?"

"I assumed that's what we were doing here." Erika was pleased she managed to sound, if not as calm as he did, far calmer than she felt. "If you're going to tattle on me, why wouldn't I return the favor?"

He tilted his head slightly to one side, his dark eyes focusing on her so intensely she thought she might bruise. But that wasn't half as scary as the way he did nothing but…breathe. One breath, then another. She watched him visibly relax. Gaining his control, then slamming it back into place, she realized as she watched.

It was the hottest thing she thought she'd ever seen. No yelling. No insults. No other reactions—just Dorian handling himself.

She wondered what it would be like to be handled *by* him.

Her knees went rubbery. And far worse—or perhaps *worse* was not the right word here—it made her pussy clench, then ache.

"You are an inventive, insolent girl," he said quietly enough after a moment.

It was not a compliment. And it took her a beat to understand what that note in his voice was, tangled up with the darkness in the disapproval.

She could swear that was disappointment.

Her heart thudded hard against her ribs at that, and there was something almost dizzying that tore her up, then settled in her stomach like regret.

Erika tried to ignore it. "So you keep telling me."

"You are reckless. Immature and impetuous. And in so far over your head it's a wonder you haven't drowned yet." He said those things calmly. As if he was making a grocery list, when she could see that particular intensity in his gaze that indicated otherwise. It was too controlled to be temper, but it lashed at her all the same. "You come into my club, you claim you're there to play, but you can't handle even the lightest conversation. That's breathtakingly foolish."

"I thought that was what exhibition nights are for."

"What if it hadn't been me?" he demanded. "What if it had been some other dominant who hasn't known you all your life?"

"Then I imagine I'd be coming my brains out right now," Erika shot back. "Instead of being lectured to death by my older brother's irritating friend. You don't know me at all, Dorian. You know Conrad. Maybe you haven't noticed, but I'm not the little girl he thinks I am."

"Then I invite you to stop acting like one."

His voice was rougher then. Much darker in a way that made her breasts feel full again, with that sharp pinch in each that meant her nipples were already hard.

Why did everything Dorian do get to her like this? When he clearly thought so little of her?

"I don't know what makes you think you get to tell me what to do." Erika eyed him, then dug into her story, because she had no intention whatsoever of telling him the truth. Not now. "Everyone knows that Walfreiheit is the best BDSM club in Berlin. Maybe in the world. How was I supposed to know that Conrad's school friend would be there the night I got in, flinging a whip around, and then up for a spot of bullying?"

"Oh, little girl," Dorian said with a dark amusement that licked over her, then knotted up inside her. "I haven't begun to bully you."

"You're the one who keeps threatening me with my brother. Do you run back to him and tell him every last thing that you do? Or do you only feel you need to report on me? I'm all grown-up, Dorian, and Conrad lost his right to comment on what I do with my life when he kicked me out of my own family."

This time he really did roll his eyes. "Your mother seems to have cushioned that blow nicely."

"And look at that. One more thing that's entirely my business and not yours. At all."

"You have no idea what you're doing," Dorian told her. In that calm way that made her want to scream, though she didn't. "Do you? Standing in my home and hurling accusations at me at three in the morning is not a particularly smart way to convince me of your maturity, Erika."

"I don't have to convince you of anything, *Dorian*. You're not my friend. You're not my brother. And when I tried to do the BDSM thing like anyone else might have in that club—"

"You safe worded out."

But his voice changed. It took on that ruthlessly uncompromising quality she remembered from the club. And more, it had an instant effect on her. Her breathing changed. Her chest felt tight.

Suddenly she couldn't seem to tear her gaze away from his.

"I was momentarily overwhelmed." She said it distinctly. Almost loftily, trying to convince herself as well as him. "I didn't realize that using a safe word meant being dragged out of the club into the street. You should have made that clear."

"Careful," he advised her. "Or you might get what you're asking for. And then what?"

"Then let me be more explicit," Erika threw at him. She stood straighter, ignoring that pulling sensation in her breasts, her pussy. Her whole body. "I went to that club for a BDSM experience. Not an older-brother's-best-friend-acting-like-a-dick experience, because I've already had that, thanks. So if you'll excuse me, I think I'm going to leave, go back and tell them I was spirited away against my will."

"Really." There was even more of that amusement then, so dark and dangerous she could feel the edge against her skin like a blade. "And what will you do when you're there?"

"Whatever I feel like doing." She smirked at him and knew the moment she did it that it was a mistake. But she committed to it anyway, because she was nothing if not brazen when it was only going to get her in trouble. "You don't get to decide how I behave, Dorian. You don't get to decide a damn thing I do."

"Erika."

His voice was a crack, like that whip of his. Erika felt her breath go out of her in a rush. All he'd said was her name, but it hit her like a command. Like his hand wrapped against the nape of her neck, guiding her where he wanted her to go.

All she could do was stare back at him, mutely, entirely too aware of her pulse going wild and her breath sawing in and out of her lungs.

"You don't need to go back to the club to have a BDSM experience," he told her. "Lucky for you, I'm a BDSM experience all by myself."

"Lucky me," she said. Faintly. Because the floor

appeared to be tilted beneath her feet and she knew that couldn't be real. It only felt real. "But maybe I want...a different experience. Far away from you and your threats to involve Conrad."

His mouth moved into a curve that was in no way a smile.

"Tonight you have two options. Me, or sleep."

She hoped he couldn't see the way she quivered deep inside, and stood straighter to hide it. "This is Berlin. There are clubs everywhere. I can—"

"Erika, hear me on this if nothing else. You will not get into any BDSM club in this city. Tonight or ever again. It will take one call."

Her breath went a little ragged, but she believed him. She'd heard entirely too much about his reputation over the past two years to think he couldn't do exactly what he said he would.

"Me," he said again. He angled his head toward the hallway that stretched off behind her. "Or sleep. Choose now."

She was choosing sleep, obviously. She would meekly shuffle off to a bedroom like the biddable girl she'd never been, count to a hundred or something, then leave. Or maybe she would just leave now, without the charade. Because there was no way she was taking the other option. No way in hell. That little scene in the club had been more than enough—it had been too much, thank you.

But...something deep inside her whispered. *But what if...?*

After all, she'd spent so long getting here. And

she might find this—him—more overwhelming than she'd expected, but there was no denying the fact it turned her on. Just as he did. And he was supposed to be the best. Maybe here in the privacy of his home, he wouldn't scare her the way he had in that hallway. Even if he did, there wouldn't be a crowd of witnesses.

And she still couldn't think of a better way to stick it to her obnoxious older brother.

Blah, blah, blah, that voice inside her commented. *What matters is that you're wet. And very, very hungry.*

Maybe that was the real point of all of this. The things that had happened tonight had left her balanced precariously on the edge of a very high cliff, and despite everything, Erika…wanted to jump.

She met his gaze again and wasn't at all surprised to find him watching her in that intent, edgily patient way of his.

He didn't pressure her. He didn't have to. He was a wall. All she had to do was walk toward that wall or away from it.

"Have you decided?" he asked, as if he'd offered her a glass of water.

She nodded. Jerkily.

"Use your words, please."

Erika swallowed, but her throat stayed dry. Half of her screamed at her not to do this—to get the hell away from him—but the other half was far too curious. And much too focused on that need between her legs.

That and the dangerous gleam in his gaze that she could feel *inside* her.

"You," she said. "I choose you."

And this time, the smile that spread over his stern mouth washed over her like heat. Or maybe she was already regretting her choice—

"Excellent," Dorian said, and she thought he sounded pleased. It amazed her how much she wanted to please him. He didn't move farther into the room, and she could have sworn he loomed over her all the same. "Let's start by addressing your disrespectful attitude, shall we? On your knees. Eyes on the floor."

"But—"

"You will speak only when spoken to," he said, his voice that calm force that made her feel giddy and terrified at once. "You will answer any question I ask, and, Erika, let me be very clear. I expect and require total honesty. On your knees. Now."

He didn't raise his voice. He didn't sound particularly sharp or angry. If anything, he sounded even calmer than before.

And still, that power he wielded hit her like a blow. That was the only way she could describe the massive force that seemed to push her forward, almost against her will. She didn't think it through and worry over it from every angle. She sank down on her knees and found her hands on her thighs again. And it was easier than she'd imagined to cast her eyes down toward the ground.

Then there was nothing but her breath. Her panic

and anticipation, tangling around into something else. Something hot and liquid that streaked through her, lighting her up and settling like a weight in her pussy.

And because she wasn't looking at him any longer, he seemed bigger. As if he filled the vast room, taking up all the space and air. He made her shake, and he hadn't done anything yet. She'd done it to herself.

She got it then, in a way she never had when she'd been playing with party favor floggers before. He made her *want* to do this to herself. He made her *want* the roller coaster of sensation and emotion.

It was like an adult magic trick. And she was still shaking.

"Very nice," he said from across the room, and his approval made her flush, then feel as if she was *blooming*, somehow. "Obedience looks good on you."

She thought he was goading her, but she was determined that he wouldn't succeed. She glared at the floor and ordered herself to keep her hands *out* of telltale fists.

"Let me be clear about what is going to happen now," Dorian said, almost conversationally. If she ignored that kick of command and heat wrapped up in his words and the way he delivered them. "I'm going to spank you. Your behavior tonight has been disgraceful. Keep those eyes down, please. And I would strongly caution you not to say whatever it is you're about to say."

Erika jerked her head back down, her heart

pounding hard in her chest. She felt outraged. Insulted. How dare he call her *disgraceful*?

Her mind veered away from the *spanking* part.

"I want you to listen to me, Erika," he continued, pitiless and relentless, and in exactly the same calm tone. And the steadier he sounded, the more wildly out of control she felt. Her eyes were blurry, and she told herself that was why it seemed as if her hands were shaking. "Ignore the noise in your head. Ignore all those lies you like to tell yourself and everyone else. Focus on me. Only me. Here, now, and until I say otherwise, the only thing you have to worry about is doing exactly what I tell you to do. Do you understand me?"

She sucked in a shaky breath. "Yes, but—"

"*Yes* is a complete sentence, kitten."

She had to bite her own tongue, actually bite it, to keep from snapping back at him. He was maddening. How could he sound so blasé when he was saying something so...

But she was the one who was still kneeling. She was the one who kept doing as he said. She was the one he'd threatened to *spank* and here she was, still kneeling here like she had no choice. When she had every choice. When this *was* her choice.

"We will use the same safe-word structure as before. I want you to tell me what that is, now. With no editorializing."

"*Green light* means everything is good, fine. *Yellow light* means I'm not sure about something. Or I want to pause. And *red light* means stop."

"Very good."

He moved then, and she could track the sound of him, but she didn't dare look up. It was more than that—it felt as if his hand was on the back of her neck again, holding her head down, when he wasn't even near her.

It was only when she heard the sound of his big body against leather cushions that she realized he'd sat himself down on the wide couch that faced her.

"Come here," Dorian commanded. "And I want you to crawl."

Was she really going to do this? Erika slid her hands off her thighs, not surprised to discover they were damp. She leaned forward, putting her palms on the ground, and then she froze.

"Now, Erika," Dorian said in that same implacable way. "And I already told you how I'd like it to look. I want to see that ass bared. There's no one here but me, but go ahead and imagine you're back in the club. The only thing you should be focused on, there or here, is me."

She told herself he was a narcissist. A lunatic. An asshole of the highest degree.

But she was the one who slid her hands forward, then dragged her knees along behind. Once. Again. And then, without even meaning to, really, she was crawling across the floor.

She couldn't say she remembered the last time she'd crawled anywhere. She felt foolish. Exposed again, and it didn't matter that they were alone here. Her skirt slid to her waist, and she couldn't seem to keep herself from imagining the picture she made: a wanton little slut, crawling across the floor to obey him.

The thought nearly made her come again.

She made it over to him, and found herself at his feet.

"Look at me."

His voice was gentle enough, but with that steel beneath that made her feel as if she was on some kind of leash. She lifted her head.

And the look in his eyes took her breath away.

Dorian reached over and brushed his fingers over one cheek, then slid his palm to hold her there. Once again, the touch of his hand got beneath her skin. It made her want to squirm. Or worse, beg.

"Thank you for doing as I asked," he said, and again, the approval in his voice made her heart skip a beat.

His palm was warm, but the gleam in his dark eyes was hot. And she felt stretched between the two, flushed and obvious and so needy it hurt.

"I expect you to take your punishment exactly like this," he told her, as if he could read her mind. Or her greedy pussy. "I'm going to spank you. It's going to hurt. This is not for your pleasure, though I expect pleasure might be one of the things you feel. You don't understand boundaries, and I'm going to teach them to you. Thank me."

She had to fight the wave of dizziness. Of shame and fury and still, that horrible curiosity that she was afraid was the truth of her.

"Thank you," she gritted out, somehow.

His gaze was cool. One brow rose. "Thank you, who?"

At least she knew this one. "*Sir.* Thank you, *sir.*"

"I find that grudging tone disrespectful." But his thumb moved over her cheek almost tenderly. "Such a pretty face, and yet, so deeply insolent. You told me you were a grown woman, did you not? Now is your chance to prove it."

She opened her mouth, but something in the way his eyes gleamed stopped her.

"You have said a great many things tonight." Dorian's voice was even quieter, like thunder that rumbled so deep inside her only she knew what a catastrophe it was. And she couldn't tear her eyes away from him. She couldn't seem to do anything but breathe too hard, too fast, and burn. "But that's what you do, isn't it? You've spent your whole life writing checks with that mouth that your body can't cash. Tonight, we're going to settle your accounts."

He dropped his hand, then sat back. "You may stand."

Suddenly, crazily, Erika didn't want to stand. She wanted to stay where she was, there on her knees at his feet, where it was safe.

When she knew full well there was nothing safe about kneeling in front of this man.

Dorian watched her intently. With that armored, intense patience that made her want nothing more than to do what he wanted. However he wanted it.

Something spooled out inside her, then, that had

nothing to do with the way her mind raced. It felt long held. Secret and certain.

And the more it unwound itself within her, the less jittery she felt, even when she knew he wasn't kidding around. Dorian had every intention of hurting her. Deliberately. Spanking her like a child, because he thought that would teach her something—

No, that thing inside her corrected her. *Not like a child.*

Because this was about sex and this was about submission, and ultimately it was about her choice to combine those things and let him pick the path they took. She could use her safe word at any time. She could be up and walking away from him right now.

The issue wasn't that Dorian wanted to spank her. It was that deep down, Erika *wanted* to let him spank her.

Or she wouldn't be here, at his feet, fighting herself while he waited. And watched.

And Erika couldn't tell if she was shuddering because she couldn't bear the thought, or because she was terrified of what she might actually learn from this. Who she might become when he was done with her.

But either way, she stood.

"Lovely," he said, and it made her flush with that same strange pride. Then he patted his thighs, his dark gaze its own command. "Now lie down."

CHAPTER FIVE

ERIKA MIGHT HAVE thought she was on the verge of being sick, if it weren't for that blazing fire in her pussy that made a lie out of all the other sensations that sloshed around inside her. Her heart jolted, her stomach dropped, her skin felt stretched too tight... But still she burned.

And all Dorian did was sit there, almost lazily, watching her intently as she battled herself.

He did nothing to encourage her. He did nothing to hurry her along.

He only waited as if he was in absolutely no doubt that no matter her struggle, she would do exactly what he'd told her to do.

Because you want *to do it*, something in her whispered.

She was that hard, small stone in his palm, and he would make a fist only if she admitted it. If she allowed it. If she laid herself across his lap and submitted the way she wanted to, with every last part of the melty, swoony thing currently burning up inside her.

"Were my instructions unclear?" Dorian asked, mildly enough.

But nothing about the intensity in his dark gaze was mild.

Erika let out a breath that turned into something like a sob, and then she lowered herself over him.

It was awkward. His thighs were much too hard, and she was too…*aware* of everything. The way her breasts pressed into the leather cushion and how weird it was to crawl over another person like this in the first place. Much less for the reason she was doing it.

"I want you to lace your hands behind your head," Dorian said, and she instantly felt calmer and more on fire at the same time.

It was like the more she melted, the more of her there was to melt.

And it was a lot different to hear him talk now. In this position. She shifted, and his hand came down to the small of her back, holding her there. Firmly, yet light enough that if she'd wanted to, she could have rolled away from him. Thrown herself on the floor, run for the door—

But she only exhaled. Loudly.

And stayed where she was.

"Hands, please," he said calmly. But there was no mistaking the power in his voice.

God, that *power*.

Erika had spent her whole life careening about from one so-called authority figure to the next, always laughing when they tried to control her, because they couldn't. They always backed down, or lost track of her, or proved easy enough for her to control. They had the position of authority, but not the power to back it up.

Dorian had the power. And she'd given him the authority, hadn't she?

And she knew without having to ask that there was no possibility that she was going to control this, or him, or anything at all unless and until she uttered that safe word.

But she really didn't want to do that.

Her skin was so oversensitized she thought she might come from the faintest breeze, and it seemed to get worse with every breath. Or maybe she meant *better*. She threaded her fingers together behind her head, and that changed things all over again. It thrust her breasts into the leather cushion beneath her, abrading her nipples through the strappy top she wore and making them pull tighter.

But she was far more focused on Dorian. His rock-hard thighs beneath her, muscle like stone, that made her feel deliciously weak. And that hand in the small of her back, holding her in place so easily—though it felt like a heavy length of chain to her. She could feel his heat. His strength. That power that she'd already spent two years chasing. She felt surrounded by him, and it made her body shudder in reaction. Or longing. It was hard to tell.

It was all the same, and she melted, and everything was much too hot—

He smoothed his other hand over her ass, flipping up that tiny skirt. She tried to imagine what he saw. Her bright red lacy thong stuck between her ass cheeks, painting him a picture. She could *see* herself and it made her hips rock a little, as if that could help her aching clit.

It didn't. Especially when he widened his legs, effectively preventing her from rocking herself against him for any kind of relief.

More than that it reminded her, wordlessly, that he was in control. Complete and utter control, and saw everything. Every little wriggle she tried to make. Every expression on her face. Every flush that stained her skin.

For someone who had spent a whole life being both too visible and yet forever ignored, it was... gratifying. Terrifying. *Electrifying.*

"I'm going to pull your thong down," he told her matter-of-factly, as if he was narrating the weather to a disinterested party. "I want your ass entirely exposed. It looks as if it's never been touched. Has it?"

"No one's ever really spanked me, sir," she said to the leather beneath her. "If that's what you mean."

"I'm not surprised to hear that," he said with what she thought might be a measure of satisfaction. "You've needed a good spanking as long as I've known you."

She shuddered at that, and his hand moved, rolling her thong down over her hips. She expected him to pull it all the way off her, but he only left it tangled there above her knees.

Confining her, she realized. Making her feel dirty,

tied down and, for some reason, so turned-on she wanted to cry.

Then he didn't say anything. He stroked her ass in silence, warming each cheek with his palms. Roughly. He explored her, running his hands where he pleased, even delving into the furrow between her cheeks to press against the opening there.

Something arced through her, white-hot and greedy, a dark little gas fire of fear and longing.

"Has anyone taken you in the ass before?" he asked with that damned calm.

"N-no."

"What a shame. Why not? Is it a hard limit for you?"

She wanted to kick him, but she couldn't seem to move. "No. I don't know."

"Pick one or the other."

"It's supposed to hurt," she said, scowling at the cushion beneath her. "Why do something that hurts?"

Though it occurred to her that the question was pretty silly, given her current situation. To his credit, though she had the sense he smiled, Dorian didn't laugh.

"Because pain is temporary and, if employed deliberately and well, enhances pleasure." He pressed against her tight bud again, then moved on. He rubbed his palms restlessly over her upturned cheeks, laying in a pinch here, there, then holding her down when she jumped. "I promise you that if I hurt you, when I hurt you, I'll also make you come. Eventually. You may thank me."

"Th-thank you, sir," she managed to say, while she melted and burned, raged and wanted to sob.

"And you didn't answer my question. Is anal play a hard limit for you?"

Erika felt the strangest trickle of something like relief then, when that didn't make any sense. Why would she feel *relieved* when she was still waiting for a spanking of all things? And he was going out of his way to make sure she knew he never forgot a damned thing?

But in the next too-quick breath, she understood. That was why. He didn't forget. He didn't let things go. If he asked her a question, he expected her to answer.

He would not forget her or any detail about her, down to the dress she'd worn two years ago at a party in Greece.

He would not, for example, swan off to Cap Ferrat for the season as her mother had done one winter, forgetting that she'd left Erika alone on the estate south of Melbourne where they'd spent a span of years. She'd been seven. The staff had been lovely, but her mother hadn't deigned to return until Erika lit a fire in one of the old, empty barns and the butler had finally given his notice, as he wasn't a babysitter.

Erika had no idea why that weird, old memory was cropping up now. While she was close enough to naked and tossed over Dorian's lap all these years later and in Berlin.

"Erika. Don't make me ask you again."

"No," she whispered. "It's not a limit. I would try it."

"If I asked."

"If you asked," she agreed, her heart so loud inside her it hurt. "Sir."

She felt humiliated and excited in turn, and the contrast lurched around inside her, making her squirm. And pant. And want to die—but not before he kept that promise that any hurt he dished out would come with a hefty dollop of pleasure, too.

Erika thought she might die if he didn't keep his promise.

And then, to her horror and her delight, he reached beneath her and cupped her pussy in his hand. That was all he did. He simply…held her there.

She was the one who was quivering, sensitive and sweating with the force of a need that felt like madness.

"Look at this," he said, sounding dark and approving all at once. "You can't wait, can you? You're desperate. Soaking wet. As if you've been waiting your whole life for someone to finally take you in hand. Is that what you want, Erika?"

She wanted to fight. She wanted to argue. And more than both of those things, she wanted to thrust herself backward and somehow make him move his palm hard against her, because she knew it would take only the slightest graze of her clit against him to make her explode.

But she didn't dare misbehave like that. And he

didn't move his palm. As if he knew exactly what it was she wanted most.

"Yes, sir," she made herself say, squeezing her eyes shut as storm after storm rampaged through her. She kept her cheek pressed hard against the leather, gripping her own fingers behind her neck—even though all that did was press her breasts harder against the sofa beneath her.

Everything she did made it worse. Or better.

"I want to hear you say it."

"Yes, sir," she said again, desperation making her voice shake. "I've waited my whole life for someone to take me in hand."

"Not someone. Me. You want me, specifically, to teach you boundaries. To demand respect. To be the only person you've ever met who doesn't allow your insolence to go unheeded. Don't you?"

"Yes, sir."

And it came out a moan, though he hadn't really done anything yet.

All she was doing was lying here, in this re-markably exposed position, with his hand resting gently in *almost* the perfect place. And yet she was as turned-on as if he was fucking her. She'd had orgasms that were less intense than this. She was stretched out, gripping her own hands too tightly behind her neck, every part of her tense and waiting and so, so needy—

"You are in luck, little girl," he told her, with a certain erotic menace that made her pulse kick at her even as she melted all the more. "Because I have no intention of going easy on you. I'm going to spank you. You're going to count. You can sob, but you will lie still. You can cry out, but you will not fight me. If you use words, they will be of gratitude or your safe word and nothing else. Do you understand me?"

It was all storms and riot inside her. Why wasn't she calling this off? Why wasn't she rolling away from him, protecting herself, doing something to stop this?

Erika had played games before, with handcuffs and funny little floggers that tickled, and she'd thought she was practicing for this. But she'd never doubted that she was in complete control. Not once. The men she was with had teased her, but never hurt her.

This was different. Dorian wanted to hurt her. And would.

Or maybe it wasn't that simple. He wanted her to *allow him* to hurt her, because the crazy thing was, she wanted him to do just that.

He saw her. He could list her sins, and had. He was the only one who could punish her for them—and then grant her absolution, too.

She might not be in control of him. But she was here because she wanted to be here.

It was as simple and as wildly, impossibly con-voluted as that.

"Yes, sir," she said and shuddered with the force of what she was agreeing to—but it felt as if she *needed* this. As if he was right, and she'd been look-ing for it all her life.

"Are you a reckless, thoughtless, selfish girl who needs this punishment?"

It was as if he could read her mind. She tried to control her breathing, and failed miserably. "Yes, sir."

"Do you trust me to punish you as you deserve?"

She gave up on her breath, because she was sobbing. Big racking sobs rolled up from somewhere deep inside her, and made her body convulse. Her eyes were wet, her fingers so tight they were cramping behind her neck.

And still, all she could focus on was that blazing heat between her legs.

And him. Dorian.

At this moment, he was the whole of her world.

"Yes," she managed to get out. "Yes, sir."

He moved his hand from her pussy, and did it without so much as grazing a single part of her that would have kicked her deeper into that fire. And when his hand moved over her ass again, she could feel her own wetness.

The first smack shocked her.

It *hurt*.

"Count, please," he ordered her.

"One," she managed to get out. "Thank you, sir."

"Excellent," he said, and he was already rubbing the place where he'd smacked her, almost soothing it. But not quite enough to keep that deep red ache at bay. "Just like that."

And then he got to work.

It was shocking. Excruciating. His hand was big

and impossibly hard. And he was thorough. The pain of each precise smack jolted through her, making her kick her legs, but she didn't roll off him. She stayed where she was, no matter the sting and the ache of it.

Erika counted. And thanked him.

And cried.

And he kept going. First he spanked one cheek, then the other. He smacked her in the crease where her ass met her thighs. He continued until her whole butt felt bright red and agonized, and then he started the same painful pattern all over again.

Again and again, until she wasn't even pretending that she was doing anything but sobbing her eyes out.

She sobbed and she sobbed and he spanked her, and it fucking hurt. And she was strung out somewhere between the white noise in her head and the way her nipples were still too hard as they moved with the force of his smacks against the leather beneath her. Her ass was on fire, the pain outrageous and bright, and still, her clit ached and her pussy was so wet she hardly knew what to do with herself.

Dorian, by contrast, did not thrash about. He spanked her, that was all, but he did it in the same calm, considered rhythm as when he'd started. He didn't speed up. He didn't hit her harder or taper off into something lighter. He was laying down a lesson.

And all Erika could do was count. And sob for all the memories she didn't want in her head right now, but seemed lodged in her chest anyway.

Though Dorian seemed determined to spank them right out of her.

When she counted all the way to twenty, he stopped.

It took her a moment to realize that, because she was still sobbing. He picked her up, so easily that it occurred to her he'd wanted her to crawl into that position with as much strained awkwardness as it took.

But that was something she would have to think about later, when she wasn't so beside herself. He pulled her to him, cradling her against his chest. And then he murmured words that didn't quite penetrate as he held her there, her ass sore and hot against his thighs and her face tucked against his collarbone.

For a long time, Erika cried. And it wasn't until she was sniffling and calming herself, that it actually hit her that she was in Dorian's arms.

And not only that, all the pain in her ass seemed to be radiating out and setting that raging fire in her pussy into some kind of inferno.

"If you keep squirming against me like that," Dorian said, his voice so close, so dark, it made her shudder, "I will take it as an invitation to continue the lesson."

She shuddered out a breath and stopped.

And then he lifted her, gripping her by the upper arms and holding her just far enough away from him that he could stare directly into her eyes.

The world outside had disappeared. There was only sensation, Dorian and that intense gleam in his eyes.

"You please me, Erika," he told her, his voice grave. "You took that well."

She couldn't seem to think. Or speak. All she could do was hold his words close, unexpected light that made her heart feel bigger than it had been.

She pleased him.

Maybe that was enough.

And then, all she could focus on was that ache between her legs, made ravenous by the hot red ache he'd given her.

He set her on her feet then, there between his legs. Erika cast her eyes down without being asked, but she could feel the smile in his voice when he spoke.

"Turn around, please. I want to admire my work."

She shuddered, but obeyed.

"Hold up your skirt, please."

And she could hear her own breathing again—not quite a sob any longer, not simply a breath—as she stood there, staring at those books again. Pretending she wasn't holding her skirt up high, her thong still tangled around her knees, baring the ass he'd spanked to his view. And also unable to think of anything else.

She knew he sat forward when he gripped her hips, then moved his hands painfully over her ass cheeks again.

"Stay still," he ordered her.

And she tried. She really did try.

"Your ass is beautifully red and hot," he told her after a moment. "I like all those tears on your face, Erika. I'm feeling magnanimous and very well pleased. Ask me for what you want. I might just grant it to you."

She didn't even think. She didn't have to think. She knew exactly what she wanted.

Erika couldn't have imagined that it would all go down like this, that he would scare her, then spank her and make her purge herself of some ugliness she wasn't sure she even wanted to look at straight. But she knew what she wanted.

She'd only ever wanted one thing from him, above everything else. It was funny how clear it was now. All the world had seemed to narrow down to just one thing.

"Look at me," he said, and she did.

She looked back over her shoulder to find his dark eyes blazing with the same intense heat she could feel coiled so tightly inside her.

"Ask me," he ordered.

"Please, sir," Erika said softly in a voice that sounded like belonged to someone else, but she couldn't think about that now. "Please. Fuck me."

CHAPTER SIX

DORIAN HADN'T MEANT to do anything but scare her.

But then she'd stuck her chin in the air, gave him that challenging look, talked about finding herself a different kinky club and… No.

He couldn't allow it.

And somewhere in there, it had all changed from a lesson he could have imparted to anyone who needed to understand what a firm hand and some discipline could do, to…this.

His cock was so hard he thought he might burst. When he was never, ever out of control. Never with submissives. Never anywhere, for that matter.

She's different, something in him whispered, but she was Conrad's little sister, so that was impossible.

But at the moment, he couldn't bring himself to think about all the ways he had already betrayed his oldest and best friend tonight, because he wasn't done yet. He had made Erika a promise.

And Dorian did not break his promises.

She couldn't possibly know the picture she made,

Dorian thought as he gazed at her now, or how badly he wanted her.

He had spanked her hard and she'd pinkened beautifully, so that high, round ass of hers was bright and getting redder by the second. He could see the pouting lips of her pussy when she bent forward slightly, still holding up that skirt to give him a better view. Her blond hair was a tousled mess from all that thrashing around on the couch, her face was tearstained, and her eyes were wide and glazed.

But best of all, bratty little Erika Vanderburg was looking at him as if she'd seen God. And better still, wanted some hard, wild communion.

He was so hard it hurt.

He'd never intended to do more than spank her. Teach her a lesson.

Liar, something in him laughed.

But she was looking at him with awe and greed and he felt the same thing return—and then some. And he couldn't think about all the reasons why he shouldn't do exactly what she'd asked him to do.

"Hands and knees," he ordered her in a growl. "Right there."

She rushed to obey him, and he almost laughed at the sight. She was so wound up, it hadn't yet occurred to her how much she'd changed between the hallway at the club and here. How eager she was to obey him, with her pupils dilated and her pulse wild.

Erika liked a hard hand, he'd discovered. She bloomed under discipline. He made a note of that as if he planned to expand on that discovery—

But this wasn't the time to second-guess himself.

Dorian reached into the drawer in his side table and pulled out a condom. He knelt behind her, freed his aching cock from his trousers and sheathed himself. Then he gripped her lush hips, making sure his hands pressed into her reddened flesh. She made a whimpering sound, but pushed back to get closer to him.

It made him smile.

"I'm going to fuck you," he told her, wanting to sound cool but coming out gravelly instead. But that worked, too. "You may come whenever you like, but if you do not, you're out of luck. You can't touch your clit. You can't rub yourself against me. I want you to submit, take it and see what happens. Do you understand me?"

Her head fell forward, as if she could no longer hold it up. As if the idea of submission on that scale made her weak.

"Yes, sir," she whispered.

Dorian lined himself up with the entrance to her pussy, pressing his fingers into the curves of her ass because he knew it would sting. And remind her what she'd already taken. She shuddered, and he could smell how wet she was. How ready.

God help him, but she was a wonder.

He took a split second to admire her, there on her hands and knees, her ass red from his hand and her pretty pussy on display and ready to be split wide-open by him.

It was almost perfect.

"Put your face on the floor," he told her. "Hands behind your back, please."

She blew out a breath, then obeyed with a certain graceless alacrity that pleased him more than studied grace would have—because it meant she was too excited to contain herself. And better still, his grip on her meant he kept her pussy right there, pressed against his wide cockhead. As she shifted, he coated himself in her and had to hold himself back, hard.

When her hands were behind her back and her forehead was nestled against the oversoft, cushy rug beneath them, he wrapped one hand around her wrists and held them there. Maybe a little higher than she would have naturally, to make it fun.

"Thank me," he commanded her. "For showing you this consideration and allowing for the possibility of your pleasure in the midst of this punishment."

He felt the shudder work its way through her, and he loved the way goose bumps prickled all over her skin. She was so responsive. He was already thinking of all the wicked things he could do to make her shudder like that, over and over again.

Dorian hadn't been this pleased and impressed by a submissive in a long, long while.

"Thank you, sir," Erika moaned. "Thank you, thank you."

And with absolutely no warning, he slammed himself home.

She came instantly, violently, with a scream that was like music to him.

He didn't wait for her to ride it out. Dorian pounded

into her, hard and deep, claiming her and taking her over and over. He fucked her through the wallop of that first orgasm, then straight on into a second one.

Erika kept screaming, prettier every time.

And still he kept fucking her at the same, ferocious pace, until her sobs and screams changed. And turned into his name.

"Please, Dorian. Please, sir. Please—please—please—"

He couldn't have said what she begged for. Only that he took it.

Again and again, he took and she gave, and that was the beauty they made between them. That was the discipline and the desire, the coming together of two halves to make something much hotter, much brighter than either one of them alone.

Dorian made her come once more, and then, with a roar, he took his own pleasure at last.

And as he fell, he had the distinct notion that this time, he was well and truly damned.

Dorian did not typically spend a lot of his time questioning himself, his motives or his actions, because he'd spent a lifetime committed to honesty and openness in all things and that generally meant there was very little to question.

He was renowned for ferreting out secrets in the club and in the boardroom by dint of…simply asking. Then demanding honesty in return.

It was amazing how rare that was. So rare, in fact, that he'd heard it discussed in his office as his superpower. He'd always rolled his eyes at that, because if he had a superpower, he was pretty sure it had more to do with the kind of sex he preferred than a simple round of honest conversation.

Some people liked to claim he had been born confident, and he couldn't dispute that. Dorian had always had a deep, invariable sense of who he was, what he wanted and what he was prepared to do to get it. That had come to him honestly. His father had been the disappointment in the Alexander family, lazy and addicted and good for nothing at all—but his inability to live up to the standards set by Dorian's grandfather had merely given Dorian a good example of what best to avoid.

He did not lie because that was all his father ever did. He did not cheat because he had seen the pain his father's various forms of cheating had caused, whether in his relationships or in the business. He was bracingly honest with everyone he came into contact with—especially himself.

But that was before his best friend's little sister had turned up in his favorite club, sank to her knees and made something deep inside him hum.

As if he'd been waiting all this time to truly come alive.

He shook that unsettling notion off. And he concentrated on the practicalities instead.

Erika lay on the floor in a heap. Her eyes were closed, her face was still flushed, and her lips were parted. She was in the position he'd left her, as if she'd simply…folded into herself. Fully surrendered, fully his.

The woman of your dreams, a voice inside him pronounced.

Dorian rubbed a hand over his face, amazed to find he was less steady than he ought to have been.

He tucked himself back into his trousers, amazed that he had come so hard. He couldn't remember the last time a woman had gotten to him like that. And he didn't feel empty and restless the way he did more and more these days, especially after sex. He wasn't already thinking about the work he had to do or what his next extreme BDSM feat would be should he find a willing submissive to test it with him. He wasn't already thinking about who that might be.

He wasn't thinking about anything except Erika and that was…new. Like the feeling of deep stillness inside him that he knew he'd never felt before—and yet recognized, somehow.

Dorian didn't know where the hell to put all that yet, so he shoved it aside. He reached down and plucked her up from the floor, shifting her to hold her in his arms. Then he carried her up the stairs to the master suite that took up most of the second floor. Her head was a soft and welcome weight tucked there into the crook of his neck, making the stillness in him feel like something else. Like religion, maybe.

He moved down the hall past his study, personal gym and sauna, and he didn't bother to turn on any lights. Berlin was bright outside the many windows, casting the room in a dim kind of glow. And when he looked, he could see the first signs of dawn in the sky.

It should have been no more than another well-spent night in this anything-goes city. But that wasn't how it felt.

Not when she was still groggy as he set her on her feet, there against the side of his bed with its four steel posters that he would very much like to tie her to. So groggy she hadn't arranged her features in the usual way. She looked sweet. Defenseless. Wide-open and guileless, and Dorian's ribs seemed to shrink. It was hard to breathe for a moment.

He couldn't say he liked that at all.

Erika murmured something incoherent as he stripped her few clothes from her body. He laid her out on the mattress and left her there, murmuring a quiet order for her to stay where she was.

And she was exactly where he'd left her when he came back. He'd gone downstairs to the kitchen to fix her a little snack and a glass of water, with an electrolyte powder mixed in for when she was recovered sufficiently to tend to the inevitable postscene drop. He'd also found his preferred salve in the play bag he brought to the club, though he hadn't used it in a while.

But that was one more thing he didn't want to think about, because it felt…fraught. Fragile, almost, in this strange blue light of almost-morning with a woman he shouldn't have touched soft and undeniably his in his bed.

Dorian shouldn't have touched her, but he had.

And that meant he had responsibilities. The kind of sex—and sex games—he liked meant there was no hit-it-then-quit-it option afterward. Especially not when things had gotten so intense between them.

Some submissives didn't like to be touched afterward, but Erika had snuggled into him as he'd carried her. He wondered if she would feel that way with one of the fantasy dominants she'd imagined she'd find in the sex clubs he had every intention of banning her from—or if it was specific to him. To them, because she knew him.

Dorian really didn't want to think about how he knew her, or how long he'd known her, and he was all too aware that the things he didn't want to think about were starting to feel a lot like lying to himself. He wasn't all the way there yet, but he had the creeping suspicion it was gaining on him. His jaw clenched on its own accord and he made himself loosen up as he sat down next to her on the bed.

She was soft and warm beneath his hands, and she smiled as he turned her over onto her belly. He took his time rubbing the liniment into the marks he'd left on her ass, taking more than a little satisfaction in the heat of her reddened flesh beneath his palm.

"I can't decide if that hurts or feels good or both," she said softly, as much to the mattress as to him, and when he looked up, her eyes were closed. As if she was talking in her sleep.

"Then it's working." He finished with the lotion and set it aside, then ran a hand down the elegant line of her back that had entranced him for a split second long ago—and that he had the sneaking suspicion would haunt him for a lot longer now. "Are you okay?"

Her eyelashes fluttered as she blinked at him. "Define *okay*."

"Do you feel exposed? Vulnerable? Emotional?"

Her gaze was steady and much too blue. "Yes."

And to his surprise, Dorian found himself smiling. "Good."

"You wanted to make me feel things," she said after a moment. "Didn't you?"

"We can talk about it later," he told her gruffly.

And normally he was remote, if caring, during aftercare. He tended to any wounds and made sure there were no physical complications. He held subs on his lap if necessary, made sure they got their energy levels up again. But he was not cuddly. He was Dorian Alexander. He did not *snuggle*.

And still, without thinking too much about why he was doing it, he crawled up onto the bed beside her. He pulled her to him and held her there against his chest. Which meant he was going to have to find another word to describe what it was he was doing, because it felt too good to be *snuggling*.

She shifted, and for another moment that made his chest too tight, he thought she might pull away. But she didn't.

Instead, she settled against him, tucking her head against his chest and letting out a long, slow exhale.

And a knot in Dorian's chest he would have insisted wasn't there, because it never had been before, eased a little.

Unfortunately, that gave his mind leave to spin about at will.

Dorian had accepted his particular kinks and quirks a long time ago. Unlike some of the dominants he knew, he had never agonized about the things he wanted. His only concession to his supposed deviance had been to go out of his way to make certain that whoever he played with wanted the same things he did. The dynamic. The exquisite give to his take.

He took joy in the initial negotiation, the setting of terms and expectations. He reveled in building scenes and taking submissives on a ride. And even if he'd begun to feel more like one of those shabby old American theme parks of late, that didn't change what he liked or who he was. All it did was make him more selective. It was edging up on a month, maybe two, since he'd gone to the club before tonight— when there had been a time he couldn't get enough.

Dorian knew people thought it was a sickness, even in these so-called enlightened times. His father, for example, who had discovered his son's predilections early and had spent years throwing it in Dorian's face—and not only when he was out of his head. Dorian had been grateful for that, all things considered, because it had made it that much easier to cut his father out of his life. The way his mother and grandfather had done before him.

For him, always, it all came down to this moment. After the storm of play and passion, the simple trust of a well-pleasured, well-spanked woman. It was everything to him. It was the point.

And he had always enjoyed this moment, when surrender was absolute, and only trust remained. He didn't *snuggle* through it, normally, but he always liked it. And tonight he couldn't help noticing that he'd never felt so complete before. As if she wasn't the only one who'd put an integral part of herself out on the table here tonight.

As if she wasn't the only one exposed.

He didn't like that thought at all.

And he *really* didn't like, once it took hold, how that thought bloomed. And cascaded, because this wasn't a random submissive woman he could have met in a club. It wasn't only a surprisingly intense scene that had veered off and become something he hadn't quite intended.

There was no getting away from the fact that this was Erika in his arms, naked, with a red ass he'd given her himself. Erika Vanderburg. Conrad's little sister.

Dorian had never hidden his nature from his friend. There was no point when his father liked to trumpet it to the world at every opportunity. And, in fact, Conrad shared a number of his inclinations.

But he doubted very much that Conrad would find it even remotely acceptable for Dorian to be exploring those inclinations with Erika.

Erika seemed to be in some doubt about the situation with her older brother, but Dorian knew what she didn't. Conrad loved her. Fiercely, stubbornly and

perhaps too sternly—but he loved her. Dorian had
been with him when he'd received news of their father's death. And Dorian knew that one of Conrad's
major concerns, then and now, was how he was going
to raise his spoiled, fragile little princess of a sister
the way his father would have wanted.

Conrad had done his best to fill his father's shoes.

Erika had flounced off and started referring to
him as her enemy.

And Dorian, who had witnessed his friend's
struggle and had taken a dim view of Erika's behavior himself, had repaid his friend's trust and
friendship by defiling the little sister Conrad almost
viewed as more of a daughter.

Plainly, Dorian was fucked.

In his arms, there against his chest, Erika stirred
again. Dorian needed to distance himself. He needed
to repair the walls he should have kept between his
cock and what he owed his friend—and fast.

But her face, her beautiful face, was open and
vulnerable when she tipped it up to his. Her blue
eyes were sleepy. And suddenly he couldn't abide
the idea of any walls.

"Lie down with me," she said, and though she
phrased it like an order, he knew it was a question.
And an uncertain one at that.

Obviously Dorian didn't cuddle up with his subs
and sleep with them that way. He'd always imagined that kind of thing was better left to long-term
relationships—which he had always been deeply allergic to.

Allergic? asked that same voice inside him. *Or uninspired?*

But all that unfettered emotion on her pretty face was easily the most beautiful thing he'd ever seen.

And the fact he was digging his own hole was clear to him. But he didn't do anything to stop it. He set her aside and rolled from the bed, and she curled into a ball against his pillows and watched him strip out of his clothes.

He waited for that restless itch to wash over him, and told himself he would handle it for however long she slept because it was the least he could do for this woman he shouldn't have laid a finger on—much less spanked and fucked and made cry. But it didn't kick in.

Not when he crawled into the bed and pulled her tight to his front, one arm slung over her soft warmth. Not when they lay there like that, wound together like roots too tangled to ever be pulled apart.

She sighed a little as she burrowed beneath the covers, and he knew that sound. Surrender and safety. *Beautiful*, he thought.

And just this once, just because it was Erika, he let himself go.

Dorian held her close, matched his breath to hers and then, for the very first time, fell asleep with a woman in his arms.

CHAPTER SEVEN

DORIAN WOKE UP with Erika wrapped around him, tangled up in every possible way with her legs between his and her mouth against his neck, and stopped lying to himself.

She slept heavily and deep. He knew her scent now, and the heat of her skin, as if she was tattooed on him. And the memories of what they'd done the night before were now interspersed with what it was like to sleep in a sweet knot with her, turning this way and then the other as if they'd choreographed it.

As if he, a man who never slept easily or at all with another, couldn't sleep unless he was in contact with her.

As if you will never sleep well without her again.

He could feel that weight in his chest, thick and deep.

But this morning, steeped in the reality his body had already accepted—since he had slept with this woman tucked up next to him and wound around him as if they'd done it a hundred thousand times before—Dorian stopped pretending he didn't know what that weight was.

He had always been honest to a fault. It was part of what attracted him to BDSM and why he flourished in a subculture that prized communication, candor and authenticity above all else. He saw no reason to stop now, no matter that this kind of sudden awareness wasn't exactly what he'd planned for this weekend. No matter how inconvenient the truth that lay there, beautifully naked beside him.

He took his time easing away from her because he wanted her to stay right where she was, her cheeks flushed with the force of her dreams and that ass of hers still red from his hand. He was hard, but then, he suspected that might simply be the Erika effect. If he claimed her, if she was his, he could look forward to mornings like this. To waking her up in whatever method he could devise to best take advantage, and his imagination when it came to the care and erotic torture of women who liked to kneel before him was boundless. And endlessly wicked.

Something thudded through him, and he had the distinct impression that it was the last of his defenses disappearing.

In what felt to him like a plume of smoke. Or maybe a bonfire.

There was no *if* about it, he acknowledged.

He had every intention of claiming this woman. If he hadn't, he would never have fucked her.

Because deep down, he knew what he wanted. He always had.

His restlessness of recent months—the past year—had been because he'd stopped believing that he could get it. It seemed impossible that he could ever combine the two parts of his life. The heir to the Alexander shipping fortune needed to marry an appropriate wife. Dorian had always known that. Even his own father had done his duty in that respect, though Dorian doubted his brittle, elegant mother—now married to a sedate London financier who she could depend on to bore her in exactly the same way for the rest of their stodgy lives—would thank him for it. And Dorian had certainly met his share of kinky, delightfully debauched debutantes over the years, God bless them.

But none of them had inspired him for more than a night. Or in his case, a part of the night. The ones who played as hard as he did weren't interested in anything but playing. And the vast majority of them were better at playing *at* debauchery than really giving themselves over to man who could lead them through the darkness of anything real.

He stood there, one hand on the steel post that he really was going to tie her to, one of these days. It was almost as if he could see it. As if it had already happened, when he knew it hadn't.

Yet.

That word echoed in him like a premonition. Like a vow.

He pulled a light blanket up and over Erika's body, little as he liked covering such mouthwatering nakedness. He would much prefer to lie back down, roll her over and lose himself in her again and again…

But he had some thinking to do. Some serious thinking to do.

And he doubted very much that he would get any of that done while he stood here, *this close* to slipping back into that bed, holding her hands over her head so her breasts jutted toward his mouth and waking her up the way he wanted to do.

Dorian showered, and toweled himself off, choosing not to handle his cock—because he had plans. He grabbed a pair of jeans and a T-shirt on his way toward the stairs, and dressed before he jogged down them. When he reached the main floor, he found his mobile and checked his messages and email. There was the usual influx of work-related things he intended to ignore as much as possible. And there were also three messages on his personal voice mail.

All from Conrad.

And if he'd had any lingering doubts about the conviction he'd woken up with, it vanished then. Because Dorian knew he needed to have a frank conversation with his best friend today, but what he didn't feel was any sense of guilt or shame.

Fuck that.

He padded into his modern, streamlined kitchen, and set about fixing himself his morning coffee. He answered the one or two emails that couldn't wait, then tossed his phone onto the counter. Then he stood there, drinking his coffee and staring out his windows at his beloved Berlin. His grubby, beautiful, sprawling and unknowable city. He had lived here over a decade, had no plans to relocate and still found something new every time he walked down the street.

That was what BDSM had always been for him. Adventure and home in one. A refuge for a boy who had grown up on a steady diet of his father's chaos, and a place where the man he'd made himself—uncompromising, brutally honest and as demanding as he was protective—was appreciated. Lauded, even.

And still, lately, he'd been thinking he was going to have to give it up. Because he needed to marry to carry on the family line in the time-honored fashion, he had no intention of treating any wife of his as shabbily as his father had treated his mother, and he didn't believe that there was any possibility he would be lucky enough to find an heiress to please his grandfather who would also please him.

After all, it was notoriously difficult to please Master Dorian. His entire reputation was built on that essential truth.

And then here, last night, with the least likely person he could ever have imagined, he'd felt that particular stillness inside him.

Erika had pleased him. Deeply and completely.

And as she had told him already last night, his grandfather already loved her.

Dorian might have preferred a direct blow to the face rather than the sucker punch that realization felt like this morning, but he was nothing if not capable of rolling with what he found and making the best of it. It was what had made him his second fortune. It was also what made him popular at the club.

He didn't have to glance at his mobile to see his best friend's name again. Conrad's name was emblazoned inside him, and the idea that a man he considered a brother would hate him for this disloyalty ate at him—but Dorian had never been one to hide from hard things. Hiding was akin to lying as far as he was concerned.

And the liar in his family was his father, not him.

He made himself a second cup of coffee and started thinking about solutions.

Conrad was an issue, but bigger by far than his best friend was the issue of Erika herself. Dorian knew she'd needed what had happened between them last night—desperately. Her submission to him had been real and raw and truly one of the most beautiful things he had ever seen. He wanted nothing more than to protect her. Help her.

And get them both off while he was at it. Repeatedly.

It was what he was made for.

He wanted to do his level best to use this particularly kinky spark between them to make them better people together than they could ever be alone. It was the sweetest, most dangerous game. It was the crux of the power exchange. He dominated, she submitted, and somewhere in there, her strength humbled him even as his power melted her.

It was Dorian's favorite kind of fire, and he had never felt it burn as hot and as wild as it had last night.

Because while clubs like his existed all over the world to create safe spaces for like-minded individuals to play at burning, it was still just play.

And what Dorian had discovered last night, when that fire had led him places he'd never thought he'd go, was that he wanted real. He was done with play-time.

But was Erika?

Because he could sit here and think through a thousand different scenarios to energetically explain his point of view until she surrendered the way he liked best, but if the only reason she was here was because she wanted to hurt Conrad… Well. That didn't exactly fit in with all the futures he was building in his head.

He sat with that for a moment. And didn't like it. Not when she'd given herself over into his hands so beautifully, so completely.

Dorian was hard just thinking about it. Hard and something more—in a kind of awe, really, at her ability to kneel. To submit. To bend to his will, and find herself brighter and more beautiful on the other side.

Fundamentally, he didn't believe—maybe he *couldn't* believe—that what had happened between them hadn't gotten to her.

He figured it was possible she'd come after him for revenge, then found herself on her knees, significantly more compelled by their dynamic than she'd planned. Because the bedroom games she'd played before weren't the same thing as the true, real connection that had blazed between them. No game could touch it.

And that connection was worth anything and everything, as far as Dorian was concerned. Especially when, until last night, he had truly believed that he would have to pack these needs of his away, meet a perfectly nice girl by regular means instead of in his club, where he could ask her for a list of her soft and hard limits, and sentence himself to a life devoid of all this glorious color.

He could get off by having vanilla sex, if he had to, as he'd told Erika last night. He had before, and he'd told himself that he would again. There had been times when he'd assured himself it wasn't even a great sacrifice. Not when he had found it so difficult to find that true connection he craved out there in the clubs, and Lord knew that even vanilla sex was better than going without.

That was what he'd told himself. And he'd been more than halfway to convincing himself that he really, truly believed it. He'd even assured his grandfather that this would be the year he would start looking seriously for an appropriate wife.

And he had. He'd gone on a few perfectly nice dates with lovely women who did absolutely nothing for him. And he'd been gearing himself to simply… choose one and commit himself, if not to his own happiness, then to hers.

But today he found himself standing in a life that looked exactly the way it had yesterday, but was wrecked from the inside out. Changed entirely.

By one mouthy, spoiled, impossible brat who made his cock hard and his heart kick, even now.

Dorian set down his second cup of coffee, ran his hands over his face and accepted his fate. It was done, as far as he was concerned. And Master Dorian did not dither when he'd made up his mind.

He set about getting what he wanted.

And one thing Dorian was very, very good at was getting what he wanted.

He needed to get Erika to admit what had happened here between them, by whatever means necessary, and no matter what revenge fantasies she might have been cooking up in that fascinating little mind of hers.

He also needed to call his best friend, tell him what had happened—or at any rate, a highly sanitized version of what had happened, complete with a full accounting of Dorian's intentions—and accept whatever reaction Conrad might have. Even if it was violent.

Dorian fully expected it to be violent.

But he was prepared to accept the consequences. If he hadn't been, he wouldn't have done it.

He blew out a breath, picked up his mobile and dialed Conrad's number.

Because there was no way he would be able to conduct the conversation he needed to have with Erika in the way he wanted until he talked to her brother.

"You're not going to believe this," Conrad said when he answered his phone. In the background,

Dorian could hear the sounds of a major city. Paris, if Conrad was at home. Though in truth, the man traveled as much as Dorian did, and could be anywhere. Dorian hoped, given what he expected Conrad's reaction to be, that it wasn't Berlin. "Really. You're not going to believe it. I'm getting married."

"Funnily enough," Dorian said, because there was no point doing any of this unless he was all in, "that was what I called to talk to you about. And I'm pretty sure you will believe it even less."

Erika woke up when sunlight streamed in the windows, bright and warm on her face.

She knew exactly where she was.

Berlin. Dorian's massive penthouse. *Dorian.*

For a moment, she let herself lie there as she was, curled up naked in his bed with the most extraordinary feeling that she…belonged there.

That she was safe at last. Cared for the way she'd always dreamed. And right where she was supposed to be.

But Erika knew better than to let herself get carried away with dreams that could never come true, no matter how at peace she felt in this bed. In this home.

She sat up gingerly, expecting there to be pain, but the ache in her butt was minimal and really almost… pleasant. Her pussy felt sensitive. Not exactly fragile, more…greedy. If anything, she wanted more of it.

More of everything. More of *this*. And more of him.

She shoved her hair back from her face, looked

around and wasn't surprised to find herself alone in the massive bedroom.

Images from the night before chased each other through her head, one more vivid than the last. Different emotions buffeted her, but it was as if she'd stuck her head out the window in the middle of a storm. She could feel the wind, but it didn't sweep her away. And when she took a deep breath, then let it out again, she found herself smiling.

Because she felt like a new person.

She crawled out of the bed, running a hand down one of the dauntingly thick and sturdy posters, pretty sure she knew exactly what Dorian did with them. To her surprise, even after everything that had happened the night before, the notion sent a thrill spinning through her, pulsing its way down into her greedy pussy.

When she would have sworn up and down, her body rejected the very idea of morning sex, as a matter of policy. Apparently not Dorian's kind of sex.

She padded into the bathroom and took her time in the oversize shower, letting all the many showerheads send hot water pounding into her as she slicked a body gel over her skin that made her smell like him.

She smoothed her wet hair back from her face when she got out, and wondered if it was because she knew Dorian that she felt so comfortable helping herself to his hairbrush. His products. And even one of his shirts. She tried to imagine what it would be like to wake up like this in the house of the random dominant man she'd pretended she wanted to find last night, but she couldn't. She doubted very much that she would have stayed overnight. And if she had, she certainly wouldn't have slept like that, crashed out in the deepest sleep she could remember having since she was a child.

Because when have you ever felt safe? a voice inside her asked.

Erika didn't want to answer that. Because she knew the answer, of course, and it made her sad. She pressed a hand against her belly as she wandered downstairs, cataloging the faint pull here and whisper of something there, reminding her that she'd had a long and eventful night.

Had she ever.

She wished she was a lot more sore, she realized as she crossed the great room where she'd cried and come and had learned things about herself she'd never known were there. She wished her ass was far more sore than it was. She wished she could *feel* him, so long and thick and demanding as he'd pounded into her. The scrape of her breasts and her cheek against that rug as she'd come and come, his cock hammering into her to make sure she kept on going.

Erika wanted to wear him on her skin.

And she didn't really want to ask herself if that was healthy, because it felt right.

She was too warm again when she padded into the kitchen, so bright with all the light of midday pouring in, and found Dorian there.

He was dressed in a T-shirt that made a symphony out of those arms of his that she appreciated a whole lot more this morning. And in new ways. Because of the pain he could inflict, the pleasure he could wring out of her, and the safety she'd found only and ever there.

But she kept that to herself as he fixed her with a dark, simmering look.

She could feel the tumble inside her. Something defiant that lit her up, and made her want to poke at him—though it was at odds with that shimmering thing that wound around and around, settled in her pussy and made her knees feel weak.

"How do you feel this morning?" Dorian asked, his voice polite. Cool.

Irritating, she thought and glared at him.

"I'm *great*," she said. "Never better. You?"

"Erika. That wasn't a random pleasantry. I want you to provide me with a detailed and honest inventory of your feelings. Can you handle that?"

And all that light tumbling around his sleek, pristine kitchen made her silly. Or bold. At the very least, it reminded her that it wasn't last night. Not anymore.

"While I'm cataloging my feelings, maybe you can ask yourself why it is you have to be so incredibly patronizing."

"I'm not patronizing you. You seem euphoric. I want to make sure you're not peaking on your way into a serious drop."

"I thought that's why you brought me a snack last night."

"What happened was intense," he said gently, as if she might not have noticed. "Emotional responses to that kind of intensity and vulnerability often show up later."

It was the way he said that, maybe. As if he knew things she didn't—about herself. Erika found herself crossing her arms, even though she knew it made that shirt of his ride up her thighs.

Or maybe she wanted to linger for a moment in the way his dark gaze moved over the extra bit of skin she'd revealed. Because she felt a little bit like a junkie, desperate to see that flame blaze in his eyes again.

"If you have feelings about last night that you'd like to share with me, this is a safe space to do that," he said in a remote sort of way, as if he was conducting a seminar on BDSM and was modeling appropriate behavior. And suddenly Erika was flooded with emotion, all right. Assuming fury counted. "No need to observe protocol. You can simply tell me how you feel, ask me questions or share any thoughts you might have that you think I should know."

"I *feel* that you're being unnecessarily condescending to a woman you had sex with when most people pretend to exchange numbers, have three seconds of awkward conversation and then leave. Will there also be a questionnaire? An exit interview?"

His dark eyes gleamed, and the power there almost made her gasp. But all he did was smile. Slightly. "Is there a way that you can share those sentiments without resorting to name-calling and insolence, do you think? Right now that's a question. The next time I get you naked and on your knees, however, you may find there are consequences for such responses."

Erika hugged herself a little bit harder. "All your life, you've been just like this. Aloof. Arrogant. Even when you were a teenager."

"I'm delighted you were paying attention."

He moved to an espresso machine that had its own countertop, and pulled two shots. Then he pulled out a carton of cream from his great steel refrigerator, poured a hefty dollop into the cup and slid it to her.

And Erika's stomach twisted a little as she stared down at it.

"How do you know how I like my coffee?" Her voice was faint.

"You're not the only one who pays attention."

She felt shaky, suddenly. She wished she had something better to wear than one of his shirts with the sleeves rolled up. She wished her hair wasn't still damp and clinging to her neck. She wished she could, just once, control herself *before* making a mess.

"I really am fine," she made herself say. She lifted the coffee he'd made her and took a sip, then forced a smile. Because, of course, it was perfect. Exactly how she liked it. "Better than fine, now."

"Why am I not surprised to hear that?" Dorian asked, and the lightness of his voice was at distinct odds with all that intensity in his gaze. It made her worry. It made her wet. "Most people have intense reactions to their first real BDSM experience, but not you, of course. Not Erika Vanderburg, recklessly careening through life, heedless and untouched by anyone or anything."

And she might have described herself that way yesterday, but she didn't like him doing it. Not today. It felt like a slap of his hand, and not because he was teaching her a lesson, but because he wanted to hurt her. A crucial distinction.

"I do not *careen*. I travel. I *explore*."

He smiled again, but it didn't exactly soothe her. He slid a plate in front of her, and it took her a few moments to realize it was...food. He'd put together a typical German breakfast of rolls, cheeses, meats and sausages. There were jams and honey, butter and mustard. Even boiled eggs.

And as she stared at the feast he quietly set out before her—matter-of-factly, really, as if he served her food every day of her life—Erika realized she was ravenous.

He'd known that, somehow. He'd known it in the same way he'd known exactly how to touch her last night to make her break, then burn.

Something deep inside her quivered.

But it didn't keep her from eating.

"Why did you leave university?" Dorian asked, conversationally.

It was a strange question, but she had warm German bread and she couldn't seem to concentrate on anything else.

"It wasn't the right place for me," she told him.

"Was it not for you or was it another way for you to practice self-sabotage?" he asked, his voice so mild she was starting to smile at him before his words penetrated. "That is what you like to do, is it not? You were a decent student, by all accounts. I believe your brother even praised you after your second-year marks came in—and you couldn't have that. You only like attention when it's negative."

She swallowed, carefully, and set her roll down. Suddenly she wasn't hungry any longer. "What is this?"

And though she was standing there at the counter across from him in his bright and happy kitchen, she felt as if she was back in that hallway. What was wrong with her that she wanted to kneel while he took her apart? *Again?*

Yes, please, something in her whispered.

But he wasn't finished.

"When your father died, you went off the rails. Your brother took on all the responsibility, and you chose instead to make certain you were the enduring thorn in his side. I assumed that was because you were as thoughtless and empty-headed as you've acted over the years, but you're not, are you? You only want people to *think* you are."

"People think what they want." She scowled at him. "And I never asked Conrad to take responsibility for me. It seems to have escaped both his notice and yours that I actually have a living, breathing parent."

"Your mother might be the most truly self-centered human being I've ever met, and my father is an addict."

He wasn't wrong about Chriszette, and yet hearing him say that about her felt like a betrayal. Erika might complain about her, or want to complain about her, but she didn't like Dorian doing it. Especially because he was right.

Now he was studying her like she was a book he was reading and finding lacking. Deeply, profoundly lacking.

For once in her life, Erika didn't know what to say.

And the longer she stood there, gazing at him— or scowling at him—the more that feeling of well-being that she'd woken up with eroded.

Stupid, she thought, the sharp little voice in her head far too much like her mother's. *Always so stupid.*

Because it really hadn't occurred to her until this moment that while she had gone on a significant journey last night, he'd been…doing what he did. To Dorian, there was no connection between a moment in a ballroom two years ago and today. He wasn't the one who had taken it upon himself to search her out. He hadn't done "research" all over the globe, trying to figure out how to get next to her. While she felt profoundly altered by what happened last night, he didn't.

Clearly.

Because the Dorian who stood there across a granite countertop from her looked exactly the same as he had when he'd tried to cut her down to size in Greece.

And suddenly, everything that had happened between them seemed dirty. And not in the hot way. *Soiled*, not sexy.

Why had she gotten on her knees? Why had she *crawled*? Why had she, a grown woman, let this man spank her like a child and then fuck her like some kind of whore?

And how had she curled up in his arms like all of that was a gift, then slept more soundly than she had in years?

She could feel her pulse everywhere, her heart in her throat as if she might get sick.

"Oh my God," she said, soft and horrified, her eyes wide. "You *hate* me."

Something changed, there in the intensity of that dark-coffee gaze. "I don't hate you."

"I think you do," she said, shaken. "I should have realized. Here I was, thinking this was some kind of connection, and you were just…"

Dorian leaned forward, keeping his gaze trained on her, and she wanted to run away. Get away. But she couldn't seem to move.

"Were you chasing a connection when you came into the club last night? Or was it something else?"

She laid her palms on the cool countertop, hoping it looked as if she was doing literally anything but what she was actually doing, which was holding herself upright. "What other reason could I possibly have?"

"I've wondered that myself since the moment you showed up," Dorian said in that same relentless way of his that made her want to cry and made her want to touch him and left her messy straight through. "And the only conclusion I reached was that you really, really want to stick it to your brother and thought you'd use me to do it."

Her heart was stuck in her throat. Or pieces of it were. And she didn't understand why it was involved in the first place. "Because nothing could possibly be worse than getting tangled up with me, obviously, whatever the reason."

"You're beautiful," Dorian told her, and what was *wrong* with her that she felt like the sun had come out from behind a cloud. "You're smart and quick and funny. And I watched the strength you have in you, Erika. Over and over again. I watched you fight yourself. I watched you struggle and suffer, and I'm not being patronizing when I tell you that it was truly humbling to see you give yourself wholly and completely. To me."

Her throat was dry, then. And her heart was a lost cause.

"But," she prompted him.

Because if she knew anything, it was that when it came to her, there was always a *but*. Always.

You could be so lovely, Chriszette had sighed at her father's funeral, *but you're so* emotional. *No one likes that much* drama, *Erika*.

I know we've been friends for years, her supposed best friend ever had told her in boarding school, *but I don't really* like *you, actually*.

I like fucking you, a great many of her lovers had

told her, in one way or another. *But that's all it is. You know that, right?*

You're my sister and I love you, Conrad had said, frowning, after she'd announced she wasn't returning to Oxford after all, *but I can't support this wasted life you want to live.*

There was always, always a *but*.

"But I don't understand how you can be the woman I saw last night," Dorian said quietly, "so courageous in your surrender when you want to be, when the rest of your life is such a disaster."

The more he spoke, the further away she got without moving an inch, and that was a blessing. Her own, personal gift. After all, she was used to being dressed down. Shouted at. She was everybody's convenient punching bag, and there were only two ways to take that. You either curled in on yourself, a sad sack in every regard. Or you practiced your enigmatic smile in the mirror, pretended everything was a *madcap adventure*, and that it all rolled right off you.

Erika had always opted for the latter, because nobody got to see her suffer.

But you already suffered, something in her contradicted. *For him. And happily.*

"What about my life is a disaster?" she made herself ask. And she even smiled. "I have more social media followers than most celebrities."

Because she couldn't help but poke at the wound. Because it wasn't bad enough that she'd woken up feeling safe and at peace, and it was ruined. He'd made an offhand comment to her two years ago and it had changed everything. She'd done nothing but think about him, all this time, and it had all led here. Where she was inviting him to make further cutting commentary, and...then what?

Did she really want to let him haunt her all over again? And probably worse this time?

"I've seen both sides of you now," he said quietly, his gaze so intense it made her *hurt*. "And the woman I met last night was extraordinary. I spent hours this morning trying to reconcile her with this show you put on. You're doing it right now. Why is getting attention the only thing that matters to you?"

"Because it's the only way I matter to anyone."

She said it without thinking. And instantly wished that she could claw those words back, shove them inside her mouth. Chew them up, swallow them down.

Her chest was heaving, and for a split second, Erika honestly and truly wished that she would die right there. Just keel over onto his kitchen floor, and be done with this.

Because surely that was better than suffering through that intent look on his face that she was certain would tip over into pity at any moment.

But it didn't.

"Bullshit," he said. Succinctly.

She felt it like one of those blows he'd rained on her ass last night. Sharp, shocking. Then the sharpness changed, into a dull ache that was almost worse.

When she had been naked before him, her hands

behind her back and completely in his control, she hadn't felt this exposed.

"You're afraid," he told her, his gaze steady on hers, though his voice was soft.

"Oh, please," she threw at him, and it didn't seem to matter anymore that she felt so...ruined. Ripped open, with the stuffing removed and no hope of ever shoving it all back into place. *What the hell*, she thought. "You should talk."

"Me?" Dorian laughed, and it stunned her that she felt *so many things* and he seemed...fine. Just having a conversation while her world was on fire. "Little girl, flailing around throwing out accusations isn't going to change the facts. You live a useless life by choice. I do not."

"Of course not. My mistake. I thought this was supposed to be an honest conversation, not a self-congratulatory stump speech about how virtuous you are, when I'm standing right here, have known you for far too long and certainly know better."

"I talked to your brother earlier," Dorian said. Calmly.

Casually, even.

"Wh-what?"

"Conrad is getting married, Erika," Dorian told her in the same unbothered tone, though his gaze stayed on hers. "He got engaged last night and his soon-to-be in-laws are throwing them a party. In England at the end of the month."

Erika made herself laugh, though it felt like cut

glass in her mouth. "Who would actually marry Conrad?"

And she felt a trickle of something like foreboding as Dorian studied her. For much too long.

"Lady Jenny," Dorian said. He waited, and Erika was sure he could *see* that name fall through her like a sickening stone. "But you know her, do you not?"

Jenny Markham had been on Erika's stair at Oxford when they were first years. They'd become fast friends, had spent their summers together, texted regularly and always got together when they found themselves in the same place. Given that the last text Erika had gotten from Jenny had been a week ago, with no mention of Conrad whatsoever, Erika was skeptical—to say the least—about this news.

But Dorian, who had not looked at her pityingly yet, seemed to be doing so now.

"Of course I know Jenny," Erika said stiffly.

"Here's what I need to know," Dorian said quietly. "Is there any possibility that you can attend their engagement party and be supportive of your brother? And your friend? Or will it be business as usual for you, instead?"

People had thought very, very little of her all her life. There was nothing new in it. Nothing shocking.

But Erika found that further evidence of Dorian thinking the same as everyone else just made her want to sit down on the floor and cry.

She would never know how she managed to stay standing instead.

And he had an idea of who she was in his head,

clearly, so she smirked at him. *Useless. Disastrous. Afraid.* She stuck her hand on her hip as if she was trying to be provocative. Just another example of stupid, attention-seeking Erika Vanderburg. Just what he wanted to see.

"I have no idea," she said, not politely. "Are you going to make me?" She waited for his brows to rise, and that thunder to roll in across his stern, hard face, then made a face she knew he wouldn't care for at all. *"Sir?"*

CHAPTER EIGHT

EVERYTHING WAS GOING as planned.

She'd walked into his kitchen with her hair wet, making her blue eyes look even bigger, wearing nothing but one of his shirts. He didn't think she'd been trying to provoke him. Quite the opposite, this morning. She looked sleepy and sweet, and she gazed at him like he'd personally made the sun rise.

He hadn't known how much he wanted to see her look at him like that. How it made everything in him settle. Then hum.

Now he wanted to see it all the time.

Conrad had not been amused. He'd been silent at first. That had been far better than the lethal clip to his voice when he'd spoken again.

My...sister, he'd repeated. *My little sister and you. In your club.*

Dorian had winced, but that was the thing about taking responsibility, wasn't it? Sometimes it sucked. Sometimes it made people hate you.

But it was always the right thing to do.

I don't know if this will make you feel better or

worse, Dorian had said gruffly. *But I have nothing but good intentions where she's concerned.*

I don't feel anything, you prick, Conrad had snapped, *except homicidal.*

Dorian was glad the conversation was happening over the phone, or he imagined Conrad would have swung on him. And he would have taken it as his due, because he'd not only crossed a line, he'd done it in his own inimitable way. What older brother wanted to think about that?

You can try to kill me all you want, Dorian had told him. *But that's not going to change anything.*

Conrad had made a frustrated noise. Then he'd gone silent.

Is she happy? he asked quietly.

I intend to make her happy, Dorian had promised his best friend. The only brother he had or wanted. *I intend to dedicate myself to the task.*

It had been a vow. And he'd meant it.

But that was the easy part, all things considered. Now he had to do the hard part, which was convincing this dragonfly of a woman—always alighting here, then buzzing off there, always moving, always changing—that he'd found everything he'd wanted in her. In one night. That yes, he knew his own mind and heart. That he'd spent his entire adult life committed to extreme self-awareness.

It was that or follow his father's path. The lies, the self-deception.

Dorian had chosen to face himself in the mirror,

no matter how unpleasant the sensation of cataloging his own flaws and working to change them.

He expected no less from the very few people he let into his life. Conrad had always been one of the few men alive who lived up to Dorian's standards. He had no doubt that Erika would, too. He'd seen what she could be for him and with him last night.

And while he was busy celebrating that unexpected connection that had rocked him to his core, he also needed to make her see that she was worthy.

Of his interest and devotion, which he planned to lavish on her—in the way a man with his particular appetites did, that was—but also of all the other things she'd walked away from. The relationships she pretended didn't matter. The empty life she pretended made her happy. All those things she'd made sure to ruin herself before anyone could take them away from her.

He aimed to give her the tools to take them back.

It didn't take a psychiatrist to understand that a woman like Erika, who hid her truly sweet, soft, longing heart beneath so many layers of attitude and armor, had set out to destroy her relationship with her brother after their father died because that way, she lost him on her terms.

Dorian was ashamed he hadn't recognized that years ago.

Then again, maybe he had. After all, he'd mentioned spanking to her in Greece. Had he sensed, even then, where they would end up?

"I can't make you do anything," he told her now,

watching intently as her bravado faded. "You must choose, and accept the consequences of the choices you make. Are you prepared to do that?"

"Are we talking about my brother's engagement party—or sex?"

"On some level, Erika, I think you and I are always talking about sex."

Her eyes dilated and her lips parted, telling him she'd lost her breath. Dorian felt that intensity snap into place between them, stronger today. Because they both knew where it went. And that meant imagining where else and how hard it could go.

"I thought we were talking about a party," she said, blinking like she wanted to clear her head. *Good luck, little one,* he thought. "And for some reason, you seem to think you can dictate my behavior."

"You should know that I have every intention of dictating a hell of lot more than that." He smiled at her faintly, over his granite counter and the food he'd prepared for her. He liked this. He liked her here, looking uncertain and mulish—and safe. "I'm a bossy man, Erika. Some people pay for the privilege of having me tell them what to do with their business affairs and their messy lives. All I require from you is that you let me. And thank me. Is that so much to ask?"

"Yes."

"Are you sure? You seemed to enjoy it last night. Or were all those orgasms a decoy for your true feelings?"

She scowled at him. "Sex isn't life. It's just sex."

But he could see the way she gripped the counter, her knuckles turning white, and he knew she didn't believe that.

"Not the way we do it," he said. "If I were you, I'd look at last night as a lesson."

"Which part was a lesson?" she asked. "The spanking? Or when you fucked me, came hard enough to take the back of your head off and then cuddled with me all night long? Or maybe you mean *you* learned a lesson."

Dorian was around the counter before he meant to move, and then it was too late. For her. He trapped her there, taking far too much pleasure in the little squeaking sound she made as she found herself with her back against the granite, his arms on either side of her like a cage.

He watched her face flush and her eyes go glassy. He studied the pulse that hammered in her throat. And the rich, sweet scent of her arousal spiced the air between them, making his cock even harder than before.

"I don't like your tone." He leaned closer, smiling when she jumped. He put his mouth on a set of goose bumps that rose along her neck. "Rethink it."

"I don't see why I can't talk to you any way I like," she retorted, sounding awfully tough for someone who was trembling slightly between his arms. And making no attempt to get away from him. "Or do you not see the difference between in a scene and out of a scene?"

"You called me sir, Erika. Do you?"

She flushed at that, and he saw some of that bravado leak away from her. "I was kidding."

"Were you? Or were you trying to goad me into reacting negatively, the way you like to do in all areas of your life?"

Her mouth dropped open, and temper chased something like misery across her face.

"I wanted to explore extreme sex acts, not engage in a group therapy session," she threw at him.

"Too bad, little girl. It's one-stop shopping with me."

She lifted her chin, and her struggle was all over her face. "You're a terrible therapist. News flash—you're not supposed to hate the client."

Dorian stared her down, the dominant in him roaring in triumph when she flushed and lowered her eyes.

"I don't hate you," he told her, using his darkest, most dominant voice, because he knew she would hear him. Even if she didn't want to. "Quite the contrary. I've been waiting for you for a long time, Erika. And now that I've found you, I have no intention of letting you go."

"What do you…?"

She was trembling, her eyes were wide, and she seemed to lose her train of thought halfway through. He liked it.

"But nothing comes easy, does it?" He shook his head sadly. "You found me. And guess what that means? Now you have to contend with me and all my demands. And believe me, Erika, they never get any easier."

"I don't want to *contend* with you," she managed to say. "I just want to fuck you."

"You can't have one without the other."

"Then I'll fuck someone else, Dorian. Many someone elses. Repeatedly and enthusiastically."

He smiled. "And how has that been working out for you so far?"

She flushed a deep, betraying red at that, pleasing him so deeply that it took all he had to keep from hauling her up against him. Her eyes got wetter and he knew that if he reached down between her legs, her pussy would be soft and hot and greedy for him.

"Surrender, baby," he told her quietly. "I'm not letting you go."

And he didn't tell her how fully he meant that. He didn't have to—not when she reacted as if he'd electrocuted her. He could see the fear on her face, and how quickly she covered it up with temper. Dorian had never wanted to wrap a woman in his arms so badly before, for the simple pleasure of holding and soothing her.

Without even paddling her first.

Necessarily.

"If you have such a poor opinion of my character," she gritted out at him, though her eyes were too big and much too dark, "and this driving need to psychoanalyze things you know nothing about, why would you want me to submit to you in the first place?"

His smile deepened. "Because I want you to be the best version of you. I want you to make choices out of strength, not fear."

And it shocked him a little as he said it, because he realized this wasn't new. He'd been uniquely disapproving of Erika Vanderburg for as long as he could remember. But until she'd appeared in his club, he'd never been able to fully imagine her as anything but Conrad's little sister.

"Not that you're a wild egomaniac or anything," she threw at him.

He let his smile cool and his gaze darken, and saw her shiver in response. It was that instinctive response she couldn't control, no matter how disrespectfully she chose to speak to him.

"You have two choices now," he told her with quiet menace. "You can leave. I won't stop you or chase you. I had the concierge find you some more appropriate clothing should you require it, and I'll have a car take you wherever you wish to go. No harm, no foul."

Once more, he watched misery move over her face and had to order himself not to help her. It was her struggle. It was his job—and his pleasure—to make it all that much more pointed, sure, but he couldn't do it for her. No matter how much he might want to.

He'd never experienced this so acutely before. He'd led many a submissive through a scene. But this was her life. And his, if he had his way. *Theirs.*

"Or?" Her voice was husky with emotion, just one of the many ways her body told him truths she wouldn't. Or couldn't. "What if I have a taste for harm and foul?"

Dorian straightened, pushing back from the

counter. He stood at his full height, aware of the way her mouth softened. He could see her pulse in her throat, rapid and obvious. Beneath his shirt, her nipples hardened to needy points.

Her body knew whom she belonged to.

"I'm going to leave the room for a moment," he told her. "When I come back in, you can be dressed in the clothes I left for you on the chair. You can eat. Drink more coffee. I'll leave you to it."

Her breath was a scraping thing between them. "Or…?"

"Or you will be sitting on the table, completely naked with your legs spread wide, eyes closed and your hands behind your back."

He watched her shudder.

"Maybe I have things to say to you," she said, though her voice was thicker now. As was the scent of her need. "And I'm not sure I want all of my sentences to end in *sir*."

"Noted."

He didn't say anything else. He didn't give her permission or argue the point, he just walked away. He went back out to the great room, where he'd left his bag, pulled out the item he'd found earlier and then took his time coming back.

And he wasn't *surprised* to find her right where he wanted her. But he was pleased.

Everything in him went still, then hot. His predatory focus kicked in, hard. He wanted to eat her alive.

He intended to do just that.

"Don't hold your breath," he told her as he moved closer. "I won't be happy if you pass out."

"I'm not going to—"

"Baby, we're deep in it now. Your usual safe word applies. If you continue to speak to me disrespectfully, I'll respond. And I don't think you'll like it."

He roamed toward her, feeling the sweet kick as the beauty of her splayed-open position flooded through him. She sat exactly as he'd imagined she would, stark naked on his table like his very own feast, her body flushed and soft against the hard black granite of the tabletop. Her hands were behind her back, just as he'd asked, making her breasts jut forward and up. Her eyes were shut tight, as if she had to frown to make herself obey. And in between her wide-open legs, he could see her pussy glistening with need.

She was perfect.

All he had to do was prove it to her.

"The only time you seem to behave is when I tell you to," he said as he came closer. "Do I have to parade around an engagement party with you on a leash to make you behave appropriately? Because I think you know I will."

When she only breathed, hard and fast, he reached out to run his palm over her shoulder. Then he took one of her pebble-hard nipples between his fingers. And pinched it.

She hissed, then squirmed, telling him she'd felt it in her pussy, too.

"Answer me, please."

"No…no." She panted. "I don't need a *leash*."

But he doubted he was the only one imagining it, then.

"I'm not punishing you, Erika," he said as he continued to pinch her nipple, raising his other hand to treat her other one the same. She was instantly responsive, arching her back to press her breasts more completely into his palms no matter what expression she wore on her face. "I'm encouraging you. It would please me greatly if you did not take the occasion of your brother's engagement party to make a spectacle of yourself." He frowned when her eyes shot open, mutinous and mad. "Eyes closed. Now."

She shut her eyes again, even as she flushed a bright red that he took for temper. And her reaction to her obedience, if he had to guess.

"I want you to wear something conservative that will cause absolutely no comment at all, unless it is a quiet compliment. The only attention you should be interested in is mine."

She shuddered, hard.

Dorian continued, "I want you to congratulate Conrad, and his fiancée, and if while you're doing it you can work in an apology for past behavior, I will be delighted. Do you understand what I'm asking of you?"

"I understand it," Erika said after a moment while he plucked at her nipples. "But I don't know what makes you think that after you spent all this time insulting me I would do a single thing for you."

"I'll tell you why," he said.

Dorian moved between her legs, enjoying the contrast between her total nakedness and the fact he was dressed. He ran his palms over her thighs, then gripped them to yank her closer to the edge of the table. Only when her ass was on the edge did he again cup her lovely breasts in his hands. He moved his thumbs over her nipples, rougher than before, and enjoyed the way it made her squirm. Then he leaned forward, and put his mouth to her ear.

"You will do it because I want you to," he told her. "Because it will please me. Because I want you to be the person I know you can be."

Goose bumps marched down her neck, toward her collarbone. And below.

"Or I could gently suggest that you go fuck yourself," she said, defiant to the last.

"Let me convince you," he said, his voice a dark ribbon of sound.

Dorian bent down and took one of her nipples in his mouth, sucking hard. She arched into him. Her head fell back, and she made a helpless sort of noise when he moved his demanding mouth to her other nipple, and treated it with the same erotic roughness.

He indulged himself with her taste. She was velvet and rose and he was addicted. He pulled away, then used his hands again until both nipples were dry again. She was so responsive, he entertained himself imagining all the ways he could make her come with nipple stimulation alone.

But that was for another day.

Today, he had other goals. He pulled out the tiny

evil clamps he'd retrieved from his bag. He clamped one nipple, and laughed at the noise she made. Then he clamped the other one, not at all surprised that she lost her head completely, jerking as if she couldn't decide whether she wanted to get away from him or move closer to him, or something in between. Her hands were no longer behind her back, but in those adorable fists at her side.

"Hands behind your back," he ordered her. When she obeyed, he rewarded her. "Open your eyes."

And when she did, all that pretty blue was glazed over.

"That hurts," she said, as if he'd betrayed her.

"You can take it." And to prove it, he tugged gently on the chain that connected the two clamps, making her gasp again. "You will take it."

And before she could say another word, he wrapped his other hand around the back of her head, and then took her mouth with his.

Finally.

He kissed her hungrily, thoroughly. He invaded her mouth, wet and dark and encompassing, the next best thing to fucking her.

And she kissed him back the same way.

Making him wonder why the hell he'd wasted all these years and all this time *not* doing exactly this.

Dorian kissed her until she went limp, and he kept going. He tried one filthy angle after the next until she was trembling beneath his hands, making needy and helpless noises in the back of her throat, and seemed to have forgotten about the clamps entirely.

So he tugged on the chain again, to remind her, and lapped up every greedy little noise she made.

He pulled away then, and stared down at her. She fought to catch her breath. Her eyes looked appealingly dazed, while her mouth was damp from his. Her color was high and good. She looked thoroughly debauched, and the clamps on her breasts made him so hard he almost hurt.

"What was it you wanted to say to me?" he asked her.

Politely.

"I don't…"

"If memory serves, you suggested I was a coward."

He watched her fight to access her brain again. He reached down and pushed her thighs farther apart, to the point where she had to strain the slightest bit to keep them open. Then he held her there, and waited.

"Why so quiet?" he asked her, a gentle taunt. "You came downstairs filled to the brim with insults. I'm beginning to think that all the trouble you cause with your mouth could be averted if you used it to do something other than talk."

An image that made his cock pulse with his own dark need. But she hadn't earned the privilege of sucking him off yet.

"Your rules are convenient," she said, focusing enough to frown at him. "You change them to suit yourself."

"Of course I do. Suiting myself is the whole point. If you concerned yourself less with following or not following the rules and more with pleasing me, it wouldn't matter, would it?"

"But you don't want me to please you," she said, holding herself very still, no doubt because every breath made those clamps tug on her nipples. "You want me to break your rules so you can punish me."

"Baby, I'm going to punish you one way or another no matter what you do." He grinned. "That's kind of the point."

"Not for me," said the woman who was dripping wet and trembling on the edge of an orgasm, all because he'd clamped her nipples. "I'm here for the sex."

"You like your sex with some pain to accentuate the pleasure," he said. He reached behind her and moved her arms, setting her hands down flat on the tabletop. "Ask me how I know."

"Maybe as an experiment," she lied, her eyes wide and full of shit. "Once in a while, as an adventure, and not because I *need*—"

"I think that's enough talking, kitten," Dorian said. Then he bent down, hauling her legs up over his shoulders and bringing his mouth down hard on her pussy in a single, swift movement.

He could feel her reaction go through her as she caught herself on the hands he'd moved for precisely that purpose, but that wasn't quite enough. So he reached up, and tugged on that chain, knowing that it would send that exquisite pain narrowing through her body, lighting her up.

That was how he wanted her.

Lit up, bright red, sweet and soft against his tongue. He tugged on the clamps again, and she got wetter, like dessert.

So he ate his fill.

Dorian ate her hard, as demanding as everything else, because she made the most delicious sounds. Her clit was stiff and proud beneath his tongue, and when he took it between his teeth, she screamed.

He took her to the edge again and again, throwing her over every time, until he had to slide his hands around to hold her steady because she couldn't seem to keep herself upright. He sank two fingers deep into the molten heat of her pussy, curling them around to rub against that rough spot tucked away in there. She made a keening kind of sound.

Then he leaned over her, kissing her so she could taste herself.

She came again, short and hard, with a deep groan that was like poetry to him.

"Promise me you'll do what I want you to do," he said. "Promise me now, Erika."

Her head thrashed from side to side. "I don't want to."

"Do it anyway," he growled.

And he reached down to free his cock, rolled on a condom, then slammed himself into her.

She made herself into a bow, arching up off the table like every wet dream he'd ever had. She was gorgeous, glorious, so he took her hard. She wrapped her legs around him, and met him, thrust for thrust.

And watching her fuck him back was so hot he was tempted to come himself.

But he wasn't quite done.

"Promise me, Erika," he said.

"I thought we were supposed to be done with talking," she managed to gasp out.

And he couldn't help himself. That made him laugh.

And as an extra incentive, he pulled the clamps off.

He knew that the pain would go through her like a shock, and he knew it did exactly what he wanted it to do when she screamed.

Dorian was deep inside her, pounding into her at a relentless pace—long and hard and deep—and he watched her shake like she might fall apart, as if the pain was picking her up and carrying her further.

She came beautifully. She was perfect.

And when she came back down, he picked her up, holding her there against him with his hands gripping that ass of hers that still bore his marks.

"Come," she begged him. "Please, Dorian. Come."

"Please, who?" he gritted out.

"Please, sir," she panted at him. "I want to feel you come inside me."

"Then you know what to do." He pulled out, then slammed himself back in, and her eyes went fuzzy. But she dug her fingers into his shoulders, and held on. "You know what I want."

"I promise," she said, as if it hurt her. "I promise. I'll do it."

For you, she didn't say.

But he heard it.

And when he let himself go at last, deep inside the tight fist of her pussy, she came with him, sobbing out his name.

Already his, he thought with profound satisfaction.

Whether she knew it or not.

CHAPTER NINE

THE FIRST WEEK after Berlin, Erika was…angry.

If that was the right word to describe the intensity of the emotions that jostled around inside her, fighting for supremacy, shifting and changing and sandbagging her every time she thought she had a handle on what was happening inside her.

Because she refused to accept that it had been a full-scale sea change.

She had spent two more days with Dorian.

Two more days filled with…more. With him.

Playing the kind of games she learned were called *playing* and *games* when they weren't really playing at all. Not when they could change a person so completely. So profoundly.

Dorian had tied her up. He'd experimented with cuffs and collars and other binding things. He arranged her on that massive bed of his, attaching her wrists and ankles to the handy chains welded to those steel posters, and he taught her things about herself that she hadn't known were there.

Over and over again.

And afterward, when she was lost in that buzzy, intense space that only he could put her in—where her mind and her emotions and her body were all one, all his—she told him stark truths she'd spent her whole life hiding from.

That she'd thought her father had left her, specifically, when he'd died. She had been the last one to see him and she had learned, during his illness, that good girls were quiet. Silent. Diffident and biddable at all times. And somehow, once he was gone, she'd decided that there was no point in being a *good girl* when people went ahead and died.

So she went in the opposite direction.

Hard.

She told him things she'd never really put into words before. That yes, as he'd suggested, a major part of why she'd dropped out of university was because she'd actually been good at studying and it made her feel like her old self again. Like that good girl she'd lost along the way, or not *lost*. That made it sound like something that had just happened. When she'd deliberately set about exterminating any traces of that girl who longed to please, bit by bit and year by year, until no one remembered she'd ever existed except Erika herself.

And though she never would have put it into words the way Dorian had, she'd shoved Conrad away, too. Because the people who loved her—who genuinely cared for her—died. Her mother was a safe space in that regard because as far as Erika could tell, she truly cared only about herself. Everything else was window dressing. Erika didn't expect anything from her and the beauty of it was, Chriszette never disappointed.

She couldn't believe the things Dorian got her to talk about.

He'd introduced her to a real flogger, not the hennight jokey versions she'd thought were real before. He taught her the exquisite fear, twined as it was with an almost overwhelming sense of delirious need, for that arch of his brow that promised exactly the pain, punishment and pleasure she wanted.

She discovered she liked anything—sooner or later, and sometimes only because of where they ended up—if Dorian delivered it.

Erika found he could read her body with a fluency that should have terrified her. That did terrify her, sometimes. He knew how far to push her, and it was always further than she thought she could go.

He always asked her if she needed her safe word.

And then, when she gave him the green light, he used it push her limits. Over and over again during those two days that seemed like so much longer to her. Several lifetimes, at least.

Erika found herself caught between her own worst impulses, as if he'd tied her there. Deliberately. She wanted to run. She wanted to kneel. She wanted to lose herself in him on the one hand, and on the other, she wanted to prove her independence. Leap to her feet, storm out and make him regret that he had ever pretended to know her.

In his hands she was made of passion and dark

greed, and rewarded for both. He made her cry and he made her come, and then he held her against him as she sobbed and slept and told him the stories she kept deep inside her and had never told another living soul.

She felt like a different person with him, and that was the real betrayal. In that brief span of time, a single weekend, she felt like the woman she'd secretly always wanted to be. Beautiful. Capable.

Lovable, something kept whispering inside her.

Dorian didn't tell her he loved her and she wouldn't have believed it if he did, but still. There was a look in his dark gaze. A certain gleam when he looked at her that made her wonder what it would be like. To always be here, with him, and a part of this powerful thing they shared. Part of this beautiful dance of mirroring, reflection and awareness.

Mixed in with blistering-hot sex and too many orgasms to count.

It would be a very lucky woman indeed who found herself kept forever by this man, she found herself thinking on that final morning. He'd bent her over the couch, where he'd spanked her that first night, burying his hands in her hair to hold her head where he wanted it. And he'd taken her with a brutal elegance that had left her wrecked in his wake.

Dorian had gazed at her before he'd left, tucking himself away into a three-piece suit that made him almost look like a stranger after the days of T-shirts, jeans and his dominance—were it not for that intensity and power of his that no suit could hide. He filled rooms with every breath, confidence and assurance stamped deep into his bones.

He looked at her as she panted and shook through the aftershocks. He looked *through* her, his mouth unsmiling and too much knowledge in his gaze.

He hadn't said goodbye. He hadn't said he would see her soon, indicating that he expected her to be there when he got back from his business meetings in Zürich.

"When I ring you," he said in that tone that made every hair on her body feel as if it was standing on end, "I expect you to answer."

It was almost as if he knew what she was going to do.

First, Erika had sobbed, there on that leather couch, where he'd first introduced her to herself.

Then she'd left, wearing the clothes she'd come in that first night and not capable of giving a single shit that she was on the streets of Berlin at midday on a Monday with her thong visible, her ass cheeks hanging out and a tiny, strappy little top that might as well have shouted her interest in bondage to everybody she passed on the street.

But it was Berlin, so nobody paid her the slightest bit of attention.

And that stung, too. Because it was impossible to discount everything Dorian had told her when there she was, prancing down the street as if she wanted some stranger to pay her some mind.

He had introduced her to herself, then confronted her with all that meant, and she didn't like it.

She'd gone back to her hotel, packed up her things and gotten the hell out of Germany.

But another fun fact about her madcap existence, about which she bragged to all and sundry as if she loved every second of it, was that she didn't have anywhere to go. Not really. She lived out of hotels, or in the guest suites at friends' houses. She'd been doing it so long that she'd long since stopped thinking too closely to be...rootless.

Untethered. Unattached.

If asked, she called it freedom. *Pure happiness*, she'd said a few weeks back. She'd been on her way to Berlin with a small stopover in Copenhagen to see the sort of friends who asked deep questions over wine, not because they were deep themselves, but because they liked to compete with their answers. The better to pretend their shallow lives had depth.

Erika was fantastic at pretending to be the happiest.

Are you happy? Dorian had asked her. Mercilessly. *Or have you wrapped up* hapless *in a curated social media feed and forgotten that the core of all that glossy performance is emptiness?*

In retrospect, what Erika was happy about was that she'd been gagged when he'd asked that question, because she still didn't know how to answer it.

Nor did the answer come to her as she landed in England, and made her way to Devon, where her mother was living it up in a country manor with her latest conquest, who claimed a Windsor connection and spent as much time tramping about his property with his dogs as he did tending to his gout flare-ups.

Not that Chriszette was ever in the mood to entertain a full-grown daughter for more than the odd meal.

Erika was dispatched to a renovated carriage house far enough away from than main hall that Chriszette could pretend she wasn't about, where she assured herself that she was *perfectly fucking happy*. And then fumed, like it was her job to prove it.

She was angry with herself for putting herself into that situation in Berlin in the first place. What had she been thinking? She was angry with her brother in general for being an overbearing asshole, and specifically for having such terrible taste in friends. She was angry with her mother, who could have taken maybe five minutes from her own narcissism to do a little parenting, back in the day, when her daughter was clearly acting out her grief—but hadn't bothered. And certainly felt no compulsion to make up for that now.

And she was deeply, volcanically angry at Dorian.

Because she couldn't help feeling that the only revenge taken had been against her. By her, which was worse, because she'd been correct in her initial assessment, if nothing else. Dorian was an excellent weapon.

"You'll forget him in about forty-eight hours," she told herself, out loud and with great confidence, when she sat down on the side of her carriage house bed, high in the eaves. "Less, probably."

Because forgetting about men was something Erika was very, very good at. But Dorian wasn't like other men. He didn't fade away, out of sight and out of mind.

For the first time in her life, Erika was plagued with insomnia, hollow-eyed and up at all hours, because her body wanted what it couldn't have. It wanted Dorian's body next to hers, holding her tight, when she'd spent her entire previous life asserting with great confidence that she was the kind of person who didn't like to cuddle while she slept.

She never had, before.

But then, there were a lot of things she'd never done before that weekend in Berlin with Dorian.

And toward the end of that first week and into the second week after she'd left him, Erika mostly just cried.

She felt tossed out to sea and abandoned while wave after wave of old, ugly emotion found her and sank her. Over and over again.

She almost thought it would be easier to drown.

But Dorian didn't let her.

He didn't call every day. Perhaps every other day. Sometimes he sounded terse, busy, and she hated that she felt particularly special that he made time for her. Other times he sounded tired, and she wished she could have the opportunity to soothe him. But he always sounded like *him*. Dark and richly textured and *him*.

"I don't want to talk to you," she said when she picked up the phone, the way she often did. Because even if that was true, she still obeyed him. He'd told her he expected her to answer and here she was, answering. Every time. "But you asked me to answer when you rang. Behold my obedience."

"I never doubted you, Erika." His voice did magical, terrible things to her body. Her nipples pinched so hard she could feel that line of sensation spiral down into her clit. She was wet instantly. Soft and ready for whatever he might do to her. "Are you ready to talk about your feelings yet?"

"I talk about my feelings all day every day," she lied, and pretended she didn't feel a little kick of pleasure when he laughed. "It's true. I stop people on the street and download my every last emotion. I've already made a lot of new friends that way."

That was slightly less of a lie, if a person counted storming about in England's greenest hills and shouting at passing sheep.

She doubted very much the Dorian would count that at all.

"It sounds to me like you've taken a little emotional dip and have stayed there," he said. "I told you that you might."

"Not everything is a pageant of intensity," she snapped, and she was aware as she said it that she clearly didn't believe that herself. Because if she did, she wouldn't be sitting in her carriage house bedroom on her mother's lover's estate, with all the curtains closed tight against the drizzle of another English afternoon. God, she was so sick of her own shit. "And here's a fun fact. Not every emotion I have has something to do with you."

"I'm delighted to hear it," Dorian said smoothly, but still, there was that undercurrent that kicked at her and made her sit a little straighter. "I just landed in London. Your brother's party is this weekend. Now that you're so marvelously recovered from all the intimacy we shared, I hope you remember the promise you made me."

"Go to hell."

Dorian made a tsking sound that blazed through like the warning it was, making her body light up. Wet, needy, naughty—and desperate for the discipline only he could administer.

She wanted to hate herself for that but she couldn't quite get there. Not with his voice in her ear.

"That does not bode well for you, kitten," he said, with that soft, amused menace that made her...glow.

She cleared her throat. "What I do or don't do concerning my brother is no business of yours."

"If you say so."

And she could swear, if she closed her eyes, she could see the look he was wearing on his face when he sounded like that. All that dark, dangerous patience in his gaze. That unyielding power stamped into that unsmiling mouth that made her feel weak in all the best ways. What was it about this man that made her silly straight through?

"Are you touching yourself?" he asked, his voice stern.

Erika froze, because sure enough, she'd reached

down between her legs with one hand, and was pressing the heel of her palm against her throbbing clit. How the hell had he known that? "No."

"Don't lie to me."

Her hand fell away from her pussy as if he'd ordered her to stop touching herself. As if he'd reached over and physically removed her hand, more like.

"I'm not lying," she said. And his silence felt as sharp a rebuke as a slap on the ass. She sighed. "Now."

"Good," he said, and she could hear laughter and satisfaction then. And all that glorious heat. "Don't. As far as I'm concerned, that's my pussy and you can't touch it without my permission. I'll know, kitten. And there will be consequences."

"You can't just say things like that to people, Dorian. Are you insane? I can do anything I want with *my* body."

"What's that?" he asked, sounding mild and stern at once. The combination made goose bumps rise all over her skin. "Was that your safe word? Or was it another round of predictable complaints because you like to deal with your uncertainty by shooting off your mouth?"

She wanted to hang up on him. She didn't. And she hated herself for that, too.

"I'll see you this weekend," he promised her. Though it sounded a lot more like a threat. "And I'll expect you to remember every detail of the promise you made me, Erika. Because you can be certain I do."

And he cut off the call before she could protest. Deliberately, she was sure.

But something about his voice galvanized her. She got out of the bed where she'd been conducting her experiments in insomnia and petulance. She threw open the curtains and glared out at the gray day. She went down into the kitchen of the carriage house and stared around, uninspired, at the dry cereal boxes that had provided her with the bulk of her nutrition since she'd arrived. Because her mother certainly didn't want her grown daughter taking meals at the big house with her lover. Erika's very existence was a testament to Chriszette's age.

Erika had learned that lesson the hard way. And years ago. Now she accepted the fact that her mother liked to control her in between affairs, but never during them. A situation that had suited them both since Erika had left university.

Does it suit you? a dark voice that sounded suspiciously like Dorian's asked inside her. *Or do you put up with it because she treats you the way you think you deserve to be treated?*

"Shut up, Dorian," she muttered into the empty kitchen.

Her body was still flushed, and wound up, and she thought that maybe she should go ahead and handle her own needs. Because fuck him. Who cared what he ordered her to do? He wasn't the boss of her.

But even when she sat down, then slipped her hand back between her legs, she couldn't do it.

Because you want to be his, something that was

all her whispered, telling her more truths she didn't want to face.

Erika went on a long, punishing walk. When she'd exhausted herself, she trudged back to the carriage house and took a long bath. She soaked in the hot water until she was so heartily sick of herself and her own endlessly cycling thoughts that she thought she might scream.

She wrapped herself in a bath towel, then padded back to the bedroom. She picked up her phone, scowled at it for a while, and admitted that what she really wanted was for Dorian to call her again. Especially now that they were in the same country again.

I'll see you this weekend, he'd said, and she shivered now, because she would see him again.

But that meant she would be seeing other people, too. Maybe it was time to stop recovering from Berlin and start handling her actual life. The one that went on no matter how many hard truths Dorian had marked into her skin that weekend.

Erika pulled up Jenny's number.

So, she texted, what do you think I should wear to your ENGAGEMENT PARTY to MY BROTHER?

Her phone rang almost immediately.

"Oh my God, Erika," Jenny cried when Erika picked up. "I thought you were blanking me."

"I wasn't *not* blanking you."

"Where are you? Are you still in Germany?"

"No," Erika said, her body flushed from her bath. She looked down at herself, caught by that same awareness that had haunted her since she'd left Berlin. That this wasn't *her* body any longer. That he'd made it his. And why was that the only thing that seemed to soothe her? "I'm in Devon with Chriszette and her latest fling. Lord Something or Other. I only stayed in Berlin for that one weekend."

The way she often had, over these last six months. Jenny would think nothing of it. Another weekend clubbing, that was all. And Erika would let her think it, because she couldn't articulate what had happened between her and Dorian to herself. There was no way she could explain it to anyone else.

And maybe that was why, when the silence stretched out between them, she let it. Because she understood it.

"It would be better to see you in person—and before the party," Jenny said after a moment. "Can you come up to London?"

Erika looked around at the carriage house that had become a prison of all the emotions she'd told Dorian she wasn't experiencing. She thought about the fact she'd be seeing Dorian himself this weekend, and all the anticipation and anxiety, need and longing that kicked up. She thought about the promise she'd made him and what that would mean—could she really apologize to her brother?

Her brother, whom Jenny was marrying, for reasons unclear.

"As a matter of fact," Erika said, "I would love to come to London. I could use a break."

She did not add *from me*.

Because that would require explanations she didn't want to give, not even to her oldest friend.

But if she could, she thought the next morning as she caught the train from Cranbrook to London Waterloo Station, she would have left herself behind.

CHAPTER TEN

THEY MET IN the breathtakingly posh bar of an extraordinarily luxurious and exclusive hotel where they'd liked to sneak away to during their Oxford years and imagine what their lives would be like when they graduated.

Erika could almost squint and see all those dreams dancing there in the dimly lit, aristocratically plush surroundings. It made it impossible not to engage in a game or two of what-if.

What if she'd lived these last years differently? Where would she be now? What would have happened if she'd stayed at Oxford and done as Jenny had—because Lady Genevieve Charlotte Elizabeth Markham, Jenny to her friends, was nothing if not dutiful.

In the flattering light of the cozy, quiet bar, Jenny looked as if she could still be the teenager she'd been when they'd met as first years. She sat across from Erika looking as disarmingly approachable as ever, which had always been her secret weapon. She radiated warmth even when she wasn't feeling the slightest hint of it herself. Erika had been drawn to it. Who wouldn't be?

Maybe Conrad could use a little warmth, too, came that dark voice inside.

She told her inner Dorian to go fuck himself.

And then she marinated in memories and more what-ifs while Jenny set about ordering them wine.

Dutiful, well-behaved Jenny had taken the requisite job in an appropriate charity after she'd graduated with her first in classics. Like many girls of her station, saddled with a father consumed with notions of bloodlines and the consolidation of hereditary lands, her charity work had only ever been meant to be a stopgap. A pretty little notation on her résumé. One that she could toss aside the moment she assumed her true duties as a wife of a worthy, wealthy gentleman. Preferably one of her father's choosing.

"You haven't posted a single thing on any social media site in weeks," Jenny said when they were both properly fortified with glasses of wine and a tray of spiced nuts. "I was starting to think the announcement might have killed you."

She smiled as she said it, though her gaze was wary.

"The announcement was a surprise," Erika agreed. And she'd received it not only from Dorian, but from Jenny, Chriszette—and even Conrad's assistant. Lest she complain that she hadn't been invited or informed, she supposed. Things she couldn't imagine doing now but she certainly might have done a few weeks back. She could admit that. "But I survived it intact."

Jenny sighed as she played idly with her wineglass. And Erika couldn't keep herself from studying the enormous, sparkling ring that didn't quite fit on her slender left hand. It slid as she moved, tipping the great stone this way, then that.

Silence had never been their thing. And Erika was suddenly struck by the unpleasant realization that it was because she'd always filled it. She'd always been perfectly happy to twitter on about herself, hadn't she? Especially in recent years, when she'd viewed every in-person meeting with anybody as an opportunity to deliver highly curated press releases on how wonderful her life was.

Confront yourself and you conquer your fears, Dorian had told her, the dick.

"Jenny," Erika said softly now, with more self-possession than she'd ever thought she had. "Tell me how this happened."

She'd wanted to say *this tragedy*, which she certainly would have before. But something stopped her tonight—possibly the fact that Jenny certainly didn't look *tragic*. And more to the point, hadn't asked Erika's opinion.

It was another little prick of shame that the pre-Berlin version of Erika would have steamrolled right in and bludgeoned half of London with her opinion without caring if anyone had solicited it. How charming.

"As I've mentioned before, I'm sure, my father

has never appreciated my passion for charity work," Jenny said, smiling wryly over her glass of wine.

"I would be astonished if your father appreciated passion in any form."

Jenny's smile deepened. "He's quite fond of his dogs."

Erika drank from her own glass. "I'm not sure I can figure out how we get from passionate charity work that benefits children in war zones to... Conrad."

Jenny's smile faded. She frowned down at her wine, but didn't take a sip.

"We were at an event in Stockholm. My father likes me to play his hostess even when it's not his party, so I was with him when he met Conrad. They started talking business, my father liked him, and a few days later he announced that he'd taken it upon himself to set us up on a date." She lifted her gaze. "Which isn't unusual. I've complained about this before. Any day now I expect him to simply announce that he's sold me off."

Erika smiled. Then returned to the subject at hand. "And you went on the date, clearly."

"I didn't dare say no," Jenny said. "I assumed Conrad had either been pushed into it, or thought he could go on a single pity date and then carry on with whatever business dealings he had with my father. But instead, he asked me out on a second date."

"And again, you went?"

"I couldn't say no."

"It's simple, Jen. *No.* See? I did it."

"Erika." And her friend leveled a frank, sad sort of look at her. "Please stop pretending you don't know what my father's like. I've been playing this game for years. He sets me up on a date, and yes, I go on the dates, because that's the price I have to pay for my independence."

"You shouldn't have to pay a price for your independence."

Jenny's smile was sad. "*Should* doesn't have much to do with it, I'm afraid. It never has done."

Erika remembered this from their university days. Jenny's sense of unwavering duty to her stuffy, unsupportive father—or maybe, more realistically, to the nostalgia she'd been raised on. The grand stories about what had made the Markham family great. And wealthy.

Not so long ago, she would have railed at her friend about this. Tonight, she kept her mouth shut instead.

"I know that I could rebel," Jenny said quietly when Erika didn't speak. "Sometimes I dream of it. But that's not who I am. So yes, I went on that second date, because my father expected me to. And I went on the third, and when Conrad brought me back home to my father's house, he stayed for a drink. And proposed marriage, there and then, with this honking great ring and all that… Well. You know what your brother is like. So *sure* of everything."

"I do indeed."

Jenny sent her a reproving look. "And it's all snowballed since. My father was the happiest I've seen him in years. Certainly since my mother died. Later that night, after Conrad left, he fairly waxed rhapsodic about putting me in safe hands at last."

"But, Jen." Erika's voice was soft. Not quite imploring, but close. "You don't love him."

Jenny took a breath, but her gaze was steady when it met Erika's.

"He's kind to me," she said simply. "We want the same things, more or less. He's perfectly happy if I continue working, which isn't something I could say for all the cavemen my father's sent me on dates with. I'm going to have to marry one of them. Conrad is by far the best option."

"Jenny..."

"And besides," she said hurriedly, "sex is not a motivating factor for me the way it is for you."

"That's because you've never been fucked properly." Erika laughed at Jenny's expression. "You know it's true. Or maybe you don't, which is sad, but *I* know it's true. Wait a minute." She narrowed her eyes at her friend. "Are you saying that Conrad's bad in bed? Or are you saying you haven't sampled the wares yet?"

"I can't imagine that you would want me to answer that question either way. About *your brother.*"

Erika made a face. "I really don't. But as your friend, it's my duty to ask."

"I haven't slept with him, no," Jenny said, her cheeks red in the dark of the bar. It made Erika wonder how her friend would react if she found herself standing in the Walfreiheit Club one fine night. Or what she'd do if faced with a man like Dorian.

But she couldn't let herself think about Dorian. Not now.

"There's hardly been time," Jenny was saying. "It's all been a whirlwind and my father insisted on throwing this party—"

"You can't marry a man if you don't know what he's like in bed," Erika said. "Really, you can't."

"People have been doing exactly that for centuries."

"And they've been wildly unhappy."

"Not always." Jenny shook her head, and her grip on her wineglass tightened. Visibly. "I don't expect you to understand this decision, Erika. It's a bit like being on a runaway train, if I'm honest. But what's the harm in it? He's not pretending to love me. I'm not pretending to love him. And, you know, there's lots of research to prove that arranged marriages are happier, on balance, than marriages based on romantic love."

"I'll be sure to make that toast at the wedding. Here's to a sexless union of people who don't love each other, but whose financial portfolios match well enough to plod along. Three cheers."

"Just as long as you come to the wedding." Jenny reached over and grabbed Erika's wrist in a fully out-of-character move that made Erika both love her more and worry for her at the same time. "We might not be love's young dream, but we're going to be all right. And I would very much like your blessing."

And a few weeks ago, Erika would have lost her shit. She knew it. She would have said terrible things to Jenny that she'd never be able to take back. She would have called up her brother and shouted a whole lot more things, likely uglier by far. And she certainly wouldn't have been able to sit here and listen to this breakdown of what had to be one of the stupidest reasons to marry another person she'd ever heard in her life. Especially coming from Jenny, who had always been a romantic.

But then, romantic or not, Jenny thought she didn't like sex. Erika had always thought that wasn't quite the truth, and that, really, Jenny had a thing about the man she called her best friend and had therefore never touched that way. Dylan Kilburn had been a first year with them at Oxford, had been brooding in Jenny's direction since day one, and yet Jenny had resolutely refused to see him as anything but a friend. For years now. Erika was chock-full of theories as to why.

A couple of weeks ago, she would have hammered her friend with each and every one of those theories, but she was different now. And Erika wasn't sure she liked that strange awareness deep inside her. She wasn't sure she approved of it. But that didn't matter, because either way, she wasn't the same.

She had always wished that she could choose not to make a mess rather than always and forever trying to figure out how to clean it up. And tonight she found she could put it into practice. She put her hand on top of Jenny's and kept her gaze steady. And she set aside her own feelings on the topic, because it didn't matter what she felt or thought. Jenny hadn't asked her for her theories, she'd asked for Erika's blessing.

"You couldn't keep me away from your wedding," Erika said very distinctly. And found as she spoke that she meant it. "It doesn't matter who you're marrying or why. I will be there, with bells on. You can count on it."

Later, as she was lying in the hotel room she'd taken for the night—curled up on her side with that ravenous hunger between her legs that still she didn't take care of because Dorian had told her not to—she remembered Jenny's face. And how stunned she'd looked that Erika had given her blessing.

And hadn't made the whole damn thing about herself, more likely.

Erika wrapped herself up in her coverlet and pretended it was Dorian's arms around her.

What if this was the strength you brought to every part of your life? he had asked her after another one of his wicked, ingenious scenes. He'd turned her inside out, left her gasping and half-mad, and yet convinced on a deep level that she could take anything he dished out. *What if you controlled yourself out there, and only let outside forces control you when those forces were me?*

And she felt too full there, in another anonymous hotel bed. Alone. Close to bursting and too thick with it for it to be anger. Or anything as straightforward as a sob.

Dorian had held up a mirror to her life and she couldn't pretend she hadn't looked into it. And seen.

Somehow, in surrendering herself to him, he had given her the control now. Out here, in the world. Because she knew what true surrender was like, so there was no reason to submit herself to every passing whim.

Erika had chosen to give herself completely to Dorian because he was powerful enough to keep her safe while she did it, and having done that, why would she bother with these lesser surrenders that never made her feel anything but alone?

She could have a host of emotions about her friend and her brother, but she didn't have to succumb to them.

She could *choose*.

She felt as if she'd been struck by lightning, so bright and hot was the jolt of awareness that hit her then.

Dorian had taught her how to choose.

Erika ran with that over the course of the next few days. She stayed in London, searching for the appropriate outfit. And this time, she didn't want attention in a general sense. She wanted his attention. Only his.

Not just his attention, if she was honest. His approval.

And when she tried on the perfect dress, cut to enhance rather than expose, it felt like his hands on her body. As if he lounged there in the corner of her dressing room, his eyes ablaze and his mouth that unsmiling line that made her heart flip over.

The night of the engagement party, she was

dressed, her hair pulled back into a neat chignon at her nape, and ready to go long before it was time to leave Devon and make the drive to the Markham family's stately home in Wiltshire.

Possibly, she thought wryly, *you are a little over-excited.*

She waited in the ancient gallery in her mother's lover's sprawling house. She stared at the dark portraits that lined the walls, each featuring some ancestor or another of his with the same red jowls he sported himself, and found herself very thankful indeed that her mother's taste in men had been much better when she was younger.

"My goodness, Erika," came her mother's stilted, affected voice from the stairs—as if she'd sensed Erika was entertaining uncharitable thoughts about her and had rushed to remind her why each and every one was true. "Are you ill?"

Erika turned to watch her mother come toward her. As ever, Chriszette was resplendent. An ice sculpture best enjoyed from a safe distance. Her blond hair was swept back from her smooth face and secured with combs. She wore a sweeping, elegant gown that made the most of her trim figure. She was a striking woman with a regal bearing and flashing blue eyes that made everyone around her feel as if really, they ought to curtsy.

And she certainly liked it when they did.

"Do I look ill?" Erika asked lightly. Because there was no telling how her mother would strike. Chriszette was like a snake. She was quite happy coiled up in the sun, until she wasn't. And sometimes she moved so fast you never even saw the strike coming until you bled.

"I have never seen you look so…appropriate," Chriszette said, her accent making her sound sharper than she perhaps meant. Then again, perhaps not.

"I'm going to take that as a compliment," Erika said with perhaps more determination than enthusiasm. "Thank you, Mother."

Chriszette did not like to be called *Mother*. Her blue eyes cooled considerably, which was always hard to imagine as she started out so devoutly frigid. She glanced toward the stairs, and Erika knew that she was looking to see if her lover had heard Erika admit to their relationship. A fate worse than death.

"Darling," Chriszette said with a smile that heralded the coming venom, "only very beautiful and very clever girls can afford to hide their assets. I assumed you knew that." She swept her eyes up and down, taking in every inch of Erika's body. "If you don't put on a little show and make sure they're looking at all that bare skin, they might remember that you're a university dropout who shuffles aimlessly from one place to another, effectively homeless. What is cute in one's twenties is a character flaw in later years. You'd do well to remember that."

The old Erika would have screamed back at her, which was what Chriszette wanted. The more of a mess her daughter was, the more she could make herself the maternal victim. The old Erika had known this as well as the current Erika did, but this was the first time that Erika did nothing but smile back at Chriszette. And fail to otherwise react.

A faint frown creased her mother's brow. "No one likes a born loser, Erika," she said. "But as you know, they are often dazzled by a whore."

"Thank you, Mother," Erika said, and she was shaking a little, but she didn't let it own her. The choice was hers, and she chose to let far more powerful things make her cry. Because *he* always sweetened that pot with a few orgasms. She nodded her mother. "I bow to your example, as always."

And her mother's lover appeared then, cutting off whatever vicious reply Chriszette might have planned to make.

The car swept them off for the long drive to Jenny's father's estate, where the party was being held in as much ancient, feudal splendor as possible. Right down to the selling of the bride, if Erika wanted to get technical.

And it wasn't until she'd followed her mother up the grand stairs that led into the soaring hall, then waited her turn while Chriszette left her coat and fluttered all over her lover, that Erika found herself attacked by her own nerves.

She told herself not to be silly.

Which...didn't really work.

After handing off her own coat, she drifted toward the grand ballroom. Chriszette liked to make an entrance, so the party was already in full swing as she swept inside.

Erika, for perhaps the first time in her life, didn't

particularly want to make a scene. So instead, she
headed farther into the house, toward one of the less
trafficked entrances to the ballroom. Then she stood
there for a moment. Jenny was moving through the
crowd, looking beautiful and bright and elegant, as
always. Jenny's father trailed along with her, looking puffed up and proud—an upgrade from his usual
puffed up and pompous.

And then Erika saw her brother, looking as grim
and determined as always.

It had been one thing to find a lovely dress. To
take on faith that her mother was wrong and Dorian
was right. That she had more to offer than too much
skin on display at an otherwise excruciatingly proper
party like this one, teeming as it was with the sorts
of people who appeared regularly in *Tatler*, yet found
their presence in its pages appalling.

She found it was one thing to do the things she'd
done with Dorian, and admit the truths he'd wrung
out of her.

But it would be something else again to look her
brother in the eye. Then apologize for not only disappointing him, but for going out of her way to disappoint *herself*, too. And then taking it out on him.
For years.

Her stomach twisted, then plummeted to the marble floor at her feet.

She must have been kidding herself. Or so hopped-
up on endorphins that she'd forgotten that Conrad
was hardly anybody's idea of the sweet, genial older
brother. He wasn't the sort to kick a football about or

help his younger sister with her maths. On the contrary, Conrad was a dark cloud of a man. He was so severe. So exacting. And he had a way of looking at a person that reminded Erika of their mother when she was poised to strike. Only worse, because Chriszette prized meanness.

Conrad valued accuracy.

And either way, Erika would end up with a hole punched straight through her.

There was absolutely no way that she could march up to him, make herself vulnerable and expose herself before that piercing blue stare of his.

The very idea made her want to curl up and die. Here and now.

She whirled around, thinking she would just grab her coat, call a car and leave all of this behind her—

But she slammed into a wall.

Except it wasn't a wall, she realized as two hands caught her shoulders, and she tipped her head back to look up acres of broad chest packed into black tie.

It was Dorian.

CHAPTER ELEVEN

"ARE YOU GOING SOMEWHERE, Erika?" he asked, his voice a dark, amused rumble, and with that dangerous gleam in his eyes. "Surely not."

And Erika…burst into flames.

She hadn't seen him since Berlin, and she'd thought his voice on the phone was too much. But this…

She couldn't hold his commanding gaze. Her whole body was a mass of flame and desire, that swamping, impossible need, and something that felt like shame. But it was much darker and less destructive than that, and somehow connected directly to that pulsing greed in her pussy.

Erika hated that they were both dressed in all these *clothes*. She yearned for the simplicity of his penthouse in Berlin, all those modern edges. And the quiet reality of her nakedness before his demands.

She could see those days laid out before her like a tableau. Like a fantasy. Like a wish made real, though she'd already experienced it.

God, how she wished she could go back.

Wasn't that what the past two weeks had been

about? Hating and wishing and wanting, desperate
to be in his presence again—

And now she was.

And it was here, at Conrad and Jenny's engagement party. Where he wanted her to do this thing
that would break her in half. She knew it would.
It would destroy her, and if she was destroyed, she
could never, ever go back. She could never have Berlin again.

She could never have *him* again.

Erika felt his fingers on her chin, and then he
tipped it up, forcing her to meet that dark, simmering gaze of his. She quivered. And thought she saw
the hint of a smile.

"You look beautiful, kitten," he said quietly.
"More than beautiful. You look like who you are."

That made her feel more than simply hot all over.
It made her want to sigh, maybe. And lean into him.
And it felt as if she already had.

"My mother disagrees," she said, concentrating
on his strong fingers pressing into her chin. "De-
mure clothing like this is for very beautiful women
or very clever ones. Dumb whores like me need to
put on a show. Tits and ass, presumably."

She wasn't sure why she'd said such things to a
man who had, until recently, been the most likely to
agree with Chriszette's take on her. Until she saw his
temper flash across his face, and not at her.

"Your mother is a very small, very jealous
woman." Dorian's brow rose, and Erika was condi-
tioned now. She felt the blaze of it go through her,

settling heavily in her oversensitive clit. Her nipples
ached for his mouth. She *hurt* for him. There was no
other way to put it. She already hurt for him, and she
would hurt more if he wanted, because the pain was
a blessing. It made everything bloom. Especially her.
"And I thought we covered this already. The only
opinion you need to consider is mine."

"I can't do it," she said breathlessly. "I can't apologize to him. You don't understand."

"I do understand." He was unyielding and it made
her melt even as it made her stomach twist again. "I
never told you it would be easy, little one. I only told
you that I expected you to do it."

Misery slammed into her, another tidal wave she
could do nothing to prevent. "I can't."

She expected him to look angry, but he didn't. He
looked only disappointed, which was worse. "That
is a choice."

And he had taught her all about choices, hadn't
he? He had taught her how to choose. But this didn't
feel like a choice. This felt like a death sentence.

"You want to humble me," she said. "Humiliate
me. I get that. It's important to you."

And to her surprise, Dorian laughed. "When I
want to humiliate you, kitten, you will know. You
will not be clothed in full view of the richest men
in Europe, one of whom is your brother. You will
very likely be on all fours, at my feet, and very, very
naked. Understand that first."

She was breathless as he dropped his hand from
her chin and then maneuvered her in front of him,

away from the crowded ballroom and deeper into
the house. He rested a hand on the nape of her neck
as if it belonged there, and Erika relaxed into it. The
weight of his palm felt right. Good. And after all the
turmoil of the past weeks, wave after wave of too
much emotion, it took her a moment to recognize
what it was that suffused her now.

Peace. Safety.

There was something about this man that felt like
home.

He opened a door, and ushered her inside, and it
took her a moment to allow her eyes to adjust to the
different lighting. It was a very small study, or sitting
room, that Erika had never seen on her previous visits
here. It was the kind of place the ladies of the house
might have retired in latter days to keep up with their
embroidery or correspondence. There were delicate,
ebullient furnishings, heavy on scrollwork and filigree.

In the middle of so much unrestrained femininity,
Dorian was like a brooding, lethal fist. All threat and
masculinity, and that uncompromising power that
blazed out of him like his very own sun.

That power that she took into her, gloried in and
made her own.

Dorian closed the door behind him and then stood
there, a narrow, assessing look on his beautiful face.

Inside, Erika felt fizzy. Bright.

He lifted one finger and twirled it in the air, indicating that she should turn for him. And she did,
different sensations scudding through her, but all of
them ending up in the same place. That delirious,

delectable heat between her legs that pulsed out into everything else.

"The trouble with you, Erika, is that you are too beautiful already. And far too clever."

His voice was almost more beautiful than he was, if such a thing was possible. It was his voice that had stayed with her in the time they'd been apart. She'd heard him on the phone and in her head, as if he had a direct connection to her body no matter where he was. As if he owned her, body and soul, mind and pussy, and everything in her exalted in that notion.

Not least because, if he owned her, surely she could own him in return. It was a power exchange after all. Not a power grab.

"When you walk around with your gorgeous body on display, people get silly," Dorian said, his gaze steady on her. "Stupid. They say jealous, small-minded things, as your mother has already amply demonstrated tonight. And people are not always as good as they should be about holding two ideas in their head at once."

"My mother holds a great number of ideas in her head, all of them nasty."

"It is easier to believe that stunning blonde woman with a smile that can light up a room and blue eyes the color of summer must be dumb," he said quietly. "Foolish, at the very least. An easily dismissible whore. I'm not surprised that the people in your life who feel threatened by all that you are would encourage you to dress and act as if you are far less than that."

He pushed off the door at his back and came toward her at last. And then, finally, he was touching her again. He ran his hands over her the way he'd done so many times before, as if he was memorizing her shape. This time, he skimmed his palms down her arms and then held them out at her sides.

"Dressed like the powerful heiress you are, you give all of these vipers no choice but to see the real you. I'm sure they won't like it." He shrugged, that dark intensity in his gaze never wavering. "But as we keep discussing, it only matters if *I* like it. And I do. Very much."

And she couldn't have said why that mattered so much to her. Only that it did. And that further, his praise felt like a crackling fire on a cold night.

"Dorian," she whispered. "I don't want you to be disappointed in me, but you will be. Because I can't—"

"Quiet, please."

It was an order. And on some level, Erika wanted to demand that he make these boundaries between a scene and life clearer to her. But then, she didn't want them clear. She wanted this, the poignancy and sharpness, the intensity and color, and the possibility that every moment with him was a scene.

And only sometimes would actual cuffs, whips and chains be involved.

But she had to shake that off, because she was thinking in terms of tomorrows and she doubted very much that he would want much to do with her by the end of the night.

Because she couldn't give him what he wanted.

"I want you to do something for me," Dorian said, sounding casual when his expression was anything but. "It's not an order. I'm going to tell you what I desire, what I wish, and you may choose or not choose to do it. What are you wearing under that dress?"

It felt as if he'd rocked a boat she hadn't known she was standing on, and she almost felt like she had whiplash as she fought to keep her balance. She expected him to bring up Conrad again and almost asked him why he hadn't...

But his gaze was intent on hers, and over the course of her time in Berlin, she had learned that it was better not to test his patience. She bit back a shiver, remembering the creative things he could do when a naked woman didn't respond quickly enough to an order he'd given her while they were preparing dinner together. One piece of peeled ginger inserted into the right place left indelible memories—and a healthy respect for the limits of his patience.

"Um," she said. She blinked. "A thong?"

"Is that a question? And who are you addressing, kitten?"

She cleared her throat. "A thong, sir."

"Remove it."

She blinked at that, too. Dorian only stared back at her while his brow slowly began to rise.

Erika started to pull at the long skirt of her dress while he stood there and made no attempt to look away. She pulled the skirt up to her waist, then wriggled out of her thong. And when she pulled it down and off, she straightened again to find him holding out his hand.

"I'll take that, thank you."

And it was ridiculous, given the things she had already done with him, but handing him her thong while it was still warm from her body made her cheeks burn. She could tell from the gleam in his dark eyes that he was enjoying it.

She handed them over and was acutely aware, then, that she was suddenly going commando under her dress. Not that it should have mattered to her in the least, when she was normally dressed in much less. But then, that was why the things he did were so diabolical. They could be over-the-top, like a dark pageant in his club. Or they could be as simple as this. Wearing a pretty dress, but knowing she was naked underneath—at his command.

He pocketed the thong, and then pulled something else out of a different pocket, holding it there in his palm like a gift. Erika knew what it was. It was a particularly high-end anal plug, complete with a be-jeweled button on the end.

"I bought it just for you," he said, a wicked amusement in his voice. "Thank me."

"Thank you," she whispered, but she couldn't take her eyes off the *thing* in his hand.

"Let me tell you what I want," he said while her heart pounded and her skin seemed to shrink. She would have called it fear or revulsion were it not for her traitorous pussy that ached, soft and hot. "I want you to bend over that breakable-looking chair behind you and lift your skirt for me. Then I want you to thank me when I slide this deep inside your ass. When I'm done, we both know you'll be so slippery that something will have to be done before we go back out there, so I'll have absolutely no choice but to fuck you, hard. You'll want to come, because you always want to come, but you won't, Erika. This time you'll hold it back, for me."

He hadn't moved. He still stood there, doing absolutely nothing but holding his hand out with the plug gleaming there in his palm. And yet Erika was gasping for breath as if he'd thrown her over his lap and paddled her again.

"I told you, this isn't an order," he said. "This is my desire, nothing more, nothing less. You can choose whether or not you want to do it. It's up to you."

And something in that scraped at her, though she couldn't have said why. She felt the way she often had in Berlin, as if she was too big inside, too bright and hot and expansive, and all because he looked at her like that. With that firm, infinite patience that made her believe she could do anything at all. Anything he asked. Anything he dreamed up.

Anything he thought she could do.

They weren't in that apartment of his, with all those clean lines and vast spaces, as if to make room for his dirty imagination. And still, everything else fell away. She forgot that they were in a tucked-away room in Jenny's house. She forgot that her entire family was out there, just down the hall, at a party filled with people who wouldn't take a lot of convincing to think the worst of her.

She didn't care, she realized. Even if they'd all been standing right here in front of her, watching and judging from the fragile-looking settee, she still wouldn't have cared.

Erika saw nothing in Dorian's gaze except confidence that she could and would do anything he asked of her, and that was all she needed. His confidence in her gave her confidence in herself—or maybe that wasn't quite right.

It was more that he saw in her what she had always believed was there, and because he believed in it, she could, too.

She jerked slightly, as if she was coming out of a spell. And still, Dorian watched her as if he could wait forever. And would. She turned to the chair he had indicated, and she flipped her skirt up as she bent over. The arms of the chair were low, and she had to tilt herself at a sharp angle to hold on to them. She was wearing heels, and the simple act of bending over tilted her naked ass high into the air.

"Very nice," he said.

And she dropped her head down, let out a small sigh of satisfaction and waited.

Dorian moved behind her, and she felt his hands on her body again. There had been times over the past couple of weeks that she'd thought she would never feel him again, and she'd never been so happy to be wrong. Her eyes drifted shut as his palms traced down her back, then over the curves of her butt.

Warming her. Greeting her. Both, maybe.

He removed his hands, but his legs were still there, brushing against hers and obliquely reminding her of his strength. His control.

And the particular sweetness of her surrender.

Because giving herself over to Dorian felt like real freedom—not like loneliness.

She felt his hands move into the crease of her ass, rubbing her opening in a way that told he was going to take what she was offering and more, that he expected her to like it. It felt rude and hot at once, especially when she felt something slick and cold on his fingers. He rubbed at her, dipping his finger in and laughing slightly when she made noises she couldn't seem to bite back.

Then she felt the tip of the plug, narrowed for entry before it widened to that thickness her mind shied away from, and she pulled in a deep, scared sort of breath. Scared, electrified—she couldn't really tell the difference.

"Push out," he told her, but he didn't wait for her to obey him. He simply began pushing the slicked-up item deep inside her.

It didn't exactly hurt, though it wasn't at all comfortable. Still, it was thrilling at the same time, because he was relentless. It wasn't about the butt plug. It was his will and her surrender, and the struggle wasn't between her and him, but inside herself.

And the more she accepted that, the wetter her pussy got and the more she pushed herself back against the plug to help him seat it inside her.

"Someday, baby, that's going to be me," he told her, low and fierce.

It made her shudder, her clit pulsing as if she was dangerously close to coming already.

She fought it back, but she was breathless by the time he got the plug all the way in. And she couldn't have said if it was from that cartwheeling, delighted thing inside her because he was here and this was happening, or the laughter she couldn't quite hold back, or all the other things she felt for him—because God, what didn't she feel for him?

And then it didn't matter, because she heard the tear of a condom wrapper.

One hand rested on her low back, keeping her in place. And his cock was there at the entrance to her pussy, as broad and thick as she remembered it.

He thrust himself inside her, hard and deep, and Erika had to bite the tufted pillow in front of her face to keep her scream inside.

"I didn't hear you thank me," he said, and she heard her own crazy breath as she pulled it in, high-pitched and wild.

"Th-thank you…" she managed to get out.

"Who are you thanking, kitten?" came his voice, a dark and silken thread that wrapped around her and pulled tight.

"Thank you, sir," she said.

And she meant it.

His cock was a revelation inside her. The plug in her ass made her tighter, and him bigger, and he was not a small man. She wanted to explode on the spot, so crammed full of him—of Dorian and his demands and his desires—that she shuddered right there on the edge of a climax—

But only in the last moment, remembered that she was not to come.

"Oh my God," she whispered under her breath.

Dorian laughed, and then he began to fuck her.

He took her hard and deep, the way he always did. As if she wasn't tighter than usual. And he didn't slow down. Or speed up.

It was that same, unyielding, relentless rhythm that haunted her in her sleep. It was a greedy, glorious pounding, and normally she would have come twice already.

But she fought it. Erika could feel every inch of him in Technicolor, but she held on.

Her clit ached, and her thighs quivered, and she thought there were tears tracking down her face, but somehow, she held on.

"You're such a good girl," he said, leaning over her, his voice a dark taunt, giving her back those words that no one had said to her since she was a child. Making them new. And his. "You're trying so hard to please me."

Erika couldn't speak. She couldn't do anything but hold herself as tightly and as carefully as possible, because the slightest wrong move—

"But I told you before. Sometimes, no matter how good you are, I'm just going to want to punish you. Because I can. And because it's fun."

And his wicked, terrible hand snaked around, took

her plump, desperate clit between his fingers and pinched. Hard.

Erika went nuclear.

She didn't pass out. Not quite. She was aware that he'd sneaked a hand up and covered her mouth, which is the only reason she didn't scream the house down around their ears. She felt him come hard with a low groan.

But she was ruined. Already destroyed and beyond saving, and she couldn't seem to care.

He pulled out, and she moaned again, because the plug was still there. And she could feel him, still too big inside her even as he removed himself. He laughed again, and she didn't have the energy to do anything but stay where she was, draped over the chair with her ass in the air, completely exposed.

She heard him moving around, and assumed he was disposing of the condom, putting himself to rights. She focused on trying to breathe. Then he was beside her, pulling her to her feet and holding her there before him.

And the look on Dorian's face made the whole world seem to slip to one side.

Tenderness. That was what she saw in those dark, dark eyes of his.

It made her feel inside out. Stripped raw, made new.

He rubbed his thumbs beneath her eyes, and she had the distant thought that she must look a mess, but she didn't care. Not when he was looking at her like that. As if she was his world.

And here, in this sacred space they'd made between them, Erika believed it.

"I don't want you to apologize to your brother for me," he told her, his voice steady. Utterly certain. "I saw him earlier this week. He took a swing at me, and I let him."

She frowned. "That's not right."

"It hurt like hell, and I deserved it." Dorian shook his head. "I'm a grown man."

"Still—"

"I don't need you to get along with my best friend, however nice I might find the idea," Dorian said intently. "I want you to apologize to him for you, Erika. He's your brother. Considering the kind of person your mother is, he's the only family you have. And I know you think he doesn't care about you, but I'm telling you—you're wrong."

"You don't understand."

"I understand completely," he said quietly, and his fingers brushed over her cheek. "You don't think anyone can love you."

Erika felt as if he'd punched her. Revealed her. Destroyed her all over again.

"But I know they can," he said, still gazing at her with all that intensity and power that made her hum inside, then melt. She had no choice but to listen to him, no matter how ruined she felt. "I know it because I do."

It was everything she'd ever wanted and more, because it was him. It was beyond anything she could have imagined. It was every gift she hadn't gotten.

It swept away every time she had been forgotten, thrown away, cast aside. Belittled or ignored.

But it was also impossible.

"Don't tell me it's too soon," he warned her. "You're already in trouble for coming when I told you not to."

And he smiled when she glowered at him.

"Dorian—" she began.

"No, it's not fair," he said, cutting her off. "And yes, Erika, I'm in love with you. I don't need more time to make up my mind. I already know. I've been waiting for you for years. I knew when we woke up that first morning in Berlin that I was never letting you go, and, kitten, I keep my promises. You know this."

It caused Erika actual physical pain to hear him say these things when she *knew* how it would go. How it always went.

"When you get to know me better, you'll regret this." She had to force herself to say it. But the fact was she knew. She knew better than him because she'd seen it play out so many times before. "When you see the truth, you won't be able to get away quickly enough."

And she said it simply. Matter-of-factly. Because she knew it was the truth.

"I've already seen the truth." His hands rested on either side of her neck, his fingers on the nape of her neck and his thumbs on her jaw, holding her where he wanted her. And what he wanted, she delighted in giving him. "What do you think we've been doing?

BDSM is never just the sex, kitten. Not the way I do it. Not if it's right. And this? Us? It's beautiful."

"I chased you all over the planet," she confessed, her eyes filling with tears. "You told me you would spank me in Greece, and I wanted it. I wanted you. Maybe I knew that if I could just find my way to you, you could fix me."

"You don't need fixing, baby." Dorian shook his head, his gaze fierce. "You're not broken. A little lost, maybe, so I gave you a compass. But the journey you take is up to you."

She wanted to fall into his arms and hide there. Instead, she made herself look at him straight on. "How can you love someone you hardly know?"

But Dorian laughed. "You were quick to tell me you've known me all my life," he pointed out. "And even if you didn't, you know all kinds of things about me now. Deep, intimate things. That you can trust me. That if I'm hard on you, I reward it. That I care enough about you to give you the boundaries you've wanted all your life. I demanded total honesty. And you gave it to me. What else do you need?"

Erika swallowed, hard, aware of her heartbeat in every part of her. Even her fingertips. "And if I go out there and apologize to my brother, then we can…continue?"

He muttered something, then leaned forward to press his forehead to hers.

"Baby. I'm not letting you go. If you don't apologize to your brother, I'll be disappointed. And I might take that disappointment out on that fine ass of yours. That's your choice." He laughed when she shuddered. "But you and me? There's only one thing you could do to end this. You'll have to tell me to go, and you'll have to use your safe word, so that I believe it. Is that what you want?"

"No," she breathed. "I don't want that at all."

"Make a choice," he ordered her.

"You," she said, and she didn't even think about it. It didn't require thought. "Of course, you."

Dorian tilted her head up then, and dropped his mouth to hers and gave her the sweetest, most delicious kiss, like something out of a fairy tale. And then he raised his head, his eyes went wicked and he dropped a hand down to her butt and squeezed.

Making her jump, because the plug was still in there.

"Try not to walk as if you have a stick up your ass, kitten," he told her, amusement making his voice that much richer. "You wouldn't want to raise suspicions."

Erika scowled at him, but when he took her hand, she laced her fingers tight with his and felt nothing short of giddy.

She took a quick peek in one of the mirrors they passed out in the hallway, and hardly recognized the person she saw looking back at her. Because finally, after all these years, she looked alive. She wasn't hiding. She wasn't afraid.

She was just...Erika. Herself.

At last.

Dorian drew her back to that same doorway where he'd found her earlier and they stood there a moment, looking in on the assembled crowd. Erika found Conrad quickly in the middle of the throng, looking as buttoned-up and unapproachable as ever. Her stomach twisted, predictably.

"Are you ready?" Dorian asked from beside her.

Erika looked at her brother. And she looked down at her hand entwined with Dorian's.

And she knew it didn't matter what she chose. That he would express any disappointment in her honestly, and present her with consequences, but he wouldn't cut her loose. She could make any choice at all, and he would support her. And possibly paddle her if he didn't agree with it.

But after all this time, after so many years out there, alone, she'd finally found her home. He was her home.

Dorian would keep her safe. He had the power to lead, to demand. But she had the power to surrender. And between them, they had the power to do absolutely anything.

Even fall in love too fast, and then stay there forever.

But she didn't tell him that. Not now. She was certain he would much rather tie her up and make her say it later, when he ran out of patience.

She could hardly wait.

Erika looked up and found herself there in the bright gleam in his dark eyes that was all for her. Only and ever for her.

"I would follow you anywhere," she told him.

And then she smiled, as bright as the sunshine

he made her feel even here, inside and at night. Everywhere. That was the magic they made between them, and always would.

She believed in him. In them. In this, no matter how new.

In the home they made between them, and carried wherever they'd go.

And before he could prompt her, she leaned closer and whispered his favorite word in his ear, so no one else could hear.

"Sir."

CHAPTER TWELVE

ERIKA APOLOGIZED TO her brother, with an openness and vulnerability that made Dorian fall in love with her all over again. And more deeply.

But then, she was good at that.

They'd made a commitment to each other in that frilly, prissy room in the Markham family manor house, but Dorian knew better than to take his skittish little kitten for granted.

It took him two months—and his favorite swing, which he could suspend from his bedroom ceiling— to get her to admit she was in love with him.

He already knew she was in love with him. But he liked hearing her tell him so.

It took him sixteen more months to get her fully moved into his penthouse. Or to be more precise, he moved her in almost immediately because he didn't see the point of being without her, but it took her all that time to finally admit that was what was happening.

He expressed his feelings on her reticence in the language they both understood best.

And Erika set about making his life better in a
thousand little ways that had nothing to do with sex.
She taught him to feel sorrow for his father's wasted
life, instead of outraged about it. She charmed his
grandfather and had the old man sparkling like a
teenager whenever she was around. Her life had been
unconventional in the extreme, but that made her the
perfect sounding board for all of the business issues
Dorian had never been able to talk through with anyone else. Not completely.

In turn, he taught her how to stand up to her
mother—or at the very least, choose not to engage
with her cruelty.

She had spent so long acting a part, but the more
comfortable she became with him and the safety of
the life they made together, the more she began to
shine. And she took care of him. She worried about
him. For once, Dorian didn't have to be responsible
for holding up the whole damned sky and everything in it.

With Erika, Dorian was safe, too. He could allow
himself the vulnerabilities he'd always before seen as
weaknesses. He could share all of himself instead of
chopping himself up into necessary compartments.

He could let her soothe him, too. He could grow,
more and more each day, without worrying that the
slightest crack in his confidence would send her running.

Because she loved all of him. The dominant, the
man and the partner he became, just for her.

Dorian had known he wanted her, permanently,

after that first night. But even he couldn't have foreseen how beautifully in sync the two of them would become over time, until he found that he could no longer remember what life had been before she'd wandered into his club and claimed him.

And now that he had Erika, Dorian lost his taste for club games. He practiced his favorite hobbies on her. He had no need to bring anyone else into it. And more to the point, he had absolutely no interest in sharing her with anyone. He liked all her exhibitions to be for him alone.

Six months into living together officially— meaning six months into getting her to believe that he wasn't going to throw her out, she wasn't going anywhere the next time the whim took her and he really did love her to distraction—she looked at him over the top of the book she was reading one evening. She was curled up beside him, naked as she usually was when they were at home. He sat next to her with her legs on his lap, wearing his typical jeans and T-shirt.

And Berlin was there outside their windows, always beckoning, always bright and unexpected. Much like his woman, Dorian thought.

"I want to do something," Erika said. "But I don't know how you'll like it."

"If I don't like it, I'll tell you so and I will proceed from there." And he grinned at her when she scowled at him. "Is that is advisable way to look at me?" he asked idly. "I haven't played with my whip in a while."

Erika shivered beside him, but her eyes gleamed. She liked to pretend she hated the whip… But they both knew better.

"I want to finish university," she said, surprising him. Because he never knew what she would say or do next, and that was one more reason why he loved her. "Oxford has offered me a place, if I want to do my third year. But it would mean…"

Dorian set aside the papers he was reading, already forgetting whatever tedious report he been making his way through. He reached over and settled his hand on the nape of her neck, calming them both. Connecting them. "And what will you do with this fine Oxbridge education should you finally receive it in full?"

And her smile was hopeful and almost scared, as if she couldn't believe she was daring to do this. To even discuss doing it.

It made his heart hurt.

But then, she was good at that, too.

"I'm not sure," she said. "Anything and everything. Isn't that the point?" Then she bit back her smile, and looked down at her lap. "But Oxford is… in Oxford, not Berlin."

"Let me guess. You want to have a discussion about what it is you think I want. And if I tell you that I forbid it, that gives you something to rebel against, which is far more comfortable than simply telling me what you want. Is that about right?"

She let out a sigh that was half a groan, tilting her head back to lean into his hand. "You know, sometimes, Dorian, I just want to have a conversation. I don't want to scrape back every layer and expose my raw and beating heart to the air."

He pulled her face to his and kissed her. "Tough luck, baby."

"I want to do this," she said, lifting her gaze and keeping it steady on his. "But the idea of missing you, even if it's only during the week and I fly back here on weekends, or whatever, makes me feel... sick. What if I ruin this? I don't think I could bear it."

"You can't ruin this," he told her, keeping her face close to his. "It's not up to you. If you want to go and do this thing, I want you to do it. Not everybody gets the opportunity to reset their past. I'll support you completely."

"My God," she said, there against his mouth. "Do you have any idea how much I love you?"

He did. But he used his whip that night anyway, to measure it.

They found a flat in Oxford, and they made it work. Sometimes she flew out to meet him at his various business affairs. Other times, he came to her. And it wasn't the same as living together 24/7, but it was fine. It was temporary, and they made it good.

And one night, when he waited for her in a pub not far from her last lecture of the day, he patiently turned down the advances of several women. And when he looked up, he found her watching him.

"Jealous?" he asked when she came to him, an odd look on her face.

"As a matter fact...not at all," Erika said, and then

she laughed. "I've worried so much about our separations, but I see now that I shouldn't have."

He traced her lips with his thumb, and felt himself harden, right there on the bar stool.

"Because you strust me implicitly?" he asked.

"That, and the reality of what we are to each other."

She smiled at him, and he felt it then. That she finally saw what he'd seen in her, and helped her bring to the surface. Real power. Their power. And damn, if it wasn't beautiful.

Just like her smile. "A random girl in a bar could never give you what I do."

"Amen," he said, drawing her closer. He made sure to pull her hard against his thigh, so he could press into her pussy, right there where anyone could see them if they looked hard enough. "And remember, please, that your flat is not soundproofed. I wouldn't want your neighbors to call the police this time."

And she still blushed, which was yet another reason he loved her to distraction. But these days, she also smiled. Wickedly.

"Promises, promises," she said.

And then paid for that impertinence, later.

Dorian was there, along with Conrad and his wife—but mercifully not her mother—when Erika walked across the stage and got her degree at last.

Because she could do anything, and would, and he would be right there with her every step of the way. He would put his rings on her finger. She would make him some babies. He knew what he wanted his happy-ever-after to look like, because he was already living it.

She was his. And she was perfect.

Especially when he knew that underneath her graduation robes, Erika wore nothing but his favorite plug that he'd greatly enjoyed inserting earlier—and his handprints, all over her extraordinary ass.

* * * * *

PURSUED BY THE DESERT PRINCE

DANI COLLINS

To my sisters, who often live far away, but remain close, close, close in my heart.

Love yous. Xoxo

CHAPTER ONE

ANGELIQUE SAUVETERRE PICKED up a call from her exterior guards informing her that Kasim ibn Nour, Crown Prince of Zhamair, had arrived to see her.

She slumped back in her chair with a sigh, really not up to meeting someone new. Not after today.

"Of course. Please show him up to my office," she said. Because she had to.

Hasna had said her brother would drop by while he was in Paris.

Angelique didn't know why the brother of the bride wanted to meet the designer of the bride's wedding gown, but she assumed he wanted to arrange a surprise gift. So she didn't expect this meeting to be long or awful. Her *day* with Princess Hasna and the bridal party hadn't been awful. It had actually been quite pleasant.

It was just a lot of people and noise and Angelique was an introvert. When she told people that, they always said, *But you're not shy!* She had been horribly shy as a child, though, and brutally forced to get over it. Now she could work a room with the best of them, but it fried her down to a crisp.

She yearned for the day when her sister, Trella, would be ready to be the face of Maison des Jumeaux. An ironic thought, since her twin wore the same face.

As she freshened "their" lipstick, Angelique acknowl-edged that she really longed for Trella to be the one to talk to new clients and meet with brothers of the bride and put on fetes like the one she'd hosted today.

She wanted Trella to be all better.

But she wouldn't press. Trella had made such prog-ress getting over her phobias, especially in the past year. She was determined to attend Hasna and Sadiq's wed-ding and was showing promise in getting there.

It will happen, Angelique reassured herself.

In the meantime… She rolled her neck, trying to massage away the tension that had gathered over hours of soothing every last wedding nerve.

At least she didn't look too much worse for wear. This silk blend she and Trella had been working on hadn't creased much at all.

Angelique stood to give a quick turn this way and that in the freestanding mirror in the corner of her of-fice. Her black pants fell flawlessly and the light jacket with its embroidered edges fluttered with her move-ment while her silver cami reflected light into her face. Her makeup was holding up and only her chignon was coming apart.

She quickly pulled the pins out of her hair and gave it a quick finger-comb so her brunette tresses fell in loose waves around her shoulders. *Too* casual?

Her door guard knocked and she didn't have time to redo her hair. She moved to open the door herself.

And felt the impact like she'd stepped under a mid-night sky, but one lit by stars and northern lights and the glow of a moon bigger and hotter than the sun could ever hope to be.

Angelique was dazzled and had to work not to show it, but honestly, the prince was utterly spectacular. Dark, liquid eyes that seemed almost black they were such a deep brown. Flawless bone structure with his straight nose and perfectly balanced jawline. His mouth— That bottom lip was positively erotic.

The rest of him was cool and diamond sharp. His country was renowned for being ultraconservative, but his head was uncovered, his black hair shorn into a neat business cut. He wore a perfectly tailored Western suit over what her practiced eye gauged to be an athletically balanced physique.

She swallowed. *Find a brain, Angelique.*

"Your Highness. Angelique Sauveterre. Welcome. Please come in."

She didn't offer to shake, which would have been a faux pas for a woman in Zhamair.

He did hold out his hand, which was a slight overstep for a man to demand of a woman here in Paris.

She acquiesced and felt a tiny jolt run through her as he closed his strong hand over her narrow one. Heat bloomed under her cheekbones, something his quick gaze seemed to note—which only increased her warmth. She hated being obvious.

"Hello." Not *Thank you for seeing me*, or *Call me Kasim*.

"Thank you, Maurice," she murmured to dismiss her guard, and had to clear her throat. "We'll be fine."

She was exceedingly cautious about being alone with men, or women for that matter, whom she didn't know, but the connection through Hasna and Sadiq made the prince a fairly safe bet. If a man in the prince's position was planning something nefarious, then the whole world was on its ear and she didn't stand a chance anyway.

Plus, she always had the panic button on her pendant.

She almost felt like she was panicking now. Her heart

rate had elevated and her stomach was in knots. Her entire body was on all-stations alert. She'd been feeling drained a few seconds ago, but one profound handshake later she was feeling energized yet oddly defenseless.

She was nervous as a schoolgirl, really, which wasn't like her at all. With two very headstrong brothers, she had learned how to hold her own against strong masculine energy.

She'd never encountered anything like this, though. Closing herself into her office with him felt dangerous. Not the type of danger she'd been trained to avoid, but inner peril. Like when she poured her soul into a piece then held her breath as it was paraded down the catwalk for judgment.

"Please have a seat," she invited, indicating the conversation area below the mural. There were no pretty views of actual Paris in this windowless room, but the office was still one of her favorite places for its ability to lock out the world. She spent a lot of time on her side of its twin desks and drafting tables.

Trella's side was empty. She was home in Spain, but they often worked here in companionable silence.

"I just made fresh coffee. Would you like a cup?"

"I won't stay long."

That ought to be good news. She was reacting way too strongly to him, but she found herself disappointed. So strange! She took such care to put mental distance between herself and others. The entire world would have this effect on her if she didn't, but he only had to glance around her private space and she felt naked and exposed. *Seen.* And she found herself longing for his approval.

He didn't seem to want to sit, so she pressed flat hands that tremored on the back of the chair she usually used when visiting with clients. "Was there something particular about the wedding arrangements you wanted to discuss?"

"Just that you should send your bill to me." He moved to set a card on the edge of Trella's desk.

She turned to follow his movement behind her. So economical and fascinating. And who was his tailor? That suit was pure artistry, the man so obviously yang to her yin.

He caught her staring.

She tucked her hair behind her ear to disguise her blush.

"Her Majesty made the same offer and you needn't have troubled yourself. It's a wedding gift for Sadiq and the princess."

He noted the familiarity of her using Sadiq's first name with a small shift of his head. "So Hasna said. I would prefer to pay."

His gaze was direct enough to feel confrontational, instantly amplifying this conversation into one of conflict. Her pulse gave a reflexive zing.

Why would he be so adamant—?

Oh, dear God! He didn't think she and Sadiq were involved, did he?

Why wouldn't he? According to the headlines, she'd slept with half of Europe. When she wasn't doing drugs or having catfights with her models, of course.

"Sadiq is a longtime friend of the family." She retreated behind the cool mask she showed the world, ridiculously crushed that he would believe those awful summations of her character. "This is something we want to do for him."

"We." His gaze narrowed.

"Yes." She didn't bring up her sister or what her family owed Sadiq for Trella's return to them. The fact that Sadiq had never once sought any glory for his heroism was exactly why he was such a cherished friend. "If that was all…" She deliberately presumed she'd had the last word on the topic. "I should get back to the final arrangements for your sister's things."

Kasim had to applaud his future brother-in-law's taste. Angelique Sauveterre had grown from a very sweet-looking girl into a stunning young woman. In person, she had an even more compelling glow of beauty.

Her long brunette hair glimmered and shifted in a rippling curtain and what had seemed like unremarkable gray eyes online were actually a mesmerizing greenish hazel. She was tall and slender, built like a model despite being the one to dress them, and her skin held a golden tone that must be her mother's Spanish ancestry.

Cameras rarely caught her with a smile on her face and when they did, it was a faint Mona Lisa slant that allowed her to live up to the reputation of her father's French blood: aloof and indifferent.

She wore that look now, but when she had first greeted him, she had smiled openly. Her beauty was so appealing, Kasim had forgotten for a moment why he was here and had been overcome with a desire to pursue her.

Perhaps this captivating quality was the reason Sadiq was so smitten?

"About those arrangements… Today went well?" He had understood it to be the final fitting of his sister's wedding gown and the bridesmaids' dresses as well as a private showing of other clothes made for Hasna, all taking place on the runway level of this building. Once the last nips and tucks were completed, the entire works would be packaged up and shipped to Zhamair for the wedding next month.

"You would have to check with the women who were here, but they all seemed pleased by the time they left." So haughty and quick to keep the focus on his sister.

From what he'd heard around his penthouse, the consensus had been a high level of ecstasy with everything from the clothes to the imported cordial to the finger sandwiches and pastries.

"Hasna doesn't seem to have any complaints," he downplayed. "Which is why I'm willing to spare her the nuisance of replacing all that you've promised her."

Angelique was tall in her heels. Not as tall as him, but taller than most women he knew, and she grew taller at his words, spine stiffening while her eyelashes batted once, twice, three times. Like she was filtering through various responses.

"All that we've *made* for her," she corrected, using a light tone, but it was the lightness of a rapier. Pointed and dangerous. "Why on earth would you refuse to let her have it?"

"You can drop the indignation," he advised. "I'm not judging. I've had mistresses. There is a time to let them go and yours has arrived."

"You think I'm Sadiq's mistress. And that as his *mistress*, I offered to make his bride's gown and trousseau. That's a rather generous act for a *mistress*, isn't it?"

She repeatedly spat the word as if she was deeply offended.

He pushed his hands into his pants pockets, rocking back on his heels.

"It's a generous act to arrange a private showing for such a large party at a world-famous and highly exclu-

sive Paris design house." It hadn't been only his mother
and sister, but Sadiq's mother and sisters, along with
cousins and friends from both sides.

The cost of something like today wasn't so high as
to imperil his riches, of course. The groom's family
could equally afford it and given the extent of the Sauveterre wealth, and the rumors that the family corpora-
tion had underwritten this folly of an art project in the
first place, he imagined Angelique wouldn't be too far
out of pocket, either.

"Had this afternoon been the only line item offered
at no charge, I wouldn't have batted an eye," he said.
"But the gown? I know my sister's taste." He imagined it had easily run to six figures. "And to throw in
wedding costumes for the rest of the party? Including
mothers of the bride *and* groom?"

"Sadiq's parents and sisters are also friends of the
family."

"Plus a full wardrobe for Hasna to begin her married life," he completed with disbelief. "All at no cost?
This is more than a 'gift' from a 'family friend.' If I
had learned of it sooner, I would have taken steps long
before today."

Hasna had been chattering nonstop about her big
day, but what did he care about the finer details? He was
glad she was marrying for love, he wanted everything
to go well for her, but the minutia of decor and food and
colors to be worn had meant nothing to him. It wasn't
until he had noted she was grossly under budget—not
like her at all—that he had quizzed her on when to expect an invoice for the dress.

"If I'm Sadiq's mistress, then I should want the fat
commission off this! I would have told him to *make* his
bride come to us as a payoff for losing his support—

which I don't need, by the way." The hiss in her tone sliced the air like a blade. "That is *not* the way it went at all. Hasna didn't even know Sadiq knew us. She said we were her dream designer and he arranged it secretly, to surprise her. *We're* the ones who decided not to charge him."

"Yes, funny that he would have kept this tremendously close 'friendship'—" he let her hear his disdain "—such a secret from the woman he had been courting for a year and professed to love. I might have understood if he *was* paying you off." He wouldn't have condoned it, not when Hasna had fought so hard for a love match and had managed to convince him that Sadiq returned her feelings, but at least he would have seen the why of this ridiculous arrangement.

"Have you discussed this with Sadiq?" she demanded frostily, arms crossed. "Because I am as insulted on his behalf as I am on my own."

"Sadiq is plainly not capable of doing what is needed. I will advise him after the fact."

"I am not sleeping with Sadiq! I don't sleep with married men, or engaged ones, either."

"I'm fairly confident you stopped sleeping with him once the engagement was announced. I can account for his whereabouts since then."

"He knows you're watching him like that? With these awful suspicions about him?"

"I don't judge him for having lovers prior to settling down. We all do it."

Although it annoyed him that his brother-in-law had slept with this particular woman. Kasim didn't examine too closely why that grated. Or wonder too much about how such a soft-spoken man had managed to seduce her. Sadiq had always struck Kasim as being more book-smart than street-smart, earnest and studious and almost as naive as Hasna.

This woman was surprisingly spirited. She would dominate someone like Sadiq.

Which more than explained why Sadiq hadn't been able to end things as definitively as he should.

"And I'm…what?" she prodded. "Trying to coax him back by outfitting his wife? Your logic is flawed, Your Highness."

Her impertinence took him aback, it was so uncommon in his life. The most sass he heard from anyone was from his sister and she typically confined it to light teasing, never anything with this much bite.

He found Angelique's impudence both stimulating and trying. She obviously didn't understand who she was dealing with.

"Why are you arguing? I'm offering to *pay* you for the work you've done. The more you resist admitting the truth and promising not to see him again, the more likely I am to lose patience and pull the plug on this entire arrangement, Hasna's tears be damned."

"You would do that?" Her jaw slacked with disbelief. "To your sister?"

She had no idea to what lengths he would go—had gone—to protect his family.

He wouldn't allow himself to be drawn into yet another inner debate about his actions on that score. It still wrenched his heart, especially when Hasna still cried so often, but he had done what he had to. Ruthlessly.

And would do it again.

But he would not see his sister's heart broken again. She loved Sadiq and Sadiq would be the faithful husband she desired him to be. If that meant fast-tracking a new wedding gown, so be it.

He let Angelique read his resolve in his silence.

She stood there with her chin lifted in confrontation, trying very hard to look down her nose at him. "All I have to do is say that I'm Sadiq's mistress and this goes away?"

"Plus send me the bill and never contact Sadiq again."

"I can give your money to charity," she pointed out.

"You can. The important thing is that you will not be able to hold the debt over Sadiq's head."

"Ah, finally I learn my real motivation." Her arms came out in amazement. "I was beginning to think I was the stupidest mistress alive."

"Oh, I'm quite in admiration of your cleverness, Angelique."

His use of her name made her heart, which was already racing at this altercation, take a jump and spin before landing hard.

"Have we arrived at first names, Kasim?" It was a deliberate lob back, not unlike when she played tennis with her siblings and she was so well matched she had to throw everything she had into each swing of her racket.

This man! She had spent years developing a shield against the world and he brushed it aside like it was a cobweb, making her react from a subterranean level. It was completely unnerving.

His lashes flinched at her use of his given name. *Good.*

"Your insolence toward me is unprecedented. Take extreme care, *Angelique.*"

Her fingernails were digging into her own upper arms, she was so beside herself. She used the sharp sting to keep a cool head. She had training for this type of negotiation, she reminded herself. He thought he was holding a small fortune in seed pearls and silk hostage, but he was actually holding a knife to the throat of her sister's happiness along with the debt their family owed to Sadiq.

Given that, there was no way Angelique wanted to jeopardize the wedding arrangements or cause a long-term rift.

Listen. That was the first step, she reminded herself as her ears pounded with her racing pulse. Apparently Kasim felt he wasn't being heard.

"To be clear," she said with forced calm, "you believe I've orchestrated this to put Sadiq into my debt?"

"Perhaps not financially. His family is wealthy in resources and political standing as well as actual gold. You've managed to neutralize yourself in my sister's eyes, so she couldn't possibly see you as a threat if you were to move in at a later date for whatever Sadiq was deemed useful for."

"Can I ask how you concluded that I'm so cold-blooded? Because even the online trolls don't accuse me of this sort of thing." She was nice! Her family regularly told her she was *too* nice.

"If your heart was involved, you would have refused this commission altogether. If you wanted to retaliate for a broken heart, you wouldn't be trying so hard to please Hasna. No. I've told you, I've had mistresses. I understand exceedingly practical women. This is an investment in your future. I accept that on a philosophical level, but not when it risks my sister's happiness. That I cannot allow. So." He nodded decisively at the card he'd left on the desk. "Send me the bill. Do not contact him again."

He made as if to leave.

"Wait!" She leaped forward and grabbed his arm.

He froze, gaze locking onto her hand on his sleeve for one powerful heartbeat before he lifted his eyes. His face was filled outrage and something else, something glittering and fiercely masculine.

"Have we arrived at *that* level of familiarity, Angelique?" He pivoted in a swift move to face her, taking her own arm in his opposite grip.

It was the sudden dive and snatch of a predatory bird catching prey in its talons.

They stood like that in what seemed like a slowdown in time. Her heart pounded so hard her lungs could barely inflate against it.

"We're not finished t-talking." Her voice came out painfully thin. She knew she should release him and step back, but she was quite blown away by the masculine interest that flared to life in his gaze.

She wasn't falsely modest. She knew she was beautiful. It was one of the reasons camera lenses so often turned on her. Men looked at her with desire all the time.

There was no reason she should react to *this* man's naked hunger. But she did.

A very animalistic sexual reaction pierced deep in her loins, flooding her with heat and… Yes, it was reciprocal desire. He was looking at her as if he found her appealing and she certainly found him as attractive as they came. There might even be something chemical here because her gaze dropped involuntarily to his mouth. Longing rose within her.

His lips quirked.

She knew he was reading her reaction and was amused. It stung. She felt raw and gauche. It was the bane of her existence that she couldn't always stop whatever feelings were overtaking her. This was so intense it was unprecedented, touching her at all levels. Physical, mental, emotional… He held her entire being enthralled.

"We are finished talking," he said, while his arm bent against her grip. His hand arrived at her waist, hot and sure. His other hand tightened slightly on her arm, drawing her forward a half step, commanding, but not forcing. "If you would like to start something new, however…"

Don't, she ordered herself, but it was too late. His mouth was coming down to hers and she was parting her lips in eager reception.

CHAPTER TWO

HE KNEW HOW to use that sexually explicit mouth of his, firmly capturing her lips in a hot, hard kiss. He slid a hand to the back of her head, rocked his damp mouth across hers, and damn well made love to her mouth like he had the absolute right!

She knew immediately that he was punishing her, but not in a violent way. He wanted her response, wanted to make her melt and succumb to him, to prove his mastery of her and this situation.

And he was doing it, sliding right past her resistance, ready to make her his conquest.

Hard-learned shreds of self-protection rallied. She had trained to meet any attack with an attack of her own.

She kissed him back with all the incensed outrage he had provoked in her, all the frustration that he affected her this powerfully.

She didn't accept his kiss. She matched it. She stepped into his space so the heat off his body penetrated the silk she wore, branding her skin through it. Then she scraped her teeth in a threat across his bottom lip and stabbed her own fingers into his hair. It was completely unlike her to be sexually aggressive, but how dare he come in here with his accusations and intimidations?

Did this feel like she was daunted? Did it?

She felt the surprise in him, and the hardening as he grew excited.

His reaction fed hers. The quickening of arousal in her swelled, rising like a tide that picked her off her feet, washing her in heat, sensitizing her skin and making her hyperaware of her erogenous zones. Her back arched to crush her breasts against his hard chest. Her pelvis nudged into the shape behind his fly, inciting both of them.

His arms tightened around her and he kissed her harder. Not taking control so much as pressing his foot to the accelerator so they burned hotter and faster down the track they were on. His hand slid down to her backside, possessively claiming a plump cheek through silk.

The sensation was so acutely good, the moment rushing so fast beyond her control, Angelique pulled back to release a small moan and gasp for air.

He growled and ran his mouth down her throat, now angling her hips into his so he ground himself against her with blatant intention.

She let him, completely overcome by the moment. She was used to being treated somewhere between a trophy and a revered goddess on a pedestal. No man had ever kissed her like a woman who was not just wanted, but *craved*. This was *real*.

It felt earthy and elemental.

Pure.

She let her head hang back, hair falling freely, and maybe, yes, she was succumbing, but not to him. To this. *Them*. What they were creating together.

He muttered something that sounded like an incantation and his lips moved from her collarbone to the line of her camisole.

She gasped, "Yes," aching for him to bare her breasts to his mouth, she felt so full and tight. When his hand moved up to her chest to caress along the edge—

Wait.

"Don't—" she tried to say, but he had already picked up the silver disk of her pendant to move it over her shoulder.

One second, Kasim was sunk deep in arousal, well on his way to making love with a woman of exceptional passion.

Then the door crashed open and men burst in with guns drawn.

His heart exploded.

He instinctively tried to shove Angelique behind him, but she resisted, shouting, "I'm fine! Orchid, orchid! Stand down. Orchid!"

She held out a splayed hand like it could deflect bullets and tried to scramble in front of *him*, as if she could protect him with that soft, slender figure, but Kasim was pumped with as much adrenaline as the invaders. He locked his arms protectively around her while his brain belatedly caught up to recognize that these were guards he'd seen on his way in.

"I'm fine," Angelique insisted in a shaken tone. "Stand down. Seriously," she said with a look up at Kasim that was naked and mortified. "Let me go so I can defuse this." Her hand pressed his shoulder.

Kasim's arms were banded so firmly around her, he had to consciously force himself to relax his muscles.

"I'm fine," she assured her guards as she slid away from him. She was visibly shaking. "Honestly. This was my fault. He was looking at my necklace. I should have warned him to be careful."

Looking at her necklace? Her lipstick was smudged and she was bright red from her forehead to the line of her top. Her guards weren't stupid.

They were professionals, however. One said, "Second level?"

"Water lily, and did you really?" She went across to a panel and reset something, then sighed and crossed to her desk to pick up her smartphone with a hand that still trembled. "Thank you. Please resume your stations."

The guards holstered their weapons and retreated, closing the door behind them.

While her phone rang with the video call she'd placed, she plucked a tissue and leaned into a small desk mirror to hurriedly wipe her mouth. "This will only take a sec, but if I don't—"

A male voice barked a gruff *"Oui."*

"Bonjour, Henri." Angelique tilted the phone so she could see the screen. She still looked somewhere between dumbfounded and grossly embarrassed, but was trying to paste a brave smile over it.

Kasim was utterly poleaxed. That kiss had been so intensely pleasurable, all he could think about was continuing from where they'd left off. *Get off the phone.*

"Je m'excuse. Totally my fault," Angelique continued. "False alarm. Orchid, orchid. It was only a drill."

"Qu'est ce qui c'est passé?"

"Long story and I'm in the middle of something. Can I call you later?"

"I'm looking at the security records."

Angelique closed her eyes in a small wince. "Yes," she said in a beleaguered tone, as though answering an unasked question. "The prince is still here. May I *please* call you later?"

"One hour," he directed and they ended the call.

Angelique dropped the phone onto her desktop and let out an exasperated breath.

"Ramon will be next. My other brother," she provided, nodding as her phone dinged. "There he is. Spanish Inquisition." She clasped her hands and looked to the ceiling with mock delight. "So fun! *Thanks.*"

"You're blaming me?" He hadn't thought he could be more astonished by all that had just happened.

She shrugged as she acknowledged the text, then dropped the phone again.

Moving to the shelf in the corner, she said, "How about that coffee?"

Angelique moved to where the French press had been sitting so long it bordered on tepid. She shakily pushed down the plunger and poured two short cups, needing something to calm her nerves.

Yes, let's not cause a rift with the wedding, Angelique, by having the Prince of Zhamair shot dead in your office.

What had happened to her that she'd let him kiss her like that? From the moment he'd walked in here, he'd been tapping a chisel into her. Now she was fully cracked open, all of her usual defenses and tricks of misdirection useless. It took everything she had not to let him see how thoroughly he'd thrown her off her game.

"Cream and sugar?" she asked, buying time before she had to turn around.

"Black."

She finished pouring and made herself face him.

He paused in using his handkerchief to check for traces of her lipstick against his mouth and tucked it away. He looked positively unruffled as he took one cup and saucer from her, his steady grip cutting the clatter of china down by half.

She quickly picked her own cup off its saucer and took a bolstering sip of the one she'd doctored into a syrupy milk shake.

The silence thickened.

She tried to think of something to say, but her mind raced to make sense of their kiss. What had he meant about starting something new? What did he even think of her now? Her level of security on its best days had suitors running for the hills.

He wasn't a suitor, she reminded herself. He was an arrogant dictator who had his wires crossed. That's why she'd grabbed his arm. She hadn't been able to let him leave thinking the worst. *Demanding* the worst.

"I wondered about the gauntlet of security I had to run in order to get in here," he said, eyeing her thoughtfully. "I didn't realize this was still such an issue for your family."

Yes, let's talk about my sister's kidnapping and how it continues to affect all of us. Her favorite topic.

"We're very vigilant about keeping it a nonissue. As you witnessed." She was trying to forget how horrifying it had been to have her guards interrupt the best kiss of her life because she'd been too dazed by it to prevent a rookie error with the panic button.

But she supposed the kidnapping was the reason this meeting had come about, ever rippling from the past into the future, so… Very well. There were days they revisited that dark time and this was one of them.

As she made that decision, she was able to move behind her desk and set her coffee aside with a modicum of control. Flicking her gaze, she invited him to take a chair.

"I'll stand."

"Suit yourself. Either way I know I've captured your full attention." She clasped her hands on her desktop, trying to steady herself. "I mean that literally. You won't be allowed to leave until I say you may."

He snorted, but she could see she did, indeed, have his full attention. She felt the heat of his gaze like the sun at the equator.

She swallowed. Good thing she was still wearing her pendant. Too bad he knew about it. She resisted the urge to grasp it for reassurance.

"The advantage that you continue to possess," she said, trying to mollify him, "is that you're willing to refuse the clothes we've made for your sister. I've heard all you said about wanting to protect her. I feel the same toward my own sister."

Empathy. Step two of a hostage negotiation. This was good practice, she told herself. Another drill.

"You're obviously aware of the general details of Trella's kidnapping." She had to swallow to ease how quickly those words tightened her throat. Her knuckles gleamed like polished bone buttons, but she couldn't make her hands relax.

"I know what was on the news at the time, yes."

She glanced at him, not sure what she expected to see. Avarice, maybe. People always wanted gruesome details beyond the basics of a nine-year-old girl being set up by a math tutor as boarding school was letting out, held for five days and found by police before money changed hands. There'd been more than one probing question today from different women in Hasna's bridal party.

Angelique was adept at dodging those inquiries, but they rubbed like salt in a cut every single time.

Kasim was next to impossible to read, but there was

an air of patience in him, like he understood this wasn't easy for her and was willing to wait.

Great. Now her eyes began to sting. She was a crier, unfortunately. She already knew there would be tears later, when she spoke to her brothers. It wasn't because she was upset by the false alarm, just that when a roller coaster like today happened, she tended to fall apart at some point as a sort of release.

She pushed the Remind Me Later button on her breakdown and strained her back to a posture she thought might snap her in two, but was enough to keep her composure in place.

"What's never been made public is Sadiq's part in helping us retrieve Trella."

Kasim set his cup into its saucer and placed it on the corner of her desk. Folded his arms. "Go on."

"You can't simply accept that this is the reason we feel a debt to him?"

"Your brother could give him shares in Sauveterre International, if that was the case. Your other one, the one who races, could buy him a car. Why this?"

"Sadiq is very modest. He has refused all the different times we've tried to offer any sort of compensation. He doesn't brag about his connection to our family. In every way he can, he protects our privacy. That's why we love him."

She took another brief sip of her overly sweetened coffee, trying to find the right words.

"As you've pointed out, his family has plenty of money. Gifting him shares would be…a gesture, not something meaningful. He's not the least bit into cars the way Ramon is, but when your sister mentioned she was going to approach us about making her gown, Sadiq was excited that he had an in."

Maison des Jumeaux wasn't exclusive because it was expensive—although it was obscenely so. No, their clothes were coveted because she and Trella were extremely selective about the clients they took on, always protecting their own privacy first. Gossipy socialites didn't even get an appointment, let alone an original ball gown with a hand-sewn signature label.

"Sadiq only prevailed on our friendship to ask that we accept her as a client, but of course we wanted to do it and of course we wouldn't charge him. He *wanted* to pay. I think the only reason he's letting us get away with not charging is because it's really Hasna who benefits, not him. For Trella, it's a way to repay Sadiq *herself.* It's very important to all of us, for her sake, that she be allowed to do that."

It was part of her sister's healing process. Attending the wedding had become a goal Trella was determined to achieve, come hell or high water.

"Is your sister having an affair with him?"

"That's what you got from everything I just said? No! And neither is my mother, before you go *there.* Family money paid for the materials and Trella and I are doing the work. This isn't a buy off or an attempt to hold something over Sadiq. We're contributing to his special day in the way that makes him happiest. That's *all.*"

He pondered that with a raspy scrape of his bent fingers beneath his jaw.

"You still don't believe me?" What on earth would it *take*?

"How did he help solve the kidnapping? How old was he? Fifteen? Sixteen?" His voice was thick with skepticism. "How well did he even know your family? I understood he only went to Switzerland when he began prepping for university."

"I trust this conversation won't leave this room? Because the police asked us to keep it confidential and we always have. We never speak publicly about the kidnapping because there are many details we wish to keep private."

"Of course," he muttered testily, as though he was insulted she would question his integrity.

"You know Sadiq is a bit of a computer whiz? Well, the internet was quite young and few tools had been developed for online sleuthing. It probably wouldn't even be legal now, the kind of hacking he'd done, but who cares? We have him to thank for Trella's return. And you're right that he only knew *of* us. We weren't friends yet. He was in a few classes with my brothers, but when Trella was taken, he was on the steps beside Ramon. He saw it happen and was horrified. He wanted to help and used his own time, hours and hours I might add, to create software code that produced a lead that panned out for the police. If you want more information, you can take it up with Sadiq."

The truth was, Sadiq was a security specialist. He'd merely been a nerd with a passion at that time, but now it was his private business—literally his confidential side job that she only knew about because her family had introduced him to the man who had the contract for their own security. She didn't know if even Hasna was aware that Sadiq wrote code for Tec-Sec Industries.

"There aren't many people we trust unequivocally, but Sadiq is one of them. He didn't do us a *favor*. He saved my sister's *life*. So if he wants me to make dresses for your sister for the rest of my life, I will. Happily. Without checking with *you* first."

CHAPTER THREE

KASIM HADN'T EXPECTED her to admit outright that she had had an affair with Sadiq, but he hadn't expected an explanation like this, either. It shed an entirely different light on things. He couldn't help but believe her.

Of course, she had done her best to scramble his brain with that kiss, so he forced himself to proceed cautiously.

"I'll allow that Sadiq is what the Americans call a 'geek.' He *is* very modest and I've seen that do-good streak. He always seems sincere in his kindness toward Hasna. I can believe he would take it upon himself to help a stranger's family. But I will check this with him," he warned.

"Be my guest!"

Sadiq would back her story regardless. It was a far more tasteful explanation than admitting he'd had an affair with her. It was more tasteful to *him*, Kasim acknowledged darkly.

"I may have to relay some of this to my parents." He was sorry now that his mother knew anything about this. She had already used the waiving of payment to stir up his father, basking in the importance of being the one to inform the king that there might be a scandal attached to their daughter's wedding. She could easily have put the wedding itself in jeopardy in her quest for her husband's attention, ever in competition with the king's consort, Fatina.

It was exhausting and, given his father's blood pressure and enlarged heart, Kasim expected his mother to show more sense. It was almost as if she was *trying* to provoke a heart attack. Maybe she was. Hell hath no fury, as the saying went, but at least he could defuse her latest damage with this information.

"If that's what it takes to keep both our sisters from suffering profound disappointment, fine," Angelique said stiffly, rising. "I trust they will also keep that information confidential."

"They will," he promised, brushing aside politics at home as he realized she was trying to kick him out.

He wasn't ready to leave.

His mind had barely left their kiss. The way she had responded like a boxer coming into a ring had been exhilarating.

"Have dinner with me," he said.

"Pah! Are you serious?" She blinked her mossy eyes at him. *"Why?"*

It was a completely singular reaction. Women cozied up to him and *begged* for an invitation to dine with him.

"We have more to talk about."

"Like?"

He dropped his gaze to the pink-stained tissue crumpled on her desk.

She blushed, but it wasn't all embarrassment. There was memory there, too. One that made her flush into her chest. The knowledge she was growing aroused again stimulated all the latent signals of his own desire.

Angelique looked away. "That was a mistake."

"It was an effective distraction," he allowed.

Her gaze flashed back to his. "That was *not* what I was trying to do."

He shrugged. "Nevertheless, it put certain possibilities on the table." He was already imagining that same explosive passion colliding on silk sheets. Or this desk she stood behind.

"I can't," she dismissed crisply.

"Why not?" A thought struck. "Are you in a relationship?" He tensed, dismayed.

"I wouldn't have kissed you if I was, would I?"

"I don't know." He relaxed, starting to enjoy that pique of hers. It put a pretty glow in her eyes and revealed the intoxicating passion he'd tasted on her lips. "This is why we should have dinner. So we can get to know one another."

"Are *you* in a relationship?" she shot back.

"No." He scowled, not used to anyone asking questions so direct and personal.

She relaxed slightly, but her brow quickly crinkled in consternation. "Do you want to talk more about Sadiq? You still don't believe me?"

"I want to go on a date, Angelique. I would think that was obvious."

"A *date*."

How could that take her aback? She actually retreated a half step. Her brows gave a surprised twitch, then, oddly, she looked uncertain. She dropped her gaze to her desktop. Bashful?

"I rarely date."

"Then it should be a treat to have dinner with me."

She laughed, which might have been offensive if she didn't have such a pretty, engaging laugh. Her enjoyment was genuine and thorough. At his expense.

"I won't apologize." She held up a hand as she noted the way he folded his arms and set his teeth. "It wasn't your conceit that got to me so much as the painful truth of that remark. You have no idea."

Conceit? He'd been stating a fact.

She ran a fingertip beneath her eye, smile lingering.

"In gratitude for that exceptionally good chuckle, I'll spare you some pain. I attract a lot of attention. I'm really not worth the trouble to take out. I know this because I've been told so more than once." Her amusement faded to something more sincere. Resigned. Maybe even a tad wistful and hurt.

He started to say they could dine alone at his penthouse, then recalled his Paris residence was overrun by his mother and sisters and assorted female relatives.

"Your place then," he said.

She shook her head, but there seemed to be some regret there. "Trella counts on certain spaces being kept private and our flat here is one of them."

That devotion to her sister kept getting to him. The second nature of it. He understood it very well and had to like her for it.

"Dining in public it is, then."

She grew very grave. "I'm serious, Kasim. My sort of notoriety is a punishment. You would be tarred as my lover overnight."

"Since I intend to spend the night with you, where is the harm?"

"Do you?" she scoffed, flushing with indignation. And stirred sensuality.

He saw the deepening of her color and the swirl of speculation behind her gaze. The way she swallowed and licked her lips. Her nipples rose against the light silk of her top and filmy jacket.

He smiled with anticipation.

"That's rather overconfident, isn't it?" she said snippily.

"Don't act surprised, Angelique." He flicked his gaze down to the breasts that had flattened against his chest, the pelvis that had pressed into the thrust of his. "We're very well matched and both intrigued to see where this could go. If you're so eager you don't want to go to dinner first, we can progress to that discovery right here and now. Provided you remove your necklace first."

Her chin was not so narrow as to be pointed, but not so round as to be girlish. It was as perfect as the rest of her. She set it into a stubborn angle and said, "Punishment it is."

She marched past him to the door.

"Maurice," she said as she swung the door open. "A card, please. I'll be dining with the prince later. Would you be kind enough to send someone to scout the restaurant of his choosing?"

She relayed the card to Kasim as he came up behind her. If he wished to be so forward, her glare spat at him, he could suffer the wrath of her *celebrité*.

He wasn't scared. His worst family secret had been painstakingly—and yes, agonizingly—buried. Reports that he had affairs with beautiful women only aided that particular cause.

"Your men can call that number with the details," Angelique said.

He pocketed the card thoughtfully. "I'll pick you up at seven."

"No need. My security will deliver me."

"So cautious." He felt the seeds of irritation forming. Perhaps he didn't care about the notoriety she provoked, but the triple-A level of security could become tiresome. "It's a test?" he guessed. If the arrangements for a simple dinner were too much for him, he was not prepared for the rest of the way she lived, she seemed to be conveying.

"It's my reality," she said with a flat smile.

He annoyed me.

That was the only reason Angelique had agreed to dinner.

Or so she told herself.

And repeated to Trella, when her sister rang through on the tablet before she'd got round to calling Henri.

"What's going on with you?" Trella demanded with a troubled frown. "I'm feeling… I don't know. Restless. Keyed up. Henri texted that your blip was a false alarm, but was it more serious?"

She and her sister didn't keep much from one another. There was no point. They read each other too well.

Not that they were psychic. Angelique never feared Trella could peer into her private moments, but they had an uncanny connection. Despite whatever distance might separate them, they were eerily aware of the other's emotional temperature. They *knew* if the other was happy or sad, angry or scared.

It was one of the reasons Angelique was encouraged to believe Trella was actually getting better this time. The Sauveterres were all paranoid to a point, but for Trella, terror had become her constant companion and a very debilitating one. She didn't *want* to fall apart with anxiety attacks, but for years they had struck without mercy and Angelique had always been aware when they did. It hadn't helped her own sensitive nature one little bit.

Living a cloistered life had leveled out the worst of Trella's episodes, but now she was trying to overcome her fear of being in public so she could go to Sadiq's wedding. It wasn't so much fear of actually being around people or in the public eye that held her back, but fear that any change in her routine would trigger fresh attacks. So it was proving to be a "two steps forward, one back" process, but she was getting there.

Angelique was just as worried that anything could cause Trella to backslide, so she was very firm in stating, "Today was me being an idiot. That's *all*."

She didn't go into detail about the kiss, but gave Trella a good laugh describing the scene as Kasim set off her panic button.

"He said it would be a treat to have dinner with him. I'll show him a treat," she muttered.

"It's been a long time since you went on a date. Even longer since it was someone you were genuinely attracted to," Trella noted.

There went any attempt at disguising from her sister how deeply Kasim affected her.

"I don't know why I am! He's not my usual type at all."

"You don't have a type. You go out with men who make you feel guilty if you turn them down, or sorry for them."

"Well, there's no feeling sorry for this one. He's..." *Indescribable.* She was reacting to him from a completely different place than she'd ever experienced. He didn't pluck her heartstrings as Trella suggested, or tweak her conscience. It was a way deeper reaction than that. He drew her to him.

And made her feel too transparent just thinking about him. She quickly mentioned she still owed Henri a call, but lingered to ask Trella, "Have you noticed… Is something going on with Henri and Cinnia?"

Trella tilted her head in consideration. "He hasn't said anything to me, but now that you say it…"

Henri didn't peep a word about anything unless he wanted it known, but if he did confide a secret, it was to Trella first. They were all close, but they each had their own special relationship with each other. It went all the way back to the day Angelique and Trella were born. Their twin brothers had been allowed to name their sisters and it had created a sense of responsibility in each boy for "his" baby sister.

Ownership, Trella and Angelique had often called it in a mutter to each other. Half the time the boys acted like their sisters were kittens picked up from the animal shelter, but it was a dynamic that had colored their entire lives. They all loved each other equally, but when it had come to holding a sister's hand or pushing her on a swing, they had naturally divided into Henri and Trella, Ramon and Angelique. Oldest with youngest, middle with middle.

Which wasn't to say that Henri was any less protective of Angelique than he was of Trella, or that Ramon was more. Trella's kidnapping had sent the boys' instincts off the scale. Their father's death six years later, when the men were barely twenty-one, had added yet another layer to their self-imposed yokes of responsibility.

Thus both men would insist on an explanation for today's false alarm.

Angelique hung up on her sister and placed the call to both brothers at once, opening with, "I can't talk long. I have a date."

Their identical faces stared back at her, Henri in the

London flat that he often shared with Cinnia, Ramon in the corporate office in Madrid. They both gave her their full attention, but Henri's expression was marginally more severe, Ramon's a shade amused.

"Do you really expect us to believe the 'looking at your necklace' story?" Ramon asked.

"Do you really want a different one?" she challenged.

"Soyez prudent, Gili,*"* Henri said. "He doesn't keep his women long and he has publicly stated that his father will choose his bride—a traditional virgin from Zhamair, no doubt. I wouldn't recommend a romance."

"Hear that, Ramon? Don't get your hopes up."

No smile out of Henri. He really was a grump these days. Angelique scanned behind him for Cinnia. She usually dipped into the screen for at least a quick hello.

"I have to go to Beijing for a week, but I'll be back in Paris after that. You can explain properly then," Henri stated.

Good luck, she thought, suppressing a snort, and took note of how permanent that sounded. *Back in Paris after that.* Henri usually divided his time between Paris and London with occasional popovers to New York and Montreal. More often than not he said "we," meaning him and his companion of two years, Cinnia.

Ramon only introduced his lovers to the family if they happened to bump into each other at a public event. Women were a catch and release sport for him and he was forever on the run anyway, covering Spain, Portugal and all of South America for Sauveterre International. The men were actively working on acquisitions in Asia and Australia, but as Ramon sometimes joked, "We're only one person."

"Trella told me not to bring her tomorrow," Ramon

said abruptly, dark brows pulling into a frown. "Did she tell you that?"

"What? No!" Angelique was taken aback. "I just spoke to her. She said, 'See you tomorrow.' We're going to finish Hasna's gown and start packing everything." Had she blocked her sister from airing some misgivings, too focused on herself and her date with Kasim?

"No, I mean she said she wants to travel to Paris alone. With guards, of course, but she doesn't want me to come with her." Ramon scratched his eyebrow. "It started because I said I was heading to Rio right after and that I had to be there until Sadiq's wedding. She said I shouldn't have to double back and she would go to Paris alone."

"Go with her anyway," Henri ordered. "I'll change my schedule and come get her, if you don't have time. Where is Mama?"

"No!" Angelique interjected. "Boys." They were thirty, but sometimes calling them that was the only way to pull them out of their patriarchal tailspins. "We've always said that Trella has to be allowed to do things in her own time. That meant not pushing before she was ready, but it also means not holding her back when she *is* ready. You know how hard she's trying."

"Exactly why she shouldn't push herself and trigger something. No. I don't like it," Henri said flatly.

"Neither do I," Ramon said.

"Too. *Bad*," Angelique said, even though her own heart was skipping and fluttering with concern for her sister. "I'll be here," she reminded. "It's a couple of hours on the private jet. I do the trip all the time."

"It's different," Ramon grumbled. "You know that."

"Let her do this," Angelique insisted, ignoring the sweat in her palms as she clutched her tight fists. "I'll text her so she knows I can come get her if she changes her mind."

She signed off with warm regards to both her brothers and finished getting ready for her date.

Angelique had to give Kasim credit. He did his homework—or his people did.

He chose a restaurant she and her family frequented for its excellent food and location atop the Makricosta, one of Paris's most luxurious hotels. The staff was also adept at protecting her privacy, not forcing her to walk through the lobby, but willing to arrange an escort from the underground parking through the service elevator.

It always amused her that the most exclusive guests of fine establishments wound up seeing plain Jane lifts and overly bright hallways cluttered with linen carts and racks of dirty food trays.

To her surprise, Kasim was in the elevator when it opened. That instantly sent its ambiance skyrocketing. He was casually elegant in a tailored jacket over a black shirt that was open at the throat.

Her blood surged, filling her with heat. What *was* it about this man?

"I didn't realize you were staying here," she said, trying not to betray his effect on her as she and Maurice stepped in.

"I wasn't. Until I had a date with you." His gaze snared hers and held it.

A jolt of excitement went through her as the suggestiveness in his comment penetrated. *Don't act surprised. We're very well matched...*

She'd never progressed so fast with a man that she'd contemplated sex on a first date. In fact, her advancement to the stage of sharing a bed was so slow, she had only got there a couple of times. Each time she had arrived with great expectation and left with marginal levels of satisfaction.

Now her mind couldn't help straying into sensual curiosity. What would it be like to sleep with Kasim? Their kiss had been very promising. She grew edgy just thinking of it.

"In case you wished to dine unseen," he added almost as an afterthought, with an idle glance at the ever stone-faced Maurice, but with a hint of droll humor deepening the corners of his sex god mouth, like he knew where her mind had gone and was laughing at her for it.

Wicked, impossible man. He had *made* her think about sleeping with him. Deliberately.

She didn't let on that his trick had worked, although her pink cheeks probably gave her away. "The restaurant is fine. I'm rarely bothered there."

The maître d' greeted her warmly by name and assured Kasim it was an honor to serve him. He showed them to a table at a window where a decorative screen had been erected prior to their arrival, enclosing them in a semiprivate alcove.

Kasim held her chair and glanced at the screen as he seated himself. "Apparently we dine unseen regardless."

"Did you want to be seen with me? You wouldn't be the first."

"I wouldn't be ashamed," he said drily. "You're very beautiful. But if you're more comfortable like this, by all means."

Angelique tried not to bask in the compliment as their drink orders were taken. She had freshened her makeup and vetted her outfit over the tablet with Trella, settling on an ivory cocktail dress with a drop waist that ended above her knees in a light flare. The sleeves were overlong and held a belled cuff while the entire concoction was embellished with some of Trella's best work in seed pearls and silver beads.

Public appearances were always this fine balancing act between avoiding being noticed but wanting to show Maison des Jumeaux in its best light if she happened to be photographed, all while trying not to look over-or underdressed for the actual event.

"Judging by what you said today, I didn't think there'd been recent threats. Is this just the vigilance against them that you spoke of?" He nodded at the screen.

"That's me trying to maintain some level of mystery," she joked, but her voice was flat. "Yet another reason I don't bother dating," she expanded. "You already know far more about me than I do about you...not that whatever you've read online is true." She *so* hoped he knew that and wondered why it mattered so much.

"You haven't stalked me?" His brows angled with skepticism. "Asked Hasna about me?"

"I rarely surf at all. Too much chance of running into myself. And no. I'm too protective of my own privacy to invade someone else's." She didn't bring up that Henri had been more than happy to check him out on her behalf. "In my months of working with your sister, she only volunteered the information that you insisted she finish school in exchange for supporting her desire for a love marriage and that you refuse to sing at the wedding, even though your voice is quite good."

He snorted. "It's not. And she's lucky our father is allowing any music at all, let alone a handful of Western tunes. That's it?"

She debated briefly, then admitted quietly, "She told

me you lost your brother a few years ago. I'm very sorry." At least her sister was alive. She was grateful for that every single day.

Kasim looked away to the window as though absorbing a slap.

"I shouldn't have brought it up," she murmured.

"It's public knowledge," he dismissed, bringing his attention back to her with his thoughts and feelings well hidden.

She instantly felt like a hypocrite for claiming she didn't invade others' privacy. She desperately wanted to know what he was thinking behind that stony mask. He fascinated her. That was why she had come to dinner. There. She'd admitted it to herself. She wanted to know more about him.

"It seems I do have the advantage." He shot his cuff as he leaned back to regard her. "In my defense, even the weather and financial pages have click-bait links with your name in them. I can't help but see whichever headline is making the rounds."

"Which is why I look out the window to see if I need an umbrella and ask my doorman for the news. Thank you," she murmured as their wine was poured.

When they were alone, he said, "The story was very compelling. I was about your brothers' age. Hasna was yours. I couldn't help feeling invested in the outcome. I suppose the entire world presumed it gave them a stake in your lives."

The world had presumed a stake in their lives long before her sister was kidnapped. It was one of the reasons her family had been targeted.

She didn't bother lamenting it aloud. Her family had learned to accept what couldn't be changed. Identical twin boys born to a French tycoon and his Spanish aristocrat wife had been fairly unremarkable, but when a pair of identical girls had come along six years later, and the four together had won the genetic lottery on good looks, well, the children had become media darlings without being consulted. She had never been Angelique. She was "one of The Sauveterre Twins."

Which she would never for a moment wish to change. She adored her siblings and wore the designation with pride. It was the attention they relentlessly attracted that exhausted her.

"It's been fifteen years. I would have thought the fascination would have died down," she said with a self-deprecating smile.

"With your sister living in seclusion? It only adds to the mystery." He eyed her as though he wondered if it was a ploy to keep the attention at a fever pitch. "The free exposure can't be hard on business."

"You're wrong," she said bluntly, amused by the way his expression stiffened at being accused of such a thing. "Discretion is one of the most valuable services we offer our clients. The planning of a maternity gown for the red carpet, for instance, when the pregnancy won't be announced until closer to the event. Or a wedding gown when the engagement is still confidential. Sometimes the wedding itself is a secret affair. Trella and I live under such tight security it's fairly easy to extend that amenity to clients."

She sent a pithy look at the screen beside them.

"Until a tourist wants a selfie with me like I'm a historic fountain. Or a shopkeeper wants instant publicity and posts the brand of toothpaste I prefer. And yes, I know I can stay in and buy online. That's what Trella does. But I like to be human and walk in the sun, browse shops for housewares and books. Being followed and photographed while doing it is far more nuisance than benefit and just makes poor Maurice's job harder."

Kasim flicked his gaze beyond her to where she knew Maurice would have been seated at a table with a sight line on her. He was likely sipping a coffee while awaiting a light meal, gaze monitoring the restaurant's employees and patrons.

"It's the reason I don't date," she said, noting where he was looking. "Men don't care to be watched while they attempt to romance a woman."

"It would be a special predilection, wouldn't it? One I don't possess, I'll admit."

She had to chuckle at that, relieved he had a sense of humor about it.

"And if I were merely attempting something that had little chance of success, I might be self-conscious," he added, gaze clashing into hers. "But I'm not."

Oh.

"You're a very confident man." She allowed herself to lean into the fire, to let the heat of his interest warm her cheeks and glow in her eyes. "You come on very strong."

"I didn't expect to find you so intriguing." He held her gaze without actually looking into her eyes. Instead he visually caressed her face, touching her loose hair with his dark gaze. She couldn't look away as he studied her like she was a painting. "A meeting in your office would have sufficed if you'd been less… impassioned. You're not like anyone I've ever encountered."

She had expected another compliment on her looks. This was far more disarming. It made her feel like he saw within her, to the real woman inside, the one few noticed or understood. Plus it was an acknowledgment of something she'd had to work on most of her life: being unique from her sister and being comfortable with her own powerful emotions.

If she wasn't careful, she would be seduced without realizing it. He was very good at it.

"I like your sister, you know. I wouldn't want to hurt her. She's delightful." She waited a beat, deliberate with her timing as she added, "Not much like you at all."

His mouth twitched and he took a thoughtful sip of his wine. His lashes were so thick and long, they were almost pretty, but he was undeniably masculine as he lifted them to regard her. There was nothing soft in the dangerous air he projected.

She held her breath.

"Feel privileged, Angelique. I'm letting you get away with a lot."

She bit the inside of her lip, wondering if she should apologize. Was she ruining this little bit of rapport they'd arrived at?

"Hasna is a lovely person," he agreed. "And you're right. She and I are opposites. Women lead different lives in our country so they grow up with gentler personalities." Something about that statement made him briefly pensive. "At least that's what I've always thought made her so tenderhearted and me more practical and assertive."

"Now you're not so sure?" She tried to read his inscrutable expression. "Supporting her desire for a love marriage sounds rather sentimental, if you ask me."

His cheeks hollowed as though he considered his words carefully.

"She was very upset about losing Jamal. I'm not incapable of compassion. I want her to be happy in her marriage and we've established that we both wish to protect our sisters from heartache, have we not? Is that how you came to open a fashion house with yours?"

She heard that as the shift in topic it was, which intrigued her because something about the way he was trying to compensate Hasna for their brother's loss struck her as guilt. Or responsibility, maybe.

Because she was the sensitive, intuitive one. In some ways it was her burden, but she couldn't deny that she often picked up on things others missed.

"Trella started making her own clothes," she began, then recalled why. Those early years of recovery had been so brutal. As if the kidnapping hadn't been traumatic enough, the press had crucified Trella, dubbing her The Fat One among other things.

"It's not that interesting a story, actually. Just something that both of us enjoyed. We have an artistic flare and work well together so we gave it a shot."

Trella was actually The Smart One. Her business plan had been excellent. The boys would have underwritten anything she'd proposed, to spoil her and give her something she could control and succeed at, but she had been determined to make her mark on the world in a very specific way. Feminine strength imbued every aspect of Maison des Jumeaux. Angelique was deeply proud to be part of it.

"The press makes a lot of the fact that family money gave us our start, but we've paid back the initial loan. I don't know why it's important to me that you know that."

"So I don't think you're chasing Sadiq's money, presumably."

"No." She couldn't help smirking at the way he stiffened every time she contradicted him. "I think it's because I know you respect women who are ambitious and independent. Isn't that why you were so adamant Hasna finish school?"

"No." He waited out the delivery of their appetizers before expanding on his reply. "The more accurate reason is that I didn't want to give my support too quickly or easily because, in order to broker that deal with my father, I promised that my own marriage would be an arranged one. With a suitable bride from my own country, one he could choose. You understand why I'm telling you that."

CHAPTER FOUR

"THAT'S QUITE A SACRIFICE." Angelique's eyelids shimmered with golden tones, shielding her thoughts.

"It's duty. My father is not what anyone would call progressive. I have visions of a modern Zhamair. It would be good for our people, but I will never be given the chance to steer it that way if I don't play by his rules. My uncle would be more than happy to accept the crown if my father decided I was too liberal. My uncle is even more of a throwback than my father. So I have agreed to my father's condition. But I'm not in a hurry to give up my freedom."

He let himself admire her smooth skin with its warm glow, her mouth gently pouted in thought. Their kiss was still branding a permanent pattern into his memories—exactly the sort of freedom he was loathe to relinquish by tying himself down.

"You intend to be faithful to your wife, then, once you're married?"

"Certainly until heirs have been established. After that…" He scratched beneath his chin. "My father has two wives. I have not observed having more than one woman coming to your bed to be as idyllic as it sounds."

Her lashes came up, gaze curious as all Westerners were when he mentioned it. "Jealousy?" she guessed.

"How did you know?" Kasim said drily.

He privately thought the polygamy was the reason his father was so ferociously implacable, refusing to evolve with the times or even hold a rational conversation. He consistently asserted his will and slammed doors on further discussion. If he didn't control every aspect of his life with an iron fist, his wives might tear him in two.

That emotional turmoil bleeding all over his childhood was the reason Kasim had grown such a thick shield of detachment. How else could he have withstood the helpless agony of witnessing his brother's struggle? How else could he have been ruthless enough to end it? Taken altogether, it was the reason he was just as happy to marry a stranger. Love provoked madness and pain of every variety.

"Was your father's marriage to the queen an arranged one?"

"It was." He knew where she was going with that. "And it was a contented one until he brought Fatina into it. Which is why I don't intend to do anything similar."

"Because you want to rule," she murmured, gaze narrowed as she weighed that.

"That concern you feel for your sister's well-being? That's how I feel for my entire nation," he explained quietly.

He had never put it in so many words. As her lashes widened at the magnitude of what he was saying, he experienced a lurch in his heart. He had always thought of it as a goal, not a sacrifice. Suddenly he saw it differently.

"None of us are in a hurry to marry," Angelique mused, dropping her gaze again. "We're a tight bunch, my siblings and I. Letting someone into my life means opening all our lives. That demands a lot of trust and we've all been stung at least once, so we're all wary. It's why I don't even bother with affairs anymore, contrary to reports online." She flashed him an admonishing look. "Don't you dare say that if I don't have affairs, it should be a treat to spend a night with you."

"Oh, I'm starting to see the honor will be all mine." He meant it. Everything she had shared pointed to a woman who lived within her own restrictions. No wonder she had exploded in his arms. She was a powder keg of suppressed passion.

She sputtered with laughter, shaking her head. "You are an incredibly arrogant man."

"There is an expression, isn't there? About a kettle and a pot?"

"I'm not arrogant." She dismissed that with a shake of her loose hair and a haughty elevation of her chin.

"You are," he assured her. It was as captivating as the rest of her.

"No." She looked him right in the eye. "My sister is the brash one. Deep down." Her irises reflected the candlelight between them, mesmerizing as the glow of a fire in the blackest night in the desert. Tears gathered to brim her lashes. "I pretend to be."

She blinked to clear the wetness and her eyes widened with forced lightness.

"I am her and she is me. At least, that's how it feels sometimes. Can we talk about something else?"

"I wasn't talking about her. I was talking you into my bed," he pointed out, made cautious by that moment of acute vulnerability. Was it concern for her sister? Or an indication of a deeper sensitivity in her personality?

He recoiled inwardly from that. He had enough emotional drama in his life. He needed her to come to this with as light a heart as he had.

"I want *you*," he stressed. "What will that take, Angelique? Reassurances about your security? I see you've changed your necklace. Is that one rigged?" He winced as he recalled her talk of suitors having to tolerate being constantly under observation. "We're not being recorded, are we?"

"No. This one requires two hands to twist and set it off." She ran the teardrop pearl back and forth on its chain. "So I rarely wear it. In terms of physical safety, I have no concerns about being alone with you. I'm not even worried you would write a tell-all afterward."

"The sting you mentioned? A man did that to you?"

"One did. You can find him living under a false name in whichever Eastern European slum men use to hide when they've been financially ruined by defamation litigation and threatened with castration."

"Your brothers went after him?"

"*I* went after him," she said crossly. "Give me credit."

"Is that a warning? I would never do such a thing," he promised her. "I may be nonchalant about spending the night with a woman, but I don't degrade myself or my partner. You can be assured of my discretion."

Her shoulder hitched in acceptance, but she wore her Mona Lisa expression.

"You're resisting temptation. Why?"

He reached across to take her hand in his, cradling her knuckles in his palm. He used his thumb to catch at hers, pressing her hand open so he held the heel of her palm gently arched open to his touch. He smoothed his thumb to the inside of her wrist, pleased to find her pulse unsteady and fast.

"Is it because it's only one night?"

"No," she said softly. "That's actually a plus. Like I said, I don't fit others into my life very well."

"If you weren't reacting to me, I would finish our meal and send you home, but I can see your struggle against your own feelings. What's holding you back then? You clearly want to."

He caressed that sensitive area at the base of her hand, where a former lover had once told him life and fate lines had their root. *That's why it's such a sensitive place on a woman's body,* she'd said.

Angelique caught her breath.

He didn't believe in the supernatural, but he did believe in nature's ability to create sexual compatibility. That sort of gift should be relished when it was offered.

"My room is just down the hall. Anyone who sees us leave the restaurant will think we're going to the elevators."

He lifted her hand and pressed his lips into her life, into her fate, as he tasted and grew drunk with anticipation.

Oh, he was good.

Her pulse went mad under the brush of his lips and she had to concentrate to draw a breath.

"I told myself I was only coming out to prove to you I wasn't worth the trouble."

"To scare me off? I don't scare."

I do, she wanted to say. She wanted to go to his room so badly it terrified her. And she didn't understand why this want sat like a hook in the middle of her chest, pulling her toward him with a painful sting behind her breastbone. She didn't know how to handle any of this because she wasn't the bold, confident one.

What would Trella do?

It was a habitual thought, one that harked way back to her earliest years when her sister had been the one to stride eagerly forward while Angelique hung back.

She brushed aside thoughts of Trella. She shared almost everything with her twin, but not this. Not him.

That was what scared her. Who was she if not Trella's other half?

An internal tearing sensation made her touch her chest. She immediately felt the beading on her dress and wondered why she had worn Trella's creation. Armor, she supposed, but this wasn't about Trella. That was what made this situation so starkly unique and put her at such a loss.

In this moment she was only Angelique. Except she didn't know what Angelique would do in a situation like this. Her other lovers had wanted one of The Sauveterre Twins and the fame or influence or bragging rights that came with it. She had gone with them hoping for a feeling of fulfillment, but had never found it.

Kasim wanted *her*. That's what made him so irresistible.

And she had a feeling this would be more than fulfilling. Profound. Maybe life-altering.

Which was terrifying in its own way, seeing as it was only for one night, but if she refused him out of fear, she knew she would regret it for the rest of her life.

The lights were set low in the opulent suite. Champagne chilled in a bucket next to an intimately set table overlooking the Eiffel Tower. The muted notes of a French jazz trio coated the air with a sexy moan of a saxophone, subtle bass strings and a brush on a drum.

Angelique was walking into a setup and wasn't even sure how she had arrived here. It felt like she had floated. There had been a conversation with Maurice, who had escorted them down the hall. She had instructed him to go back and finish his own meal and put theirs on hold. Charles, her second guard, stood post at the door of the suite. He had assured her as she entered that he had inspected and secured these rooms prior to her arriving at the restaurant and had been at this door ever since.

They were very mundane details that were decidedly *un*romantic, but they had each been one of the many tiny steps that had carried her toward this moment.

"I am fascinated with this dress," Kasim said, picking up her hand and carrying it over her head, urging her to twirl very slowly before him. "It is a work of art. I'm afraid to touch it." He lowered her hand, but kept it in his, so they were facing one another. "But I want to touch you."

His words made her heart stutter. She tugged free of his grip and walked to an end table where she set down her pocketbook.

"I'm not used to being touched."

"I'm not going to chase you through these rooms, Angelique. If you've changed your mind, say so."

She turned to face him. "I haven't. I'm just nervous."

"Don't be. I won't rush you."

He didn't have to. She was rushing herself, not ignoring misgivings so much as refusing to give in to the natural hesitation that had held her back one way or another most of her life. If her sister hadn't pressed her toward this fashion house idea, she never would have had the nerve.

So part of her was saying, *Don't be impulsive.* But the truth was, this moment had been brewing since their kiss this afternoon.

This was why she had come to dinner with him. She was a person of deep feeling and what he made her feel was too strong to resist. She had never felt so much like herself as she did with this man.

But she wanted to be herself. She wanted him to want Angelique.

She lowered the zip on the back of her dress, slowly drawing the shoulders down her arms and very carefully stepping out of it without letting the skirt brush the floor.

Kasim's inhale was audible over the quiet music, sounding as a long, sharp hiss.

"You, however..." he said in a rasp. "Seem in a big hurry."

"You said you were afraid to touch it." Avoiding looking at him, she took great care with folding the dress in half lengthwise, then gently set it on the arm of the wingback chair.

She was naked except for her high silver shoes and a pair of lavender cheekies that cut a wide swath of lace across her hips and the top half of her buttocks. She had done enough quick changes backstage alongside half-naked models that she wasn't particularly self-conscious.

Nevertheless, it was intimidating to turn and face him. At the same time, it was a rebirth of sorts, standing there naked and vulnerable. Tears flew into her eyes at the significance of shedding the shield of her sister and being only Angelique.

Would he like her?

"What's this?" Kasim murmured, coming forward to cup her face and make her meet his gaze with her wet one.

"I don't often let myself *be*." Life was far easier when

she kept her thoughts on the future or her sister or a piece of fabric. Allowing the moment to coalesce around her, so she experienced the full spectrum of emotions he provoked—impatience and sexual yearning, uncertainty and deep attraction—it was huge and scary.

She smoothed her hand down the lapel of his suit jacket, then warily looked up at him, fearful of what she might find in his gaze.

What she saw made the ground fall away beneath her feet.

His eyes were hungry and fierce, but there was something tender there, too.

"I'll take care of you," he promised in a low growl, then dipped his head to kiss her.

She started slightly as his arms went around her and a jolt of such acute pleasure went through her it was almost like a shock of electricity.

He paused briefly, gentled his kiss. Then, as she pressed into him, encouraging him to continue, he deepened it, sweet yet powerful, making her knees weaken.

They quietly consumed one another. She speared her fingers into his hair and met his tongue with her own and let herself flow wholly into the kiss.

Releasing a jagged noise, he pulled away and threw off his jacket. Yanked at the buttons on his shirt. "Damn you for being so far ahead of me. You do this."

He left his shirt open but tucked in and set his hands on her bare waist, capturing her lips with his as he ran his hands around to her lower back, making her shiver then melt as he molded her closer. They were chest to chest, hot dry skin to hot hairy chest.

A sob of broken pleasure escaped her. More. She needed more of him, and pushed at his shirt, smoothing her hands over the powerful shape of his shoulders.

With a brief pull back, she yanked his shirt free of his pants, then they were embracing again, her hands free to steal beneath the hanging tails of his shirt to caress the warmth of his flexing back.

Skin. Lips. A cold belt buckle against her bare stomach and a hard shape behind his fly that made her both nervous and excited. She had never abandoned herself to desire, had never allowed herself to be so vulnerable, but she didn't have a choice. Time stopped. All she knew was the feel of him stroking her skin, pressing her closer, fondling her breast then looking at where her nipple stabbed at his palm.

He bent and covered the tight bead with his hot mouth, tongue playing in a way that had her shuddering as ripples of pure delight went straight down her middle to pool in her loins. When he moved to the other one, she ran her hands through his hair, loving the feel of the soft spiky strands between her fingers, and spoke his name like an endearment.

A moment later, he dropped to his knees, taking her underpants as he went and leaving them twisted on her shoes as he stroked his hands up and down her thighs, gaze so hot on the flesh he had bared that she felt it. Her inner muscles tightened and a press of moisture wet her lower lips in anticipation.

She closed her eyes, blocking out anything but the sensation of his light touch, so delicate she barely felt the caress at first, but she was so sensitive it took nothing but the graze of a fingertip to make her throb.

Her breath rasped over the music. He stole one taste and she fisted her hand in his hair. Her stomach muscles knotted with excited need.

His caress deepened and she sobbed as glittering sensations poured through her. Her knees wanted to collapse, but she held very still as his lovemaking intensified and her arousal doubled upon itself until she was saying his name over and over, pushing her hips in an erotic rhythm and she was dying, *dying*, because it was so good.

Climax arrived as a wave of pleasure that had her tipping back her head to release her cry of joy toward the ceiling, body shuddering, hard hands on her hips the only way she remained standing.

"Your guards might have heard that," he said with smug lust, rising before her.

Her heart lurched.

His command of her and the moment stung. Not so much the guards hearing, although that was hideously embarrassing. No, it bothered her more that Kasim was significantly less affected by what had just happened than she was. She ought to be feeling like the selfish one, but it felt quite a bit like he had benefited from her giving up her self-control so thoroughly.

He guided her backward onto the sofa. She was so weak she fairly wilted onto it, body still shaking with aftershocks, but she was clearheaded enough to know she wanted him as carried away as she was.

He opened his belt, unzipped his fly and brought a condom from his pocket, all the while studying her like he had every right.

He covered himself and knelt between her knees, drawing her hips to the edge of the cushions and moving a pillow to the small of her back.

"That's very pretty," he said in a lust-filled voice.

The pillow arched her back so her breasts came up a few inches and he bent to suck her nipples again. It was proving to be her greatest weakness, making her close her thighs on his hips and urge him to soothe the ache he incited.

"Do you want me, Angelique?" He kissed her throat. "I want to hear it. Tell me."

"I do," she admitted on a helpless sob, not caring about propriety or modesty. But she did care that she not be alone in her abandonment to passion. She grasped the hot shape of him, feeling the muscle leap under her cautious caress, so hard and promising.

With a determination to make him as wild as she felt, she guided him to where she wanted him and caressed her folds with his tip.

He reared back, stole a look into her I-dare-you expression, and something untamed flashed in his gaze. He hooked his arms beneath her knees and nudged her for entry, pretty much daring her right back. *Take me, then,* he seemed to challenge.

She was very aroused and arched to accept him, but the press of him stretching her made her instinctively flinch. It had been a long time.

His grip on her legs prevented her from closing them, but he felt her reaction. He paused. "What's wrong?"

"Don't stop," she gasped, grabbing at his neck and pulling herself upward against him, angling her hips to take him in and releasing a stifled groan as he filled her.

He made a feral noise and shuddered.

"Gently," he ordered, moving in small, abbreviated strokes, testing her body's arousal and willingness to accept his intrusion.

She lolled back on the cushion, smiling at him in a way she had never imagined smiling at any man, inviting him to have his way with her. Thoroughly. Completely.

"Let them hear both of us this time," she taunted,

and ran her hands over her breasts, cupping them, letting her nipples poke from between her splayed fingers. "Unless you can't wait for me."

He muttered something that was probably an accusation of insolence, but he began moving with powerful strokes, deliberate and measured, watching her to ensure she liked it. She did, unable to help moaning and arching, hands stroking up his arms. She caught at his shoulders and pulled him down while bringing herself up, so they were chest to chest. She lifted her mouth to catch at his in soft, biting kisses.

Soon it became uninhibited and wild. Sweaty and earthy and abandoned. It was incredible. She would have laughed in triumph, but her breaths were nothing but jagged gasps and cries of pleasure. She received him with joy, basked in being his vessel, and told him how good he made her feel.

"Don't stop. Don't ever stop."

The tension built to impossible levels, both of them digging fingernails into the other as they mated, the enjoyment of the act no longer enough. They sought the culmination. It was coming. They were almost there. So close. Tense. Tight.

The world exploded and he covered her mouth with his own, so they were the only two who heard the sounds of ecstasy they made together.

CHAPTER FIVE

KASIM SHOULD HAVE been fast asleep. He was utterly relaxed. Sexually replete. He certainly didn't want to move. The bedsheets were smooth beneath his back, the warmth of Angelique draped over him the only blanket he needed. Her hair felt pleasantly extravagant, spilled across his chest and neck in cool ribbons.

She was falling asleep, twitching lightly as she drifted into slumber, growing heavier against him. Equally sated.

The things they had done to one another. He closed his eyes and a banquet of remembered sensation washed over him. Smooth, soft hands. A wet, lavish mouth. Legs like silk slithering against his own. Her ripples of climax squeezing him again and again.

Not that they'd been particularly adventurous. He generally left the level of exploit to his lover, never needing fancy positions or toys to enjoy himself so long as he had an eager partner. But the sofa hadn't been enough. They had come in here to the bedroom and consumed one another all over again.

It hadn't been mere enthusiasm between them. It had been immersion. For a woman who "didn't do this," Angelique was tremendously willing to throw herself into the fire of passion. He couldn't help but burn right alongside her.

Which was such a disturbing loss of self-governance, part of him was thinking he should rise and take her home right now.

His body reacted to the thought with an involuntary tightening of his arm around her. A fierce urge rocked through him to roll atop her and have her again.

One night was *not* enough.

Sleep, he ordered himself. *Sleep and think clearly in the morning.*

His eyes wouldn't stay closed, preferring to stare at the decorative ceiling tiles, textured with shadows in the mellow light slanting like sunset from the lounge.

He likened his sleeplessness to those few times in his life when a day had been so perfect, he couldn't make himself go to bed and end it. A day in the desert with his father as a child, when the king relaxed and they only concerned themselves with basic needs. Or his last day with his brother, *knowing* he would never see him again…

His heart gave a wrenching twist and he tensed, restraining himself from rolling into Angelique and seeking more than escape into physical pleasure. Comfort?

No. He refused to be that needy.

She drew a long inhale, disturbed by the tension that kept taking a grip on him. She repositioned herself, sighed and relaxed, but he could tell she was awake. He could feel her lashes blinking against his skin.

"I'm thirsty, but I don't want to move," she said in a husk of a voice.

He was starving, but only moved his hand to her head and caressed her scalp through the thick waves of her silky hair.

With a beleaguered sigh, she pulled away and climbed from the bed to go into the bathroom.

Kasim tucked his arm behind his head, listening to the tap run. When she came out of the bathroom in a robe, he rose onto his elbow.

"Come back to bed," he ordered, voice graveled by sexual excess.

"It's already been a very long dinner," she said wryly. "I don't want to give the press more fodder than they might already have." She walked out to the lounge.

Angelique was trembling on the inside, reacting to something so intense it had left her dismantled and exposed.

She gathered her few pieces of clothing and dressed, aware of Kasim coming into the lounge behind her, but she didn't turn to look at him. If she met his gaze, if he was naked, she feared she would find herself back in his bed in a matter of seconds.

With a practiced wriggle, she got the zip fastened up her back, then swept her loose hair back and behind her shoulders. The silk liner on the dress was cool and the beadwork made it feel heavy and stiff. Her sensitive, sensual soul was firmly tucked away behind walls and guards again.

Searching out her pocketbook, she glanced at her phone and saw her brother wanted her to text when she arrived home safely. She rolled her eyes and plucked her lipstick from the velvet interior of her purse. She had already tidied the rest of her face in the bathroom and was determined to look like she had *not* been rolling around with the prince all evening if she happened to be photographed leaving the hotel.

"You don't have to go."

"I should let you sleep," she said, sending him a sly look in the mirror near the door. "You've worked hard."

"That tongue," he said on a breath of laughter, stalking close to catch at her and turn her, drawing her in front of his naked frame. "If you hadn't used it to pleasure every inch of me, I would curse it completely."

Oh, he did not just say that. She blushed. Hard. And she would *not* look to see if he was laughing. Or hardening. She stared at the flex of tendons in his neck.

He chuckled and bent his head to nuzzle against her mouth with his own, murmuring, "I'm rather fond of it, now. Let me say hello again."

He meant "good night," didn't he?

Their lips parted and sealed in a mutual coming together, like polar opposites aligning and locking. His tongue found hers and caressed, making showers of pleasure tingle down her front. She hummed a pleasured noise and pressed into him, trying to assuage the instant rush of greedy desire.

She found him hard and famished. He clutched her with increasing passion, threatening Trella's beautiful beadwork.

She drew back as far as he would let her and had to stifle a pant of pure need. His eyes were like midnight, his desire for her undisguised, from the flush of excitement across his cheekbones to the thrust of flesh pressing into her abdomen.

"Come back to bed." Implacable determination was stamped into his face.

Her heart turned over with helpless yearning.

Defensive, flippant remarks like, *I had a nice time*, threatened to come to her lips, but she found herself speaking more earnestly. Almost begging for clemency. Her stupid eyes grew wet with the conflict inside her.

"I would prefer to keep tonight private, if at all possible." Her voice reflected the arousal he incited and the powerlessness she felt in the face of it. If he pressed, she would stay the night. "If I get caught doing the walk of shame tomorrow morning, it will cheapen something that was actually very nice." She couldn't bear that. She really couldn't.

His eyes narrowed in a brief flinch. His mouth tightened and she thought he was about to demand she stay anyway.

"I'm going to London tomorrow. Come with me."

She blinked, thrown. She had geared herself up for this to be one night. A rush of hope flooded her. *Yes. More.*

Just as quickly, she thought, *No. How?*

Her mind splintered at the complexity of it. Obligation to Trella rushed in to make anything but these few hours impossible.

"I thought… You seemed pretty clear about there being no future." She searched his gaze.

His expression grew shuttered. "One more night, that's all I'm talking about."

Ouch. Right. She smiled her regret, hoping he'd take it as regret at refusing, not the very real regret that this was such a dead-end road.

"The more we see each other, the more likely we are to become a sensation."

"Still trying to scare me off? It is unrealistic to think we won't be found out, that's true. So what? If that's the only obstacle, there is none."

"It's not," she murmured with genuine reluctance, and tried to step away. Maybe when she went to Berlin next week? She would have to think about it. She was never impetuous, least of all about men and allowing them to impact her life.

He locked his arms, not holding her more tightly, but

turning his muscles to steel so she was forced to stand quietly and look up at him. She did *not* hide her disapproval at being manhandled.

"What then?" he queried.

"Trella is coming to Paris."

"So?"

"We have to finish your sister's trousseau."

"Hasna will not be wearing everything you're giving her on her first day of marriage. I will personally take responsibility for anything that arrives late."

"That's not the point." She tried again to pivot away from him.

He kept her in place, not allowing her to screen her emotions or remove herself from his thought-scattering touch. *Infuriating.*

"I never leave Trella alone when she's here." She'd never even considered it because she'd never been tempted. She set her hands on his wrists where he gripped her hips, trying to extricate herself from the lure of him. "Most especially not overnight."

"How old are you?"

"Twenty-four. And don't pass judgment." She could see opinions forming behind his eyes and it was true that they all babied Trella, but there were *reasons*.

Trella was traveling on her own tomorrow, though. Did that mean she was ready for other acts of independence?

Angelique found herself standing acquiescent in Kasim's embrace, considering her own arguments to her brothers about allowing Trella room to find her own confidence.

What if she had a rebound crash as a result, though? She was trying to justify deserting her sister. What was wrong with her?

Berlin, she thought again, because it was further into the future and gave her time to think. This man moved way too fast for her.

"Is security the issue? Your detail can travel with us," he said.

"No. I mean, yes, they would have to. And Henri keeps a flat in London that is completely secure. No, it's Trella. I could ask her…"

"I do not ask permission from strangers to go away with my lover."

"That's not— You don't understand." *Lover.* Her heart pounded with excitement at the sound of that.

"Enlighten me."

"No," she said bluntly. She never talked about Trella's experience. It was hers and nearly killed Angelique every time she revisited it. Her nostrils stung with unshed tears just thinking about it.

His fingertips dug in just a little against the soft flesh of her hips, insisting on possessing her full attention.

"Am I sleeping with you or your sister, Angelique?"

"That's the problem, Kasim. That is exactly the problem," she said as her eyes filled.

Kasim had begun to think she was playing coy, attempting a manipulation as some women were inclined, but the anguish in her beautiful features was real. It caused such a twist of protectiveness in him, he instinctively tightened his arms to draw her nearer.

The old habit of standing between Jamal and the constant threat of harm rose in him, mentally pushing him between Angelique and her sister, making him even more determined to separate her from something that was obviously harming her in some way.

She resisted his attempt to enfold her, bottom lip caught in her teeth, brow pulled into a wrinkle of angst.

With a flex of agitation at the stiffness of her, he pulled away and sought out his pants from the floor where he'd shed them.

"Explain," he commanded as he stepped into them and zipped. He reached for his shirt, slipping it on but leaving it unbuttoned.

"It's hard," she said in a small voice, one hand lifting helplessly. "It doesn't even make sense, really. But it's how I feel." She sighed heavily. "And I am the sensitive one, ruled by my emotions."

She sounded so forlorn.

He folded his arms, trying not to let that niggle at him. He had learned to shield himself against expressions of deep emotion. Too many times in his childhood he'd been bombarded by the pain of others—his mother and Fatina, the king's warring wives, trying to draw him to their side. Jamal's inner torture then Hasna's unrelenting grief...

There was no way to fix the emotional pain of others. He could only protect himself from becoming wound up in it.

Seeing Angelique had demons warned him to cut short whatever this was, but he found himself rooted, willing her to speak. He wanted to understand why she was resisting him. He wanted to help her.

"It was supposed to be me," she said, gaze naked and filled with guilty torment. "The kidnapping. I was the quiet one. The shy one. The one who was bad at math and needed a tutor. It was end of semester and our chauffeur was coming. Trella was already outside. She was the extrovert who wanted to say goodbye to everyone. My tutor called out to her. He thought she was me.

She went over to tell him I would be out soon and he grabbed her." She snapped her fingers. "Just like that. Ramon came out in time to see it happen and chased the van as far as he could, but they'd plotted their getaway very well..."

Her lips were white. Her hand shook as she tucked her hair behind her ear.

"Was she...?" He didn't want to finish the question. What kind of person assaulted a nine-year-old child?

"What happened in those five days is Trella's to tell or not," Angelique said in a voice that quavered. She knew, though. The answer was in her eyes. *Hell.* Whatever it was, it had been hell.

Kasim moved to take her cold hands in his, trying to rub warmth into them.

"You're suffering survivor's guilt," he said quietly. "I understand that." He did. Jamal should be living the life Kasim enjoyed. They were both sons of the king. There was no difference between them except those small characteristics that made every person unique unto themselves.

"The guilt is only part of it. We were already legendary, not that we ever wanted that sort of notoriety, but that's why we were targeted. The Sauveterre Twins, one of Europe's treasures, right? Of course payment would be made for Trella's return. Of course the press went mad at the sensationalism of it."

She cleared her throat, obviously struggling.

"My father had to use that circus to our advantage. I looked just like Trella so they used me as Trella's face, to plea for her return. Any tiny thing could have been the key to getting her back. It was horrible exploitation. He hated himself for doing it to me, but when you're desperate..."

Her eyes filled and she pulled her hand out of his to press the knot of her fist between her breasts.

"All the while… The connection between twins is a real thing, Kasim. It is for Trella and me. I knew she was terrified and suffering. It was unbearable. And then she came back to us so broken and I felt that, too." Her lips quivered.

He had to enfold her in his arms. Had to.

She shook like a tiny animal that had barely escaped certain death.

"She's safe now, hmm?" he coaxed gently into her hair. "Come back, Angelique. That was a long time ago and she's safe. You're both safe now."

She nodded and sniffed once, but he could feel the shudders of dark memory running through her. Her arms went around his waist, beneath his open shirt. The beadwork on her dress abraded his bare skin. He stroked her hair, imparting as much comfort as he could, rubbing his chin against her temple.

"You're afraid to leave her alone, in case something happens again," he surmised.

"I'm afraid all the time of everything." Her cheek was damp where she pressed it to his chest. "That's who I am, Kasim. I'm the worrier. I'm the introvert. But I had to become the strong one. The only way I've ever been able to do that— God, the only way I could find the courage to stand in front of cameras and beg for her return was to pretend I was her. I had to become her in some ways. How could I ever go back to being quiet, shy Angelique who leaned on her sister for confidence? My support was shattered. She needed *me* to be that person."

She wiped at her cheek and settled against him again.

"We should be two carefree young women, but she

was cheated. I know she would have risen to the challenge if it had been me so I have to do that for her. Everything I do is for both of us. Sometimes I feel like I am her and I don't know how to be just me."

Her odd comment at dinner about being each other, which he had thought was a bit of twin peculiarity, now made more sense. So did the one about her not letting herself "be."

"Who were you tonight?" he asked, cupping the side of her neck, invaded by a prickling tension as he urged her to look up at him.

She drew back, but her gaze stayed on her own fingertips as she smoothed the hairs down his breastbone in a petting caress that made shivers of delight travel up his spine.

"I stole tonight for myself."

"Good. That is the correct answer."

She tsked and gave him a little shove. He only settled her closer, pleased when she relaxed and rested her head against his shoulder again, arms looped around his waist.

"But I can't be selfish and take what I want. I can't do that to Trella. Do you understand?"

"You know you cannot live someone else's life for them, don't you?" How many times had he tried to solve Jamal's "problem" to no avail? "You cannot shelter someone forever. It's not fair to either of you. We are each responsible for our own lives."

"I know," she murmured. "Separating my life from my sister's has to happen. We both know that. But I can't force that on her and I certainly won't let you force it. And the truth is..." She tilted back her head to look up at him with a solemn expression. "I am not impulsive. I am a thinker. If you want Angelique to go anywhere with you, you have to give *Angelique* time to put it all together in her pretty little head."

He pondered that, distantly aware he didn't have much time. His father was already talking about finding him a bride as soon as Hasna's wedding was out of the way.

"How much time do you need? I was going to leave first thing in the morning and it's already…" He looked around and swore lightly. "There are no such things as clocks anymore."

Releasing her, he found his cell phone and clicked to see it was nearing midnight. He dropped the phone into his pocket, then left his hand there with it. He raised the other to pinch his bottom lip.

"I have meetings in the morning. Come later in the day. I'll make the arrangements."

"I can make my own arrangements," she informed him, but with a rueful purse of her lips. "Which I realize you just heard as agreement." She sighed and touched her brow. "I could call my mother, see if she feels like spending the night in Paris with Trella. Does anyone ever say no to you, Kasim?"

"They realize very quickly that it is a waste of both our time. You, apparently, are a slow learner."

"Don't," she said with a little flinch. "It's still a sore point for me. I can cut out a perfect square meter of fabric by sight, but ask me to add one half to three quarters and I just embarrass myself. Now I'm going to put on fresh lipstick." Her hand shook as she picked up the little golden tube and pointed it at him. "Keep your lips to yourself."

"Come here first," he commanded, compelled to reinforce the connection between them.

She paused in winding up the stick of color, sent

him a pert look. "Saying 'no' would just be a waste of a layer of lipstick, wouldn't it?"

"Look at you. You're actually very quick to learn."

She rolled her eyes, but she came across to kiss him.

CHAPTER SIX

IF I NEED YOU, I'll call.

Trella's words dogged Angelique as she stole off to London. They weren't telling any of the family that Angelique was leaving Trella for a night on her own in Paris. Better to let it be a fait accompli, they decided, given how reluctant their brothers had been to let Trella make the short flight alone.

Trella had passed her own test "with flying colors," she had excitedly said about her solitary flight, quite triumphant in her achievement.

Angelique had been so proud, she'd had a little cry about it, which had made Trella laugh and hug her and call her their sensitive little Gili.

Nevertheless, Angelique felt guilty for leaving. Trella was very safe. Situated on the top floor of the design house, the Paris flat was ultra-secure. Seamstresses and other staff came and went from the lower floors, working into the night if the mood took, but the flat had its own entrance, a panic room and a private passage to the office.

Trella had been very heartfelt in her plea for Angelique to do something for herself for a change.

I've held you back too long, Trella had insisted, then added with a sly look, *Besides, I'm curious about Henri and Cinnia. See what you can find out.*

Angelique had laughed at that, but if Trella had a setback, she would never forgive herself.

Deep down, however, she was anxious to see Kasim again. It was a foreign state of mind for her. After Trella's experience, she'd spent her adolescence wary of boys and sex. When she finally started to date, she had been hard-pressed to find men who measured up to the standards her father and brothers had set. When her suitors had fallen off because her life was too restrictive, or proved to be social climbers or other opportunists, she'd been annoyed and disappointed, but never truly hurt.

She had never been taken with any man. None had engaged her feelings very deeply and she had never, ever, allowed a man to come between her and her family.

In some ways, she was terrified of the influence Kasim was having on her. He fascinated her and thus had power over her. He was confident and secure in himself, almost brutally honest, but that lack of subterfuge was as seductive as the rest of him.

And oh, did he seduce! From a physical standpoint, she was completely infatuated. Her blood raced as she silently willed the driver into London after the family jet landed at the private airfield.

She hadn't given Trella many details about her evening with Kasim, but her sister had said with a sensual lift of her own hair, *I know you slept with him. Don't deny it. I'm kind of jealous, actually. In a good way. It makes me realize what I'm missing.*

That had made Angelique very self-conscious, but she knew Trella was interpreting her body language. They had the same expressions and mannerisms so even though Angelique could disguise her thoughts and feelings from many, her sister would read the indolent stretch or the warmed cheek and soft gaze of pleasant memory without effort.

Trella didn't tease her for it, and when Angelique studied Trella, she saw nothing but determination in her sister at being left alone this evening.

Kasim had been right about Angelique suffering survivor's guilt. She wondered if it was the reason she had given up so easily on her previous relationships. Being happy when her sister had been struggling had always felt incredibly disloyal.

She still felt disloyal, haring off to London to be with a man, but it was only one night, she told herself. Kasim hadn't promised anything else and neither had she for that matter, even though she felt a yearning for more.

Not that she'd defined exactly what "more" would be. The artist in her appreciated that whatever they had was too new and special for close examination. Deconstruction could kill it. Sometimes you had to go with instinct, then determine after the fact what you had.

Was this instinct? Or greed and selfishness? Or old-fashioned blindness to obvious facts?

Exactly the type of scrutiny she had to avoid, she thought with a stifled sigh.

Whatever it was, it drew her inexorably. Her pulse was racing over a single text from Kasim, promising to meet her at her brother's flat within the hour.

It was actually the family flat. Knowing Henri was in New York, Angelique assumed Cinnia was staying in her own flat, but texted her as a courtesy, mentioning that she was in town and asking if Cinnia wanted to get together for a meal.

Cinnia's reply came through as Angelique was letting herself in. It was a simple regret that she was staying with her mother and was sorry she had missed the chance to visit.

Angelique put her bag in the room she and Trella used, checked that there was a decent bottle of wine in the fridge and moved restlessly into the lounge, wondering if she and Kasim were going out for dinner and if so, where? What should she wear?

Paparazzi. Ugh, she thought with another sigh, but for once she wasn't filled with as much dread as usual. She would have hated to have her night with Kasim reduced by the online trolls to a one-night stand, sullied and mocked, even though she'd gone to his room last night convinced it would be only that.

Having this affair extend into a second night made it feel— Well, it still felt so rare and precious she wanted to guard it jealously, but she was so thrilled to see him again, she was willing to pay the price.

"Oh, no," she murmured, jerked from introspection as she caught sight of the coffee table.

A courier envelope had been torn open and the contents spilled out. It was at least a hundred thousand euros in jewelry, probably more. It looked like the contents of Ali Baba's cave, glittering and sparkling innocently against the glass tabletop.

Angelique sat down hard on the sofa, chest tight. She thought about texting Trella, but Henri was the most private of all of them. He would kill her if he knew *she* had seen this. She couldn't share it like tawdry gossip, not even with Trella.

But what had gone wrong?

Henri was adamant in his decision never to marry, but he and Cinnia had seemed so good together. Angelique would have bet real money that Cinnia genuinely loved him. How had those tender feelings become something as harsh as throwing his gifts back in his face?

It was a cool, disturbing reminder that relationships fell into one of two categories: those with a future and those that ended. Her heart chilled, starkly confronted with the kind she had with Kasim.

There wouldn't be a moment of callous rejection between them, though. Not like this. She and Kasim were never going to spend two years together the way Henri had with Cinnia.

Upset for Henri and Cinnia—and disturbed on her own behalf—she pushed the jewelry into the envelope, but the artist in her was drawn to examine the tennis bracelet. She'd never taken a proper look at it. It was a string of alternating pink and white diamonds, one Cinnia had always seemed to be wearing. Angelique was really shocked she'd given it up, especially now that she saw how exquisite it really was. The craftsmanship in the setting was extraordinary. She searched it for an insignia that might tell her where it had come from.

When the door opened behind her, she stood with surprise, expecting Maurice, but it was Kasim. She had told Maurice to expect him, but had thought she'd have to ring him through the main doors downstairs before he would appear up here.

"How did you get in the building?" she asked as she moved to meet him, flushing uncontrollably with instant pleasure.

His mouth tilted with a hint of smugness, as if he read her infatuation and knew how slowly the minutes had passed for her before seeing him again. It was disconcerting, making her feel defenseless and obvious, but she still found herself crossing toward him, tugged by an invisible lasso around her middle.

He waited for the door to shut before he hooked his arm around her and kissed her.

It was proprietary and given how fleeting this affair was likely to be, she should be keeping better control over herself, but her heart soared. She quickly melted into him, instantly transported to the languorous memories of last night and anticipation for more of the same incredible pleasure he'd delivered.

"You missed me," he said when he drew back.

"You didn't miss me?" She tried to sound blasé, tried to pull away, but she was hyperaware of how needy that sounded. How completely easy she was being.

His hand slid to her tailbone and pressed her hips into his enough that she felt how he was reacting to her. "I've been thinking about you," he allowed.

Fluttery joy invaded her abdomen and she tried not to reveal how quickly and thoroughly he'd bowled her over.

"Good to know," she said lightly. "But I am genuinely curious how you got into the building. It's supposed to be locked down for residents only."

"It is. I was given the codes when I bought my flat this morning. Shall we go look at it?" He finally released her and stepped toward the door with a low wave for her to accompany him.

"You—you bought a unit in this building *this morning*?" She had grown up with wealth, but they only owned a flat here because her father had bought it during the design stage, just before his death. The address was obscenely exclusive with a wait list a mile long of international dignitaries and techno-billionaires trying to get in.

Perhaps she had underestimated *how* wealthy and

powerful Kasim was. The cost to jump queue must have been exorbitant.

"It's a good investment. My mother likes London," he said with a shrug. "She'll use it if I don't. Mostly I thought you'd appreciate the privacy. By some miracle, there is nothing online about us. I thought we'd celebrate our lack of infamy by staying in and extending our lucky streak. I've ordered dinner to be delivered in a couple of hours."

"We could have stayed here!" she pointed out.

He offered a pained frown. "I do not steal into a girl's bedroom at her parents' home."

No, he dropped a few million pounds on a suite he was only using for one night. *For her.*

She urged herself not to let that mean too much.

"Shall I change?" She was still wearing her travel clothes, a dark blue jersey skirt with a pale yellow top, both her own design. They were quietly feminine, breezy yet classic and a tiny bit waifish.

"You look beautiful." He skimmed his gaze down and back. "And whatever you wear is only for the elevator."

"You're not even going to pretend you're inviting me to look at etchings?" She planted her hands on her hips, only realizing as she did that she was still holding Cinnia's bracelet. Shoot. She was instantly self-conscious on her brother's behalf. "Um. I just have to put this down and grab my phone."

"What is it?" Kasim asked, catching at her wrist as the snaking sparkle caught his attention.

She opened her hand. "Something Henri bought for Cinnia," she prevaricated.

Her brother's long-term relationship was well documented in the press, but she wasn't going to be the one to start the rumors about its demise.

"I want to ask him where he got it because the work is outstanding. Look at the detail here. You can tell each of these claws has been crimped individually to create this effect all the way along. I'm in awe at how painstaking that would be. Have you ever seen anything like it?"

Kasim's nostrils flared as he picked up the bracelet and gave it a thorough study, his expression pulling into a tension that bordered on agony. As if suddenly realizing how hard he was staring, and that she was watching him, he quickly straightened his features and handed her the bracelet.

"No," he answered belatedly and rather abruptly. "Let's go."

Her heart did a little thump. The mood had definitely shifted. "What's wrong?"

"Nothing."

She was hurt that he would lie so blatantly to her, but moved across to tuck the bracelet into the envelope and picked up her phone.

The silence in the elevator was not precisely thick, but it was significant.

Kasim's cheeks were hollow, his mouth flat.

Maurice was with them, so Angelique kept her own counsel. Her guard went through Kasim's new flat ahead of them, even though Kasim's team had been here all day, ensuring it was not only clean and secure, but furnished and well stocked.

The layout was similar to her family's suite with a lounge opening onto a balcony overlooking the Thames. She imagined the door next to the wet bar led to the kitchen, as it did in their own. Down the hall would be the bedrooms and baths.

This one smelled faintly of paint and was filled with contemporary furniture and a handful of decent

art pieces. His decorator was competent, if unimagi-
native, having fallen back on the latest issue of *Colors
of the Year* for lack of inspiration.

The moment Maurice left them alone, Kasim drew
her into his arms again and kissed her quite passionately. Almost aggressively, questing for a response. It
was as if he was trying to propel them into the mindless
state they'd experienced last night in Paris.

It was breathlessly exciting, yet made her feel... She
wasn't sure and, as her blood began to heat, started not
to care.

"Do I not even get a chance to explore the place myself?" she gasped when his mouth traveled to the side
of her neck. Arousal suffused her, but she had the sense
she was being used as much as desired. It scraped her
insides raw.

"If you like," he said, straightening and not looking pleased.

"Have you even seen it?" she asked, trying to recover
and stung by the distance she sensed between them.

"I'm more interested in this." His lashes cut downward as he slid his gaze to her toes and came back to
her lips.

His ravenous gaze made her skin tighten, but her
heart squeezed at the same time. She *knew* he was sub-
limating something.

"Kasim." She cupped his jaw. "What has upset you?"

"I'm not upset." He pulled away from her touch and
moved to the bar. "Children get upset. Do you want
wine?"

He was speaking shortly. Irritably. Like he was upset,
she thought drily.

"Something about the bracelet bothered you. Did you
recognize it?" She was intuitive that way. She just was.

"You can tell me what it was, or I can make up stories of my own to explain your reaction."

"I've never seen it," he said flatly, setting out two wineglasses. "But the workmanship reminded me of Jamal's. He designed jewelry."

He wound the screw into the cork with a little squeaking noise and pulled it out with a pop, movements jerky, facial muscles still tense.

"My father hated it. He took it as a reflection against his own masculinity. An insult. He was ashamed to have a son who was…artistic," he pronounced with disdain. "My mother used that to her advantage."

"What do you mean?"

He poured, steadying the bottoms of each glass with two fingers as he did.

"Jamal is—was Fatina's son. My father's second wife. My mother…"

He set aside the bottle. For a moment he was a man on the verge of exploding, wrapped tightly, but packed to the eyebrows with dynamite, fuse burning in his eyes.

"Children should not be used as weapons, but my mother loved to find fault with him. To his face, to my father, in public. However she could humiliate him and Fatina, she did it. In sly ways, though. Small little stabs. Death by a thousand cuts," he said grimly.

"That's horrible."

"It was. And my father was determined to turn him into something he could be proud of. That was his way of countering my mother's attacks, by telling Jamal he was to blame for her criticisms. If he only changed, we would all have peace. I'm furious every time I'm reminded of how it was for him."

"You couldn't make your father see reason?"

He snorted. "This?" He lifted his glass and touched

it to the rim of hers. "I don't care one way or another for alcohol, but it is completely outlawed in Zhamair. It's not a religious restriction. We have as many citizens who are Christian or Jewish as we do Muslims in our country, but my father's word is rule. My father is a dictator in the way that political scientists define one."

"But you do what you want when you're away," she noted with a glance at his Western clothes. "Couldn't your brother have done that? I'm sorry, I know it's very easy to say that he should leave his country and turn his back on his father. It's not something anyone would do without deep struggle, but…"

"No," Kasim agreed in a hard, grim voice. "It's not. Especially since it meant leaving his mother and the rest of his siblings. Fatina has four younger children, as well. And he felt my father's rejection very deeply. He wanted desperately to earn his respect. It was an impossible situation for him."

"That's so awful." Her heart ached for not just his brother, but for Kasim. No wonder he wanted to take the reins from a man who possessed no hint of compassion or empathy. No wonder he had fought so hard for Hasna to have a love marriage.

"How did he die?" she asked softly, then clutched where the pang in her chest had intensified. She could see the anguish still fresh in Kasim's face. "It wasn't suicide, was it?"

Kasim didn't speak, only stared into his wine for a long moment. His fingernails were so white where he clutched the stem of his glass, she though he would snap the crystal. His gaze came up and she thought he looked about to say something.

In the next second, he shut down, mouth flattening into a sealed line before he finally said in a neutral, almost practiced, voice, "It was a car crash. We were in Morocco on business. He was out on his own along a stretch of road near the ocean. He wasn't reckless by nature, but he was under a lot of pressure from my father to give up the jewelry design, work with me full-time and marry suitably."

His expression was filled with perturbed memories.

"The car went through the guardrail into the rocks below. Calling my father with the news was hard, but facing Fatina and Hasna, and my younger brothers and sisters…"

The torment in his expression was too much to bear. So much guilt, but how could he have prevented it? It was just a terrible accident. He shouldn't blame himself.

She set aside her glass and came around the bar to slide her arms around his waist. "I'm sorry."

"Why? You had nothing to do with it." He continued to hold his glass, his other arm hanging at his side, stiff and unresponsive to her embrace. He looked down his nose at her.

"I shouldn't have forced you to revisit his loss."

She felt the flinch go through him. He sipped, stony as a column of marble that didn't give under the lean of her weight, only supported her with cold, indifferent strength. "The bracelet did that."

"And you wanted me to help you think of nicer things." She traced her fingertips up the line of his spine through the back of his shirt, trying to reach him through physical contact since he seemed to have shut her out emotionally. "Now I will. If you like."

"What about your great explore?" He didn't bend at all.

"I've seen a flat just like this one. But this…" She brought her hands around to climb his chest and brush his suit jacket open, nudging it to fall back off his shoulders. "This territory is still new to me."

She was trying to be bold, to find the affinity they had shared in Paris, but was highly unsure when he failed to respond. Self-doubt, her great nemesis, twisted through her.

"I plan to be very thorough in my mapping of it," she said, voice wavering as she became convinced he was about to reject her.

"You're liable to see nothing but this ceiling for the next hour," he warned, setting aside his glass and clasping her hips in heavy hands.

"Maybe that's all *you'll* see," she said with a tremble of relief. "Did you think of that?"

Kasim had almost told her the truth about Jamal. It was a stunning break in his normal vigilance against any woman's intrusion into his inner world.

Idly caressing from the back of her thigh over the curve of her buttock to the hollow in the small of her back, he wondered how this smooth golden skin had come to get so far under his own in such a short amount of time.

He didn't regard women as a Western indulgence he allowed himself when he traveled, but he did treat his sexual relationships much as he did his business ones. Some were brief transactions, some longer term, but they were exchanges and trades, always agreements with clear parameters. Paramours didn't cause him to rearrange his life and they rarely stimulated more than his libido.

This one, however… He had made a ridiculously large transfer this morning so he could protect their privacy, mindful of her request last night to keep the world from cheapening their association.

Why? What did he care if their association was known or in what context? He would eagerly show her off. The idea of staking a public claim held a great deal of pleasure for him, in fact.

He very carefully blocked the vision of any other man thumbing into the small dimples at the top of each of her firm, round cheeks, then he lightly traced the line that separated them, fingertips claiming Angelique's backside along with the rest of her, sweeping the back of her thigh and taking possession of her calf.

He had grown up watching his father deal with the fallout of indulging unfettered lust. Every person was susceptible to being attracted to the wrong person— or rather, an inconvenient person in relation to the life they led. Giving in to that desire was the root of whatever problems arose.

Kasim had always regarded himself as superior to his father and brother. *He* was capable of rising above the temptations that foretold complications.

Was he kidding himself, believing this thing with Angelique was a trouble-free dalliance that could end tomorrow morning with a light kiss and a "pleasant knowing you"?

An uncomfortable bolt of rejection shot through him, not just resisting the idea of walking away, but outright refusing to countenance it. His reaction was so visceral, his hand closed in a small squeeze where it rested above the back of her knee. He was literally holding on to her and he'd only *thought* about the inevitable parting that awaited them.

It was a sobering confrontation with his inner animal, the one he had always been so sure he governed without effort.

"I'm awake," she murmured on a contented sigh,

as if she took his grip to be a test of her level of consciousness.

She turned her head so she could blink dreamy eyes at him while keeping her face mostly buried in her folded arms and the fall of her magnificent hair. "Just thinking. Do you want to meet me in Berlin next weekend? I have a thing."

He had places to be, people to rise above.

"I thought we were staying out of the spotlight."

Her sleepy smile slowly warmed to something vulnerable yet elated. It made his heart swerve and swell.

"I was really asking if you wanted to see me again after tonight." The tone in her voice caused a pleasant-painful vibration through him.

He looked at where his hand was still firm on the back of her thigh. "I fear for our lives at the rate we're going, but I was going to ask you to stay the weekend. I have to escort my mother and sister back to Zhamair on Sunday, but I will arrange to take them back late." He would also cancel his lunch arrangements for tomorrow with his foreign secretary and the British counterpart.

"I wasn't planning to spend the weekend," she said, last night's troubled light coming into her eye. Her sister again.

"No?" He tensed and felt her hamstring flex against his light grip.

Guilt and longing fought for dominance in her gaze. She released a soft moan of struggle and gave a taut stretch beneath his touch.

"I will if I can arrange it." Her tone echoed with something like defeat.

He began to pet her again, blood tingling as he fondled her with more purpose. He wasn't used to a woman resisting him. It made him restless for her capitulation.

Not something forced. No, he needed her to give herself up to him.

Rolling her over, he began to kiss her, running his mouth to all the places that made her arch and moan under him, impressing on her the benefit of belonging to him. As he felt the tension in her, the clasp of nearing climax, he kissed his way back up the center of her torso.

"Tell me what you want."

"You know," she sobbed, moving against his hand, but he followed her undulations, keeping his penetration shallow and light.

"You want this?" he very slowly and gently deepened his caress, deliberately holding her on the plane of acute pleasure she occupied, not letting her tumble into orgasm. "Or this?"

He rolled atop her and loved the saw of her breath as she gasped in a sensual agony. Holding himself in a tight fist, fighting back from his own approaching peak, he rubbed his aching tip against her slick folds, nudging at her with promise.

She danced and angled her hips, trying to capture him.

He shook with want, barely able to see straight, but made himself hold off and only kiss her. "What will you do for me?"

"Anything," she gasped, but opened her eyes. They were shiny with helpless torture, a hint of resentment even. She knew what he was demanding. *Her.*

He cupped her head and slowly, slowly sank into her. Their breaths mingled as their bodies joined, both of them parting their lips to release jagged noises of intense pleasure.

How could she resent this? How?

He made love to her then, sending her over the edge, then keeping her aroused so they were damned near clawing each other when the next crest approached. He didn't think he could wait for her, but he wanted her with him. Demanded it with the hard thrust of his hips against her. *Needed it.*

She locked herself around him and released a keening noise, shuddering beneath him. The greedy clasp of her sheath triggered his own climax and he shouted in triumph as he joined her in the paroxysm.

Angelique was a little stunned by what she'd just experienced. Not just the ferocity of Kasim's lovemaking. She'd been so aroused, she had craved that intensity, but there'd been a loss of self in that joining. He had been the only thing important to her. It left her scrambling to recover her sense of autonomy, while he made it impossible by rolling back into her and running proprietary hands over her still-tingling skin.

The condom was gone along with his urgency. Now he was the tender man whose touch was soothing and reassuring. He almost lulled her back into thinking everything about him was safe, but it wasn't. He imperiled the very heart of her.

She put up an instinctive hand against his chest, resisting his effort to pull her into a sprawl across his sweat-damp body.

"What's wrong?" He picked up her hand and lightly bit her fingertip, then kissed the same spot. "I can't make promises about Berlin, but I will try. Good enough?"

He sounded languid and satisfied while she was completely dismantled.

"Is it because we might be found out?" She had been

trying to think how they could continue on the sly, but couldn't see a way, not unless he wanted to go broke buying private flats. He hadn't seemed particularly worried about exposure anyway. "Would it be complicated for you with Hasna if something wound up in the press?"

He snorted. "I don't consult *my* sister on how I conduct my private life."

There. *That* was the issue. He resented her sister. She stiffened and tried to pull away.

"That was a cheap shot," he allowed, arms clamping like a straitjacket around her. "I take it back."

"No!" She turned her face away. "You don't get to kiss me into forgetting you said it."

He sighed against her cheek.

"I'm spoiled," he stated without compunction. "Never second fiddle to anyone except my father and that is a finite situation, not that I wish his life away. I only mean that I am his heir and aside from him, I am autonomous."

"Yet I'm supposed to be content as a second fiddle in your life."

A long pause that was so loaded, she had to glance warily at him, fearful she'd truly angered him.

Maybe she hadn't angered him, but she'd scored a point. She could see echoes of his mood earlier when he'd talked about his mother's brutal treatment of his father's second wife and his half brother.

"I have meetings all next week," he said in a cool tone. "Roundtable discussions with a dozen of our region's most powerful leaders. You must have an idea of our political and economic landscape? The stakes are always high. I go so my father won't or he'll send us back to the Stone Age. The conference could easily go into next weekend. That is the only reason I am avoiding saying yes to Berlin."

"Fine." Now she felt like she'd pressured a concession of sorts from him, but it was a hollow victory. "It was just a thought."

"What are you doing there?" His tone wasn't patronizing, but she read his question as an attempt to mollify her and move past their conflict.

"A fashion awards night." She glossed over it. "There's a white tie and champagne thing after. I'm presenting so I can't skip it. You'd probably find it boring anyway."

"Do you do a lot of these things? Who do you usually go with?"

She would not kid herself that he sounded jealous.

"Colleagues. Sometimes one of my brothers. Honestly, it's fine. I'm supposed to be at a thing tonight and—" She'd forgotten to cancel, she realized. She had decided not to go once she realized Trella would be in town, but had paid the plate fee because it was a charity she liked to support. It wasn't a big deal that she was a no-show. She shouldn't be experiencing this stab of guilt.

All part of Kasim's magnifying effect on her emotions, she supposed. She frowned, aware of a cloud of traitorousness blanketing her too, along with a niggling desire to rebel. She put it all down to letting him extract that surrender to his seduction at the expense of thinking of—

She scrambled out of his arms to sit up. *Trella.*

"What—?" Kasim made a noise.

She kicked away the covers as she scooted off the bed. "I have to check in with Trella."

"Why?"

"I just do," she muttered and quickly shrugged into his robe, tying it tight then leaving to scour the lounge for her cell phone.

Angelique had put down the agitation in her belly to the sound of an invisible clock ticking down on her time with Kasim and all the things that she was doing that were out of character: engaging in an affair, leaving her sister, shunning work responsibilities.

But there was that other plane of awareness that her sister occupied in her unconscious...

Kasim came into the lounge, pants pulled on, but wearing nothing else, blanking her mind. Lord, he was beautiful, moving with economy, sculpted muscles rippling under smooth, swarthy skin. For a moment she forgot to breathe, she was so captivated.

He prowled to where the food had been received and abandoned on the dining table an hour ago. They had been too busy with each other when it arrived to do more than set it aside and get back to bed.

He opened the wicker basket and said, "We should eat before this is stone cold."

When he glanced at her, he caught her ogling. A light smirk touched his gorgeous mouth. He hooked his thumbs in his waistband, so sexy her mouth watered.

"Unless you're hungry for something else?"

She swallowed and ignored the fact her blood turned to lava. It was better that he wouldn't be in Berlin. He had way too much power over her as it was.

"I could eat." She hid her reaction by gathering their still-full wineglasses and bringing them across to the table under his watchful eye.

"Your sister?" he prompted.

"Fine." She bit her lip, flashing him an uncertain look. "She told me not to hurry back."

Take advantage of flying under the radar as long as you can, Trella had texted, but Angelique was still aware of her sister in that peripheral way. Trella wasn't frightened precisely, but she was disturbed.

They had used their authentication codes, though. She knew it was definitely Trella telling her to stay in London, coming across like an adolescent pushing for independence, insisting she was *completely fine*.

Angelique hadn't tried a video call, too embarrassed at how much she would betray, especially wearing Kasim's robe.

"So you'll stay the weekend." Kasim looped his arm around her.

"Do I have a choice?" she challenged tartly.

He stroked the back of his bent finger along her jaw, perhaps looking apologetic, but all he said was "Not if I have anything to do with it, no."

Then he kissed her until she was leaning into him, utterly spellbound.

CHAPTER SEVEN

ASIDE FROM THE odd time when she had become tipsy from having too little to eat before having a glass of wine, Angelique had never been drunk or stoned. Kasim, however, provoked a feeling in her that she imagined one felt when ingesting party pills.

She walked around in a fog of euphoria after London, mood swinging wildly. One minute she was lost in recalling how they had essentially spent two solid days in bed, rising only to eat and make love elsewhere in the flat: the sofa, the kitchen chair, the shower. It made her too blissed out to care about the lost shipment of linen or the hundreds of euros in hand-made bobbin lace that wound up attached to the wrong gown.

The next minute she plummeted into a withdrawal depression, certain she'd never hear from him again. With his hand buried in her hair, he had kissed her deeply late Sunday afternoon, both of them aware cars and planes were waiting for them. He had finally released her, saying, "You won't hear from me. I'll be tied up in meetings. I'll try to meet you in Berlin. If I can't, we'll figure out something for the following week."

Would they, though? She wished they'd made a clean break of it. She could have handled that. This veering between hope and despair was too much!

If Trella noticed Angelique's distraction, she didn't say anything. She was immersed in finishing Hasna's wardrobe, almost obsessing over each piece, working late and rising early to ensure everything was perfect. She seemed really wound up about it when she was usually the coolheaded one about deadlines and never lacked confidence that their work would be received with great enthusiasm.

Angelique had a fleeting thought that her sister was burying herself in work to avoid her, but they *were* behind, thanks to Angelique staying in London an extra day. It was probably her own distraction making it seem like her sister was off. She was grateful to Trella for picking up the slack and tried to set her own nose to the grindstone so they could ship everything as planned.

Then, even though time passed at a glacial pace, she suddenly found herself rattling around her hotel room in Berlin, phone in hand as she compulsively checked her messages for word from Kasim, behaving exactly like an addict needing a fix. She had sent him her agenda yesterday, mildly panicked at the lack of word from him. She absolutely refused to let herself text again.

Tonight's event was taking place here in this brandnew hotel. Her suite was airy and ultra-contemporary, run by a firm out of Dubai that understood the meaning of luxury. She promised herself a soak in the private whirlpool tub when she returned later. It was already filled and warmed. Tiny whorls of steam wisped from the edge of its rollback cover and candles were at hand, awaiting a match.

She would need to drown some sorrows since it looked like Kasim wouldn't turn up. She was devastated.

That shouldn't surprise her. Right from the beginning he had pulled a formidable response from her.

She fought tears as she set out her gown and did her hair, then her makeup, saying a private *Thanks, Trella*, as her sister's face appeared in the mirror to bolster her.

She wished now she had brought one of Trella's designs. Her sister's confections tended to have a self-assured cheekiness whereas Angelique's evoked more introspective moods. Hers tonight was wistful and damned if it wasn't *blue*.

A powder blue in silk, sleeveless, but abundant enough in the skirt to move like quicksilver. The bodice was overlaid with mist-like lace that split apart at her naval and fell into a divided overskirt that became a small train. She pinned her hair back from her face, but let it fall in loose waves behind her naked shoulders and painted her lips a meditative pink.

Her earrings were simple drop crystals that caught the light. A velvet choker with a matching stone collared her throat. A panic switch was sewn on the underside. She and her sister often joked about starting their own line of high-end security wear, but they didn't want to tip off anyone that they wore it themselves.

Just for a moment, as she took in her reflection, she wondered what it would be like to live without so much vigilance. In a prince's harem, for instance.

This lipstick really emphasized the pout she couldn't seem to shake. *Ugh*.

She gathered her composure before facing the masses. It was better that Kasim wasn't with her, she consoled herself. Events like this, when her presence was advertised ahead of time, were always particularly rabid attention-wise. Maurice wore special sunglasses to deal with the glare off the flashbulbs it was so bad.

Maurice was reading something on his phone when she came out the door. He tucked it away promptly, but took it out again when they were in the elevator, since they were alone.

"Je m'excuse," he said. "It's a report about some photos that have surfaced. I'm sending instructions to question their authenticity."

She dismissed his concern with a flick of her brows. "Of me with the prince?"

"It says 'prince,' yes, but—"

"I don't care," she insisted, even though she cared a great deal.

The elevator stopped, the doors opened and some models joined them. One was beyond thrilled to be sharing an elevator with One of The Sauveterre Twins. Maurice put his phone away and remained alert while Angelique exchanged a few remarks with the strangers and consented to a selfie.

Moments later, the doors opened onto the ballroom floor. The paparazzi went mad as soon as they saw she had arrived.

Maurice guided Angelique down the narrow pathway toward the VIP entrance where greeters would be waiting to check off her name on a tablet and handlers would hand her a swag bag that she invariably gave to her mother.

As she approached, a man in a tuxedo turned to look at her.

Kasim.

He was asking if she'd already entered the ballroom when the madness behind him made him turn.

She was stunning. Like an ethereal creature surrounded by fireflies as a million flashbulbs went off behind her.

Even more riveting than her beauty, however, was

the way her composed features softened with surprise, then dawned into warm recognition. Her eyes sparkled and a joyous glow suffused her. Her breasts rose as he moved toward her.

He caught his own breath. Him. The man who had decided this affair was too inconsequential to mention to his father, merely stating he had, indeed, resolved the situation with Sadiq's "friend." While he'd been so far away from her, he'd been able to convince himself their time together had been merely a pleasant diversion.

Nevertheless, he'd found himself bulldozing his way through his meetings, working late to negotiate agreements and pushing hard for resolution, a mental clock urging him to leave on time to be here with her. He had worked nonstop on the plane, barely sparing a moment to put on his tuxedo before finalizing a few last details over the phone in his car, arriving at the perfect moment to watch her emerge from the gauntlet.

Bulbs were still flashing as she unconsciously posed, awaiting his approach with that beautiful, reverent look on her face. He wondered what his looked like. Irritated and possessive, he imagined, since he wanted to steal her away from this madhouse. *Now.*

Mindful of her flawless appearance, he held back on crushing her even though he ached to feel her against him. Instead, he took her hand and detoured past her lips to press a light kiss to her cheekbone.

Her lashes fluttered closed and she breathed, "I'm so glad you're here."

He almost didn't hear her, but the blush that stained her cheeks told him she'd said it and was adorably self-conscious for having revealed herself like that.

"Are you?" He straightened to bask in her look of adoration. "Because I think we've been found out."

Behind her, the paparazzi had moved to completely block the passage. They had become a wall of strobing light and a din of clicks and whirs and shouts of her name.

"Is there anyone else here?" Angelique blinked her green, green eyes, mouth quirking with irony. "I only see you."

"You're stealing my lines." Stealing something else if he wasn't very careful. "Let's get this evening over with so I can have you to myself."

They created a huge stir and for once she didn't care. She was proud, so delighted and proud, to stand beside this man. He was *here*. It wasn't the most important occasion of her life, but it was important to her that he had made an effort.

He *wanted* to be with her.

Although, that could change if the attention didn't lighten up. Kasim might not be as infamous as she was, but with those features, the camera had to love him. His air of detachment meant eyes followed him with a yearning for scraps of his notice.

"You weren't exaggerating about the attention," he said when she returned to her seat after her presentation and he rose to help her with her chair.

"No," she agreed, then had to tease, "Scared?"

"Pah!" he dismissed.

They were an "it" couple before the final speeches had wrapped. "Kasimelique," one of her colleagues teased her in a whisper as the trays of champagne began circulating and the networking portion of the evening began.

"I'm so glad to have that over with," Angelique said to Kasim once they had the first rush of introductions over with and were able to move into a quieter corner for a moment alone. "Did I sound all right when I was onstage?"

"Perfect. You weren't nervous, were you? You didn't look it."

"I told you, my trick is to pretend I'm Trella. Do you know that man?" She tried not to sound so keyed up as she flicked her glance to the right, but this crush of people was wearing on her. "The blond one with the sash," she clarified.

The stranger was tall and quite handsome with a regal bearing. He wore the red satin as a bold streak across his chest beneath his jacket.

"He keeps looking this way. Maybe he's related to a client, but I can't place him. I'm going to be so embarrassed if he comes over and I don't know his name." The Champagne probably wasn't a good idea, but she took a sip anyway. This was still her first glass.

"I don't know who he is, but I recognize the look." Kasim seemed to stand taller and more alert. He took a half step closer to her.

"What do you mean? Like, Nordic heritage? Or do you mean you know the sash?" She lowered her glass, smile fading as she read the suspicion in the way he looked down his nose at her.

"I mean possessive. He's resentful of my place beside you. *Jealous.*"

"Are you serious?" She tried a laugh, but realized very quickly that Kasim was more than serious. He was trying to see inside her head.

"Kasim." She was deeply offended. "I swear to you, I don't know him." But she could see the reel of her online exploits playing behind his eyes.

"Believe what you want," she said frostily. *Don't*

you dare, she silently railed, heart clutched in a vise. He didn't trust her? After all they'd shared?

Well, honestly, what *had* they shared? A weekend of sex and not even some long-distance afterplay via text.

She looked at him with new eyes, thinking of how much she had anticipated his meeting her here, but now she had to wonder if she wasn't simply a convenient booty call. It was so lowering, she had to remind herself to breathe.

"Excuse me." He walked away into the throng, leaving her staring at his disappearing back, confounded and trying not to panic. That was *it*? He had just broken off their affair because a stranger looked at her in a way he didn't like?

Before she could fully absorb that and succumb to fury or despondency or both, the stark white of a truly beautiful tuxedo parked itself before her. It was cut by the slash of red and there was a star-shaped pin at his shoulder with a shield inside it.

The man could have come out of a fairy tale, he was so patrician and perfectly hewn.

She hated him on sight and wanted to throw her champagne in his face, but he spoke with an exotic accent and impeccable manners.

"Your lost item, Cinderella." He offered her a cupped hand.

Inside it was a gold hoop earring with a line of diamonds down the front. It looked exactly like a pair she owned. They'd been a gift from her father for her fifteenth birthday—not something run-of-the-mill that showed up in every low-budget jewelry shop. Trella's were similar, but that one was definitely the match to her own.

She took it to examine it more closely, trying to recall when she'd worn them last.

"Where—?"

"Caught under the pill—" he started to say in a tone that was very throaty with latent passion, but he cut himself off. Something in his expression grew sharp and arrested as he studied her face. Whatever lightness might have been in his mood became something accusatory as his gaze moved restlessly over her like he was searching for something he couldn't find.

She knew that look, but refused to believe she was interpreting it correctly. It was far too outrageous to imagine—

"I knew if I walked away, he would approach you," Kasim said, reappearing beside her.

Angelique startled, not exactly guilty, but defensive. *No.* She needed time to figure out what was going on with this stranger. She searched his blue eyes, now distinctly frosted with hostility toward Kasim. *And* her.

Kasim's gaze cut to the earring in her hand, making her close her fist around it.

"Introduce us." Kasim's tone was lethal.

Angelique was distantly aware of people sidling by them, glancing their way.

Kasim's expression was positively murderous and this stranger was shifting his gaze from her to Kasim, contempt curling his lip.

"I told you," she insisted to Kasim in an undertone. "I don't know him."

Trella, you didn't.

"My timing is inconvenient," the stranger said, flicking a look to Kasim that was a silent warning. *Be careful with this one.*

It was so infuriatingly *male*, like they were lofty

equals who came across tarts like her all the time, she instantly wanted to smack him. Both of them. How dare he show up and throw her under the bus this way. How dare he touch her sister! Her heart began to race, trying to assimilate how it could possibly have happened.

Was she crazy? Could he have been with Trella? How? *When?*

At the same time she was trying to work it out, she could see she was dropping like a free fall elevator in Kasim's estimation. That *hurt*, damn it. How could he think this of her?

"If you're going to accuse me of being a slut, at least tell me who you are," she bit out.

"You picked that label," the stranger shot back derisively. "And I don't *care* that you've moved on, but those are real diamonds. I was going to send it by courier back to Paris, but I read that you were going to be here and I was in Berlin." He shrugged a dismissal, looking distinctly bored as he glanced away. "My mistake. Carry on."

But he stood there like he was waiting for Kasim to give up and leave, as if he wanted to continue talking to her.

"*Back* to Paris," she repeated, reclaiming the stranger's attention while hotly aware that Kasim was glancing away as though looking for an exit. "When exactly was I there with you? Wait. Let me guess," she insisted, because it finally hit her. It was completely impossible, but she *knew*. "Last Friday night? The charity dinner for the Brighter Days Children's Foundation?"

The stranger's cheeks went hollow. "You know it was."

"Kasim, where was I last weekend? *All* weekend?"

Finally she had his attention. His resentful, derisive attention.

"You *are* both aware I have a twin. *Aren't you?*"

Kasim couldn't say that he was relieved when Angelique cleared herself of cheating on him. He was still too gripped by residual possessiveness. Maybe his jealous rage had eased enough that he was capable of rational thought, maybe he'd ceased wanting to *kill* the other man acting so proprietarily toward Angelique, but he was still pulsing with adrenaline. The sheer force of emotion that had overtaken him as he identified a rival was paralyzing.

Unnerving.

"I'll need your name and contact details," Angelique said while signaling Maurice to approach.

"His Highness, Xavier Deunoro," Kasim supplied stiffly. "Prince of Elazar."

Angelique and the prince both turned raised-brow looks his way.

Kasim shrugged. "I asked when I walked away."

"Another prince. *Charming,*" Angelique said scathingly.

Upset that he'd been mistrustful? She should look at the facts before him: they hadn't been together all week, her sister was never seen in public and this man had brought her damned earring from what was no doubt his *bed.* Shared intimacy was the only reason he would want to return it personally.

"She said she was you," the prince said as he reached to an inside pocket of his tuxedo. "The resemblance is remarkable, but there is something…" He narrowed his eyes. "I can't put my finger on it, but the moment I saw you tonight, I knew something was different."

That made Angelique stiffen and flash a wary glance at the man, but she recovered quickly and took the prince's card, relaying it to her guard with a hand that shook.

"That explains the photos you were questioning," she said to Maurice. "My brothers will want that, but wait until I've spoken to Trella. I'll head upstairs to do that now." With a hard glance at her sister's lover, she said, "If you tell anyone it was her and not me, I will personally hunt you down and unman you." She looked as gloriously provocative as she had the day Kasim had met her.

"You can try," the prince drawled. "Give her my regards."

Angelique turned away only to be confronted by a Hollywood starlet.

"I'm sorry," Angelique said with tested graciousness, briefly clasping the actress's hand. "I've been called away. I'm looking forward to our appointment next month, though. We'll talk then."

"My people will need a copy of the press release before it's sent," Kasim said, taking out his phone as he fell into step with her, winding toward the nearest exit.

"What press release?"

"The one clarifying her identity."

"That won't happen."

He checked briefly, not faced with any physical obstructions, but walking into the wall of his own ego.

"You will," he informed her. "Or I will."

"Do not make threats in that direction, Kasim."

"It's not a threat. It's a statement. I can't allow people to have a wrong impression." His father would find Kasim's means of putting Sadiq's problem to bed rather crude as it was.

"After what you just thought about me, you might be surprised how little I care about how this reflects on *you*. I would rather the general public think the worst of me than know the truth, however."

"Why?" he demanded.

"Reasons."

They approached the melee of reporters. He was forced to table his questions as they pushed their way through the chaos to the elevators.

Her guard efficiently plowed them a way and barred anyone from coming into the car with them, but Angelique still had the gall to look at Kasim like he was a hitchhiker who had hopped on from the highway.

"I'm going to my room to call my sister. You're not invited," she said.

"It's my room," he stated.

She shot a look to Maurice who was instantly alarmed. "That shouldn't happen," her guard said, reaching for his phone. "I'll call—"

"I know the owners," Kasim said tightly. "I pulled strings to take over the reservation. It's *fine*."

"It really isn't." Angelique sailed out the doors as they opened, striding down the hall with her elegant dress trailing behind her like a visible whorl of her cloud of fury.

One of Kasim's own guards had joined Maurice's partner at the door to the suite, leaving Kasim's bag just inside on the floor. Angelique gave both a baleful look and walked straight through the lounge into the bedroom where she quickly shut the door. Seconds later Kasim heard the dull ring of her placing a call and a greeting in a muted voice that held a tone that sounded much like her own.

He took out his own phone and searched for the most

recent photos of Angelique Sauveterre. Most were from tonight, first the ones of them greeting each other outside the ballroom, then mingling within. A few showed her onstage, and one grainy snap across the restaurant last weekend was obviously a belated effort to pile on tonight's revelation that they were dating.

Then there were a handful of images that showed her—it damned well looked *exactly* like her—in a clinch with the Prince of Elazar in a ballroom in Paris.

And someone had managed to snap her very tense expression as she had defended herself against two-timing right before they'd come up here.

Kasim gritted his teeth as he weighed Sauveterre security protocols against his own reputation. He could spare Angelique an hour to address this scandal in her own way, he allowed generously. After that, he would turn down the heat on this particular conflagration himself.

Twenty minutes later, Angelique emerged from the bedroom, cheeks flushed, brows pulled into a distraught line. Opening the door, she said, "Maurice, can you send a snapshot of that card I gave you to Trella? *Merci.*"

She closed the door firmly and turned to glare at Kasim.

"Does she do this often?" Kasim asked.

She pursed her lips as though deciding whether to answer. Then she huffed out a breath and crossed her arms defensively, but her shoulders fell a notch.

"It's something she's tried a few times in the last year, basically since she knew Sadiq was getting married. She wants to attend the wedding and is determined to get over…" She stopped herself. Sighed again. "It's a way for her to test the waters of moving in public again. If she appeared as herself, the press would go stark raving mad. If she poses as me, however, and goes to Ramon's race with Henri and Cinnia or something like that, it's run-of-the-mill attention."

Tonight was run-of-the-mill?

"Shouldn't she get it over with? Coming out at my sister's wedding is liable to take attention away from the bride and groom. Has she thought of that?"

"It will be a closed ceremony and don't judge how she's doing this."

"Her actions deserve to be judged. I look like a fool. If you had had an actual affair with that man last *year*, I wouldn't care." That was a small lie, but he would be able to convince himself he didn't care. "The fact you've been photographed with both of us in the same week makes all three of us look bad."

"We're all going to have to grin and bear it, aren't we?"

"No," he told her sternly. "You warned me about attention. You didn't say your sister would ridicule me. I will give her the chance to come clean. If she doesn't, I will make the completely true statement that you were with me in London all of last weekend."

"No!" Her fists hit the air next to her thighs, arms straight and angry. "Don't *do* that to her."

"I didn't take the photographs, Angelique. She's bringing this on herself!"

"It could do so much damage, you can't even comprehend." She paced with agitation across the lounge. "The press was horrible to her for years after the kidnapping, printing every lurid scrap, fact or fiction, on what happened while she was captive. True or not, those things assaulted her every time, victimizing her again and again. Then, as if that wasn't bad enough, they called her unstable and a drug addict and *fat*. She was barely a stone heavier than me, but there was this magnifying glass on her so she couldn't buy a stick of gum without it being a cry for help, or a sign she was suicidal... It drove her to go the other way, until she was underweight and we were scared she would disappear completely. I'll tell you, if anything is designed to break a person's spirit, it's that sort of relentless, vicious criticism."

She paused to take a few panting breaths. Her face contorted in a wince of distant memory.

"Then, after my father's funeral... I guess we finally looked like young women by then. It's not like we were dressed for clubbing, you know, but photos circulated of us at the service and men stalked both of us online after that, saying the most disgusting things. Sending us—" She waved a hand toward her crotch. "*Those* sorts of pics. It was even worse for Trella. She knew what men like that are capable of." Her voice broke on the last words, eyes haunted.

"Angelique," he breathed, and started toward her.

She bent to unfasten her shoes and kick them away, then kept moving, restless with heightened emotion, dress swirling like a cape each time she turned.

"She started having panic attacks because of it. That is *not* public knowledge." She pointed at him as though warning him not to speak of it. Then she whirled away again. "She was terrified all the time. It was horrible for her. For all of us. It was like watching someone who is depressed to the point of being suicidal, or in chronic pain, and listening to them scream. You can't do anything except sit there and watch. She spent, God, a good two years stoned on medications, trying to get it under control. Finally she left the public eye and it took a while, but she was able to stabilize. That was so hard-won, none of us rocks the boat. We don't want to throw her off again."

She hugged herself, gaze fixed on the past.

"For years, one of us has always been with her, never farther than the next room. We all know it's not healthy. We *want* a normal life for her. Our version of normal, anyway," she muttered, then waved with exasperation toward the guards in the hall.

"Even Trella is balking at how she lives. I just asked her how this happened and she told me she feels like she's been doing time on a prison sentence for a crime she didn't commit. What did she do wrong, Kasim? Are her kidnappers half so tortured? They might be in jail, but have they suffered one-tenth as much as she has? And even through all of what she has faced, she *tries*."

Her eyes were wet and gleaming. She was visibly shaking with intense emotion, making his heart feel pinched and tight.

"She's been trying so hard to get over all her mental blocks. She flew to Paris alone. You have no idea what a big deal that was for her. And then, when she realized you and I were keeping out of the spotlight and I was expected at that dinner, she stole the chance to go out as me. To see how she felt going out *alone*. It was a spur-of-the moment thing, which is exactly like her when she's at her best. In certain ways this is such thrilling news."

She began pacing again, her dress flaring around her as she pivoted, but halted to press a hand to her brow.

"Not the part where she went home with a stranger, of course. I asked her how *that* happened, but she didn't want to talk about it, only apologized for not telling him who she really was. My brothers are going to kill me for not being there to stop her."

Kasim folded his arms, observing drily, "She took acting like you to the highest level, didn't she?"

Angelique jerked her head up, eyes narrowed with antipathy. "I had dinner with you first!"

They hadn't even finished their drinks, let alone started on the appetizers, but *okay.*

"That has to be me in those photos, Kasim. If the press gets wind that it was her…" She pinched the bridge of her nose. "Trella is a tiny baby sea turtle making her way to the water. If we can just give her time to get there before unleashing the crabs and gulls…"

He snorted. "Laying it on pretty thick, aren't you?"

"What do you want me to say? That it's okay if you traumatize my sister by causing the hell of public attention to rain down on her again? It's not."

"What do you want *me* to say? That it's okay if the world thinks you've slept with both of us? It's *not.*"

"Who cares so long as you're the one in this room with me tonight? Or, wait, am I invited to stay in the room I booked for myself?"

He scowled. "Don't get bent out of shape about that. I don't book weekends with women then ask them to foot the bill."

"I see. That's interesting." She gave a considering nod, shoulders setting in a stiff line. "You realize that by mentioning these legions of other women for whom you have paid hotel bills, you're saying it's okay that you have a past, but not me. Is that what you were doing this week, by the way? When you were not texting me? Paying for hotel rooms with other women? Just because no one returned a cuff link downstairs doesn't mean you weren't making a fool of *me*, but do you hear me complaining? No. Because I'm well aware we haven't made any commitments to each other—"

"Enough," he cut in. "I paid for the room because I will put up with your pain-in-the-ass security protocols, but you will stay in *my* room. I will not ask permission from *your* guards to enter. As for the photos, I don't want people to think that's you because I'm jealous. All right? Is that what you need to hear?"

Her shoulders went back, but he could see he had finally pulled her out of her own interests into *theirs*.

"Which I might have hesitated to admit if you weren't acting like a green-eyed shrew yourself. No, Angelique, I was not sleeping with other women. I was working. Nonstop. So I could come here and be with you. Future or not, we are damned well exclusive to one another until we're over. Is that clear? Now, go warn your sister I won't be so forgiving if she does this to me again."

The line of her mouth softened. "You're not going to expose her?"

"Do I look like someone who takes pleasure in feeding baby sea turtles to the gulls?"

She threw herself at him.

CHAPTER EIGHT

ANGELIQUE GLIMPSED THE velvet box on the romantically set table when she arrived at Kasim's Paris penthouse.

She was getting to know him very well, but wouldn't have pegged him as a man who celebrated a one-month anniversary. His sentimentalism touched her. It told her he valued what they had as deeply as she did.

"We're staying in tonight?" she asked as she kissed him without even taking off her jacket or setting down her purse.

He had already shed his suit jacket and tasted faintly of Scotch and…tension? He lingered over their kiss, drawing it out with a quest for her response, waiting until they were both breathless and hot before drawing back.

"Do you mind?"

"No." She tossed her purse toward the sofa then hugged her arms around his waist again. Nestled her mons into his hardness, pleased with the evidence his desire wasn't letting up any more than hers. "It's been a long week. I missed you. I'd rather have you all to myself."

"Me, too." His voice was sincere, but…off. He started to pull her into another kiss.

She hesitated. "Are you angry?"

A flash in his eyes, then, "Not at you."

He combed his fingers into her hair and gently pinned her head back, so her neck was arched, her chin tilted up for the press of his damp lips. The stamp of hot kisses went down her throat, making her skin tighten and tingle.

"And you can't talk about it so you want to forget it. Perhaps I can help with that," she allowed with another press of her hips into his groin. It was her cross to bear that she was the lover of a man with great responsibilities.

His breath hissed in and he straightened to his full height, seeming to wage an inner debate. He bit out a soft curse and his hands fell away from her.

"We will have to talk about it," he said, twirling his finger to indicate she should turn and let him help her with her coat. "Much as I'd rather make love to you first, you probably wouldn't forgive me if I did. Let's get it over with."

Wary now, she watched him drape her jacket over the back of the sofa and move to the chilled wine in the bucket.

"A votre santé," she said when he brought her a glass.

He only made a face of dismay and said bluntly, "You can't come to the wedding."

Angelique held the wine in her mouth until it was warm and sour. She swallowed.

"Sadiq and Hasna's wedding?" *Obviously*, but she couldn't process how he could say such a thing. "I know we can't…be together when I'm there. I wasn't expecting—" To stay in his room. Maybe she'd fantasized about it. "I mean, I thought I'd stay with my family and you and I could…" She shrugged. "Dance?" Steal time somewhere? They were very adept at that.

"My father is inviting the woman he would like me to marry. It would be awkward and disrespectful for my mistress to be there."

And the hits just kept on coming.

His marriage was supposed to be some far-off thing that would happen one day, but in the mists of a distant future, like death. Unavoidable, but not something the average person worried about as an immediate concern.

"Did you explain my family's relationship with Sadiq?" Her hand began to shake. She leaned to set her glass on the coffee table before she spilled wine all over his antique Persian rug.

"My father is still convinced you had a personal relationship with him. Bringing up the complimentary wardrobe does more harm than good."

"I'm not going to miss Sadiq's wedding, Kasim. He asked us to be there. It's a big deal for all of us, especially if Trella is going to be with us. I have to be there for *her*."

"I'm not happy about it either, but it's *one* day."

"Does Hasna know?"

"I'm not about to play those sorts of politics," he said, sharp and hard. "That is my mother's game, to stir up tears to manipulate my father. Hasna understands our father very well along with my promise to marry the wife he chooses for me."

"Why—?" Why had he ever agreed to such a thing? But she knew. So he could rule differently. Better.

That selflessness on his part ought to inspire her to make peace here and act in the greater good, but she was too appalled at how casually and callously he was brushing aside her feelings in this.

He set down his wine and grasped her arms. "Angelique, it's one day. Then we can carry on as normal."

"Normal being this." She broke away from his hold to wave at the room.

The impermanence of their association penetrated. What she had seen as a relationship, one where she could reveal her deepest thoughts and worries, was nothing more than a convenience for him.

She caught sight of the table and its narrow velvet box. Its significance struck like a bludgeon.

"Silly me, I thought that was for our anniversary," she said dumbly.

"Anni—?" He pinned his lips shut. Such a man. One hundred percent oblivious.

She walked around the far end of the sofa and moved to open the box.

The necklace was a stunning confection of thin chains and cushion-cut emeralds set in gold.

This was all she would be left with when their affair was over. Some token of his. It wasn't even affection, was it? Appreciation? For the orgasms she'd given him?

And this affair *would* end. She had managed to ignore that reality these past few weeks of meeting him in hotel rooms across Europe.

He was marrying. Sooner than later. And his chosen wife would be at the wedding.

It was absolutely true that she couldn't meet that woman then carry on with Kasim until… When? The day his engagement was announced? Days before he married? Her heart was pulsing like a raw wound just thinking of it.

Each breath she drew felt like a conscious effort and burned both directions. In and out. Her throat closed and her eyes swam. Her voice came out strained with insult.

"I'm not a woman you buy off, Kasim."

She looked up in time to see him flinch and avert his gaze.

"I know you're disappointed," he began. "That is not—"

She cut him off with a hoot of disbelief. "Is that what I am? *Disappointed?*" Her chest was caving in on itself. "Are *you?*"

"It's *one* day."

"It's you turning me into your mistress, then letting your father call me a whore who's not good enough to be seen in his palace. One who is paid well, I admit, but no thanks. I'm not interested." She gave the velvet box a thrust of rejection so it tipped off the table onto the floor.

"You're overreacting," he bit out, trying to catch the necklace.

"No, *you* should have told me this could happen before you took me to your bed! That is information I needed because you know what Sadiq means to us."

"And what? You would have passed on all of this so you could attend one damned wedding?"

"All of what?" she charged, waving at the necklace he now held. "You've just reduced our relationship to an exchange of sex for jewelry. Do you know what I've given up so I could be with you? The sacrifices I've made? I've pushed Trella *away* so I could be close to you. What have you given up? *Nothing.* And now I know why. Because I mean nothing to you. So, yes, the wedding is a deal breaker. Tell your father your mistress won't be there because you no longer have one."

She turned toward her coat.

He caught her arm. "Angelique—"

"Don't," she said in the deadly, assertive voice she'd been trained to use, free hand snatching up her pendant in warning.

His mouth tightened and he lifted his hand to splay it in the air, like she'd turned a gun on him.

"Really? You'll call in your guards rather than have a civilized conversation about this?"

"How do you see this conversation ending? In your bed? Yes, I will call in my guards rather than let you seduce me into accepting this kind of treatment. You had chances to end this before my—" *Don't say "heart."* "Before my emotions were involved." Her voice shook. "Did you really think, after all that I've shared with you, that I was only here for a *necklace*?"

The control that she had cultivated through a lifetime of having to buck up and be strong was never harder to find. She shot her arms into her coat and picked up her purse.

"You're as emotionally tone-deaf as your father."

If she had been trying to stab him in the heart, she had picked up the most efficient knife with which to do the job, then snapped it off against the bone for good measure.

As he gathered the necklace from the floor, he thought of Jamal showing it to him a decade ago. It was one of his brother's first efforts at a big piece, not perfect, designed with more passion than attention to the finer details, but it was genuinely beautiful. Jamal had been rightfully proud and Kasim sincerely impressed.

Kasim had bought it, wanting to be his brother's first patron, declaring, *Someday it will be worn by a queen, as it should be.*

But lately, as he regularly saw green and gold tones in the eyes of his lover when she woke beside him, he had decided to give it to Angelique. He had known she wouldn't like what he had to say today, but he had hoped to soften the blow by giving her something that was genuinely precious to him, that was hard to give up because it was one of the few remnants of his brother he had.

Of course she wasn't aware of that. There had been no point in trying to explain. He had let the door slam and the quiet set like concrete around him.

Because they had no future. His father was choosing him a wife. The goal today had been to keep her from attending the wedding and that task was definitely accomplished.

Sometimes hard choices had to be made. Jamal had been one of them and Angelique another.

It made him furious and sick, but it was done.

Angelique heard the door, but didn't get out of bed. She was too devastated. Her eyes were swollen and gritty, her throat raw, her nose congested and her heart sitting in a line of jagged pieces behind her breastbone.

She had tried to brave it out on her own, but sometime in the darkest hours of the night, when her sister had texted, asking if she was all right, her willpower had collapsed.

Please come, she had texted.

Trella hadn't asked why. She had only texted back that she would leave as soon as the family jet could be cleared for takeoff. Now her sister's shoulders fell as she walked into the bedroom and took in the shipwreck that was her twin.

"What happened?" Trella asked gently.

"We broke up," Angelique said in a voice rasped by hours of crying. "I've been so stupid."

"No." Trella came to the bed and swept away the crumpled tissues to lie down in front of her. "You fell in love. That's not stupid." She stroked Angelique's hair back from where it was stuck to her wet cheek.

"I didn't mean to." Fresh tears flooded her eyes. "I never let anyone in. You know I don't. It's too painful."

"You were always so full of my suffering there was no room for anyone else."

"No."

"Yes, Gili." Trella stroked her hair, petting and soothing. "I tried not to put it on you, but you carry it because that's who you are. I'm not surprised you fell for him when he was the first person who didn't lean on you emotionally. When you finally felt like I didn't need you every minute. That must have felt like such a relief."

"He didn't lean on me because he didn't love me!" Angelique pushed a fresh tissue under her nose and sniffed. "And I feel so pathetic, crying like this when a bruised heart is nothing compared to—"

"Shh…" Trella said, stroking her hair. "Don't ever compare, *bebé* angel."

Angelique closed her eyes and tried to level out her breathing. "I thought I had learned how to be strong and I'm so…" *Sad. Scorned. Heartbroken.*

"Do you know how I get through my worst moments?" Trella's fingers gently wove in and picked up Angelique's hair, combing to the ends. Her voice was pitched into the tone they had used as children, when telling each other secrets in the night. "Every time I've wanted to give up, I've always thought to myself, I have to be there when *she* needs *me*. You gave me a gift, asking me to come. You're telling me I'm strong enough to be your support. It was worth fighting through all that I have so I could be with you here, in your hour."

Angelique had seen her begging Trella to come as pure weakness, but wondered now if she had failed to see what a comeback her sister was really making— because she'd been so wrapped up in Kasim.

"You didn't hesitate, even though I've been letting him come between us." Her lips quivered and she looked at her twin through matted lashes. "That was wrong. I'm so sorry."

"No," Trella crooned. "Don't apologize for offering your heart to him. It's his loss that he didn't see how tender and precious it is. And no matter what happens, we will always be us. I *will* be here for you, Gili."

Angelique's smile wobbled and she let out a breath she'd been holding for years. "I love you, Trella *bella*."

"I love you, too."

Angelique wasn't going to Zhamair. She wasn't buckling to Kasim's demand that she stay away, though. It was the other way. She couldn't bear to see him, fearing she would make a fool of herself at the first glance.

Or, at the very least, have to face what a fool she already was.

She had always seen easily through men who asked her out. They wanted to date her because she was beautiful, a prize. Some had wanted to get closer to her brothers, others had been so overcome in her presence it had been a burden to live up to what they imagined her to be. It had been fairly easy to maintain a certain distance.

Kasim had been different. He was strong, confident, *honest*. She had felt safe with him and it had allowed her to put her true self out to him. That inner soul of hers was as shy and hesitant as she'd ever been, only coming out when she trusted she wouldn't be hurt.

Yet he had treated her like one more mare in the stable and she should have seen it coming, which left her feeling like she'd set herself up for this heartache. She had failed herself.

Be the tough woman Trella is, she kept urging herself, but she had never managed to be that woman when it came to Kasim. That was her downfall.

So she finished drafting her email to Sadiq mentioning the "terrible flu" that had her deeply under the weather and hit Send.

She was fooling no one. Her family knew that things were over between her and Kasim. Hasna had to be aware of it, as well.

She sniffed and glanced at her red eyes in her desk mirror. She certainly looked like she was battling a serious ailment. Heartsickness took a toll.

Trella, bless her, was doing everything she could to support her.

It was the great reversal Angelique had longed for and it wasn't nearly as relieving or satisfying as she'd imagined. For starters, her brothers looked at her reliance on Trella as a small betrayal of their unspoken pact. They had all worn the mantle of protector for so long, they couldn't put it down long enough to see that Angelique's pulling back had actually been a good thing for their baby sister.

Trella was stepping up on her own volition now. She had planned to attend the wedding, but it was her suggestion that she take on the wedding day with Hasna so Angelique could skip going to Zhamair. This morning, Trella had even volunteered to make a quick run to London *by herself* to meet in private with a certain longtime client who belonged to the royal family and had a confidential occasion coming up.

Trella was also talking of doing more of the front end work once she returned from Zhamair, which was something to look forward to, but for now the task of greeting prospective clients still fell on Angelique.

Thus, when her guard rang from the front doors, stating that her eleven o'clock was here, she could only sigh and agree to come downstairs.

As she rose, she glanced at the appointment details. Girard Pascal. Something about a gift for a bride. Since she had no other reference on this prospective client, he would be shown into the small receiving room off the front foyer.

The room was a quaint little conversation area filled with Queen Anne furniture that served as a border crossing of sorts. Technically inside the building, it was still on the perimeter. Staff and accepted clients went through a second controlled door to enter the hallowed interior.

The reception room had two doors and a window onto the foyer, giving the illusion of a more spacious chamber, but the glass was really there to allow the guards to monitor her safety if the doors happened to be closed.

Girard Pascal looked Arabic, that was her first impression, but there were many Parisians with Middle Eastern heritage who had been here for generations. With that name, she assumed he was French.

He looked like Kasim, was her second thought, as he stood to a height that was very close to her former lover's. The resemblance was only in his coloring and ancestry, she told herself. Maybe something indefinable across his cheekbones. His eyes, too. That bottom lip. His build and the commanding way he held himself.

She ignored the leap of her heart and told herself she

was making more of the superficial similarities because she missed Kasim. That was all.

Then he opened his mouth and spoke with the same accent, almost the same tone and intonation. "Please call me Girard. Thank you for seeing me."

He smiled warmly, looking nervous in a way that she almost thought was male attraction, but it wasn't. Nor was it the fan-based giddiness some people showed in meeting a Sauveterre. It was affection and admiration and a searching of her expression for something she couldn't define.

"I'm Angelique. Please sit and tell me what sort of gift you had in mind. If I can't help you, I'm sure I'll be able to suggest someone who can." It was her stock greeting, something to give her an out if she decided not to take on a client.

She was already leaning toward not. She didn't feel threatened, precisely, but she did feel prevailed upon. He wanted something from her. Not just a spring ensemble, either.

He held up a finger and went to the door, waiting while one of her guards brought over a black pouch smaller than his palm.

"Nothing showed on the X-ray. It's fine," her guard told her.

"Do you mind?" Girard said as he stepped back into the room and started to close the door.

Angelique moved to close the second door, then joined him at the coffee table, sitting in the opposite armchair from his.

"My request is very..." He frowned, searching for words, then poured out the contents of the pouch onto the coffee table.

It was a necklace, the chain three delicate strands of

white gold, the pendant complex and simple at once. The stones were blue, set into a graceful sweep that almost looked like a cursive letter.

"Arabic?" she guessed, caught by both its whimsy and the suggestion of joy.

"It means 'with.'" His smile flashed.

"It's beautiful." She was instantly taken by it and moved to the settee so she could examine it more closely.

"May I?" She reached out, adding in a murmur, "You want me to design something to go with it?" She would love to. The well of her creativity began to burble just feeling the weight of the piece against her fingers. It had a certain magic that penetrated her skin right into her blood.

"I believe you already have."

"Pardon?" She dragged her stunned gaze off the crimping on the claws, experiencing a shiver as she recognized the workmanship. "Did you make something for my brother, Henri? A tennis bracelet with pink and white diamonds?"

"I don't discuss my clients." His mouth twitched as if he knew that she'd said that same thing more times than she could count. "But my work is carried by a jeweler here in Paris and one in London. And I did make something like that when I first moved to France. It's quite possible the bracelet is mine."

"I meant to ask him where he got it," she murmured, but her brother wasn't speaking to her, primarily because she had dared to invade the family flat and discovered that Cinnia had left him. "I would love to work together," she blurted. "I'm bowled over by your skill."

He smiled with shy pleasure, eyes gleaming. "That touches me. You can't imagine how much. But let me ask my favor first. Then we'll see what you think of working with me on something else."

"Yes, right. Did you see a piece of mine somewhere? You know it's just as likely designed by Trella?" She looked at the pendant again, trying to imagine how she could have inspired something so beautiful. She was utterly in love with it.

"I made this for my sister. I was hoping you could take it to her."

"Your— Oh, my God!" If she hadn't been so enthralled with the necklace, she would have put it together sooner. Now she quickly dropped the pendant on the table and jerked to her feet, backing away from a ghost. "Oh, my God!"

Charles shot in.

She held up her hand.

"I'm fine. Just a shock," she insisted to her guard. "What is today's word? I can't even remember. Daffodil?" She touched her forehead. "Honestly, I'm fine. I just need a moment with…"

She waved at *Kasim's dead brother*. Her hand trembled.

"I'm so sorry," Jamal said with a wince. "I thought you might know."

"How—? *No*." She had to be white as a sheet, but managed to shoo Charles out.

He continued to watch her closely through the glass.

"Oh, my God, Jamal," she breathed. "How on earth would I know? Your whole family thinks you're dead." She held her hand to her throat where she felt her own pulse thundering like a bullet train.

"Kasim didn't tell you? He helped arrange it. The death certificate and name change…"

"No he didn't tell me!" It caused her quite a pang to

admit it, but she had already processed that however much she had thought she meant to Kasim, she had actually meant a lot less.

"Good God, *why*?" She moved to the settee and sank down, wilting as the shock wore off and her mind jammed with questions. "I mean, he told me that your father didn't like that you were an artist, but—"

"Is that what he said?" His smile was crooked and poignant. "Our father couldn't accept that I was *gay*."

"Oh," she breathed. More secrets with which Kasim hadn't trusted her. She had been so open about her own family. It made her feel so callow to think of it. Where had her precious speech gone? The one from her first dinner with Kasim, when she had told him she was reticent out of respect for her siblings. But had he entrusted her with Jamal's story? *No*.

"You couldn't just…live in exile? Here?" she asked.

"My lover was already here and beaten to within an inch of his life for…leading me into that life."

"No! Oh, dear God. Your father couldn't have arranged that?"

"People in his government. There are those in Zhamair who are still very prejudiced. They said they were protecting the reputation of the crown, but my father did nothing to prevent or punish them." Deep emotion gripped him for a moment and he struggled to regain his composure, swallowing audibly before continuing. "Either way, I couldn't risk Bernard's life again. I feared for my own. Merely leaving wouldn't have been enough. I was afraid to even see Kasim again, in case it made things difficult for him, or exposed us."

He propped his elbows on his thighs, back bowed with the weight of the world, expression weary. He rubbed his hands over his face, then looked at her over his clasped fingers.

"My mother's life is not easy. The queen is very resentful of her. If my mother had had a gay son living flagrantly abroad..." He shook his head. "No. It was terribly cruel to tell her I was dead, but if the queen picks on her now, my father stands up for her out of respect for her grief."

"I can't imagine," she murmured, appalled anew at the ugly aggression Kasim had grown up in. "I'm so sorry, Jamal."

"Why?" he said, looking and sounding so much like Kasim, her throat tightened. "You had nothing to do with it."

"I wish I could do something, I guess." She realized immediately that she had backed herself into a corner.

His smile was sharp and amused. "Thank you. I would like that."

She shook her head. "You're so much like him it's unnerving. But I can't take that to Hasna and tell her it's from you. You think *I* was shocked!"

"No," he agreed. "She can't know I'm alive, but Kasim could tell her it was in my old collection and that he had been saving it for her wedding day. It would mean a lot to me for her to wear this. I know she would."

"We're not, um... Kasim and I aren't seeing each other anymore." The press hadn't quite caught on, so she wasn't surprised he didn't know. The words still abraded her throat. "I'm not going to Zhamair."

"Ah. I didn't realize." His expression fell. "I'm sorry. From the photos I saw, you both looked quite..." He didn't finish, only looked at the necklace, crestfallen.

She looked at it, too.

With. He wanted to be with his sister in the only way he could.

She couldn't tell this to Trella or one of her brothers. It was Kasim's secret. Jamal's *life.*

I am a sucker, she thought. Trella would have a far better sense of self-protection. Kasim didn't even want her there. She would be an embarrassment. He might even throw her out.

But Jamal looked so disconsolate. And Hasna missed her brother so much. It would mean the world to her to have this...

She closed her eyes, defeated. "I'll go. I'll go to Zhamair and give this to Kasim."

CHAPTER NINE

THERE HAD BEEN many times over the years that Kasim wondered how his father could be such a pitiless, dictatorial bastard. These days, he understood the liberation in such an attitude as he adopted the same demeanor, contemptuous of those around him for being ruled by their emotions. What did the desires of others' egos and libidos and hearts matter when his own had to be ignored? Everyone made sacrifices.

Don't think of her.

Were it not for his sister marrying in *two days*, he would ride into the desert and take some much needed time to regroup. Instead, he was part of a ceaseless revolving door of relatives and dignitaries. One branch of the royal family had no sooner arrived and joined him and his parents for coffee, when a foreign dignitary was in the next room awaiting a chance to express felicitations.

This morning the parade had begun with an ambush. The king had introduced him to the father of the woman he thought would make a fine queen someday—when she grew up. Did his father seriously expect him to marry a child of barely eighteen?

To his prospective father-in-law's credit, a concern for the age difference was expressed. Kasim smoothly stated he could wait until she completed her degree if that was preferred. It would serve the kingdom better if the future queen was well educated.

The king had correctly interpreted it as an effort to put things off and took him to task the minute they were alone.

"Did you give me your word or not?"

"I cleared the field for her, didn't I?" Kasim replied in a similar snarl. A glance over the guest list a few days ago had shown that Angelique had sent her regrets. "Surely we can get one wedding over with before we host the next?"

Sadiq's family were announced, cutting short the clash. Kasim sat down with Sadiq and their fathers to sign off on the marriage contracts, then they joined the queen and Sadiq's mother.

"Hasna isn't here?" Sadiq said, morose as he glanced around the room.

"The gown has arrived," the queen said with a nettled look toward the king. "Fatina has been pestering to see it. Such a nuisance when Hasna has guests. What if she ruins it?"

"The girls will not let that happen," Sadiq's mother soothed. "They have been ever so careful this week, watching the unpacking of Hasna's wardrobe."

"The Sauveterres were staying with you?" the queen asked in her most benign yet shrewd tone.

"Oh, yes," Sadiq's mother said with a smile of pleasure. "The men went into the desert for what the Westerners call…a stag? Is that correct, Sadiq? I had a nice visit with their mother. We are all friends for many years."

"And they all came with you here?" the king asked, gaze swinging like a scythe to Kasim. "Both girls?"

"Yes, Trella was the one we worried wouldn't make it, but then Angelique came down with the flu. She recovered, though, and…" Sadiq's mother lost some of her warm cheer as she sensed the growing tension. "Is there a problem?" She touched the draped folds of her hijab where it covered her throat. "I know we said she was not coming, but she shares a room with her sister so I didn't think it would be an imposition when she made it after all?"

"It's no problem," Kasim said firmly, aiming it at his father.

Get rid of her, he read in the flick of his father's imperious glance.

If she had left things as they'd been in Paris, Kasim brooded as he strode down the marbled hall of the palace, he would be resentful, but not furious.

This. This was unacceptable. Now he would be in for it with his father. Threats would be made. His uncle and several cousins were coming to the wedding. Tensions were high. Impulsive autocratic decisions could easily be made in a fit of temper.

Not only was he now courting *that* disastrous possibility, thanks to Angelique coming here against his orders, but he was raw all over again. Her rejection stung afresh and his intense feeling of being hemmed in by impossible circumstances was renewed.

He had resigned himself to never seeing her again, damn her! Now she was *in his home.*

He started to ask a passing servant which suite the Sauveterres had been given, but glimpsed a face he knew down near the end of the hall, standing outside the door to his sister's apartment.

His heart rate spiked as he approached the guard.

"Charles," he said, ears ringing. Angelique was behind this door.

"Your Highness."

Kasim knocked.

Female laughter cut off and his youngest half sister cracked the door to peer out at him. Her smile beamed as she recognized him.

"Kasim!"

"Is Hasna dressed? May I come in?" He fought for a level tone. Distempered as he was, he would never take out his bad mood on a six-year-old.

There was a murmur of female voices, then Hasna called, "Yes, come in."

He entered, picking up his baby sister as he did, kissing her cheek and using her small frame to cushion the rush of emotion that accosted him as he anticipated seeing Angelique.

Hasna's suite was half the size of his, yet still one of the most opulent in the palace, decorated in peacock blues and silver, with high ceilings and the same sort of delicate curlicue furniture his mother favored.

She was in her lounge and stood on something because she was a foot taller than normal. He couldn't see what it was because her wedding gown was belled over it, flaring a meter in each direction. A filmy veil was draped over her dark hair and all of it was covered in more seed pearls than there were in the ocean.

Fatina rose from her chair and came to kiss his hand, tsking as her older daughter charged at him, arms raised in a demand to be lifted and hugged.

Kasim concentrated on setting down his one sister and lifting the eight-year-old so she could squeeze his neck with her skinny little arms and press her lips to his cheek.

"You're growing too fast," he told her. "You'll be wearing one of these soon and then who will draw me pictures? You look very beautiful, Hasna."

He set down his sister and pretended he was taking in the extravagance of the gown when he was far more focused on the flash of movement behind the flare of her skirt.

The veil rippled slightly and Angelique rose, her attention remaining stubbornly fixed on her creation.

His heart skyrocketed as he took in the graceful drape of her pink dress and the way she'd covered her head in an ivory scarf so she looked like she was a part of his world—

She turned her head to meet his gaze.

The mercury shooting to the top of his head stalled and plummeted.

Trella.

He didn't know how he knew. The resemblance was remarkable and he couldn't say that her eyes were set closer or farther apart, or that her face seemed wider or thinner. He just knew this wasn't Angelique, even though her greenish-hazel eyes stared at him.

Given the antagonism he sensed coming off her in waves, the straight pins poking out of her mouth were unabashedly symbolic.

He knew how she felt. He was ready to spit nails himself. Where the hell was her sister?

"Angelique has done an amazing job, hasn't she?" Hasna said. He could hear the lilt of trickery in her voice, hoping to fool him.

"I understood this to be a collaboration between the twins. Hello, Trella. It's nice to meet you. Is your sister here?" He looked around the lounge, returning to a state of tense anticipation.

"Oh! You can't tell this is Trella!" Hasna accused. "I can't. I still think this is Angelique and she's tricking me."

Trella pinned a place on the veil that she had marked with her fingers, then removed the rest of the pins from her mouth to say lightly, "I showed you my passport."

Hasna chuckled and Trella glanced at Kasim, smile evaporating.

"She went back to our suite."

He couldn't stop staring, feeling as though he was looking at a film of Angelique. She was a faithful image of her sister, but there was a sense of being removed by time or space. She made him long to be in the presence of the real thing.

"Still recovering from her flu?" he said with false lightness. "Perhaps she should have stayed home after all."

"It was minor. She's over it." Trella's glance hit Kasim with pointed disparagement.

Did she recall that he had done her a favor, hiding her night with the Prince of Elazar? An attitude of deference wouldn't be amiss here, he told her with a hard look, but he didn't have time to teach her some manners.

He had to get her sister on the next plane back to Paris.

Angelique was normally at her most relaxed around her family, but not today. She was wound up about being here, feeling like she was smuggling drugs, that pouch of Jamal's was so heavy on her conscience.

Ramon was not helping. He was growing restless away from work and began badgering her to play tennis.

"I thought Henri said he would?" She was actually

dying to see more of the palace. As they had come in by helicopter with Sadiq's family, Angelique had been awestruck. And taken down a peg. What had made her think she had any place in Kasim's life when his home sprawled in opulent glory over more area than a dozen football fields against the stunning backdrop of the Persian Gulf?

She told herself that it was the heat of the desert sun that caused her to sweat as they were taken by golf cart along a palm-lined path overlooking a water feature. It was actually anxiety. Kasim was here. Somewhere behind those columns and tall windows, beneath the domes and flags, he was carrying on with his life, perhaps already having moved on to another lover, completely unaware she had defied him and come to Zhamair after all.

She searched across the gardens, noting small gatherings in gazebos and colorful tents, trying to see if he was among any of the groups. Guilty and eager at once for a glimpse of him.

Maybe she wouldn't see him until the wedding. She'd been trying to decide whether to contact him outright and request a meeting prior to the wedding—and probably be asked to leave—or just hope she came across him and was able to say her piece before he deported her.

Being special guests of the groom and traveling with the groom's parents, her family was given a luxurious suite of four rooms with a stunning stained glass window set high on the exterior wall of the lounge. It poured colored light onto the white tablecloth of the dining table, where fruit, cordial, sweets and flowers had been waiting on their arrival.

"Gili!" Ramon said. "Are you listening?"

"Are you? I said you and Henri should play. I have to

hem these for Hasna's sisters." She lifted the silk dresses she'd brought back from Hasna's suite.

Fatina had cried when Hasna revealed that her daughters hadn't been overlooked in the wedding preparations.

Now that Angelique had met Jamal and had an even broader understanding of the family's painful dynamic, she was thrilled to be part of including Fatina's children in the wedding. And, as much as it pained her, she had accepted payment from Fatina for them. Fatina had insisted, worried what the queen would say if she didn't. Angelique had kept it very nominal, doing what she could to keep the peace.

Ramon sighed.

"You have to come with us so we can talk to any women we meet." He spoke like he was explaining it to a child. "I don't know how Sadiq survived these restrictions," he muttered, resuming his pacing.

Ah. It wasn't work he was missing so much as his extracurricular activities.

"Ask Mama to go with you," she suggested drily.

"Siesta or I would," he shot back. "Desperate times."

She shook her head at him.

Henri emerged from his room. He had changed into light gray sweatpants and a white long-sleeved tunic. He made a small noise of disgust as he saw that was exactly what Ramon already wore. They didn't try to dress alike, but it happened constantly. Even their panama hats had been purchased on two different continents, but their tastes were so in sync, they had each brought one to Zhamair.

When they set them on their heads, they did so facing each other, moving like mirror images—because that's what they were. She and Trella were stamps, both right-handed, both wearing their hair parted on the left because that's where their crowns were.

The boys were left and right, but were still difficult to tell apart for most people. They wore their hair in the same short, spiked cut, favored the same clothes and had such even features they easily passed for the other, not that they played that game.

Well, Ramon had tried with Cinnia a couple of times, because he was a tease, but she had always caught him. Her ability to tell both sets of twins apart from the get-go was one of the reasons Angelique had been so sure Cinnia was right for Henri.

Her brothers left and she sat down to work.

A knock sounded a few minutes later.

Most of Trella's security detail were women so they'd been given much-deserved vacation time, rather than coming to work where they would have been hampered in performing their regular duties. When the family was together like this, in a secure location, they needed fewer guards anyway.

Maurice was outside this door and she paused to listen, expecting him to ask for identification.

Nothing.

Weird. Unless he already knew the person knocking?

Angelique faltered, suddenly paralyzed with nerves, then forced herself to rise and open the door.

She caught her breath.

He looked so exotic in his *bisht* and *gutra*.

She had studied menswear to design her brother's wedding cloaks, but even though she'd taken great care with them, Kasim's was obviously of royal quality and tailored by hands that were intimately familiar with the engineering of such garments. His robe fit his shoulders perfectly. It was stark black with its V opening trimmed in gold, his white *gutra* framing his face and secured with a cord of matching gold.

He had let his beard grow in, but it was trimmed to a sexy frame that accentuated his mouth and the hollows of his cheeks. The contrast of white and black and gold made his eyes look all the more like melted dark chocolate.

He stole her breath.

His expression flashed something that might have been exaltation as he looked at her, but it was quickly schooled into the stern, confrontational look he'd worn the day she had met him.

"You can't be here," he said.

She searched for the woman she'd been in her office that first day, the one who had stood up to this man, but it was far harder to find her backbone when he looked right through her and saw all her weaknesses.

Her weakness for him.

Somehow she managed to speak despite the earthquake gripping her.

"You'll feel differently when I tell you what brought me here."

Instantly alert, he stepped in, crowding her into stumbling backward. His expression was grave as he firmly closed the door behind him and left his hand flat on the carved panel. His lips barely moved as he said in an undertone, "Pregnant?"

"What? *No!*" Her heart fishtailed, then did it again as his mouth tightened.

Disappointment? *Don't be stupid, Angelique.*

He smoothed his expression into something aloof and pitiless, sweeping his gaze around the empty lounge. He tensed and swore under his breath.

"Are you alone?"

As his gaze slammed back into hers, practically knocking her onto her back, her skin tightened with anticipation and a rush of heat hit her loins.

"My m-m—" How was she supposed to speak when he looked at her like that? "Mama is asleep in her room," she blurted, pointing to the one closed door. "Trella will be back any minute." *Quit making me think you still want me*.

His nostrils flared and he swung away, moving into her lounge like he owned it, which he did. He cast a glance around to take in the litter of tablets and purses, her open mending kit and his young sisters' dresses in vivid green and yellow.

"Damn you for coming," he said, pitching his voice low, but it was still overflowing with restless emotion. "What do you think you're accomplishing?"

Angelique moved to her purse and dug for the velvet pouch, hand shaking as she offered it to him.

Kasim hadn't been able to stop thinking about how they'd ended things, the bitterness of it. He hated that the acrimony would be even deeper after this. He had lived in that sort of thorny forest all his life and knew how unpleasant it was.

That Angelique had forced his hand and was making him reject her outright, forcing her to leave his country, seemed cruel on her part—which was the last word he would use to describe her. He hadn't expected this of her and that made it doubly hard to accept and behave as he knew he must.

Yet there was only the anticipation of pain as he stood here. Duty and reputation hung like anvils and pianos over his head, but in this moment, the bleak anger that had consumed him had become radiant light in her presence.

Angelique turned, expression solemn, and stood where the stained glass poured colors over her golden skin and pale blue dress.

He drank in the picture she made. Memorizing it.

Then she offered something to him and her expression was so grave, so filled with deep compassion, it made his heart lurch. All the hairs on his body stood up as he took the pouch and poured its contents into his hands.

He recognized the workmanship if not the piece. New. Better than anything else he'd made yet. His brother had definitely found his calling in this.

The piano landed.

She knew.

"Your family knows this is why you came?" His mind raced while cold sweat lifted in his palms. He tried to imagine how he would contain this, but his mind was as empty as the shifting dunes in the desert. Old protectiveness warred with fresh, fierce aggression while betrayal washed through him.

"No," she dismissed, barely speaking above a whisper. Her eyes stayed that soft, mossy green. "They think I decided to brave the wedding. That's all."

"How did you find him?"

"He came to me. Asked me to bring that to you for Hasna."

Trella walked in, making both of them start guiltily. Kasim let his arm fall so his sleeve fell over his fist where he clutched the pendant. He slipped it into the side pocket of his robe.

Trella's gaze flicked between them, sticking upon her sister's pale face. "Shall I come back?"

"No," Kasim said on impulse, probably a self-destructive one. "You can tell your family that she's with me." He clasped Angelique's hand in an implacable grip.

"Kasim—"

"We have to talk." He had to ensure Jamal would stay dead. That's what he told himself, even though he knew at a cell-deep level that he could trust Angelique with this secret. She hadn't told her family, had she?

"Gili, your phone," Trella urged, handing it to Angelique as Kasim tugged her toward the door.

There's no point, he thought, as he decided on the fly where they were going.

CHAPTER TEN

A LIFETIME OF taking precautions and Angelique had been kidnapped anyway. Maurice had been left in the dust. Fat lot of good her panic switch would do a hundred miles into the middle of nowhere.

But they were *some*where. As the helicopter lowered into an oasis, tents fluttered under the wind they raised.

Kasim was in the copilot's seat and unhooked his headgear as they settled on the ground, glancing back to signal she could do the same. The whine of the rotors slowed and dwindled.

"No wonder you were so offended by my audacity that first day." She leaned to see more of what looked like a scene from an epic Hollywood tale of Arabia. "You are a future king, Kasim. I didn't fully appreciate that."

"I am aware," he said flatly, crouching to circle in front of her and push open the door. He leaped to the ground before holding up a hand to help her exit.

This strong hand had spirited her down a servant stairwell that had felt like a secret passageway. She had allowed it because she had expected to come out in a library or private lounge.

They had wound up in a break room of some kind where men watched TV and read the paper. One had been eating a rice dish. They had quickly stood to attention when Kasim appeared, all plainly shocked so she assumed he never went there and never with a woman whose head was uncovered!

They'd leaped to do whatever Kasim ordered in Arabic and moments later he had tugged her upstairs and out to the helicopter.

She had balked and he'd said, "Get in or I'll put you in."

What was she going to do? Set off her panic switch and an international incident? He wasn't going to hurt her. He didn't want to extort money from her family.

"Are you flying me out of Zhamair? At least let me get my passport."

A muscle had pulsed in his jaw. "We'll be in the desert."

We. For some reason that had been enough to make her climb into her seat. Minutes later, they'd been chasing their own shadow across the sand.

Now they were at their destination, a pocket of verdant green in an otherwise yellow landscape that was turning bronze with the setting sun. Palms loomed over the tents that showed not the tiniest ripple now the rotors were still. The water mirrored the scene, placid and inviting.

People moved, however, bustling out of one of the biggest tents to stand at the door, heads lowering with respect as Kasim drew her into it.

"This is…" There weren't words for the fantasy of draped silk and tasseled pillows that surrounded her. Candles had been lit and an erotic incense perfumed the air. A low table with cushions for chairs was set with what looked like gold plates and cutlery. In the distance, music from a lute began.

The bed was low and wide, draped with netting so

it was a tent within a tent, sumptuous in its bold colors and swirled patterns on silk sheets, luxurious in its multitude of pillows.

"Where will you sleep?" she asked pointedly.

He gave her the look that said, *Take care.*

"Well, you're taking a lot for granted, aren't you? You may be a future king, but I am not some harem girl you can order to your bed for the night."

Listen to her, talking so tough when she might as well be a concubine stolen by a barbarian for all the power she had here. And for all the strength she had when it came to resisting him. She was already reacting as she always did, hyperaware of his physique as he shrugged out of his *bisht* and tossed it aside.

He wore a light *thobe* beneath and peeled off his *gutra*, running a hand through his hair, letting go of his veneer the way she had often seen him do when they entered a private space. He was shedding the future king to reveal the man who captivated her.

"Have you ever *been* a harem girl?" he drawled. "If not, it should be a treat for you to try it. You can dance for me later."

She was standing near the door with her arms crossed, and did her best to dice and slice him with her stare, but found herself fighting a laugh. *The bastard.*

"Don't you dare act like this is funny. My brothers will be beside themselves."

"So will my father. What was that expression you used after your sister's antics? Ah yes. They can grin and bear it." He slouched into the only chair, one with wooden legs, sumptuously cushioned in blue velvet with matching pads on the arms.

Oh, this banter felt familiar and inviting. Poignant.

She wanted to let all the harsh edges between them soften.

She couldn't. He had hurt her and could again, so easily. She ducked her head, avoiding letting her gaze tangle with his.

"Why did you bring me here?"

"Because my father wanted you removed from the palace." He indicated she should move. She was in the way of the servants bringing food.

Forced to step deeper into the tent, she watched as dishes of fruit and bowls of something that smelled rich and spicy were set out for them. When they finished, they looked back at him for further instructions.

He sent them away with a flick of his wrist, as supremely arrogant as Angelique had ever seen him.

Tipping his head against his chair back, he watched her through eyes so narrow his lashes were a single black line.

She shifted her bare feet under the skirt of her dress. Her phone was still in her hand, showing zero bars of coverage. He hadn't let her pause for a scarf or sandals.

"I would make you my harem girl if I could. Keep you here. That's how my father started up with Fatina. This is her family."

"This is their tent?" She glanced at the bed, not sure how she felt about that.

"This is my mother's. She used it once when they were first married. She doesn't like the desert. I use it."

"Ah." Of course. She scratched beneath her hair where the back of her neck was damp from perspiration. At least the sun was setting. The heat was beginning to ease.

"After me, my mother was reluctant to have another child. I don't judge her for that. I watched Fatina go through several pregnancies and she carries like she's made for the process, but it still looks cumbersome."

Cumbersome. How enlightened he sounded. She bit her lip against interrupting with sarcasm. The way he was being so forthcoming had her staying wisely silent, curious to hear how much he would tell her.

"When Fatina became pregnant, my father married her. If it was a son, he wanted him born legitimate. An heir and a spare. Mother was incensed. She promptly got herself pregnant with Hasna. She and Jamal are only a year apart. That's why they were so close." He had his elbow propped on the arm of his chair and smoothed the side of his finger against his lips. "My father was ambivalent toward Hasna. Still is. He sees little value in females. They are expensive."

"She's so sweet," she was compelled to say. "It's his loss he doesn't appreciate her."

"It is. And I often think that for all the nightmare his having two wives has been, at least she had Fatina. Mother was quite content to shuffle her newborn onto Number Two. The messy years of wiping noses and offering affection. She enjoys Hasna's company now, but if mother had raised her, we would have had two shrews terrorizing the palace, I'm sure."

What a way to talk about his mother.

"If she was thrown over because she was afraid to go through childbirth again, can you blame her for her jealousy? Does he love Fatina? That must have been a blow to her, too."

"She didn't have to turn into what she did. After Jamal, she quietly fed Fatina birth control pills for years. My father was furious when he found out. He knew by then that Jamal would never—" Kasim's mouth flattened, face spasming with anguish.

"He told me," she said, pulled forward a few steps on the silken rug that covered the floor, then halted and curled her toes against the cool material. *Jamal wouldn't marry and produce an heir.* That's what he had been about to say. "It's terrible that your father couldn't accept him. Was his life really in danger?"

She didn't want to believe it. Who hated to such a magnitude?

"From my father's intolerance, my mother's jealousy, and latent bigotry in some of our countrymen, yes." His hand fisted on the arm of his chair. "Do you think I would have taken such extreme steps otherwise? Even I couldn't risk seeing him."

He was so impassioned and tortured, she was drawn forward another couple of steps. At the same time, she wondered if Jamal was still in danger and glanced toward the door.

"They have some French, but don't speak English. And they'll have given us our privacy by now."

Privacy? For what? She was here to talk. That's *all*. Wasn't she?

"How was he?" Kasim's voice was low and yearning, hopeful, yet worried. When she met his gaze, she saw that same search she had seen in Jamal's eyes. He longed for news of his family.

"Good. I think," she reassured, smiling with affection because she had been quite taken with his brother by the time they'd parted. "Homesick, maybe, but he seemed content. I gave him my private number and begged him to collaborate with me on something, but I realize it might be too risky. I won't tell a soul, Kasim. I swear."

He dismissed that with a flick of his hand.

"I know you won't, but it may not matter. If I give Hasna that necklace... His body wasn't found, obviously. She and Fatina have held out hope. I had to give them that much. But what now? Do you know how much it has weighed on me that I hurt them like that? My father is no dummy and neither is my mother. Do I come clean? Put his life in danger again? What the hell do I do, Angelique?"

There was so much torment in his expression, her insides twisted painfully and her eyes welled. She threw herself into his lap and slid her arms around his neck, hearing his breath rush in as his chest filled. He clamped hard arms around her and squeezed her into the space against his torso, allowing her to drape her legs over the arm of the chair, then snugging her even tighter into the hollow of his body.

The way he held her pressed more tears out of her so she sniffed and tucked her wet cheeks into his throat.

"Don't cry," he said. "It's not for you to weep over."

"I'm crying for you," she said as a little shudder racked through her.

"I am fine, Angelique. My life is not in danger. At worst my father could disown me. I'll survive."

She drew back, thinking that men were so obtuse at times. "I'm crying *for* you. Because you can't. Can you? Have you ever let go of any of this?"

His brow angled with great suffering and his mouth tightened. "No," he admitted, and pressed her head to his shoulder. "No, I never have."

Fresh agony rose in her, spilling from her eyes and releasing as soft, pained sobs.

He stroked his hands over her back and arms, throat swallowing against her forehead, tension easing as he held her and held her while she cried. She cried for him and for them. She cried because he was leaning his heart against hers and his was so heavy, so very heavy, and she wanted to brace it forever, but she knew he wouldn't let her.

He was strong and disciplined and had responsibilities to a *country*. She might have room inside her for him, but his life did not have room for her.

Which meant it was pure self-destruction to slide her hand from his neck down to where his heart beat. Setting her damp and salty lips against his throat was both a step out of the pain she'd nursed since their breakup and a willingness to go back to a deeper level of it.

"I missed you," she confessed, because if she didn't say that, she would say something else. *I love you.*

He brought his hand to the side of her head and tucked his chin to look into her eyes. "I missed you, too."

His face spasmed anew. "But I still can't make you any promises."

"I know." It was a knife, twisting in her heart, but she only said, "We're together now, though. Even if it's only for an hour, Kasim…"

He groaned and she tasted the longing in him as he covered her mouth with his.

Joy quivered through her, blocking out the future and fear of loss, brimming her with happiness at being in his arms again. Pain ceased and all was right in her world.

They kissed without hurry, breaking away to look into each other's eyes, caress a cheekbone or the shell of an ear, then returned to another kiss of homecoming. She couldn't get enough of him. There would never be enough.

He rose, keeping her in his arms, and moved to the bed where they stretched out alongside each other with a sigh of relief. Together again, at last.

He jerked back. "I don't have condoms. I don't bring women here. I'll have to ask—"

She touched the side of his face. "I'm on the pill. It's okay."

"You never told me that before." He frowned.

"PMS makes me really emotional. That's the only reason I take them."

She would have pointed out that she didn't have them *here* because she hadn't been given an opportunity to pack, but he smiled and kissed her again, which distracted her from anything but how wonderful it was to lie with him again.

When he drew her onto her side so he could unzip her dress, there was reverence in his touch. He took his time, took great care as he stripped her dress down to her waist and unhooked her bra. She tugged it away herself and tossed it aside, smiling as he gave her breasts the possessive, hungry look that tightened her skin all over her body.

Heat pooled between her legs and she had to press into his groin with her own, *had to*.

"You have missed me," he said with satisfaction, cupping a swell and lowering his head to capture her nipple.

She gloried in the sensation, unable to get close enough to him. As her dress rode up, so did his *thobe*. She scraped her legs against his hair-roughened ones and used her hand to climb the fabric higher. His thighs were hot steel, but she was seeking that other column of strength.

He abruptly pushed onto his knees and threw off his *thobe*, revealing his sculpted form, the dark tone of his skin seeming extra dark as the light faded.

"You were naked under there," she commented, a little dazed by the idea. Her gaze slid past his six-pack to the thrust of his erection, so aggressive and familiar.

She was compelled to reach out, claim and squeeze.

He was velvet over steel, smooth and damp at the tip. She wanted that turgid heat moving inside her, soothing and stoking.

"Ah!" He reacted with a clench of his abdominals and fisted his hand over hers, eyes glittering fiercely at her.

"I will have my way with my harem girl first," he told her, thrusting in her grip a few times before peeling her hand off him and leaning to press the back of her hand to the mattress above her head. Then he tugged to remove her dress and underwear. "So many wicked pleasures…"

He stroked his hand from her collarbone over her breast to her hip, arranging her to best please his eye.

"Kasim." She writhed, loins clenching and aching as he skimmed his touch past her sensitive folds. She tried to guide his touch back to where she wanted it. "Please."

He caught her hand and tucked it beneath the small of her back. Then he gathered the other and did the same as he rolled atop her, using his legs to part her own.

"Don't tease," she protested. Caged beneath him, she rubbed her inner thighs against his, lifting her moist center to invite the penetration she longed for.

He shifted down a few inches and stayed propped on his elbows, admiring the way her hands beneath her back arched her breasts to him.

"Better," he said, and cupped both, lifting them for his delectation. He licked and teased and sucked, moving back and forth between them until she hugged her knees to his ribcage, shamelessly offering herself, *begging*, "Kasim, *please*."

He laughed and smoothly slid down even farther, licking at her very lightly, just once. She was so aroused, she had to catch back a cry.

"Don't be shy," he ordered, drawing a circle with his fingertip. "No one is listening but me. Do you like this?"

He pressed a finger inside her and tasted her again as he did.

She groaned in encouragement.

"You do," he said with satisfaction, and pressed two fingers inside her, making her moan with intense pleasure as he set about lavishing such attention she quickly shuddered with climax. Oh, she had missed him so much.

"So beautiful," he told her as he kissed his way up her belly. "You please me very much, my little harem girl."

"Your harem girl is going to tell you to go to hell if you don't quit calling her that," she panted.

He chuckled and rolled to her side, allowing her to free her arms, caressing himself with two fingers as he looked at her sprawled next to him, slumberous from climax, but aroused and filled with desire for him.

"Do you want me to do that to you, My Prince?" She rolled into him so her breath was humid against his chin. She nipped lightly. "Would you like me to pleasure you with my mouth until you can't even speak?"

"Yes." He gathered a fistful of her hair, holding her still for his kiss, pressing over her and parting her legs with his, thrusting in and shuddering, lifting to look into her eyes as they absorbed the feeling of being joined without a barrier between them. "Later," he breathed. "Later I want you all over me. I want you to ride me and give me your nipples and I want you on your knees in front of me. I want you every way I can have you."

"I'm yours," she vowed. "All yours."

For now.

CHAPTER ELEVEN

"I'VE NEVER SKINNY-DIPPED BEFORE."

"No?" Kasim wondered how she was swimming at all. He was worn right out, barely able to sit upright on the natural rock ledge that hung just below the waterline.

He was exhausted, but knew he wouldn't sleep even if they went back to the tent. And he didn't want to miss a moment of her slick form twisting in the inky black of the water, rippling the reflection of the moon and stars. His midnight mermaid. He would remember this forever.

He wanted this night to last forever.

"Tell me something else about yourself," he coaxed.

"Like what?"

"Something about your childhood. Before." Before her sister's kidnapping he meant, when she had been carefree.

"Um…" Her voice hummed across the water like a musical note. "Oh, this is something not many people know. My father spoke French and my mother spoke Spanish, even when they spoke to each other. The boys grew up thinking that if Mama spoke to them, they had to reply to her in French and Spanish with Papa. If they spoke to each other, Henri used French and Ramon used Spanish. Then we came along and did the same thing."

"That's ridiculous."

"I know. The boys knew better by then, but they thought it was funny. We girls grew out of it once we realized it wasn't normal for other families."

Thinking of herself only as a piece of the collective wasn't normal, either. He wondered if she realized *that*.

"Now tell me something that is just about you," he commanded.

A pause, then a dreamy, but rueful, "I like birds."

"Which ones?"

"All of them. I'm weirdly fascinated and have dozens of books about them. I listen to recordings of their songs and study the patterns of their feathers. I love that they fly and always know where they're going. I'm intrigued by how they build their nests and I always imagine that when I'm old, I'll be one of those odd people squatting behind a log with binoculars, excited because I can tick off red-throated warbler in my birding book. Are you laughing at me?"

"That would make me a hypocrite. I own falcons."

The water rippled as she let her feet sink and brought her head up, swirling around to look at him. "Really?"

He had to smile at her excitement. He suspected he had just won her over for all time. For good measure, he added, "My mother has an aviary."

"Can I see it?" She skimmed closer in her excitement, then paused to tread water. "Never mind. I'd probably cry because they're caged."

He held up a hand to warn her as he noticed a servant coming toward the shoreline.

The report didn't surprise him. Nor did the apologetic way it was delivered. Fortunately he was too relaxed to order a beheading of the messenger.

He responded with a flat "Thank you," and jerked his head to indicate they should be left alone again.

"What was that?" Angelique asked, turning to watch the retreat.

"My father is not grinning and your brothers are not bearing." And he was not interested in talking about reality. They had stepped beyond time, at least until morning. He wished to enjoy it.

"Relaying my safe word didn't reassure them?" She sounded genuinely surprised. Small wonder.

"I didn't relay it."

"Kasim! Don't do that to them." She swam a little closer.

He reached out his feet, but she was too far away to catch and drag close. "Your sister knows you came with me willingly. What do they think I'm going to do with you?"

"Just tell them I'm all right," she said impatiently, looking again to where the servant had disappeared.

"My father knows where I am. He can arrange to transport them here if they need proof of life so badly."

"Or you could send a message."

"I'm just as happy to let them pressure him into having you returned to the palace."

"You're using me," she said with a lilt of outrage. "Using *them* to back your father into a corner. I thought you didn't play those games." She made a V in the water as she headed away from him, toward shore. "What would that even accomplish? He can still disinherit you, can't he? Are you going to risk that so I can stay for the wedding? For *one* day?"

She was really asking if he was fighting for a broader future with her. And she was right that he would be disinherited for *that* sort of transgression. He was playing a dangerous game as it was, thinking he could steal this night with her.

"Why can't you just enjoy what we have?" he challenged. That's what he was doing.

"I *was*. Sex and skinny-dipping is great. But apparently I'm not here for that. You want to punish your father. You're using me to embarrass him because you're angry about Jamal." As she climbed from the water, her shoulders hunched, even though the air was still velvety and warm.

"Stop accusing me of only wanting sex from you." He pulled himself up and out, pushing to his feet so water sluiced off his naked body in a trickling rush. "I brought you here because this is where I'm happiest. I wanted you to see it."

He waded along the ledge until he reached the path on the shore, then he circled through the high grass to where she stood, towel wrapped around her middle, arms hugged over it.

"Will you take me back? Please?"

"To the palace? You're going to choose a night with your family over one with me? Live your own life, Angelique! Quit hiding behind your sister."

She recoiled like he'd taken a swing at her.

"This *is* me. I don't hurt the people I love."

"Meaning I do?" Now who was delivering the sucker punch?

She dropped her gaze so he only saw her pale eyelids, not whatever emotion might be glimmering in her eyes.

"You're better at holding yourself apart from things. I even understand why you had to become that way. But I feel things, Kasim. Do you think I came to Zhamair for a midnight swim in an oasis? No. I came because my heart was torn apart by a family so broken I couldn't stand it. I came *despite* knowing I would probably wind up in your bed and be shattered at having to leave it again."

"Then *don't*," he growled, hating to hear that he was hurting her when it was the last thing he wanted to do. He thought of her sitting in his lap, crying for him, and his guts twisted.

"And what?" she challenged softly. "Become Wife Number Two? Look how well that turns out!" Her profile was shadowed with despair as she gazed over the moonlit water.

He sighed and pinched the bridge of his nose. The last time they'd had this conversation, he had fought to exclude one day from their lives. Now he saw the single day they might steal—only a night, really—slipping away.

"You want me to call your brothers with your code word, *fine*."

"Your father will still know I'm out here and resent it. Do you really want to fuel the fire? I don't want to be the reason you two went to war the day before your sister's wedding. Kasim, I *love* you."

The words struck him with such a blast of heat and light, he rocked back on his heels, speechless at how powerful the statement was.

"I know you don't feel the same," Angelique rushed to say, appalled that she had spilled her heart out at his feet like that. Crushed that he only stood there looking stunned. How could he not have expected this?

"I don't *want* to know how you feel," she added quickly. "It would make this even more impossible to deal with," she babbled on, drowning in yearning. "But that's who I am. If you think I hide behind my sister, it's because I don't know how else to protect myself from feeling so much. You get past even that and it makes me feel so defenseless."

She wanted to look at him, but was afraid what she'd see. Pity? Weariness with yet another woman falling at his feet?

"You *could* talk me into being a second wife, and we'd both lose respect for each other for it," she said, feeling as though one of his falcons had taken her chest in its talons and was squeezing relentlessly. Her voice thinned. "So I'm asking you not to wield your power over me. Be the man I love and show respect for someone weaker than you. Don't use me in your fight with your father. Take me back and make peace with him for your sister's sake."

He let out a breath like she'd kicked it out of him.

"Don't be selfish like my parents," he summed up, voice as dry and gritty as a wind off a sandstorm. "You should give yourself more credit, Angelique. You're plenty brutal when you need to be."

He took her back to the palace and let her go without so much as a reluctant "goodbye." She didn't suppose she would ever forgive him for that, even though it was exactly what she had asked for. She had hoped for some kind of miracle though. Foolishly hoped.

Henri met her off the helicopter and escorted her wordlessly back to their suite where she half expected Ramon to be waiting up. He wasn't. They were all asleep.

"Is Trella okay?" she asked as Henri firmly closed the door behind them.

"*Bien.* She's your champion. You know that." He unstoppered a bottle, smelled the contents, and set it away with disgust. "Cordial. How do they survive without a decent brandy? Do you want to tell me what you were thinking, disappearing like that?"

She lifted a hand and huffed out a breath of despair. "Do you want to tell me what went wrong between you and Cinnia?"

He jerked his head back. *"Non."*

She tilted her head. He knew how she felt then. Sometimes things were far too painful to share.

He sighed and held out his arm. *"Je m'excuse, Gili.* Come here. I hate fighting with you. It just makes me feel like a bully."

She laughed faintly. "Because I don't fight back?"

"You just did. Most punishingly." He hugged her. "But it tells me how hurt you are when you hit below the belt like that."

"I'm sorry about you and Cinnia," she murmured as she hugged him back. "It's so hard to find people we can trust. Even harder to keep them," she added in a voice that thinned to a whisper.

He squeezed her and set her away. "You should get some sleep. We may be packing to leave first thing."

They didn't. Kasim pulled strings and Angelique was allowed to stay for the wedding. At least, she assumed Kasim had arranged it, until she and Trella caught up to the bride to help her dress.

Hasna had been crying, as most brides were wont to do, and was running late while her makeup was fixed. Her suite was being cleared, everyone leaving to take their seats. Angelique offered Fatina a smile as the woman hurried past her, but Fatina didn't even acknowledge her. She was ashen beneath her olive complexion. She looked both wispy and frail, yet had an incandescent glow behind the wetness in her eyes.

Angelique's blood chilled with premonition, but she was pulled back to Hasna's reflection as she spoke.

"I told Mama to tell Papa I want you both at the wedding. I realize there are politics, but…" She touched the pendant at her throat and Angelique wondered if there were other reasons for the smudged mascara and puffy eyes, the haunted shadows behind Hasna's somewhat shell-shocked expression.

Oh, Kasim. Angelique wished, illogically, that she could have been with them when he'd given Jamal's gift to his sister, to hold his hand and bolster him as he had made his explanation.

"That's fine," Hasna said with a flustered dismissal of the makeup artist, sounding very much the princess as she said, "*Go*. I just want to be married and live with my husband. Help me dress."

The woman left and Angelique and Trella helped Hasna into her gown. She was a vision, with a distinct line of maturity setting her shoulders and running like a line up her spine. Some might see it as her wedding causing this coming-of-age moment, but Angelique knew it was the necklace she kept touching. The memories of time lost with a cherished brother.

It was another tear in the fabric of Kasim's family and Angelique silently ached for all of them.

"I don't think I've ever been prouder," Trella said, linking her hand with Angelique's. "Oh, look at you, crying over how beautiful she is! Our tender little Gili. We used to call her Puddles. She hated it."

Her sister was being Trella, giving Angelique an excuse for the tears that were filling her eyes because yes, she was proud of their work, but she was bombarded by so much emotion in this moment. She hurt for Hasna and Fatina, Kasim and Jamal. At the same time, she saw the dress as a symbol of what had brought Kasim into her life. It was exactly what she would never wear when walking toward him. In fact, today especially, she couldn't go near him. In future, it would be far too painful to approach him, not that she expected to bump into him anywhere.

The wedding reception was the last time she would ever see him and she wanted to weep openly with her loss, until she collapsed in a heap.

Trella squeezed her hand in comfort, as though she felt the echo of agony that clenched Angelique's heart.

Hasna's bouquet dropped an inch and her come-and-go smile faded into misery.

"You have both worked so hard to make this day absolutely perfect and—" Her gaze briefly met Angelique's, but she quickly shielded her thoughts with a sweep of her lashes. "I can't believe I have to ask you for another favor. Sadiq will kill me if he knows, but my mother wants a picture of the three of us. She said it's about the dress, but I know it's because she's excited to have the first photos of you both together in public."

Hasna looked embarrassed and angry, but resigned.

Angelique glanced at Trella, worried the photo request was too high a price. If Trella wanted to refuse, she would back her up, even if it meant they were both expelled from the wedding, the palace and Zhamair.

Even though it would mean not catching a last glimpse of the man she loved.

Trella smiled even as her fingers tightened on Angelique's.

"Of course," Trella said. "I knew photos would wind up in the press and I'm only sorry it might overshadow your special day. But if you're not bothered by that, then I'm not. You, Gili?"

Angelique shook her head and tried to bolster Hasna by saying, "Anything for you, because you make Sadiq so very happy. You know how much we want that for him."

Hasna's smile returned, shakily, then beaming with anticipation. She blinked. "Yes. He's lucky to have such good friends. Me, too." She touched her pendant and nodded. "I'm ready."

When it came to levels of power, there were elected officials, religious leaders, authoritarian dictators and right at the very top of that heap: Mother of the Bride. When she also happened to be a queen, she accomplished great feats with a single sentence.

"You cannot expect Hasna to give up the prestige of hosting such rare guests for a woman who may or may not join this family." Her tone implied that she would veto Kasim's prospective bride completely if she impacted the illustriousness of Hasna's day.

His mother didn't know the reason Hasna had become so insistent on having *all* of The Sauveterre Twins at her wedding. Kasim had gone to see his sister last night, when he'd returned from the desert. She had known the moment she saw the pendant that Jamal was alive. "You would have shown this to me before, with all the rest."

As the truth had come out, she had railed at him, and cried bitterly, but she understood that it had been Jamal's choice, and the people truly at fault were their parents. He hoped she had managed a few hours of sleep after that. He hadn't, too aware that Angelique was close, but essentially gone from his life.

Then, just before the ceremony, he had held out his arm to escort Fatina to her place behind the king and queen. She had been trembling, her face a stiff mask, as she'd said, "I saw what you gave to the princess."

Her eyes had held a maelstrom of emotion, topmost resentment and betrayal, but underscored by a glittering return of hope.

He would owe her some explanations, too, he supposed. At least he was able to brood unnoticed as the attention through the reception was drawn in a completely different direction.

Watching the wedding guests behave like the twins were creatures in a zoo made Kasim sick. They had all been briefly introduced at the receiving line, Angelique removing her hand from his like the contact had burned. Her eyes had remained downcast and his heart had been a tortured knot from the moment he saw her coming to the moment she'd disappeared into the crowd.

Her brothers now bookended their sisters, Henri on Trella's right, Ramon on Angelique's left, all posed in a row like movie stars to allow photographs, the men wearing dark green, the women a lighter shade, so all their eyes flashed like emeralds. Their smiles were aloof and unbothered.

They *were* a sight, so very good-looking, tall and flawless and so startlingly the *same*. An old woman touched Ramon like she wasn't sure he was real. He said something that made her cover a titter and blush. Angelique sent her brother a reproving look and pinched his arm.

Kasim's lungs felt tight as he memorized the vision of her. His heart had echoed her voice through him with every pound since she'd said, *I love you.*

Respect someone weaker. Did she not know how weak she made him?

He fantasized about having a second wife. The wife he really wanted. He loved her, too.

And claiming her would make him just like his father.

He ran a hand down his face, ensuring none of this struggle was evident as he gritted his teeth and tried to get through the hours of this everlasting wedding.

A servant touched his arm. "You must come," he said. "The king."

What now? Kasim stalked after the man, taking a relieved breath as they went through a door and the worst of the noise was closed out behind them. "Where is he?"

"The doctor is with him in the Consort's Chamber."

"Doctor?" Kasim's heart lurched. He strode past the man up the stairs to more quickly reach Fatina's suite.

Her rooms were at the far end of the wing from the royal apartments, but it didn't surprise him that his father was there. It did shock him to find his mother coming toward the same door from the other direction, expression tense. Fatina's maid was trailing behind her, obviously having fetched her with the same urgency.

This was serious.

Kasim's mind raced. Should Hasna be called away from her guests? Was it that bad? He pushed into the lounge and found his father being loaded onto a stretcher, an oxygen mask over his gray face. He wasn't conscious.

"What happened? What have you done?" The queen was quick to accuse Fatina.

Not her. Me, Kasim thought.

Fatina was crying, tail end of her scarf bunched up to her mouth, shoulders shaking with sorrow.

"Why was he even here when he should be downstairs with his guests? *You*—"

"Mother," Kasim said through his teeth. He looked to the doctor.

The royal physician wore a very grave look. "We will do what we can. Perhaps the queen should accompany us in the helicopter."

For potentially his father's last moments. Kasim's insides clenched.

As they all looked to Kasim for direction, he thought about the guests downstairs. The woman he'd used to needle his father—not to score points, but because he loved her.

The end result was the same, however. He had given his father a heart attack.

Kasim felt not just the weight of decisions that would have to be made in the next five minutes, but the weight of a nation landsliding to rest with infinite weight upon his shoulders. Even if his father recovered, Kasim was the man in power until he did.

And he didn't deserve it.

He had thought his father's censure had hung heavily around his neck. His own self-contempt was worse.

"Mother," he prompted. The word stuck in his throat. "I will follow with Hasna as soon as we can." And Fatina. He wished he could give her the honor of flying with the man she loved. She was rocking in her chair, face buried in her scarf as she tried to stifle her sobs.

Turning to a servant, he ordered them to have Hasna and Sadiq wait for him in one of the anterooms downstairs. He would tell them first, then make the announcement.

And he would say an unspoken, but final goodbye to Angelique.

I don't want to be the reason you two went to war the day before your sister's wedding.

Nevertheless, she was. She would never see this differently and neither would he.

Do you need me? I will stay if you want me to.

Angelique had rather foolishly sent the text as the wedding fell apart and Kasim disappeared, presumably to have a police escort to the hospital where his father was struggling to hang on to his life.

He didn't respond. Not that day, not before she left Zhamair, not as his nation went into mourning at the news of their king's demise, and not after his father was laid to rest and Kasim was crowned king.

She followed all of it, doing exactly what she had told him once she would never do. She stalked him online and even read what was said about the two of them, reliving their various moments together, not caring about the inaccuracies and wild theories and outright lies.

As one week turned into two, then three and more, it became obvious that he didn't need her. He took his rightful place on the throne and seemed fully in control of all he surveyed. Infinitely resilient and autonomous.

Now she felt vulgar for having sent the text in the first place. All she had wanted was to reach out to him in that moment when he must have been so anguished, but who was she to think she had anything a *king* could need?

It hadn't struck her until afterward that her presence at the wedding might have been the catalyst for his father's heart attack. Kasim had been so remote as he'd made his announcement that the king had been taken to hospital, so very stately and contained, yet she had sensed his agony.

Now she wondered—did he blame himself? *Her?*

She wished she hadn't been so quick to climb on her high horse at the oasis. She should have stayed there with him. No, that was selfish. It might have made things worse with his father. Of course, how could the outcome have been any worse than death? Still, she had been so preachy when really, she had been doing what he had accused her of. She had hidden behind her family because she loved Kasim so deeply, it scared her.

And leaving without having spent a full night at the oasis didn't mean she hurt any less now.

She hurt for both of them, so much so she went online yet again and walked straight into a statement from a source "close to the king." A marriage was being arranged and an announcement would be forthcoming.

She couldn't tell if it was an older statement made by his father or something Kasim might have said recently.

Either way, it rattled her all over again and drove her away from looking at any kind of screen for days.

She had to get on with her life.

But she couldn't make herself go back to Paris. She had come to Spain from the wedding, to lick her wounds, allowing her mother to mollycoddle her now that Trella was so much better and spending the bulk of her time in Paris.

Trella had finally confided a few details about her night with the Prince of Elazar to Angelique and was dealing with the fallout from it—big fallout—but she was fiercely determined to handle things alone and not lean on her siblings again, particularly her twin. It was both admirable and worrying, but Angelique had to let Trella muddle through and just impress on her sister that she was here if she was needed.

Even though she felt as useful as a milquetoast.

Thank God they had Sus Brazos, the family compound. "Her arms," it meant, referring to the safety of their mother's arms. They had taken to calling it that when Trella had retreated here.

Trella might have come to see the family stronghold as a prison, but Angelique needed it rather desperately. The gated compound overlooked the Mediterranean, ever inspiring with its expansive view. The buildings were a gleaming white, the main villa obscenely luxurious and up-to-date even though it had been built when her parents first married. The staff were all such long-time employees they were a type of extended family.

It made her feel safe and cosseted in every way, which allowed Angelique to relax as she ate quiet meals with her mother, walked the gardens, sunbathed and sketched, turned in early and tried to heal her broken heart.

The days were very predictable here, which was part of its charm. And it was also why she was so stunned when she was interrupted while watching seabirds diving into a churning pool out on the water. She had a guest at the gate, she was told.

"The King of Zhamair."

CHAPTER TWELVE

Angelique wore a summer dress in pale pink with tiny ivory polka dots. It had a high neck, but bared her golden shoulders and accented her slender waist and long legs, falling in layers of tall slits and sharp points. Her hair was in a high ponytail and she pressed her lips together over what he suspected was a fresh coat of lipstick. She seemed breathless as he was shown into their lounge.

"Welcome," she said, pressing her palms together. "My mother isn't here, I'm afraid. She had a luncheon with friends. She'll be sorry she missed you. Shall I order coffee? Your Highness?"

Kasim felt like it was their first meeting all over again. She was treating him like a stranger and was too beautiful for words, emptying his mind of all but base masculine thoughts. His perfectly tailored suit felt too tight.

Still, he found himself letting out his breath, relieved to finally see her, but exasperated by the fact he'd had to chase her down in Spain when he'd expected to find her in Paris.

"Excellency," he corrected absently. "And no to coffee."

Her mouth twitched, probably thinking he sounded

pretentious. She had never been particularly impressed by his station, which was part of her charm for him.

She sent a jerky nod to dismiss the maid and said, "Let me guess. You'd prefer to stand?"

"I would. Why is that funny?" he demanded as he heard the tiny noise she tried to stifle. "I've been sitting for hours, traveling to Paris then here."

"Paris?" The news arrested her.

"To take Fatina to see Jamal." It had been a bittersweet joy to embrace his brother again. As he'd met his brother's partner, and left Fatina to reunite with her son, Kasim had felt as though his last barrier to being with Angelique had been removed.

But now, as he entered the inner sanctum of her world, and recalled how she'd been treated like a museum exhibit at his sister's wedding, he wondered if he was taking too much for granted. The wife of a king was not exactly a low-key profile. Why would she want to take on such a position? He was struggling with the elevation in circumstance himself and it was only one notch.

"He does live in Paris, then? I wasn't sure," she said.

"Hmm? Oh. Jamal. No, he doesn't. It was complicated." A cloak of weariness fell over him. He wanted to throw off his *gutra* and shave his beard and be the man of lesser responsibilities he'd been when they'd first met.

But he was king now. And was expected to marry.

"It has been a very complicated, demanding few weeks."

"Of course. I'm so sorry about your father. I should have said—"

"Your mother's card was among the rest," he cut in. "My mother appreciated the gesture."

"She must be devastated. And poor Hasna, to lose her father on her wedding day. How is she?"

"Grieving. We all are. They curtailed their honeymoon." But he was glad his sister had such a stalwart support in her husband. It was one less weight on his own shoulders.

Angelique nodded, mouth pouted as though she wanted to say something, but knew there was nothing to say. As she looked at him, her eyes brimmed.

"Don't." He flinched, took a step toward her, then veered away, running a hand down his face in frustration. "I'm so tired of tears, Angelique."

She swallowed, trying to choke back the emotions swamping her. But she couldn't take it in! He was *here*, and so blindingly handsome. His eyes were dark and unreadable, but riveting. His mouth was stern, tension pulling at that sexy mouth of his.

He wore his beard, precision trimmed to frame his face, and also his *gutra*.

He had come to her world, but still had one foot in his.

Her heart panged because she felt firmly shut out of that side of his life. Shut out of all of it, really.

She drew a breath, but didn't know what to say.

He looked her over in the way he did sometimes, like he was taking in her hair or clothes or the set of her shoulders or the angle of her foot, but really, he was seeing what those things revealed. Like he was reading her. Seeing *her*.

It made her feel so transparent it was painful. She struggled to hold on to her composure. "This is just really…confusing. I'm not sure why you're here."

"After ignoring your text, you mean?"

She shrugged a shoulder, cheeks stinging with embarrassment all over again. "It wasn't appropriate of me to send it. I realized afterward that our going to the oasis may have contributed..." Her voice dried up. She didn't want to think she was to blame for his father's death.

"Maybe it did." His shoulders lifted and fell. "I certainly believed I'd killed him when I was being crowned."

"I'm so sorry," she whispered, hating herself for being his weakness, the thing that he'd gone after to the detriment of his father and his relationship with him.

"He had a heart condition. His heart had been failing for years." His mouth curled with irony. "But I didn't respond to your text because I blamed myself for his death. I blamed *us*."

Her worst nightmare. Her heart plummeted. There went the small dream she had formed at his arriving here, the one she hadn't really let form.

"I even blamed you for bringing that damned necklace from Jamal. I was not the man you asked me to be," he said with self-disgust.

And this was his punishment. The ultimate sacrifice, losing his father. He wasn't trying to dump that on her shoulders. She saw he carried it alone, but she felt awful all the same. Wanted to help him.

"What I didn't know, until he was dead and I was king, was that Fatina had fought with him that night herself. I was so busy in those first days after he passed away, it was two whole weeks before I could sit down and talk with her privately about her future. She fell apart, completely racked with guilt."

"They fought about Jamal?"

"She told him she wanted a divorce. I won't break her confidence by repeating all she told me, but... I do believe he loved her in whatever way he was able. Losing her, realizing he had lost her love by failing Jamal, was more than he could bear."

"But he had a heart condition," she hurried to repeat. "Please tell me you didn't make her live with that guilt."

He cast her a look that demanded some credit.

"I told her she was a generous wife and a good mother. I was unsurprised she would fight for the happiness of all my brothers and sisters, particularly Jamal. I told her she shouldn't blame herself and that I wanted to arrange for her to see Jamal as soon as possible."

"You're a good man, Kasim."

He made a dismissive noise. "I would have preferred to bring Jamal home, but I don't think that would be safe yet. I'm afraid to resurrect him. But I was able to reach him through the jeweler and we met him in Paris. He says hello and that he is still interested in working together if you are."

"That's why you're here? To deliver his message?"

"No." He gave her a look that suggested she was dense, then paced across to the windows that looked out on the sun-drenched sea. "I am here because I am under a great deal of pressure to go through on the promise I made to my dead father, to marry the woman he chose. But if I succumb to an arranged marriage, I know I would take you on the side and turn into him."

He slashed his hand through the air.

"I will not repeat history. I will not have you end up hating me as Fatina did my father. Not when I need your love so badly. I *will* need that love in the years to come, to keep me human. Ruling a country is not easy."

"Kasim…" This was heaven and hell wrapped up in one moment. She dropped her head so she wasn't looking at him. She was so tempted. "If you loved me—"

"Angelique. Look at me."

She lifted her head. The fierce determination in his features made her heart skip while the tenderness in his eyes stole her breath.

"What have I learned from my family? You love who you love. If you fight it, if you try to force it in another direction, there will be nothing but pain. You asked me once to give you up for the sake of my country. I'm coming *after* you for the sake of my country. Without you, the one I love, I will be as frustrated as my father. I'll become bitter and my heart will shrivel into a pitiless husk. Save my people from that. Save me from turning into that."

She let out a small laugh. "You're overstating, aren't you?"

"No. I watched it happen to him. He was much kinder in my youth, but his being trapped with my mother while wanting Fatina twisted him."

Her ridiculously tender heart pitied his father for the position he'd been in. Still, "Would your country have accepted her if he had married Fatina?" She'd seen Fatina's family. They were modest people of the desert. "I don't want to be a source of unrest in your country. I have a reputation, true or not. People will think you should have found someone more upstanding."

"In choosing my wife, I will be the authoritarian that my father was," he said with a point at the floor. "I will not compromise. I could engage myself to the woman he chose and tomcat through Europe for the next four years until I marry her, but I don't want that sort of freedom. I don't *want* other women. I don't want *her*. I want *you*. I will have you. My uncle and my advisors and anyone else who disapproves can…" He showed his teeth. "Grin and bear it."

She couldn't take it in, especially now she'd seen the scope of his life. If she had thought being a media darling was onerous, she couldn't imagine flouting his country's conservatives and becoming his wife.

"I'm not someone who thumbs their nose at the establishment. They'll tear me apart."

"They'll try." His mouth tightened. "But you'll win them over. God knows you'll be well protected until you do. I swear to keep you safe, Angelique."

"But you're overestimating what I'm capable of."

"Like hell," he said softly. "You think you're only brave if you pretend to be your sister. You are bravest when you're defending her because you *love* your sister. That love of yours is such a well of strength. I've seen it and I want it beside me, supporting me. I know that *my* love for *you* will make me a better man. Provided I can indulge it," he added with a look that was both sensual and tender.

Oh, he was such a seducer. Her heart fluttered like a caught bird and her eyes stung with moved tears. She cupped her hot cheeks.

"How could this be a surprise to you?" he chided, coming toward her and increasing her excited turmoil.

He took her wrists and drew them down so they stood face-to-face. She had no way to hide how overcome she was.

"I didn't think you loved me," she confessed in a daze. "I thought maybe if we had had more time you might have come to care…"

"I *care*," he admonished. "I always cared. And I am not someone who needs a lot of time to know my own mind." He shifted his grip and caressed the back of her knuckles with his thumbs. "But we will have to take things slow. Announcing an engagement this soon after my father's death— You're not pregnant, are you?" he asked with a sharpening of his expression.

"What? No! How could I be?"

"We didn't use anything at the oasis."

She huffed out a disbelieving laugh. "I'm on the pill, remember?"

His mouth twisted. "Shame. It would have given us a reason for shortening our timeline, but it's probably for the best if we do things in the right order." He sighed. "I want to make so many changes in my country, relax restrictions and change attitudes, but it has to be done carefully or there will be chaos. Is that the reassurance you need, Angelique? You will have time to put all these pieces together in your pretty head."

He was teasing her, reminding her of their first night together when he had tried to railroad her into extending their affair. She wanted to duck into him, maybe have a little cry because this was so much to take in. She was trying to smile, but her lips were trembling.

"I didn't bring a ring. I asked Jamal to make one for you."

She had to choke out a little laugh and pull one hand free to swipe at a tear that leaked down her cheek. "You don't have to *bribe* me."

"No? Well, I brought this anyway, hoping it would be an inducement." He released her other hand and reached inside his suit jacket, bringing out a velvet box she recognized.

Her heart did a little bump and roll as he flipped the lid to show her the emerald necklace he'd tried to give her in Paris.

"I should have explained that day that it was not a pay-off. Jamal made this years ago, before he left Zhamair. I told him that one day my queen would wear it."

"Queen!" Her knees wilted and Kasim quickly hooked his arm around her, catching her into him. Which didn't help at all because finally being back in his arms was such a relief she melted against him completely.

"What did you think?" He leaned to drop the necklace on the side table and scooped her under her knees, moving to sit on the sofa with her in his lap.

"I just wanted you to love me. Yes, I had fantasies we might marry, but because I want to be your *wife*. I want to see you every day and share my life with you."

"Finally she says yes."

She curled her arm around his neck and laugh-cried against his throat at his presumption. *So* like him.

But she loved him. So much.

Tipping back her head, she set her trembling hand against his bearded cheek, gazed into his beloved eyes and said, "I would be honored to be your wife."

"And my queen."

"Harem girl, if that's what you need me to be," she said, barely able to see him, her eyes were so full. She swiped at her silly leak of tears. "Good thing I had no time for makeup. I'm trying not to do this, you know. You said you were tired of tears, but I'm just so *moved*."

"The sad tears are killing me. The angry ones. I trust these are happy ones?"

"They are. Oh, Kasim." She lifted to press her mouth to his, unable to hold back her expansive feelings.

His arms tightened to gather her closer and he kissed her with deep passion and infinite tenderness. Love imbued the moment, sending a rush of joy and heat through her. Desire. That delicious, sharp desire that only he ignited in her awoke to make her burn.

He was reacting just as instantaneously. She felt his

hardness against her thigh and he slid to press her beneath him on the sofa.

As his mouth slid down her throat, he lifted his head and frowned at her bare neck. "No panic button."

"I wasn't going to put one on for *you*."

"Even though I intend to steal you from your family?"

"That part will be hard for me," she admitted. "It's good I'll have time to do that in stages. But there are times when I'm impatient, you know." She loved the feel of his stubble against her palm and absolutely had to trace his bottom lip with her thumb. "I don't want to go to a hotel," she whispered.

"No?" He was reading the hunger in her and answering with a growing heat in his own gaze. He shifted so he was between her legs, pressing his hardest flesh against her softest.

"It will take too long to drive there and have it scouted. I want to sneak you into my bedroom so you can ravish me there. *Now*."

He pulled away, drawing her up as he went. "See how good you are at encouraging me to compromise? Lead the way, my beautiful future wife."

EPILOGUE

Two months later...

ANGELIQUE WAS ALWAYS happiest when her whole family was together, but she felt a little guilty for being *so* happy today. It was her engagement party, however, so she was entitled to be elated.

And it wasn't a huge party, which made her even happier. Just those closest to them gathered at Sus Brazos for a weekend to celebrate what amounted to a secret engagement since they weren't officially announcing it for another few months.

She was making other people happy with this small party, too. Sadiq and Hasna were here and Jamal had just arrived with his partner. Kasim was sequestered with the four of them while his brother and sister took a few minutes to reunite in person after being in touch again since the wedding.

It gave Angelique a few minutes to study her sister, who was arguing heatedly with Ramon on the far side of the pool. Of the four of them, those two were the only combination to descend into yelling matches. They weren't there yet, but it was only a matter of time before one of them completely lost their temper and pushed the other into the water to cool off, evening clothes notwithstanding.

The way Henri was glaring at them, it might very well be both of them taking a swim—by his hand.

"What's going on?" Kasim asked, coming up behind her and wrapping his arms around her waist.

"They have Mama's hot Spanish blood." She leaned back into him. "Henri and I have our father's French temperament, you lucky duck. Our silence speaks volumes. Their volume does."

"What are they fighting about?"

"Unclear and probably not important," she said with a fatalistic sigh. She suspected Trella had picked this fight to let off steam. Her sister was troubled. Angelique had been feeling it, but couldn't do a thing about it. Trella was being that delightfully frustrating shade of her true self: stubborn and ferociously independent.

She had even come up with a plan to transition Angelique from the day-to-day operations at Maison des Jumeaux, while allowing her to keep her foot in the door, submitting designs and indulging her artistry around her duties as queen—oh, she would never fully grasp that!

Trella was determined for Angelique to move on with her life without feeling held back. It made Angelique wistful, even though she was also grateful. She loved Kasim so very much and wanted to be with him without guilt.

"How is Hasna?" She turned in his arms to ask the question.

"Good. They'll be out in a moment, but I couldn't wait to show you... Come here."

He pulled her a little farther along the veranda to a corner where the light was soft and the view was nothing but starry night and glittering sea. The fragrance off the early summer blooms came up from the garden below and the warm air caressed her bare shoulders and calves.

She had a feeling she knew what he wanted to show her, but was still overcome as her future husband caressed her arms before he went down on one knee.

"Angelique, my love."

"Oh! You don't have to do that." She instantly choked up and lost sight of him behind a film of emotive tears.

"Arrêtez," she heard Henri growl at her siblings, receiving instant silence. She suspected they were being watched.

She was never comfortable as the center of attention, but she looked into the face of the man she loved and knew he would keep her safe no matter what.

"Will you marry me?" He showed her the ring that Jamal had made, the one she had been holding her breath to see. Now, in this deeply moving moment, she couldn't make herself look away from the love in Kasim's eyes.

"You know I will. I love you with everything in me. Please." She waved for him to rise. He was a king after all.

He did, suddenly tall and close. He slid the ring on her shaking hand and handed her his handkerchief so she could clear her vision enough to fall in love with the hint of a feathered design cut into the band. Claws like talons held a stunning round diamond. It was simple and elegant, pretty, but imbued with the fierceness of her husband while conveying that he did know her very well and longed to please her.

"I *love* it."

"I love you." He cupped her chin and kissed her tenderly. "This time next year we will marry in Zhamair. It's far too long to wait, but this is a step in the right direction."

A small burst of applause made them both glance in that direction and she blushed to discover not just her mother and siblings, but Jamal and his partner, Hasna and Sadiq, all beaming at them.

They would marry in a ceremony that would be big and overwhelming, and her life would be equally huge and daunting, but she would have these cherished people to help her through it.

And this man. She looked up at Kasim, her other half. Not her reflection, but her complement. Curling her arms around his neck, she went up on tiptoes to kiss him.

* * * * *

MASQUERADE

CARA LOCKWOOD

To PJ, my amazing husband, partner and best friend.
Thank you for making every day better than the last.

CHAPTER ONE

THE THINGS ONE did for love…and revenge, Asha Patel thought as she squeezed between two men in custom-made tuxedos wearing silver masks in the glittering gold ballroom of the Grand Hotel in Stockholm. Everyone, in fact, wore them, except Asha, who was—not so subtly, she realized now—crashing this shindig. Also, a small point, but it *seemed* this might be a black-and-white ball. Everyone wore some combination of one or the other, and her Chanel red strapless gown stood out like a police siren. So much for subtlety.

She moved past a golden column, past the gilded mirror windows lining the walls on either side of the opulent space, feeling like she'd fallen into a costume drama. She checked her reflection in the mirrored windowpanes. She might be standing out like a sore thumb, but she still looked like a damn fine one with the strapless floor-length gown clinging to her curves like a glove. The slinky dress with the thigh-high slit and matching red stilettos suited her perfectly, because she paid her in-demand stylist top dollar to ensure it did.

She wore her long, wavy, nearly black hair down, and it hit midback. She'd kept her makeup heavy and dramatic, her lips the same Chanel red as her dress. She scanned the well-heeled crowd, noticing a few pointed stares in her direction. Not that she cared. She was here to catch her cheating boyfriend, Connor, whom she knew was here was that empty-headed lingerie model, Kayli. She grabbed a glass of champagne from a roving waiter, who also gave her the side-eye and a slight raised eyebrow. Okay, so how was she supposed to know she should be wearing a mask? That *hadn't* been mentioned in Connor's texts to his model mistress, but then, most of his texts included dick pics, so she supposed he was busy doing more important things like trying to get the best lighting for himself.

Asha had been monitoring Connor's phone for weeks. He was the one dumb enough to use her father's app to proposition models. Enlisting the help of one of her father's engineers had been easy. And what she wanted now was to find her boyfriend and tell him to jump off a high balcony. Of course, *boyfriend* was a strong term. Although not as strong as *fiancé,* the word he'd been hinting about with phrases like "ring shopping" and "popping the question."

They'd only been dating three weeks. Hell, they'd not even slept together. Not for lack of Connor's trying. He came in hot and heavy, declaring his love, telling her she was his soul mate, smiling his legendary smile. Except, it became increasingly clear, Connor didn't like brunettes, even though he was one. Clearly, he preferred empty-headed blondes. Asha, whose father immigrated to Seattle from India, and built one of the most successful tech companies in recent years, knew from experience growing up in Seattle that she wasn't everyone's type. How often had she smiled politely when someone called her an "exotic beauty"—making her sound like she came from Mars? But the worst, by far, was discovering that the men declaring love to her were really declaring love to her billion-dollar fortune.

She was here to make Connor pay. And pay he would. Except, glancing around her, with all the guests hiding behind silver eye masks, she realized *finding* Connor and Kayli would be more challenging than she thought. And what *was* this mystery party anyway? Lord help her if she'd stumbled upon some weird kinky sex party. Was Connor into that? Well, he *was* an actor desperate for any publicity he could get. Who knew what he really felt about anything? She glanced around her and saw many of the guests whispering to each other and staring at her. She got the impression they were all talking about her. Her eyes scanned the crowd, but all she saw were masked faces. Impossible to pick out Connor's or anyone else's, unless she knew what the jerk had planned to wear.

"Ms. Patel?" Asha whirled and came face-to-face with a pristine tuxedo shirt and tie, and the dark satin lapel of an expensive black jacket. She looked upwards and saw a strong jaw and full, sensual lips, curved up in a smile. Sharp, cool blue eyes stared at her from beneath the ornate silver-and-gold eye mask he wore. Dark hair rolled back from the mask and curled beneath his ears, thick and soft enough to want to touch.

"How do you know my name?" she asked, suspicious, heart thumping in her chest, because she couldn't shake the feeling she'd been caught red-handed. Not, of course, that that meant anything. She could usually bribe or cajole her way out of any problem. Trespassing had to be among her most minor offenses of late.

"Everyone knows the heiress of The Skycloud—founded by your father?" He spoke with a faint French accent, soft and sexy. "Also, I believe you have more followers than he does on social media." Damn her social media feed, a blessing and a curse. Mostly a blessing, since her influencer powers also made her a decent amount of money. Money that she'd need if she ever wanted to get out from under her father's thumb. "Your reputation proceeds you."

It always did. She'd made her social media reputation as a party girl with loose morals, someone who courted and discarded actors and pop stars on a whim. Some people loved her, some hated her, but they were all *interested.* That's how she kept selling all those mascaras and lips glosses, and how her followers kept growing every day.

"What do you know of my reputation?"

"You're a woman used to getting what she wants." He paused. *Here it comes,* she thought, the moment when he made a remark about how *contro-versial* she was, how she hopped from bed to bed. She didn't care.

"How so?"

"You point at a man and he usually falls in love with you. Is this not so?" He grinned, slowly, and Asha knew he meant one of the pop songs written about her. It was a lie, of course. When she pointed at men, they did fall in love. Just with her money. Not her.

"That's a slight exaggeration."

"Is it? I am not so sure," the mystery man re-plied, the French accent a bit thicker now. Asha realized that a hole in the crowd seemed to form around them. People were giving them space. Oddly. And a few were staring in their direction. She wondered why. She turned her attention back to the Frenchman in the tuxedo and gilded mask.

"You seem to have me at a disadvantage, Mr...." she trailed off, trying to figure out if the slant of his mouth, the shade of his eyes, held any clue to his identity. No, she decided, she didn't know him.

"Mathis Durand," he said, and gently took her right hand. He bent over it and laid a gentle kiss above her knuckles, a warm, feather-like touch that made all the nerve endings in her arm come alive. "I am the host of this party."

"The host?" Oh, great. Now she was in trouble. "Well, you see, I'm so very sorry. I've forgotten my mask." Forgotten, or never knew she needed one— what was the difference? "The friend I came with forgot to tell me it was a costume party."

She laughed uneasily. She'd never felt more exposed. Durand didn't join her. He cocked his head to one side.

"The friend? Who is this?"

"Connor Henry."

A slow smile crept across Durand's face. "I do not believe that is true, Ms. Patel. You did not come with Mr. Henry. You are…how do they say in America? Crashing?"

All the guests ceased their own conversations and were simply staring now. Why? Who cared about a single party crasher? Every party had dozens. Didn't they?

"I…" She was about to double down on her lie, because if she knew anything it was that if she acted passionately enough about a bald-faced lie, most people believed it. "I'm a guest."

"You're the guest of no one." The direct contraction startled her. Now she realized too late that bluffing was a mistake. He was the host, after all. Perhaps he *did* personally know…all the hundred or so people who crowded the ballroom. "Shall we talk about this in private?" Durand asked. He took hold of her elbow, a gentle but firm grip, his fingers a shade paler against her golden skin.

"Sure?" she said and he steered her through the crowd, which parted like the Red Sea, the whispers following her as she went. Now, nervous butterflies flapped their wings against her rib cage. Why all the seriousness? He led her to the end of the ballroom, past the enormous crystal chandelier and to the balcony doors beyond. They passed at least three women in low-cut dresses that only seemed to have eyes for Durand. Asha got the impression she was keeping him from flirting with the gorgeous, lithe Nordic model types who were frowning at her as he took her through the balcony doors, and out into the cool summer night in Stockholm. In the distance, Asha could see Strömmen, the innermost part of Saltsjön, a bay of the Baltic Sea. Warm lights dotted the shore of the bay, making it look magical.

Durand closed the heavy, ornate double doors behind them, and then they were alone on the stone balcony, but as darkness never truly fell in Stockholm on summer nights, the ever-present never-quite-set sun meant they needed no man-made lights to see each other. Beneath the gray, slightly pink sky, she noticed the balcony had another, smaller side door, and she wondered where it led.

"Okay, you're right. I crashed your party and I'm sorry," Asha said, hoping that a little groveling might help her case. She needed to find Connor. That is, *if* he hadn't seen her already and booked it out of there. "Surely you have room for one more guest? I'd be happy to pay my way. Of course."

Durand chuckled, the smallest of sounds at the back of his throat. "I do not need your money, Ms. Patel."

"Really?" She'd discovered that the one truth in life was that money *always* talked. And opened doors. And some of the oldest money families sometimes were the poorest. After all, a few of the most famous royal families in the world were happy to use her private jets. She shifted slightly, and she watched as his eyes trailed down her bare shoulder.

"Really." He cocked his head to one side, curious. "What brings you to my party?" She caught the note of possessiveness in his tone. *My party.* There was no mistaking it. "And, please, if we could dispense with the lies and…ah…the theatrics?"

Says the man hiding his face behind a gilded mask.

She glanced up at him, his full face still shrouded by that damn mask, and was tempted to lie. *For fun.*

For a laugh. But she had a feeling this man would see through any petty lies. For once in her life, she decided she'd be honest.

"I'm trying to find Connor Henry. I do know him. He's my…" She hesitated to say *boyfriend,* since they hadn't been dating that long. Plus, after she caught him with his lingerie model, he'd be an *ex-boyfriend.* "Well, we had an understanding. He's deceived me, and he's come here with a woman he also lied to me about, and I want to catch him in that lie."

And make him grovel, and then tell him he's lost me before he ever really had me. Dramatic? Maybe, but he deserves it.

Durand lifted the mask from his face, and Asha's breath caught a little at the back of her throat. The man made gorgeous look ugly. Strong jawline, slim, straight nose, clear blue eyes that looked even darker in the grayish light of never-quite-dusk, even though she knew it was close to midnight.

"That *is* unfortunate. But I am afraid I cannot let you stay." He shook his head slowly, eyes solemn. It took a moment to realize this walking sex god was actually denying her.

"Why not?"

"This is a *members only* event. You must be a member of the Sphinx Society in order to mingle here."

Asha laughed, bright and brittle, but seeing the

serious look on Durand's face, she realized her mistake. He was *serious.*

"What is the Sphinx Society? Some kind of sex club?"

Now it was Durand's turn to laugh. "Hardly. It's one of the oldest societies in the world. We helped *build* this hotel. You know, in that ballroom the very first Nobel Prize ceremony and award banquet was held in 1901?"

"Really?" Asha faked interest. She cared little about history, unless it concerned her personally. What could dusty old facts do to help her, anyway? What she wanted to do was get into that ballroom and find Connor. And if kissing up to this exceptionally sexy Frenchman was the way to do it, then she would. She actually didn't mind, truth be told. She loved pretty things. Durand was the one who ought to be the movie star. She moved closer to the man, eyes never leaving his. If he wasn't interested in money, then maybe he was interested in her attention. Most men were. And she wasn't afraid to take advantage, either. "Tell me more."

Durand's dark eyebrows raised a millimeter. She bit her lip, and he studied her mouth. Good.

"The King of Sweden uses this hotel for his official business, as do all the Swedish royals," Durand said.

"Tell me more about the Sphinx Society." She ran one perfect red nail down his immaculately tailored lapel. He watched the bloodred tip against the black fabric. She didn't exactly care about the society, or its history, but if this man wanted to crow about it, and indulging him got her what she wanted, then she was happy to do it. Not all of her reputation was exaggerated. Men might not fall in love with her at first sight, but they often fell into lust.

"You either know about the Sphinx Society or you don't. There's no *telling* someone about it." Durand was interested, she could tell, just as she knew that now his gaze lingered a bit too long on the neckline of her strapless dress.

"How about…you help me join?" She was so close to him now that if she rocked up on her stilettos, she could kiss his lips. She took his hand and put it open-palmed on her slim waist. He let her. His eyes met hers, the dark pupils in them crowding out his gray-blue irises. *Yes, that's it. Want me. You know you do.*

"Membership is by invitation only."

She studied his eyes. "I can think of one way to get an invitation."

She reached up and slid her hand behind the back of his neck, and then pulled him down to her lips. Asha knew how to play this game—to a point. Most men turned into jelly with a kiss and little more. She'd never really had to go farther than she'd liked. And, to be honest, she'd only ever had a handful of lovers her whole life. Unlike what the tabloids said.

According to them, she was one of the world's biggest whores. Using her body and her money to get famous men to do what she wanted. She'd been accused of all kinds of nonsense, all the allegations no rich man would have to confront. After all, rich men were supposed to have revolving doors on their bedrooms. Rich women? Not so much.

Not that any of what was said about her was true, anyway.

But she used it all to her advantage. Played up the role. Men loved it. And she typically got what she wanted in the process. Now she pressed her lips to his. She was the aggressor, and yet the man took possession of her mouth as if it always belonged to him. Damn, he knew how to use his lips, gently, over hers, coaxing her mouth open, his tongue meeting hers. He tasted like fine champagne, and something more…expensive. He deepened the kiss with a gentle lash of his tongue, teasing her, drawing out her hunger, and for a second, she lost herself. Forgot *she* was the one trying to seduce *him*. He seemed to hold all the power, and she seemed to be losing her edge. All she wanted was more of his mouth. More of his body. More of everything. His mouth on hers, driving her, tasting her, made her head spin, made her body buzz with want. He opened the floodgates in her, and her desire roared out, white rapids of pure energy.

And she wasn't the only one affected by the kiss,

either. She could feel Durand's own body stiffen, feel his own lust rising as she pressed her belly against him. Yes, he wanted her, too. Wanted her badly. She pulled away at last, panting, her heart pounding in her chest, her mind buzzing with all kinds of feelings, none of them having to do with Connor or the party or anything other than Durand's talented, talented mouth. She met his gaze, and he, too, seemed a little stunned. Her chest heaved as she struggled to get her breathing under control. Hell, after a kiss like that, he'd have to let her in. She couldn't see how he could deny her entrance to this party after a white-hot encounter like that, and the promise of more to come. A small smile quirked the corner of his sensual, knowing mouth.

"Thank you for that, Ms. Patel." He wiped the corner of his mouth with one finger, the light of desire flickering in his eyes. "That was…exquisite."

The way he looked at her now made the air catch in her throat. Was he going to pull her into his arms for another kiss? God, she hoped so. Her whole body vibrated with desire for his mouth against hers once more.

"I'm afraid, however, that you can't stay at my party," he said, voice low. "I'm going to have to ask you to leave."

CHAPTER TWO

A WEEK LATER, Durand found himself staring out of his office window in his well-heeled Sphinx Society office, with a perfect view of the Eiffel Tower rising up from the Paris skyline. The breathtaking view, especially with a cloudless summer sky behind it, and his window open to the warm French sunshine, normally calmed him, but today all he could think about was the taste of Asha Patel's lips. He couldn't understand why a simple kiss would linger with him so long. But the invitation in the woman's dark eyes, the way she'd looked at him, lingered in his mind. For a split second, he'd seen right through her expert attempt at seduction, seen her true desire there on her face and felt it in her lips. The memory made his groin tighten.

"Mr. Durand?" The voice of his assistant, Madelyn, broke his reverie. The stunning blonde with her hair neatly up, carried a tray with his morning espresso. He nodded swiftly, and she moved in, leaving the tray on the small table between the two Queen Anne chairs sitting near the window. "Do you need anything else at the moment?"

She waited, red lips pursed, her hands clasped in front of her. She'd changed quite a bit since he'd first hired her, a college dropout who'd been disinherited by her father, a prominent Parisian whose wife disapproved of him supporting his illegitimate daughter. In some ways, Durand had saved her, though Madelyn was resourceful and would've done just fine on her own. Madelyn, he knew, was grateful for the chance to work with him and had, over the last five years, grown to have feelings for him. Though she'd never acknowledged them, and he'd never take advantage, he felt them there all the same.

A sticky situation, to be sure, but Durand never mixed business with pleasure. He always looked elsewhere for distraction and felt it was unseemly to take advantage of an unfair power dynamic. Many of his colleagues had been taken by surprise with #MeToo. But Durand always thought it had been wrong to abuse one's power. He always believed a woman was not truly free to consent if her paycheck was being signed by the man who invited her into his bed.

Durand picked up the small espresso cup, keeping his eyes on the tower. He thought about Asha's cheating boyfriend, that actor, Connor. "Yes. I'll need to revoke the membership of Connor Henry."

Madelyn raised a single blond eyebrow, the only evidence of surprise. "What should I tell him is the reason?"

He thought about the fact that Connor cheated on Asha. Normally this wasn't something that rose to Durand's interest. Men cheated all the time. It wasn't his job to police their behaviors. But…when a member's behavior *brought* chaos to his society, or to one of the parties, then it became his business. Connor should've known Asha would take it personally. He should've guessed Asha would follow him or should've simply taken better care to keep his whereabouts secret.

And Connor hadn't even bothered to try to clean it up with Durand himself. No, he'd taken one look at Asha and fled. The coward. Durand had heard from security that the action star had bolted out the kitchen door, his model date in tow, the second he'd seen Asha in the ballroom.

He could cancel Connor's membership for simply causing this little headache. He'd revoked memberships for less. He told himself getting rid of Connor was simply a smart move, and the one way to avoid inviting Asha and another outburst to a future party. But in reality, he simply didn't like the man. Didn't like that he took Asha for granted, and that he'd be stupid enough to cheat on her in plain sight.

"Ungentlemanly conduct," Durand said at last, turning from the window. It was a broad enough category that could include revealing society secrets, such as the location of one of the society's events.

"He might challenge your decision," Madelyn suggested.

"Let him." Durand waved a hand, dismissive, as he sipped at his rich espresso. He wasn't afraid of a man who lacked the balls to face his girlfriend and own up to his bad behavior. Besides, ultimately, this was, and always would be, *his* club, and he made the rules. There was no board, no oversight committee, no appeals court. He was judge and jury, and that's the way he liked it. He'd spent his entire life trailing after his successful but distant father, hoping for approval, which he'd never get. It had taken most of his life to realize that sad truth.

So instead, he spent his time working on proving his father wrong. He wasn't the disappointment his dour father believed, even though he'd tried hard to forget all about him after he had a string of new children with various mistresses and second and third and fourth wives across the globe. One of those other sons was named heir to his billion-dollar shipping and logistics business. Durand and his mother were left nearly penniless after his parents divorced when Durand was just

fourteen. Durand made back all of his father's fortune—and more—using his connections and his
wit to take over the Sphinx Society. Members paid
handsomely, not only for the privilege to socialize,
but also for the powerful business and political connections Durand offered. More than one billionaire-
dollar deal had been struck in a Sphinx Society
cigar room. He'd started as a board member—as
one of the only things his father gave his mother in
the divorce settlement—and had consolidated his
power, updated the once aging group into a coveted
invitation once more. He wouldn't let some lowly
action star like Connor Henry be a distraction.

"And we have more important things to worry
about. I'll be sending you potential venues for the
Masquerade Ball. That'll be all."

"Yes, sir." Madelyn bowed her head and ducked
out of his office.

The Masquerade Ball. This most opulent, most
extravagant gathering of the society all year. It also
happened to be one of the worst kept secrets among
the upper echelon. Old money and new money vied
for invitations to the ball, and not *every* society
member received a black-and-gold envelope. Only
certain members would know of the super-secret
location of this year's most coveted event. Planning
the event took months and poring over the society's
ample membership list for the best and most deserv-
ing candidates. At the Masquerade, nearly anything

was possible. Once, a live elephant mingled with the guests in Bali. In Milan, each guest received an engraved platinum bracelet designed by one of the brightest figures in fashion. In Egypt, guests sipped champagne in the shadow of the Pyramid of Giza.

Each year became more extravagant, more dazzling than the last, the guests working hard to top their extravagant costumes each year. But it wasn't just the stunts of the party that occupied Durand's mind. It was also the delicate balance of guests, the way he worked hard to deliberately pair together the right people. Sure, there was the spectacle, but the Masquerade was also where billion-dollar business deals got struck, love stories were made, and feuding families reconciled. That was the part that Durand loved the most.

Durand turned away from the window, glancing at the original Monet hanging above his polished, ornate gold-and-black antique desk, once used by King Louis XV in the Palace of Versailles. The golden clawed feet and ornate golden figures of women on either side, holding up pitchers and grapes, was ostentatious to be sure, but Durand liked exactly that about it. He also very much liked the fact that it stood as a reminder to him not to grow too egotistical, or too lazy. King Louis XV's extravagances and his weak rule, after all, helped sow the seeds of discord in France and led to the French Revolution.

As he took a seat behind the massive desk, loud voices from behind his office door captured his attention. There were at least two of them, and they were angry. Madelyn, he heard, was doing her best to shoo them out, but Durand felt the need to intervene. He wouldn't let his assistant be abused like this.

He swung open his door only to see Asha Patel, dressed in a fetching white linen strapless A-line sundress and matching strappy wedges, a large-brimmed straw hat shielding half of her face. She looked more like a starlet ready for her movie debut than an heiress. Most of them lacked Asha's striking natural beauty. They often used money to hide their flaws, but from Durand's watchful eye, he didn't see any. Her beauty, in fact, took his breath away—a cliché to be sure, one that he'd never believed possible, but the breath caught in his throat as his eyes roved her generous curves, her golden-almond-colored skin, her flawlessly lined dark, soulful eyes—a lighter brown than he remembered, a rich golden brown.

Two men in expensive suits flanked her, both carrying briefcases and the egotistical air of attorneys looking to sue. They were middle-aged and graying, with pudgy middles and faces fleshy from too much expensive wine, which meant they relished fights just like these. He'd met their kind before.

"What's the meaning of this?" Durand demanded, but kept his eyes on Asha. Asha met his gaze and lifted her chin in good old-fashioned defiance. Resentment flashed in her eyes. So, it seemed, she still had sore feelings about him for escorting her out of his party.

"I'm sorry, sir," Madelyn cried, eyes wide, a phone receiver in her hand, as she no doubt prepared to dial security. A blond hair fell loose from her normally pristinely pinned chignon. "They are insisting on seeing you. I told them you have many appointments today."

Durand eyed Asha, who glared at him, eyes flashing. He loved the way her bottom lip trembled just slightly—nerves? Anger? He wondered.

"I have come with my attorneys," she said. "And I'd like to discuss the issue of membership in the Sphinx Society."

So little Miss Disruption was back, and demanding entry into *his* club? He ought to throw her and her attorneys out on the street. Yet something about the defiant rise of her chin made him hesitate. Perhaps he could toy with her a little first. If she wanted to play a little game, maybe he'd indulge her. Cat and mouse was one of his favorite pastimes.

Durand chuckled low in his throat.

"You really think you can bully your way into my club, Ms. Patel?" He smiled slowly, almost relishing the challenge. It had been years since someone was bold enough to defy him openly. Perhaps she didn't know who she was dealing with. Yet.

"You owe me a meeting, Mr. Durand." Asha's dark eyes flashed. Look at that sense of entitlement. It was almost sexy, if it wasn't so obviously the temper tantrum of a spoiled heiress used to bullying people to get what she wanted.

"Oh, I assure you that I don't *owe* you anything." Durand made sure that people who demanded things from him regretted that decision. Even gorgeous heiresses. Or maybe, especially gorgeous heiresses.

Madelyn hovered in the background, still holding the receiver of the phone. "Shall I notify security, sir?" Her blue eyes were filled with concern as she clutched the phone.

Durand glanced at his assistant, and then back at Asha.

"I'll see Ms. Patel, but *without* her entourage." He met the gaze of each of the lawyers, who blinked back at him coldly with their nearly lifeless eyes.

"Ms. Patel," protested one of the pudgy, middle-aged men in their overpriced suits. "I strongly advise—"

She held up a perfectly manicured hand and the attorney instantly fell silent. "No, Robert. I'll allow it."

Allow it, as if she was royalty and not a new money tech heiress. Oh, my. Durand would enjoy this. New money so often lived under the mistaken impression that money, once made, lasted forever. Only heirs of vanishing old money knew the truth: you were always one or two bad investments away from losing it all. Or a single divorce, in Durand's case. A divorce that diverted his father's attention and resources to other children.

Madelyn slowly returned the receiver to the cradle, expressionless, although Durand suspected she would've preferred to kick out the beautiful heiress. Did she suspect Durand's interest?

And, so what if she did? Madelyn knew to keep her feelings under control. He'd never encouraged her, though technically, he hadn't disabused her of the notion either. He thought they understood that their working relationship had no room for tender feelings.

Durand stepped back from his ornately carved door and swept out his arm as Asha moved past, her Louis Vuitton purse clasped beneath one elbow, a trail of expensive perfume stretching out behind her. Madelyn sent him a worried glance before focusing on the attorneys in the waiting room.

"If those two so much as sneeze, feel free to call security," Durand instructed. The lawyers glowered at him quietly, but eventually sat on the gold antique love seats near the front door of his office. Madelyn gave him a reassuring nod and went back to her computer. Durand stepped into his office and closed the door behind him. Asha stood at the over-sized window, staring at the Eiffel Tower.

"That's quite a view," she said, turning around slowly, soaking it in.

"The view, mademoiselle, pales to your beauty," he said, easily. It was the truth. She glanced at him, suddenly, color rising in her cheeks. She wasn't expecting a compliment, though it was easy enough to give. She was far more beautiful than a metal tower in the distance, no matter how famous that tower might be.

"Do you think flattery will get you somewhere?" she challenged, recovering her composure. Durand liked to watch the struggle, liked to watch her try to keep her balance. This was going to be fun.

"I am simply being honest, mademoiselle," he said. "French men appreciate natural beauty."

"Do they? Is that all they appreciate?" She raised an eyebrow in challenge as she took off her sun-hat, freeing her long dark locks. He watched as they cascaded down her bare shoulders, soft enough and silky enough to beg for his touch. The sunlight danced in her hair, revealing merlot highlights. He could feel the power in her beauty calling to him, a siren's song, no doubt, an invitation to crash himself against the rocks. He'd need to keep his head. He'd need to be careful.

"Please, won't you have a seat?" he asked.

She picked one of his red velvet Queen Anne

chairs, her white dress stark against its bloodred fabric and painted gold accents.

"Quite the office you have here."

"I'm partial to antiques—to furniture with history," Durand said, indifferent, as he perched on the edge of his ornate desk, made over 250 years ago. "History is everything. Those who ignore history do so at their own peril."

"I do not care for history," Asha told him boldly. "I care about the future. Making my own path."

"And you think you can make your own path in a vacuum? Without knowing where you came from?"

She smiled at him but did not answer. Instead, she studied the golden accented desk. "Did that desk...belong to... King Louis XV?"

Durand couldn't help but be impressed. "You know antiques?"

She smiled, switching tacks, away from annoyed, entitled heiress and to...coy, flirty one. "Perhaps I just know *you,* Mr. Durand. I did a little research on you."

"About my proclivities in furnishing my office?"

"Among *other* things." She raised a solitary dark and perfectly manicured eyebrow. "You like to leave a trail of hearts in your wake."

He laughed a little. "That is not my fault if one is offered to me. I do not steal them, if that's what you're implying."

"So you just use your charms until you get what

you want and throw women away like disposable towels?" Asha shook her head slowly. "That is so... old-fashioned. Maybe you are a little *too* obsessed with history. You act like a relict, a playboy of the 1950s."

Durand laughed, unable to stop himself. Since when had a woman openly insulted him so? Not that he could recall. "You think I'm a relic?" An amused smile danced on his face. "And you believe that insulting me will get you what you want?"

Asha shrugged one shoulder. "I do not believe in flattery, as you do. Flattery is kissing someone's ass. I believe in a more direct approach."

"Is that so? Is that why you lied to me in Sweden? About being Connor's date."

Asha swept her black hair off one shoulder. "I didn't say I *never* lied. I said I don't believe in kissing asses."

He almost laughed but caught himself. "So you are trying to insult me?"

"Wouldn't you have to have *shame* to be insulted, monsieur?" She grinned.

She was using her wiles again, just like that night at the party on the balcony. The way she sat now, her head tilted just so, leaning forward just a tad so he could see the hint of cleavage in her square neckline. Leaning forward to give him the best possible view, that she no doubt practiced before one of her mirrors in her hotel room. He tried not to linger too long there. He couldn't afford to get distracted. He needed to stay on his toes. She wasn't going to get the best of him. He'd make sure of that.

"You have a reputation, too." He met her dark-eyed gaze. "A man-eater. A woman who leaves broken hearts in her wake. How many pop stars have written heartbreak songs about you? Too many to count, and on at least three continents."

She picked a piece of lint off her skirt, looking nonplussed. "And?"

"And... I'm not sure how much of the gossip should be believed, but I've read you are a woman who has appetites even...greater than most men."

A small flush colored her cheekbones, a bit of color that most might have missed, but Durand prided himself on reading people, on being able to detect even the slightest hint of emotion. She was... embarrassed. Not quite the reaction he'd expected from the world's most famous and unapologetic party girl. But she was quickly trying to hide the shame with bravado. She squared her shoulders and looked him in the eye.

"What is wrong with a woman wanting what a man wants?" she challenged.

"Absolutely nothing," Durand said.

Asha leaned forward even more, revealing more of the top curve of her golden-tan breasts, her skin the color of a perfect creamy latte. He tried to avoid her neckline, but found himself drawn to it again and again. By design. She knew what men liked. That much was obvious. He studied it all: the ridge of her collarbone made him want to lay feather kisses on it, the flawless golden-tinted skin, the cleavage—plunging. Still, of the traps he'd seen laid for him, this was a truly, beautiful trap. He could see why so many men fell for it. The woman's body begged to be touched. Begged to be explored.

"Well, then. We know each other at least," he added, and with great strength of will stopped staring at her flesh. He hated that it had such an effect on him. Yet he wondered if her appetites could match his. He was a man who liked to explore every crevice of a woman, who felt sex wasn't sex unless it was a complete mind and body experience. Would she be able to meet him? Keep up? He wondered.

"As much as I'd love to talk about me, I believe we have business to discuss," Asha said, shifting gears. "I'd like to be a member of the Sphinx Society."

"Yes, well, there's one problem with that," Durand said as he moved from his desk and sat in the Queen Anne chair opposite her own. Now, face-to-face, it was her beautiful, watchful brown eyes that distracted him and not her delicate tan shoulders and beautiful skin. She was so very small, so very delicate, even her hands, which she kept neatly folded on her knees. "You need an *invitation* to join, and I'm afraid you do *not* have one of those." He cleared his throat, his gaze never leaving hers.

"You seem to have a problem with always showing up uninvited."

Annoyance tugged at the corner of her mouth.
"Do I? Well, I'm not the kind of woman who waits
around hoping to be rescued," she said. "I'm a
woman who goes after what she wants."

"Indeed." One of her sexiest qualities, he thought.
Like so many brash Americans, she seemed to believe that sheer force of will could make anything
happen. Except there was wishful thinking, and
then there was brutal reality. The French knew all
about brutal reality. "But in this case, I'm afraid,
you can't just muscle your way in. No matter how
American, nor how *rich* you may be."

"My lawyers say…"

"Your lawyers have no sway here. This is a private club. I am its owner, and I decide who joins.
Period. *C'est comme ça.*" Durand leaned back in
his chair.

She reached out and put her hand on his knee, the
meaning and invitation impossible to miss. He felt a
jolt from the top of his knee to the pads of his feet,
as if her very touch was electrified. His whole body
hummed with nervous energy, every nerve ending
acutely aware of the woman's hands, of where else
he'd like them to be on his body. A hunger came to
life in his belly, a hunger for *this woman.* "Are you
sure there's nothing I can do to persuade you?"

For a second, he couldn't respond. His brain had

shut off, and in its place was just primitive, base need. A need for this woman's hands on his body. A need to put his hands on hers, a primal hunger pervading his being to taste her, to taste all of her. He wanted badly to kiss her again, to have her breathless in his arms, to make her moan.

No. To make her beg.

If she'd had so many men before him, then he'd make damn sure he was the one she'd never forget. It almost felt like a challenge he couldn't ignore. A ripe, perfect grape in need of plucking.

He studied her hand on his knee, hoping she couldn't know the effect it was having on him right now, the unsettling need she'd awakened, the yawning need.

"We could…how do you say…fuck? Right here?" He spread out his hands to show the expensive Persian rug beneath their feet. He had no intention whatsoever of taking her here, on his office floor, in full range of Madelyn and her army of attorneys, but *she* did not know that. She assumed he was an uncouth playboy relic, so he'd act like one.

The offer took Asha by surprise. He saw the flicker of—was it panic?—cross her face. She withdrew her hand from his knee. Interesting, then. The woman who supposedly had no shame, with a reputation for being the world's most vicious man-eater, might actually be…shy? When he called her on her advances…she withdrew? Perhaps that meant she wasn't as confident as she appeared. Maybe she was bluffing. Maybe all that bluster about being a woman unashamed about her appetite might not be completely true? It would explain her unease when he'd mentioned her reputation.

"Here?" Asha scoffed. "But my lawyers are right outside…"

"Let them hear us. Who cares what they think?" Durand pressed. "Surely not a woman as bold as you."

Pink crept up into her cheeks. She was *blushing*. Oh, this was perfect. Truly perfect. He'd put her back on her heels. The way she shifted in her seat made her seem like more of a prude than a party girl. Maybe it had all been an act, the worldly seductress nothing more than a blushing innocent.

And now that he had her retreating, he'd press his advantage.

"Yes, well…" Asha's attention darted to the door, which did not have a lock. So she'd clocked that. And it made her uncomfortable. She definitely wasn't the wild seductress of her reputation. Yet somehow, that fact made her…even more seductive.

"Did you not want to make this transaction? I thought that is what you came here for." He reached out and stroked her cheek, her chin, his finger trailing down the side of her neck. His motive unmistakable.

"Well, of course I do, but…" She bit her lip. She was trying to come up with an excuse. He would let her try.

"But…?" he prompted.

"Well, how can we have *decent* sex here?" She swept her hand across the sunlit room of his office. "And with people hearing."

"That makes you embarrassed?"

"No." She lied. He could tell by the way her gaze darted away from his.

"The blush on your cheeks and the way you won't meet my eye tells me otherwise, I'm afraid."

Asha coughed and stood, turning her back to him so she could glare at the Eiffel Tower. "I am not embarrassed."

"Do you always lie about such things?" This was extraordinary. A seductress with *shame*. A man-eater with performance anxiety. Oh, my, my. What would he discover about her next?

"No," she snapped. "If you want sex for the membership then, fine." She whirled, eyes furious, as she angrily tugged at the side zipper of her sundress, as if she planned to peel off her clothes and get this over with. As if it were a bothersome exercise. That was a bit insulting, to be honest. Durand didn't want to be a chore. He'd make sure he wasn't. Not to her or anyone else.

"No, no, no, ma chère." He stood and stopped

her from undressing herself in a rage. "I tease you. I do not mean to make you give yourself to me."

"You don't?" Now she was utterly confused.

"I told you that I do not accept *gifts* of this nature in exchange for membership."

"Then…" She blinked fast, her brain catching up to the reality. "You are just teasing me? Playing with me?"

He was. "I am just having a bit of fun."

"At my expense." She tugged up her zipper and angrily crossed her arms on her chest. "So I am wasting my time, then? You won't give me a membership?"

"I did not say that." He grinned. "But there might be one thing you could do." He leaned even closer to her, so now they were less than a foot apart. Her eyes grew wide, excited even, at the prospect of her trap working.

"Anything," she murmured, voice low but cautious. Her perfume filled his nose and drove him a little bit wild. How he'd love to get beneath that designer scent to her skin. Her real self.

He smiled slowly. "You are willing to do…whatever I ask?"

"Yes," she nodded frantically. "Whatever you want."

"You could say '*please.*'"

She laughed, a sexy, throaty laugh. But he didn't join her. It was time to teach this impatient, brash, *full-of-herself* American some manners. When she realized he was serious, the laugh died in her throat.

"You mean it?" she managed.

Durand cocked his head to one side but said nothing. "Those are my terms." He shrugged one shoulder. "How do you Americans say? Take them…or leave them?"

"You mock me." Now Asha's lips flattened in disapproval. Anger danced once more in her eyes.

"On the contrary, Ms. Patel. I'm only trying to see if you have any humility."

Asha stood, sweeping her white skirt across his knee. "I'll not be insulted like this," she said. "Next you'll ask me to beg."

"Perhaps." Durand couldn't help himself. He chuckled, low in his throat. Making her beg *would* be so very satisfying.

"I don't beg." Asha set her lips in a thin, determined line.

"Perhaps you have not met the man strong enough to make you *want* to beg," Durand offered. He sat back in his chair and interlaced his fingers across his knee. "Surely, saying *please* is an easy exchange for a membership you want so much?" Durand almost enjoyed watching her squirm. He could see her fight with herself: her pride on the one side, her desire to get her way on the other. He loved it. Loved watching her inner battle. She *was* intriguing, and he honestly wasn't sure at that moment which side of her would win. Durand, who could read people better than anyone he knew, couldn't predict this little heiress. Maybe that's why he found her so intriguing.

"If I say please, what guarantee do I have that you're serious? That you'll give me what I want?"

Durand raised both eyebrows. "Why, none at all. You simply will have to trust me."

Asha weighed his offer for just a split second.

"You're impossible." She snatched her bag from the chair and stomped to his door. Durand stood as well, still grinning.

"No. I believe I am just the one…how do you say…holding all the cards?"

Asha let out a disgusted grunt and, glaring at him, opened his office door with such force, it banged against the line of first edition books on his shelf. Asha swept out without a backward glance, and her attorneys, surprised, scrambled to their feet to follow her out of the office.

"How rude," Madelyn exclaimed in French as she stood, surprised. "I hope she has learned the lesson that she can't just demand everything she wants."

"Somehow, I don't think she's learned that at all," Durand said. "I have a sneaking suspicion I'll be seeing her again. Sooner rather than later."

CHAPTER THREE

ASHA SIPPED CHAMPAGNE from a crystal flute, staring out the window of one of her father's private jets as they headed upwards to cruising altitude. She stewed in the anger that still bubbled in her belly. How dare Durand toy with her? She wasn't some dumb socialite, or another kind of woman that likely had no other ambition than to worm her way into his bed. Asha studied the puffy white clouds above Paris and fumed. She'd never been so soundly rejected in all of her life. Never been so *dismissed* as inconsequential by anyone, and she'd met the Queen of England. If anyone had the right to give her the cold shoulder, it was the Queen. Not Mathis Durand. So what that his family made their fortune in the shipping business: more than a century ago, his father hadn't earned his money, but inherited it. Her father defied much greater odds to build a tech empire today.

She understood all too well the tension between

old money and new money. She *had* gone to one of the East Coast's most revered girls' boarding schools. Asha knew firsthand that money didn't solve all problems. Not among the old money elite who felt it was their job to keep newcomers out, especially ones who weren't the "right" race. She remembered the taunts some of the meaner girls had leveled at her, taunts about the color of her skin, the fact that her family came from India, the horrible nicknames that stuck with her through a whole year. She knew what they were trying to tell her: her skin was brown, she was new money, and she would never be welcomed into their social circles, circles with a legacy that stretched back generations to the families who were now household names, who'd built America. In their eyes, there wasn't any room for newcomers, especially those who looked different than them. But she'd proved them wrong. She'd survived it all. She'd outmaneuvered the bullies. She'd left that damn school as one of the most popular girls. Hell, she'd been *class president.* And she wasn't about to be laid low by the owner of a private club, no matter how entitled he believed he was. She'd come too far for that.

Asha watched Paris fade as the plane rose higher in the clouds, and the Eiffel Tower grew ever smaller until she could see it no more. The worst part of all was how easily he seemed not to care about her advances, how he seemed immune to her charms. It was insulting on many levels, but most of all because *she* was most definitely *not* immune to his. Even now, she remembered the determined and experienced way his lips had moved on hers, the way a simple kiss on the balcony in Sweden had electrified her entire body. But rather than being keen on repeating the experience, Durand seemed not to care. Was that how he kissed every woman he met? Did she really offer him nothing new? She thought of the women who eyed him at that party, as if he were a juicy steak they intended to devour. Maybe not. Maybe she hadn't made an impression on him.

Damn him, then.

Still, it was the sting of his rejection that burned. He'd hinted he wanted to take her, there in his office, but when she'd finally agreed...he'd told her no. Men didn't reject her. She rejected *them*. Did she use sex *appeal* to get what she wanted? Sure. Had she done that unfortunate fast food commercial naked, wearing only suds and playing up her sex kitten image? Sure she had, but it had just been for fun, a lark. When it came to men actually getting into her bed, she was...picky. Beyond picky. Downright particular.

Truth be known, she often rejected them long before even the first kiss. Ironic, then, she had such a reputation for sleeping around. It was all her ex-suitors bemoaning her on their social media accounts, implying more happened than did. Just like Connor. Hell, they'd only ever heavy petted across their clothes before he found the need to two-time her with a model. But it worked for his public profile: player plays the player. She didn't care what people said about her. Besides, being a bad girl had its perks. Typically, she could get away with more.

Not to mention that it was one way to rebel a little against her tight-fisted father. She didn't mind that at all.

She set the almost empty champagne glass down in the round, gold-lined holder in the polished wooden arm of her chair. Asha glanced at her phone. On her father's plane, the pilot allowed her to keep it on for the duration of the flight. One of the many perks of private travel.

I expect to see you tomorrow at the board meeting.

She sighed. She wouldn't be going to his board meeting in San Jose. She was headed to London. To one of Durand's next parties. She'd seen the party on his assistant's computer screen because she'd been too slow to hide it. She had her own priorities, and they didn't include sitting in on earnings meetings or charming members of the board on her father's behalf. Besides, her father had long since made it clear that she was to be *seen* and not *heard* at the board meetings. He called all the shots. Her father: the control freak.

I'm not coming. You know why.

Her phone rang then.

"Why can't you come?" Her father's clipped British accent came through the line crystal clear with his disapproval.

"Have you considered my proposal about cutting emissions for the entire company?" she asked him.

He sighed, irritated. "No, you know that our bottom line…"

"Or…letting our warehouse workers organize?"

Her father let out a groan. "You know that would kill our bottom line. We've talked about it and we decided."

"No, *you* decided." This was the problem with trying to work with her father. He made all the rules, and all the decisions, and wasn't much even in the frame of mind to debate issues, either. He wanted her to be a part of the business, but only as a child at the Thanksgiving table generations ago—to be seen, not heard.

"Asha. Please. Should I cut off your funds? I don't want to do it, but if you won't meet the family obligations…"

She glanced out her small window as the private plane glided over the fluffy clouds below.

"Go ahead." This was met with shocked silence. Good. She wasn't just a trophy her father got to sit at the board table. She was a smart woman with her own ideas. Her own goals.

"You can't be serious. You won't have the money to do your absurd socializing. All those ridiculous videos you make…all those parties. When are you going to settle down and get serious?"

"Those videos make a lot of money, Father." So did her new cosmetics line, and her legion of followers who wanted to know about every new outfit she donned, every new party she went to. They'd make sure she didn't go hungry. "This image you hate so much funds all those parties."

"You couldn't survive without me and you know it. You do not want me to cut you off." Her father still couldn't believe it. But then again, he'd always tried to control her with money.

"You're wrong, Dad. I don't *need* your money. I've not been living on your money for some time." That felt good to say. After years of trying to work her way out from under his thumb, of dreaming of real independence, she was finally really doing it.

"The very plane you're on is *my* plane."

She glanced around the gilded interior. Sure, she'd miss the private jets. But she could still afford to fly first class, commercial. And she would. It wasn't all *that* much of a sacrifice. She could forgo his private cars, too. There were such things as rideshares, after all.

"H-how did you…" Her father sputtered on the line, truly amazed. Well, let him be amazed. He'd been so wrapped up in trying to get her to take a more prominent role in his company that he'd not noticed she'd already struck out on her own. She didn't want to carry on his legacy. She wanted to forge her own path. She just wasn't sure what that might be—yet. If she took over her father's company, she'd just be a legacy kid for her whole life. She wanted to have something that was uniquely her own.

"Because I worked hard, Dad. I learned that from you." She glanced upwards at the roof of the private jet.

"You are making money from the social media… things you do?" Her father still sounded shocked.

"Yes. Those things make money. So do the cosmetics I sell."

Her father made a frustrated sound. "But the woman on your accounts…that is not you, Asha."

Asha sighed. "It's a persona. Nothing more. And it's very, very profitable."

"I don't understand why you have to be *someone else* to make money. I am always myself. I do not pretend to be someone else."

"You're you, Dad."

"Yes. That's the whole point." Her father sucked in a frustrated breath. "I want you to take a bigger role in The Skycloud, Asha. You know this. Please. Do it for me, if not for the money."

Her father's voice had softened, and she did realize how much this meant to him. On some level, she understood this. Knew that he only wanted to make sure the business he'd created lived on in the family. Yet this wasn't *her* dream, and she had to somehow make him understand that.

"Dad, I really can't…"

"No. Don't tell me a final no. Think about it."

"Dad." Asha sighed in frustration.

"Just *think* about it. Do that for me."

"Fine," she said, relenting, even though she knew this only delayed the inevitable. Asha had thought about it. Her answer was no, but she was still working out a way to tell her father this. He'd built the company from the ground up, and she was his only natural heir. But tech stocks and new ways to track user data online just didn't appeal to her. She wanted to do something else with her life. She just wasn't sure what yet.

"What's to think about? I want you by my side."

"Yes, but…" She wanted to walk her own path. Yet she was having trouble breaking the news to her father. She would. One of these days. Just not

now. "We'll just talk about it later. By the way, have
you ever heard of the Sphinx Society?"

"No. What is it? A restaurant?"

Asha laughed. "It's a club. For the elite."

Her father clucked his tongue, sounding disapproving. "Sounds like a reason for rich people to pat
themselves on the back." Her father didn't believe in
status or the *look* of things. He was too busy taking
over the world, one single-day delivery at a time.

"So you're not a member?" she prodded.

"No. Why waste my time with vanity projects?
I have real work to do."

Somehow, the fact that her father *wasn't* a member made her want membership even more. It would
be one more step to staking out her little claim on
the world. Besides, she wanted nothing better than
to somehow get the best of Durand. She wasn't
going to take no for an answer. Boarding school
had taught her that you either fight for your rightful place in the world or you just let the world walk
all over you.

Not to mention, reporting from one of his invite-
only parties was exactly what her followers would
go crazy over. She'd be even more popular. She'd
sell even more mascaras. Win-win.

Then she hung up and began thinking about
just how she was going to get past security at the
next Sphinx Society party that next evening at the

British Museum in London. She knew this because she'd managed to plant a bug on Madelyn's computer during her little meeting with Durand. Turns out, it wasn't all a bust.

To London, she planned to go. And she couldn't wait to see the look of shock on Durand's face when she showed up uninvited. Again.

The Egyptian sculpture gallery at the British Museum the next evening was awash in low purple light and filled with guests—in masks—wearing the trademark white and black, as they sipped champagne and chatted among themselves. Asha wondered why everyone was required to be black and white, and told herself she'd file away the question for Durand later. Was he allergic to color? Still, this time, she came prepared, wearing a tight-fitting, shimmering black dress with a plunging neckline and a matching black glittering mask across her eyes, but all she could do was gape at the surroundings: massive Egyptian sculptures dotted the exhibit, making her feel small. Ramesses II, among others, and then...the main attraction at the center of the room, the Rosetta Stone standing in a large glass display case, the very stone that made translation of the hieroglyphics possible. History here was impossible to ignore. It screamed from every glassed-in exhibit, from the statues of the

Parthenon to upstairs, where Cleopatra's mummy lay entombed in a display case. Treasures lay here from all over the world, history shouting from every corner. No wonder Durand picked this place, Asha thought. He and his obsession with history.

Asha had never been to the British Museum before, and certainly not after hours where all the rich and glittering guests wore formal designer clothes. She scanned the crowd for Durand, but failed to find him amid the many dozens of men with dark hair swept back, masks across their faces that hid most of the true identities as they moved past the giant six-feet-tall golden vases, palm fronds splayed at the top, like the world's most expensive palm trees. She stared at the enormous bust of Ramesses II, and the old black-and-white photos of the original archeologists about two hundred years ago, taking the statue from a temple. Asha wondered who gave them the right to take the statues. Why was Ramesses here at all, and not in a museum in Cairo?

"Impressive, isn't he?" a familiar voice whispered in her ear, the French accent faint but unmistakable.

She turned to see Durand, hiding behind a silver mask, his white tuxedo impeccable. Even though half his face was covered, she'd know that crooked smile anywhere. They were the perfect mix, it seemed: he in white and she in black. She felt her heart tock up a notch and hated that the very presence of him sent blood flowing straight to her thighs. She was only glad he couldn't read her mind.

"I was just wondering what gave them the right to take all these treasures. Don't they really belong at home, in Egypt?"

Durand's sensual mouth tugged up to a smile. "Ah, you Americans. Still so troubled by colonialism."

"Well, we *were* colonies. The wound's still a little fresh."

"These treasures are well taken care of," Durand said. "If they were left, they might have been destroyed."

"Or maybe it's because *history* is written by the victors, so they believe artifacts belong to them, too."

"Is that why you don't like history, Ms. Patel?"

"Maybe," Asha said, not even sure herself why seeing these world treasures bothered her so much. After all, they were spectacular, and on display free to the public. Except, of course, during glitzy parties, where the super-rich gathered with their expensive champagne and used the backdrop to socialize. "I just don't think the British Empire should decide where these treasures reside."

"The British aren't all too blame. Take the Rosetta Stone." Durand nodded behind them to the tablet in the case, the one with hieroglyphics and Greek. "It was found by French soldiers."

"And yet it's here. In London."

Durand shrugged slightly as he took a step closer. "Well, the stone belongs here. But you, Miss Patel, I'm afraid, you're once again without an invitation."

Durand put his hand on the small of her back, just a tiny bit of pressure. His hand felt big and warm and strong, and she had to fight an urge to lean into his touch. A shiver ran down her spine.

"Perhaps we should discuss your trespassing in private."

"I'd rather discuss how you'll be approving my *membership* in private." Durand smiled, amused.

"You are an optimist, aren't you?" Durand moved her away from the Egyptian statues and Asha let him steer her.

"More like I'm always determined to get my way," she said, as Durand led her out into the Great Court, the giant open circular heart of the museum, and as a nearby sign proclaimed, the largest enclosed "public square" in Europe. High above them, latticed steel over glass sheltered them from the night air. The stars in the sky were covered by clouds. Soon, he took her directly into the massive cylindrical building at the center, and inside, she found herself in an enormous reading room. Up above, a domed ceiling with a single circular glass window showed the dark night sky. The lights, already dimmed, gave the room a solemn feel, and large drapes across furniture and a scaffolding for construction sat against some of the shelves.

"This part of the museum has been closed for some time, and they're renovating it now," he said. "We won't be disturbed here."

He closed the brass double doors behind them, and a little bolt of excitement traveled from her head to her toes. She was alone with him here in the dim light of the circular room, most of the furniture hidden beneath tarps, and she wondered just what that meant. Could she explore the electric connection with him? Could she—finally—convince him by any means necessary that she deserved a society membership? She felt a tremor of nerves through her arms and down her fingertips. She really wasn't like her online persona, the one who jumped men on a whim. It was simply a mask she wore, like the one across her eyes right at this moment. Yet neither one was making her feel very brave at the moment. Still, she wanted this. More than she'd wanted most anything she could remember. She wanted the membership, but beyond that, she wanted Durand. His hands on her. She'd happily sacrifice her body to him if that meant getting what she wanted. And part of her knew it would be no sacrifice at all.

She turned to him and took off her mask, slowly.

"If you want to get me alone, Mr. Durand, all you needed to do was ask." She laughed at her own joke as she took a step closer to him. He didn't move and kept his blue eyes on her. She reached up and took the edges of his mask, and he let her. Might as well play to her reputation. Men loved it. She could do brash and brazen all day.

His eyes swept her slowly from head to toe, taking in her entire body, lingering at her plunging neckline. She grinned. Men. So predictable. Maybe this wouldn't be the challenge she thought. She arched her back, ever so slightly, giving him a better angle, glad she'd opted not to wear a bra beneath the thin-strapped dress. Eventually, he pulled his gaze away from her body and studied her eyes.

"I want a membership," she said, feeling confident now. "I want an invitation." Above their heads, in the circular skylight, the moon broke free of the clouds, sending a silver light into the room, brightening the dimness.

Durand slid his hands into his pockets, rocked back a little on his heels. "You cannot demand either, I'm afraid."

"I'm not *demanding.* I'm *asking.* Nicely." She took a step back from him. Now was the time to offer what most men wanted. She didn't have to give herself, not really, just a little peek, a little tease. Men were usually so easily swayed. Easily distracted. And she could play the role they wanted. She'd just pretend. Like she usually did. "I know you said you do not usually accept *gifts,* yet would you make an exception?"

Except, of course, she did expect something in return.

She'd hadn't forgotten the debacle of his office, where he'd called her bluff about sex. This time, she was ready. She wouldn't be blindsided, because this time she'd be the one to make the first move, the one to keep him off guard. Asha moved one strap of her dress down her right shoulder, slipping her arm out of it. Then, she eased the left strap down. She let the top half of the dress fall to her hips, the cool air of the room brushing across her chest, making her brown nipples stand at attention. Asha stood, topless, watching him as his eyes roved her bare skin, as his mouth tightened with want. She saw his arms stiffen, as if he were trying to fight the urge to touch her. Let him fight. It was a fight he would lose. She knew men enjoyed her body. Knew what her gravity-defying breasts did to their libidos. She knew her best angles and strongest assets and exactly how to use them. She also knew that a mere touch, a mere glimpse, and most men were putty in her hands. Men, in her experience, were simple and predicable.

Now, she stepped closer, reaching out her hand and grasping his wrist. She pulled his hand upwards to her right breast, putting his hand beneath it. He didn't fight her. Couldn't seem to fight her, as he touched her, firmly, but gently, cupping her.

He flicked his thumb across her nipple, causing it to harden even more.

"Please?" she whispered then, as he stared at her pointed nipple. "Isn't that what you wanted? Me to beg?"

Her voice was so low, almost a hoarse whisper, that she wasn't sure at first if he'd heard her. But then, he looked up at her face. She could read him like an open book, a book that spelled out want. Desire. Need. She could feel it thrumming in him, a live wire, snapping with electric power. Want was a dangerous thing, she knew. Want made people do things against their interests, made them make foolish decisions. Hadn't her father told her a thousand times that the key to being successful in business was not to let emotions rule? Durand was fighting his own desire. She could see it in his face as he struggled to keep it completely expressionless. He held her as if weighing his options, knowing the route he'd take might just be inevitable.

Then, he shook his head slowly. He lowered his hand and backed away from her.

She couldn't help but raise her eyebrows in surprise. This wasn't what she expected. Not at all. She was supposed to be the one in control, not him. Never him.

"You can't use your body to get what you want, Ms. Patel," Durand said after a beat, but his voice came out a little bit hoarse, a little strained, as if the effort of holding himself back took every bit of willpower he had. "I will not make an exception."

She moved to him, trailing a fingernail down the front of his shirt, and brushed the fly of his white tuxedo pants.

"Oh, it's not my body I plan to use to get what I want." A tempting smile curved the edges of her red lips. "It's yours."

She flattened her palm against the front of his fly, feeling him very much alive, very much ready for more. Some men needed *more* persuasion, and perhaps he was that kind of man. A hand job, then, she thought. Easy enough. As she rubbed him, she fanned the flames of his desire. She could see it in his eyes, the struggle. Could see how much effort it took for him not to move. Yet the only way for him to stop this, she knew, was to leave her in this room. Leave her, bare chested, her hand on the fabric against his cock, and she didn't know any man with that kind of willpower. She rubbed him harder, feeling him come alive, strain against the fabric. She knew exactly what would drive him wild. What drove every man wild. She undid the latch of his pants, sliding his zipper down. Her heart thudded in her chest, but she could do this. Just because she was used to playacting, flirting from afar, didn't mean she was a virgin with no skills. She reached in and found him bare, found him ready, found him so very, very thick.

She wrapped her hand around him and his lips parted, his pupils growing big and dark. She knew what she needed to do. Knew that despite his apparent sophistication, Durand, in the end, was like any other man, led by his cock. This was going to be easier than she thought. She'd have the membership in no time, and she'd be able to file Durand under one of many challenges met and answered. She worked him with her hand, delighting in how much her touch affected him. Soon he'd been begging *her* to join the society. She had no doubt about that. Good, she thought. All according to plan. A few more minutes, and the society membership would be hers.

But then, he took her by the wrist, freezing her motion. She glanced up at him, surprised, but before she could protest, he'd lowered his mouth to hers, hungry. She matched his appetite, her mouth open to his, her tongue lashing his. He tasted like champagne, and something more dangerous, a power she hadn't anticipated. But somewhere in the kiss, her game became serious. She was no longer the one in control. He deepened the kiss, pulling her to him with a strong hand to the small of her back. Her nipples pressed against his stiff tuxedo jacket, and his hardness against her lower abdomen pressed against the shimmering, thin fabric of her dress. Now he was taking off his jacket, shrugging out of it, lips still on hers. And she found herself forgetting, for a minute, what she was doing here, why she was here, and all she wanted was his hands on her.

Maybe she'd need more than a hand job. Hell, maybe she'd even enjoy it. A dirty little quickie right here in the dark. It went against her usual strategy, but this was an unusual situation. Maybe she could let herself go enough to enjoy it. Her few real lovers hadn't always been able to make her come, and too often, she'd been left unsatisfied. That's why she preferred to reject them first, before she found that her body wouldn't cooperate with her own mind, that she couldn't reach the finish line, even as her partners sprinted right past it. The irony of the fact that Ms. Party Girl couldn't really climax wasn't lost on her. She realized how ridiculous the situation was, but it was the truth. She'd worked hard to craft her persona, the face she showed to the world. But it wasn't her true self.

Durand's kiss told her that he wouldn't be fooled. He demanded her whole mouth, hell, her whole body in that kiss. He wouldn't let her hide. Wouldn't let her pretend. Maybe Durand would be different than other men. Maybe she'd even let him try.

She worked his shirt buttons, hungrily taking his mouth, and he inched down her bare lower back, finding the zipper of her expensive dress. In seconds, the dress dropped to the floor, in a pool by her red-soled stiletto Christian Louboutins.

Now she stood naked before him, wearing only a lacy thong. He still wore his shirt, though she'd gotten half the buttons undone, the muscled shape of his chest visible in the low light. She itched to touch his bare skin and wanted to put her hands in his shirt.

But then, his hands rested on her hips as he moved her backward, as she carefully stepped out of her dress. His lips demanded more of her, and they moved back into the room, until the ridge of a table hit the back of her upper thighs. In one quick motion, he'd lifted her up on the table. His mouth trailed down her neck then, down the front of her chest, and his tongue found her nipples. She gasped as he took one in his mouth, gently, the pressure of his teeth on the edge creating a pool of want between her legs. Now it was her turn to feel desire burning in her belly, to feel the rage of need churning in her.

She forgot completely about the Sphinx Society, about her little game with Durand. About how she needed to be in control. Now, all she wanted was his hands and his mouth and everything he could give her. And she wanted it now. Asha opened her thighs and pulled him closer to her. All that separated him and her was the thin little stretch of lacy fabric of her thong. In that moment, she didn't even think about consequences: about protection or about whether or not she'd actually even get the membership she so wanted. All she knew was that she burned for this man in a way she hadn't burned for anyone. Perhaps ever.

She wanted him. And she rarely wanted anyone.

She could feel him pressing against her pelvic bone, could feel the thick weight of him against her as he shifted his attention to the most delicate spot on her throat.

"Yes," she whispered as she glanced up at the full moon overhead in the circle of paned glass in the domed ceiling. "I want you inside me."

He pressed harder against the thin fabric, and his hands went to the edges of her thong. She suddenly wanted him to rip it away, the passion between them burning so hot he couldn't help himself. Yet Durand hesitated.

Why? Her brain burned with impatience. Her whole body simmered with need. Now this wasn't a game, wasn't about any membership, it was about something deeper and more primal. It was about her want.

And then, he backed away from her. Cold air hit her bare body. She blinked fast in the near darkness. What was he doing?

She struggled to understand why as she watched him tuck himself inside his fly and zip his pants.

"I'm afraid I cannot accept this…" He glanced at her bare chest, her nearly naked body, prostrate on the table. "Bribe. Beautiful…and tempting…

though it may be. Especially since I know this isn't you, Asha."

She froze then. Feeling more than naked. Feeling vulnerable. "What do you mean?"

"You are playacting. You are wearing a mask of your own choosing."

"No, I'm not." At least, she wasn't now. Maybe it had started as a game, but the pounding of her heart in her chest was real, the thumping of want in her belly as true as it got.

He took another step backward and grabbed the tuxedo jacket across a nearby chair. He dusted it off. His composure was returning, bit by bit.

"I'll allow you time to compose yourself, Ms. Patel. Then I'll have someone escort you out."

With that, he turned on his heel and left her, nearly naked, completely unsatisfied, and hot with embarrassment—and want. She panted, wondering what the hell had just happened. Somehow, he'd seen through her tactics, seen to the slightly scared, intimidated woman beneath. But how? She couldn't be that obvious. She was too good at acting for him to know the truth. Wasn't she?

But, God, the worst of it was, she wasn't even pretending. Her thighs were slick with want, and her pulse beat hard in her temples. Her body had responded to him honestly. His tongue had ignited a white-hot fire in her belly.

And then, he'd walked away. Could it be that

he found her…lacking? That he didn't want her as much as she wanted him? Could he sense that her body was somehow wrong, that unlike other women, she couldn't climax so easily? Her own insecurities ate at her.

Or…was it just as he said, that he was a man determined not to be bribed?

Asha didn't know what to believe, but the rejection burned. He didn't find her sexy? The look in his eyes told her otherwise, and yet…here she was. Alone and abandoned.

This would *not* be tolerated, she thought, as she hopped off the table and snatched her dress angrily off the floor. Her hurt and insecurities dissolved beneath a tidal wave of fury. She'd never been treated this way. She wouldn't *allow* it. Not now. Not ever.

CHAPTER FOUR

DURAND COULDN'T CONCENTRATE on anything his assistant, Madelyn, was saying in the makeshift office of the penthouse suite in the Savoy Hotel in London. His large windows overlooked the Thames, and in the distance, the London Eye circled slowly, taking tourists upwards to view the city. He barely noticed them or the inside of his posh suite with the plush white couches and golden pillows facing a green marble fireplace as Madelyn went over the last of the bills from the night before. They were supposed to be tying up loose ends from the party, but his mind was elsewhere. Durand was consumed, too busy remembering the feel of Asha's bare breasts in his hands. Heavy. Soft. Perfect.

And the bright light of triumph in her eyes when she worked him, made him hard for her.

"Mr. Durand?" Madelyn's soft voice found him. She had her hands poised on her keyboard. "Should

I reach out to our usual vendor about catering for the big ball?"

"Yes," Durand managed. "Sure, Madelyn. That would be great."

"Is everything all right, sir?" Madelyn, wearing a pristine gray wool fitted blazer and a slim-fit skirt, sat with her legs pressed together on the small love seat, her laptop perched on her knees. Her blond hair was up in a tight French twist.

"Yes, Madelyn. Sorry. I'm just a bit…distracted." That was the understatement of the year. All he could think about were Asha's big dark eyes, wide with want for him, and the taste of her delicious mouth. How he'd only barely restrained himself from taking exactly what she offered him. He'd been so very close to falling into her trap. He refused to be another one of the woman's famous conquests, one more love-struck boy in her wake. He was no boy. He was a man—a man used to being in control. A man who'd worked his entire life to consolidate power, to outmaneuver his enemies, and to show the world he had no weaknesses, especially ones that revolved around feelings and wants. He'd long since learned to control those.

And then Asha Patel strolled into his life and wreaked havoc, dive-bombed his self-control, made him second-guess everything. Because he'd never had a woman he wanted so badly before. He always prided himself on being a man who could take or leave promises of the flesh. After all, one woman was very much like another.

Until Asha.

Asha, who he guessed that the very second he gave in to her, fell into her bed and promised her a membership, would dance out of his life, laughing as she went. And he could not risk that. She was a formidable foe, and one that couldn't be underestimated.

Yet something about the way she kissed, the way she'd pressed her body against his, told him that maybe she wasn't quite as experienced as she claimed. He couldn't say how he knew, exactly, just that the reality of the woman was different than the reputation. There were layers to her that he hadn't expected. Delightful little surprises.

Maybe that was why she stirred such passion in him. Because, God, how he'd wanted her. Like he'd wanted no one in his entire life.

"So, the tallies, sir? Are they suitable?" Madelyn held the bills in her hand from the British Museum and the Savoy. Work this morning seemed pointless.

"Yes," he said, waving his hand, not bothering to double-check the totals. These details didn't interest him this morning. All he wanted was Asha. And he felt as if rejecting her last night was a mistake.

Asha was a proud woman, and he'd rejected her: twice. What were the odds she tried for a third time? But if he were truly honest with himself, he worried that he wouldn't be able to fend off a third advance. He wanted her. Wanted her the way he'd never wanted a woman before. It felt primal, chemical, like their fate was somehow entwined in their DNA. He'd never felt want this powerful before. Never felt like it was out of his control.

Durand prided himself on his self-control. He wasn't like other men who let their petty vices rule their lives. No. Durand's father had taught him to be mentally strong in the usual way rich fathers did: by ignoring him. He knew that was part of the reason he'd taken a small, meaningless society and turned it into a force to be reckoned with. To get noticed. To keep people's notice. To have a place where *he* made the rules. And he so loved the rules.

Asha, on the other hand, hated rules. She clearly looked to circumvent them at every turn. In some ways, he knew that this was all a game to her. All she wanted was a membership, and after she got it, well, he suspected she would disappear from his life forever. And he worried that he didn't want her to leave. Not at all.

"Sir?"

Durand blinked again, realizing that Madelyn had been speaking and he hadn't been listening.

"Yes?"

"Will that be all, sir? Or did you want me to fetch

you some tea?" Madelyn was standing now, laptop folded against her chest.

"No, thank you. And, yes, that will be all." Madelyn nodded once and headed towards the door, no doubt to head back to her own hotel room to finish making the calls and setting up appointments. He needed to concentrate, needed to clear his mind of thoughts of Asha, but the harder he tried, the more he failed. Madelyn hesitated at the door.

"Uh, one more thing, Mr. Durand."

He glanced up. "Yes?"

"Ms. Patel has been calling Sphinx Society board members this morning."

"Excuse me?" The Sphinx Society had a board, just like any other private firm, but it was largely ceremonial. Durand himself owned the lion's share of the company. The board really just worked to give more prominent members a larger role. Durand ultimately still made the big decisions.

"Yes, sir." Madelyn hesitated, seemingly surprised by his sudden pointed interest. "She's trying to bribe them so that she can get a membership."

"You knew about this and you didn't tell me?" Durand felt anger rising in him, uncharacteristically. Normally, he never lost his cool, but he didn't like that Asha was making moves without him knowing about it. He wanted to know everything she planned. Hell, if he were honest, he just wanted to know everything about her.

"I'm sorry, Mr. Durand." Madelyn couldn't meet his gaze. "I—I didn't think it rose to a level—" She looked up at him and swallowed the rest of her sentence. "I mean, she can't bribe the board. They work for you. And even if she did, she won't get an invitation to the club without your direct consent."

"Yes. But I'd still like to be informed." Everything Madelyn said was true, but he still wanted to know what Asha was doing, especially if she was talking to his board. What was she saying? What was she accusing him of? And more importantly...had she given up on trying to win him over entirely? He didn't like that idea. Not one bit. And yet...he admired her resolve, her determination to circumvent him. He'd seen through her playacting, and called her on it, and yet...she still wasn't giving up.

Most people would run home, embarrassed, but not Asha. She had determination. She was stubborn. Stupidly stubborn, and part of him admired her for it. The more he told her no, the more she was determined to get her way. Intriguing.

"You have taken an interest in Ms. Patel?" Madelyn asked, as she struggled to keep both face and voice neutral.

"A passing interest," he said, wondering if that were even true. Asha seemed never far from his thoughts. He was already more interested than he should be. That might be dangerous.

"Yes. Of course." Madelyn looked at the floor, once again working hard to keep her face blank. "I'll keep you informed."

He glanced at his downtrodden assistant, feeling guilty. "It's not your fault. Asha is…" he struggled to find the right words "…a unique case."

"Yes, sir." Madelyn still wasn't looking at him as she turned the knob of the door.

"Wait, Madelyn." Madelyn paused at the door, glancing back at him, hopeful.

"Yes, sir?"

"Can you get me the contact information for Asha Patel, please."

A look of confusion passed across Madelyn's face. "Are you sure, sir? If you just ignore her, she'll go away."

That's only a little bit of what Durand was afraid of. He didn't want her to go away. He wanted her in his bed.

"Just her contact information, please."

"Yes, sir. Right away." Madelyn nodded and then headed out the door, her body language stiffer, her demeanor curt. Durand knew why, but he didn't want to think about his assistant being jealous. Didn't want to deal with her crush at the moment. After Madelyn quietly closed the door behind her, he walked over to the love seat and sank into it. He grabbed his tablet on the coffee table and began doing research on Asha. Objectively, she would be a fine fit for the Sphinx Society. She was no doubt prestigious enough, and she'd created her own cosmetics company, successful in its own right, though no company right now could be remotely as successful as her father's Cloud. It owned most of the market share and seemed intent on gobbling up what was left.

The problem was that so many young, rich heirs like herself were so intent on their social media presence that Durand knew it rattled some of his more privacy-seeking members. The Sphinx Society prided itself on secrecy, after all. The masks were just one of the ways its members could mingle anonymously. The Society took its duty of keeping parties secret and its members' identities secret a top priority. Social media sensations were all but barred from the gatherings. No one trusted them to keep the Society's secrets.

Not that there were many to keep.

He didn't run underground S&M dungeons, or secret meetings for powerful people to rule the world. This was simply a fun distraction, a way for members to feel safe and secure, to let go and have a good time. He pulled up images of Asha, and immediately felt a surge of lust run through him. She was gorgeous, yes, but why this pull? Why did he want her so very badly? He pulled up an image from one of her social media accounts. She was on the beach, wearing a barely-there bikini, her beautiful, perfect bronzed skin darker beneath the sun. The curves of her body made his own respond, as he remembered how soft she'd felt in his arms. How pliant. Willing. Eager.

Eager to play you, an inner voice told him. He couldn't know whether she was really attracted to him or whether this was all a game to her.

He knew that, and yet, he still wanted her. Wanted her badly. He could feel his body stiffen, felt the urge to skim the fly of his own pants. Was he really considering *pleasuring* himself to this photo of her? Right here in his hotel room?

Maybe.

A message appeared on the screen of his tablet from his assistant, with Madelyn's phone number and email.

Durand didn't hesitate. He picked up his phone and dialed her number. He was shocked to discover that she answered on the second ring. Who answered their cell phones from unknown numbers, he wondered?

"Hello?" she said, and her voice, so smooth, like honey, reverberated through his lower abdomen. Even the woman's voice was all sex.

"Ms. Patel," he began. "This is Mathis Durand."

A pause met him on the other end of the line. He wondered, briefly, if she planned to hang up on him. It was risky calling her like this. He knew it. He had, after all, rebuffed her advances the day before. Would she yell at him? Unleash her temper? Or would she be too curious?

"What can I do for you, *Mr.* Durand?" Her tone sounded guarded. So, curiosity won out, he thought. But she was holding yelling or hanging up in reserve. He could guess that much.

"I understand you've been calling my board," he said. He stood and walked to the window of his suite. He watched a boat full of tourists sail down the Thames beneath the big white Ferris wheel.

"Does that trouble you?" The teasing note in her voice both irritated and aroused him at the same time. He fought within himself for control.

"No, Ms. Patel. You don't trouble me. Not at all." That was a lie. She troubled him quite a bit. In all the right ways. That was the problem. "I'm calling because I was wondering if you'd care to join me for dinner tonight."

"Dinner?" she couldn't keep the surprise from her voice. Good. Keep her off balance. That was the only way to win. "And why would I do that?"

"I was hoping to discuss the possibility of your membership. Into the Sphinx Society."

Asha went silent on the other end of the phone.

"What time?" she asked.

"Say 7 o'clock?"

"I think I could squeeze you in," she said, barely able to keep the excitement from her voice. She did want a membership, and badly. He wondered why it meant so much to her and told himself he'd use this evening to find out. "Where shall we dine?"

"Society business can't be discussed in public," he said.

"Is that a rule?" The amusement was back in her voice.

"So, I'd suggest my hotel suite."

"Would you now?" Durand realized too late that it sounded as if he planned a tryst in exchange for her membership. Which he wasn't. This was no quid pro quo. He would never barter for sex. It was beneath him. He never asked for sexual favors. Hell, he never needed to.

"We will only discuss business, I assure you." He felt his own face grow hot and wondered why Asha always made him feel off balance.

"Yes. Yes. Of course." She laughed, the hard edge of a challenge in it. "I'll be there, Mr. Durand."

CHAPTER FIVE

ASHA ARRIVED TWO minutes early at Durand's hotel suite door, butterflies rioting in her stomach, a swarm of them fluttering their tense, anxious wings. She pressed her hands against the thin fabric of her fitted gold cocktail dress that hit above the knee. The shiny fabric clung to her curves and the tiny straps over her almond-colored shoulders were largely decorative. She picked the dress knowing that it flattered, knowing that men would tend to stare at her when she wore it. She knew the effect it had and hoped that Durand fell under the same spell.

She wore slinky, strappy stilettos on her feet, knew that they made her calves flex in a way that men liked. She'd wrapped her dark, nearly black hair up in a French twist, and wore sparkling, dangling earrings she thought drew just the right amount of attention to the curve of her neck. Asha took a deep breath to steady her nerves. She told herself that this was exactly what she wanted: a membership, whatever the cost, and she ought to be relieved that Durand was motivated by the same things as every other man: sex and money.

Though she knew he couldn't be distracted with small things, a simple hand job or a little flash of flesh wouldn't do it. She'd have to go farther. Give her whole self. But she didn't even care about sleeping with him to get what she wanted. No. It wasn't that she didn't care. It might be that she cared too much. She *wanted* this. She worried she'd even jump into bed with him without the membership. She wanted to feel the man's hands on her body. Wanted to grind against him until their bodies became slick with sweat. She was actually *looking forward to it*. And that was a far more dangerous game. How often had men disappointed her? More times than she'd like to count. Then, when she'd fail to be pleased, it was *her* fault somehow.

Frigid.

That was the word one of them used, after, when he'd failed to make her climax. She worked hard to keep men at bay since then. She played to their fantasies of her, she remained in control, and then no one could ever find *her* lacking.

Now she needed to focus. Keep her eyes on the prize: the membership into the Sphinx Society. Durand probably wouldn't be anything special, and it was no good to get her hopes up. She lifted her fist and rapped hard on the double door of Durand's suite. Judging by the lack of doors down the hallway, she assumed the suite must take up the bulk of the corner of this floor of the Savoy Hotel.

Durand opened the door and Asha glanced up at his face, her mouth going suddenly dry. He was more handsome than she remembered, and this time, wore no mask. His dark wavy hair perfectly combed, his sharp blue eyes assessing. He wore a stiff oxford button-down, with three of the top buttons undone. She could see the hint of tanned chest there, and itched to run her hands inside his shirt, feel his smooth, muscled pecs beneath her fingers. He cleared his throat and she realized she was staring at his open shirt collar. Not exactly the best way to play her cards close to the vest.

"Would you care to come in?" He stepped backward, arm sweeping wide, to let her into his enormous luxury suite. She stepped inside, glancing about, but keenly aware of Durand's eyes as they swept her from head to toe. His gaze felt like heat she could feel.

"Wow. This is some place." Asha was used to opulence. After all, she had billions at her disposal, but this had the feel of old-world money. Mirrored walls gave the impression that the suite—largely decorated in white and gold—was much larger. She could see at least three large rooms, and none of them contained a bed. A living area, complete with green marbled fireplace adorned with golden antique statues, and two large white couches met her as she stepped into the room, framed by antique golden floor lamps. A small hallway led to a study with a glass desk and workspace with a wall of shelves containing leather-bound books, and beyond that, a dining table with four plush white chairs. The dining table was already set with a silver candelabra and fine china. Near the table sat a rolling cart with what she assumed must be dinner, hidden behind plates covered by ornate silver domes.

"I'm impressed," she managed as she stepped further inside, hesitating near the foyer table filled with a large yellow-and-white bouquet of roses. She trailed her fingers across the cool white marble tabletop. As she turned the corner, she saw a black-and-gold bar near the dining room, on it, sat a chilled bottle of open champagne.

"Would you like a glass of Dom Pérignon?" Durand asked, his French accent even more pronounced as he mentioned the famous champagne.

Asha raised an eyebrow. The butterflies in her stomach hadn't calmed, and if anything, were still flapping around like maniacs. Maybe a drink would help calm her nerves. "Yes, thank you. I'd like that."

Durand passed close on her left, and he brushed her arm ever so slightly. She felt a little chill run up her arm as she watched him stride purposefully to the bar, his legs long and lean in black pants that hugged him in all the right places. He was a man who kept himself in excellent shape. She appreciated that. So many wealthy men felt they deserved to let themselves go. Not Durand. She watched as he lifted the bottle out of the golden bucket and poured them each a foaming serving in a crystal flute. He handed it to her and her fingers brushed his as she took it. He raised his glass.

"To new friends," he said, and touched his rim to hers with a high-pitched plink.

"I hope to be more than friends," she said, feeling a little brazen as she met his gaze. If she could hide behind her persona, then maybe she had a chance of pulling this off. She knew what she was here for. She needed to keep reminding herself of that.

He stared at her a beat without answering, a playful smile tugging the corners of his lips. No matter how hard he tried to keep aloof, Asha could sense his growing desire for her, see it in the sparkle in his eye.

"Why do you do that?" he asked her and took a sip of his champagne.

"Do what?"

"Play the vixen."

"Who says I'm playing?" Her heart thudded now, the butterflies in a full-out panic in her stomach.

"I'm a good reader of people. I can tell." The

way he was studying her made her believe him. She could not read him and wondered for the briefest of seconds if he'd brought her here just to reject her once more. Her body vibrated with the knowledge that this night would end with their clothes on the floor, but now, her mind intervened. What if she'd read all the signals wrong? What if she'd come here only to be humiliated?

"We all act. After all, isn't that why you have these parties? Where all your guests can wear masks?"

A slow smile spread on Durand's face. "Touché," he conceded.

He was staring at her, and she'd forgotten to breathe. She inhaled, pushing the troubling thoughts from her mind. Surely not. Surely the man could feel the energy between them. It felt immovable, like gravity.

She took a sip of her own glass. The expensive bubbles hit her tongue with an explosion of flavor.

"This is delicious," she murmured, leaning against the bar.

"It should be. Dom Pérignon invented champagne." He held up his glass to the light, studying the bubbles flowing to the service. "Did you know he was a French Benedictine monk? His vineyard at the abbey produced phenomenal white wine in the 1600s at a time when almost all wine in France was red."

"Really? A monk?" She glanced at her own glass. "I guess he had a lot of time on his hands, what with taking all those vows of silence."

Durand laughed a little. "Probably true. Many think he also added the bubbles to the wine, but that came later."

"I like the bubbles," Asha said, taking a long sip. She'd drunk just half the glass and already she could feel a happy buzz beginning at the back of her brain. "This must be expensive."

He glanced over the rim of his glass at her. "Does everything need a price tag to be valued?"

"No," she said after a moment. "But doesn't money make the world go round? People care about how much things cost. That's why they want to drive expensive cars, and own expensive bags."

"Money isn't everything."

"Says the billionaire," she joked.

Durand laughed, showing even white teeth, as the low roar of his amusement rumbled in her belly. She liked making him laugh. She wanted to do it again.

"I think history is more important than money. It's better to know where we come from than to know how much it cost to get here," he added. "So tell me about your own history, Ms. Patel. Who made you the woman you are today?"

"Why is history so important?" The past, to her, was filled with disappointment, like the bullies who tormented her in boarding school. Much better to bury those memories than relive them.

"History is everything. Tell me one thing about you. Something pivotal."

"You first."

Durand shrugged one shoulder. "Very well. I believe history is so important because that's the only legacy my father left to me. He had many mistresses. My mother…she…well, she is French. She understood when she married him—into his very wealthy family—that he'd not be faithful. It was expected he'd stray. What she didn't expect was for him to fall in love with one of them." Durand frowned and stared at his champagne glass. "She told him he could have as many mistresses as he wanted, as long as he came back to her."

"But he didn't come back."

"That's right. One day, he stayed with one of them. Wanted to begin a new family. He divorced my mother, left her hardly anything. The only thing he ever gave me was his board seat to the Sphinx Society. So he gave me history, but…no money." Durand's mouth set in a thin line. "And just a few years after that divorce, Mother died. Heart attack, the doctors said, but I think it was a broken heart."

"That's horrible." Asha felt her heart break for Durand, a man who was all but alone in the world, his mother gone and his father absent. And he hadn't just been alone, he'd been penniless. She'd always assumed he'd inherited his money, but now it was clear he'd had to build it all up. Himself. "How did you afford this?" She glanced around the hotel suite, and at the expensive bottle of champagne chilling.

"I turned Sphinx Society membership into something everyone coveted, and I grew an empire, because of history."

Asha took a step closer to him and he glanced down at her, his blue eyes determined. She suddenly had a new appreciation for the man. He hadn't been born with a silver spoon in his mouth. Or, at least, he'd had it knocked out and had to get his own.

"That's impressive," she said.

He smiled slightly. "That's just necessity," he said. "I did what I had to do."

"What does your father think about it?"

He grinned, even bigger. "My father is not a member. So, he doesn't get a say about it." He seemed to relish the power and that made Asha laugh. She could understand wanting to buck a little against the edicts of an all-powerful father.

She was beginning to understand Durand a bit more. He was a man with something to prove. Just like she was a woman out to do the same.

"Is that so? I guess the tables have turned then. I envy you that."

"Does your father make demands on you?" Durand asked.

"Often." She sighed. "He wants me to be his one and only heir. I don't want the responsibility."

"Don't want it, or worried you can't handle it?" Durand studied her and she felt as if he could see straight through her. Why could he seem to get right to the center of her, but she managed to be able to fool so many others? His insightfulness was unnerving.

"Maybe both," she said. "But it is my father's company, not mine. I want to make something of my own."

"And you worry if you take it over, it'll be somehow diminished."

"No. Well…possibly." Was that it? Was she telling herself she wanted to forge her own path but in reality she was just worried about being measured against her father and coming up lacking? "Enough about The Skycloud. The Skycloud bores me."

"Does it? What doesn't bore you?" He grinned.

"You," she said, the honesty surprising even herself.

"Really?" The sparkle in his blue eyes grew brighter. "Then, by all means, let's sit down and talk about me."

Asha laughed.

"Would that be to your liking, Ms. Patel?" He

motioned towards the table with his nearly empty champagne glass.

"If we're going to be friends, you should call me Asha." She glanced at him and grinned, noticing his lips twitch.

"All right." He paused, the look in his eyes unreadable. "Asha." She loved how her name rolled off his tongue, how his French accent seemed to caress the vowels. "Would you care to sit?"

He gestured to the table and she nodded, walking towards it. He moved easily and pulled out a plush white chair. She sat and he walked around to the other side of the small round table. He grabbed the bottle of champagne and refilled each of their glasses. Then he opened the first silver cover and revealed a plate of chicken and vegetables.

"Coq au vin," he announced.

The warm smell of chicken in wine hit Asha's nose, making her stomach grumble. He put the plate before her, and then a plate on his side of the table. As he slid into his seat, Asha couldn't help but admire the way he moved, as his strong hands took the white linen napkin and gently laid it on his lap.

"Bon appétit," he declared.

"Bon appétit," she echoed back.

"So tell me, Ms.—" He caught himself. "Tell me, Asha." Her name in his mouth raised the hairs on the back of her neck. "Tell me why you don't care for history."

"History is in the past." She put her own linen napkin in hers. "I'm about looking towards the future."

"What's in your past that you hate so much?" he studied her. Asha felt suddenly on display.

"It hasn't been easy to live in my father's shadow." She said it softly, so softly she wondered if Durand even heard. He studied her.

"I can imagine. Money does not solve the problems most people think it does."

"And sometimes it creates new ones."

Durand laughed. "Yes, indeed. What problems did it create for you?"

"Boarding school bullies." She surprised herself with her own candor. She hadn't admitted to anyone about being bullied at boarding school. Not her father. Not her best friends at home. No one.

Durand clicked his tongue. "They were jealous of you."

"They thought very, very powerful and rich people should be blond. And blue-eyed." She remembered the endless taunts, the smirks, behind her back, the nicknames. "They called me *Slumdog Millionaire.*"

"Ah." Durand nodded, as if understanding. "People are scared of what they don't understand, and they're even more scared when it has more money than they do. Your father could no doubt buy them over many times."

Asha laughed. "Yes, he could."

"What did you do about these bullies?"

She glanced at her almost empty champagne glass. "I never backed down. Whatever group they didn't want me to be in, I made sure I was in."

Durand laughed, a low chuckle in his throat. "You thrived on conflict, then."

"I wasn't going to let them win. I had as much right to be in their clubs as they did."

Durand nodded. "True. So, then, is that why you want to become a member of the Sphinx Society so badly?"

Asha studied Durand. "Maybe." Could this be the reason she was so determined to keep going—to get access to a place denied to her? It was about a matter of principle. She didn't take "no" well.

"Initially, as you know, I wanted to catch my boy—" she stopped and corrected herself "—now, ex-boyfriend in the act of cheating."

"Yes, about Connor." Durand swiped his lips with his linen napkin. "I was curious about why you were so jealous…about a man you'd not slept with?"

Asha felt like she'd been slapped. As if Durand could see past her defenses. How did he know that? How did he know Connor was one of those men she'd toyed with, but never let into her bedroom?

"Who told you that?"

Durand's mouth quirked up in a smile. "Connor himself. It was his defense. He didn't think he ought to be kicked out of the society for ungentlemanly conduct when you were…as he said…'a tease.'"

"That's a distasteful term. That's a pillar of rape culture," she managed, her heart thudding as she felt exposed. Vulnerable.

Durand arched an eyebrow. "Yes, well, he is no gentleman."

Asha's mind whirled. Connor was telling her secrets to Durand, and she didn't like it. Also, Durand had stuck up for her? "So you expelled Connor from the club. Why?" she asked.

"Our members should have better sense than to insult someone as beautiful and intriguing as you." He met her gaze, and for a second Asha couldn't say anything. The man was definitely flirting with her, but she wondered if it was a game, or if he really believed what he said.

"Is that why you don't want me in your club? Because I'm so beautiful and intriguing?" she teased.

"Oh, I want you in my society, Asha." He paused, letting this sink in. "I want you very much."

She froze, glass halfway to her lips. Her stomach knotted as she met his stark blue gaze, the want in it suddenly real. He was telling the truth. She felt a tingling at the back of her neck. She realized it was her own excitement. Not just at the possibility of being invited into an elite group, but because she wanted to be invited into *his* life, see behind the curtain he so carefully used to block outsiders.

"Then why...deny me? You've told me no three times." The rejection, actually, still stung.

"You needed to hear a no," he said. "I doubt you've heard it very often."

She felt a flash of anger, heat at the back of her neck. This was far too close to the truth for her liking. "So you're the king then? Ordering us all around? What gives you the right to tell me what to do?"

Durand leaned forward and his knee touched hers at the side of the table. "Because I'm the one who made the Sphinx Society what it is. I say who joins and who doesn't."

"Maybe I'll form my own group then. Keep you out of it," she threatened, her fingers tightening on the stem of her champagne glass.

A slow smile spread across his face. "It won't be very interesting without me in it."

That's what Asha was afraid of, if she was honest.

"So, why am I here? If you're just going to reject me again?"

Durand reached out and touched her knee. His hand felt like hot flame on her bare skin.

"Who said I'm going to reject you?"

"Isn't that what you like to do? It's not *me* that's the tease. You're a tease."

He raised an eyebrow, amused as he withdrew his hand from her knee. "Am I?" He took a bite of his chicken and chewed thoughtfully, as she waited for what he'd say next. That she was out of the society forever? That there was no way he'd even consider allowing her entry? "I don't think you're telling me the whole truth about why you want to be in this club. I don't think it's just because you don't like being told no."

"I don't like being told no."

"Yes, but there's more to this." He glanced at her, and she felt almost naked, as if he could see straight through her clothes, straight through her defenses. He took his heavy linen napkin from his lap and patted the corners of his mouth. "I have a proposition for you."

She felt hope swell in her chest. Hope and nerves. Was this where they got down to business? Finally. Sex for membership. A simple transaction that she was more than willing to make. More than willing. She was looking forward to it.

"Yes?" She left her fork at the edge of her plate, her appetite suddenly disappearing.

"I will give you a membership... If..."

She leaned forward in her chair.

"If you admit to me that the reason you want to join this club is because you want *me*."

Asha laughed, but inside, she felt uncertain. Felt as if he could somehow read her mind.

"I want to make Connor feel bad."

"You've long since forgotten about Connor," Durand said, calling her bluff. This was true. She'd barely given Connor another thought since that day in Sweden when she'd met Durand. "Maybe I'm just here to make a transaction," she said, bluffing. "Maybe this is just all about me trading sex— or whatever you might want—for membership."

Durand's smile grew bigger as he reached out and took her hand. She felt the jolt of contact in her toes. "We both know that's not true. We both know that if I invited you into my bed tonight—no guarantee of membership—you'd come. Willingly. Dare I say…even…happily?"

Asha's heart ticked up a notch.

"You're full of yourself," she managed, but panic began to well in her stomach. Panic that he was right. And that she wasn't in control of this game. Maybe never had been.

"Maybe." He squeezed her hand. "Or maybe, I just know people. Why didn't you take Connor into your bed? He is handsome, no? Famous? Sought after?"

She didn't like being put on the spot like this. "Yes. He is."

"And you were attracted to him."

She glanced down at her plate. "Yes."

"So, why did you not have sex with him?"

So many reasons. She knew if she had sex with him, he'd stop paying attention. But, even more than that, she feared he'd disappoint her. Like every other man. Because inside, she worried that she was *frigid,* a block of ice that would never melt for any man.

"Men are more interesting before they get into my bed than after."

Durand seemed to take this as a direct challenge. "Is that so? Be honest with me. We wear no masks here."

Asha took a shaky sip of her champagne. She felt oddly unencumbered, being brutally honest for once. "I've not met a man who pleased me. Not really."

There. She said it. Her dirty little secret. Of her handful of lovers, none had ever made her come through intercourse. One had managed with his hand, after many clumsy tries. None had managed with their mouths, but, in fairness, only one had ever tried. She'd been amazed at the number of men who found it distasteful. They all expected *her* to please them. But when it came to the other way around? It always seemed a begrudging duty.

A smug smile tugged at the corners of Durand's mouth. "You mean to say, you have not climaxed?"

"Oh, I've climaxed." Asha thought about all the times she'd done it herself. "But typically only at my own hand."

Durand laughed then, a dark rumble of a laugh. "Is that why you run through men so quickly? Because all you have had are inept ones?"

"I find men are always inept in the end."

Durand's blue eyes sparkled. "You have not had the right man, Asha."

"And you are, then? The right man?" she challenged him. Men always said that. They always lied. Then, they always blamed her in the end.

"Oh, I believe I am." He said it with such confidence, even Asha partly believed him. She wanted to believe him.

"How can you be so sure?" she asked, because deep down, she always felt there was something wrong with her. That she really didn't feel pleasure with men because...she was lacking somehow.

"Do you feel the connection between us?"

Oh, she felt it all right. Asha blinked fast, clutching the stem of her champagne glass as she sat across the table from what could be the sexiest man she'd ever met. Sure, he was an egotistical maniac, but that was part of his appeal. The way he was looking at her right now, the way he was studying her, daring her to contradict him, made her want to try.

"I just want a membership," she said, lifting her hand from his. She reached over and touched his knee, the pressure she put there unmistakable. "And I'm willing to...sacrifice for it."

Durand clucked his tongue. "Oh, Asha. We both know it won't be any sacrifice. Trust me on that. You have had some pitiful lovers. But all that changes. Tonight."

CHAPTER SIX

ASHA'S HEART WAS truly beating a mile a minute in her chest as she stared at Durand. The rest of the food on her plate would go uneaten while she sat across from him in the small dining room in his hotel suite. Could he deliver on his promise? Could he show her pleasure that no other man had? She realized she wanted him to try. Had wanted it damn near since the first time he'd kicked her out of his party. Yet part of her, also a small part, rooted for him to fail. There was something about Durand, and not just his impressive physique, or his stark blue eyes, or that sexy French accent, that made her want to bring him down a peg.

"You are going to be the man who finally convinces me that they're worth something?" she challenged. "What if *I'm* the one who blows your mind? Not the other way around?"

His gaze slid slowly down from her face to her cleavage, on display for him in her plunging neckline. "I know you will, Asha."

"So?" She let him stare, enjoyed the attention. "Do we have a deal?" She let the words hang there. All he had to do was say yes. All he had to do was nod his head, and then she'd pounce. Then, they'd get on with what she'd come here for.

Durand ran his finger up her arm, raising goose bumps. "No," he said, meeting her gaze. "We don't have a deal."

"What?" Asha was stunned. Wasn't this what she was here for? Sex for membership? Cold disappointment rushed down her throat, forming a hard ball. She let his knee go and stood, pushing her seat away from the table, the legs of the chair almost catching in the carpet. She walked to the black-and-gold bar, hands shaking. Durand followed her. She could feel the heat of his body as he stood behind her, so close that his breath tickled the back of her bare neck.

"I mean, that I want *you*, Asha, but separate from any membership. Separate from the Sphinx Society. I want *all* of you. One night. It has nothing to do with the society or the membership. But you have to give your body to me. One night. You have to give over everything. That's the only way you're going to have the pleasure you deserve."

"And if I don't?" she asked, still facing away from him, still not willing to turn around.

"Then you won't know what it is to truly climax. To truly let yourself go."

Asha had to admit to herself that she was curious. Durand was so confident. More confident than
any other man she'd ever met. But all of her lovers
had failed. Granted, there hadn't been that many of
them, but even so. He laid a kiss on the base of her
neck. A bolt of desire ran straight down her back.

Asha tried to laugh, but it came out as a little
gasp. "So, you want to have sex, even though you'll
probably just reject my membership anyway? What
kind of deal is that?"

"The only one you'll get," he said and nuzzled
her neck, making all the hairs stand up there. "I
won't pay you with a membership. I'll pay you with
a night of pleasure you'll never forget. You have a
passion in you, Asha. You and I are the same. Nothing is ever enough."

That might be true. Maybe he was the one who
could make her feel something real. Make her body
work in ways that it was supposed to work. How
often had she felt shame after sex with the few she'd
taken to her bed? How often had she felt it was *her*
fault that none of their tricks would work? So often.

"You say men have not satisfied you, but I guarantee I will." He kissed her earlobe, flicking the
edge of it with his tongue. She gasped a bit, the
gentle touch sending shockwaves through her body.
She felt a want for him deep in her belly, a want
that burned hot. His words were so seductive. Did
she have a flame within her? Did she burn with

desire? Maybe she wasn't *frigid*. Maybe she just needed the right man.

"How can you be so sure?" she asked. He sucked her neck ever so slowly. She gasped. He reached up and loosened the twist of her hair. It tumbled down her shoulders. He swiped it to one side and kissed her earlobe.

"I know you," he said. "I know what you need. Give yourself to me. One night. No acting. No masks. Just you." He put his hands on her waist and pulled her to him, flattening her back against his hard stomach. She leaned into him, naturally, her body sinking into his. He reached around her, laying his hand on her bare knee. He moved upwards, ever upwards, taking the hem of her dress upwards, too. He stroked her inner thigh, his hot hand an invitation and a promise. She spread her legs, offering a path for his hand, and he found the mound beneath her expensive silk underwear. He ran a finger down the seam, and she shivered, her breath coming faster now.

"I can feel how much you want me, Asha," he murmured in her ear, as he slipped deftly beneath the fabric, the soft pad of his index finger stroking her gently. "You're ready for me. Admit it, yes? You want me, as I want you."

"I…" She didn't want to admit it. She didn't want to give in. She knew her body wanted him, could feel her want, wet between her legs, and now, his hand stoking that white-hot flame. But admitting this felt like defeat. Felt like she was handing him everything he wanted. It made her feel too vulnerable. Because what if a fire didn't burn in her? What if inside, she was, as she feared, a block of ice? Just like the other lovers had said?

"I can feel the fire in you," he whispered, seductive words. "The other men you've known have been afraid of it. That's why you tire of them so easily. I know just how you feel."

Did he? Did he know?

"Other men won't know what to do with you. With that desire. I do. I know. Let me feed those flames." He pushed against her back, showing her just how much he did want her. She could feel his hefty bulge against her lower back and it made her knees weak. He worked her with his fingers, softly, gently, with a determination that told her he'd make her his. And that's what she wanted right at this moment. Wanted him. Needed him. Something was building inside her, some deep desire, some unlocked want, with the gentle flick of his finger against her.

"I… I…" Her breath came fast. The building of pressure between her thighs. God, was she going to come right here? The man's hand beneath her skirt was going to be enough to push her over the edge? Never had a man touched her like this. Gentle, insistent, knowing. For the first time she worried he might just be the man to break through her barriers, to make her enjoy sex like she'd never done before. She moved with him, arching into his hand, her body making it obvious how much it wanted his touch, how much it needed him.

"Give yourself to me," he demanded. His voice in her ear, in her mind, taking control.

She was going to come. She was going to come right here, against the bar, Durand's hands on her. And then, he stopped, suddenly, whisking his hand away. Her body whined its discontent. She needed that release, needed what his hands would give her. She'd never felt desire like this for a man. Not with any of her other lovers.

"Let the fire grow," he growled, harsher now. She turned and now she was staring into his blue eyes, and saw the determination there, the grit. He put one of his fingers in his mouth. "I can taste you," he said. "I can taste your need."

Her lips parted then. Her thighs burned, and her clit throbbed. She knew he spoke the truth. Knew that he could read the want in her eyes, in her body. She'd never before seen a man so determined to get behind her defenses. Yes. She needed him.

"Yes," she admitted finally, her voice hoarse. "You can have me. One night." She felt like a raw nerve, exposed, and yet, her body would let her answer no other way. She was giving herself to him in a way she'd never given herself to any man. But, she told herself, it was for one night.

"Good," he said, and whisked her into his arms, kissing her open mouth, his tongue lashing hers, both in punishment and in pleasure. Her own mouth opened for him, and took his tongue again, and again, her own meeting his in the most primal of ways. He tasted like something she always wanted, something she always needed. His fingers found the side zipper of her dress and she wanted them there. Wanted all the fabric gone. He slowly moved the zipper down, almost too slowly. He moved a strap of the dress off her shoulder and kissed her bare skin there. She'd gone braless.

He stood back and studied her nearly naked form.

"You're beautiful," he said, his eyes drinking her in. She could see the want in them, the desire, and it fueled her own hunger. He took a step forward and lifted her up on the bar as if she weighed nothing. She went, shocked, as he spread her knees, the hem of her dress hiked up to her waist. His hands were on her underwear, tugging them downward. She felt her own heartbeat in her clit, thudding to an ancient beat.

"I want to taste you again," he said, meeting her eyes, and then he dipped down between her knees, his tongue finding her need. His expert tongue caressed her pulsing want and her mind went wild with desire, like nothing she'd ever felt before. The flames felt like they'd consume her from the inside out. She let out a shriek, and clutched his thick hair, holding on for dear life. Her chocolate brown nipples formed hard peaks as Durand devoured her—there was no other way to describe it. It was if he wanted all of her, stoking her fire with his tongue, building it, a wildfire that threatened to rage out of control. Her back arched, and a cry ripped from her throat. He knew what he was doing. More than knew what he was doing. She felt completely out of control. He knew what her body wanted, knew how to control it, knew how to take her home.

He whipped her with his tongue, bullying her body into submission. But she wanted this. She handed over control to him, handed him her body, and then she came. An explosion of pleasure burst in her mind, her body shuddering with the spasms of pleasure as she cried out, a hoarse cry of surrender.

Her heart beat frantically, and she couldn't catch her breath as Durand lifted his head from between her thighs.

"Now, your body belongs to me," he promised, and she believed him. Whatever she had, she'd give him. Her body was his to control. For this night, anyway. He lifted her then, and she wrapped her jellied legs around him, the muscles in them still quivering, as she held tight to his neck. He walked her through the impressive suite, into the massive bedroom, and laid her on his king-sized bed, pushing aside the white furry throw on the high-thread-count comforter. She sank into the soft bed, nude and vulnerable, feeling the soft sheets on her bare back.

"Tell me," he told her.

"Tell you what?" she asked, raising herself on her elbows.

"That your body is mine. For this night. That you will give yourself to me completely. Because I know this is what you want, no?"

He undressed himself, his nimble fingers undoing the buttons of his expensive shirt. Her breath caught in her throat when she saw his expansive, muscular chest. Lean and cut from hours in the gym. The man took pride in his body. And she admired that. Yes, she did want him. And she wanted to give herself to him—in every way possible.

She nodded. "Yes," she managed, a croak. "My body is yours."

"That's right." He stepped out of his pants, coming away with a condom he'd stashed in his pocket. So the man was planning for this. He'd come ready. More than ready, she realized, as she saw all of him, saw his want, both in his eyes and his hard cock. She leaned forward then, wrapping her arms around him. He groaned, his eyes never leaving hers.

"It's my turn," she said, and then she took him

in her mouth. She wanted to do this. Wanted to show him that she, too, could stoke his flame. She worked his shaft with her hands as she wet the tip of him with her tongue. He groaned, leaning into her, his eyes focused on every move she made. She took him deep and he groaned again, once more, growing even harder in her mouth. Then, he withdrew, gasping.

"You're going to make me come," he murmured, voice low, pupils wide, the want on his face evident. She could see his mounting desire, feel the restraint in his stiff fingertips. She wanted him to let go, wanted him to go wild. She'd make him, too. She reached out with her hand and clasped him.

"That's the idea," she growled, arching an eyebrow. "You need to come."

He pushed her down on the bed as he ripped open the condom package, and rolled the thin latex down the length of him. "No, no, ma chère. You, first."

"I—" But he was already on top of her, his mouth on hers, and then with one strong thrust was inside her, filling her, stretching her, taking her breath away. She arched her back into his movement, his delicious weight on her chest. She clawed at his back, groans of pleasure escaping her mouth, as his tongue once more found hers. He was in control, ever in control, the pace, the depth, all him, even as she rocked her hips to meet his, as she tried to take him ever deeper. She wanted to swallow him, own him, make him cry out with need.

And then, he'd rolled to the side, and she was on top of him. He clutched her heavy breasts, stroking a thumb possessively over one nipple. She arched her back once more as he clutched her, holding on tightly. She loved the feel of his hands on her, loved the strength of them. Their eyes met, and for a second, she fell into that stark blue ocean. An ocean of want. Of need. For her.

He spoke French in her ear, and it felt like a caress. So sexy. So fluid.

"Come for me, Asha," he told her in English, a soft command. "I want to see your face when you come. Burn. Burn bright."

She'd never done such a thing before. Hell, never had the chance, as she'd never had a man's cock make her come before. Could she even do it? He pressed deeper into her, raising his own hips, and she rocked harder, faster. She felt desire build in her, as it had built in the past, though she'd never made it to the end, never found a way to push through. Would she tonight?

"Your body belongs to me tonight," he reminded her, sending electric pleasure through her veins. She liked that idea. Being his. Just for one night. His fingers found her clit then, as she rocked on top of him, his expert fingers teasing her, flicking her, making her lose her mind. He played the perfect rhythm as she found herself rushing to the edge of the waterfall, in a raft she could no longer control. She hit the lip and descended downward in a white rush of heat. Her head jerked back, and her mouth fell open as she cried out, riding him ever harder and deeper until the rush faded. She collapsed on top of him, her hair splayed across his bare chest, gasping for air.

"You're going to kill me."

"If you can die of pleasure, then, yes, I will," he murmured into her hair. "You belong to me, remember?"

"Just for tonight," she told him. That's all she could give.

He pulled away, searching for her eyes. "Yes," he managed, eventually. "Just for tonight." He pushed her off him. "And tonight, I will explore every part of your body." He ran his finger down her side, and across her bare hip. His fingers roamed between her bare legs. "I will have you every way I can," he promised. And then he'd set her up on her hands and knees, and he was behind her, his flesh heavy against the back of her legs, the promise of much more to come. He entered her with a hard thrust and she gasped, as he squeezed her hips. It felt primal, animalistic, the way he drove into her, but she loved it. Loved how he took control, how he seemed to grow ever bigger inside her. Her breasts bounced with each rocking movement, heavy. Just when she thought she might come again, he switched positions once more, tossing her on her back, and pulling her to the edge of the bed. He took her legs and lifted them, putting them up against his shoulders.

She was helpless on her back, her feet in the air, his hands clutching her ankles. She'd never done anything like this before, never done much out of the way of missionary and occasional cowgirl. For all her tough talk, she'd not had much experience in the bedroom, not with a man like this, a man who seemed to know every position of the Kama Sutra, and wanted to show her every one.

"You are mine," he told her, as he worked inside her, ever harder, ever deeper.

And she forgot in that moment to add, *for tonight*. Because in that moment, she was his. Her body was his to control. And she knew she'd come again. Because he'd will it.

"Yes," she gasped, because she couldn't help it. He'd made her his. Completely.

CHAPTER SEVEN

ASHA WOKE THE next morning to a ray of sunlight streaming in through the gap in the curtains of Durand's hotel suite. She reached out her hand across the enormous bed but found it cold and empty. She sat up, blinking, realizing she was naked in Durand's bed, alone.

"Durand?" she called, but no one answered. Where was he? They'd spent almost the entire night exploring each other's bodies, and he'd made her come—again and again. He'd shown her positions she hadn't even thought about, much less tried, and she'd realized with certainty that she was not frigid on the inside at all. She was a ball of flame ready to ignite the second he touched her. All her adult life, she thought *she'd* been the problem. Now, she realized, she'd just never met a man with enough experience to please her, enough care to learn how her own body worked to satisfy her.

But now, that man was gone. She pulled herself from bed, noticing her dress from the night before hanging in the adjoining closet. Her stilettos on the floor beneath. There were no other clothes there, though. She was too groggy to wonder why, as she dragged the white cover sheet from the bed and wrapped it beneath her armpits, in case she wasn't alone. On bare feet, she padded to the bedroom door, which she found closed, and opened it, accosted by even brighter sunlight from open windows. She blinked, wondering what time it was. A clock on the wall in the sitting room said nearly noon. She'd slept six hours or so. Six hours since the weak light of dawn had filtered into their bedroom, when Durand had curled up behind her, spooning her and nuzzling her neck. Had it all been a dream? Surely not.

No. The delicious soreness between her legs told her none of it had been a dream.

"Hello? Anyone here?" she called to the other rooms of the suite. She could see the open dining room and part of the bar. No one answered, and she heard no sounds, and realized she was alone. A pit formed at the bottom of her stomach. Durand had told her he'd own her for one night. And, it seemed, he meant it. There was no sign of him. She ran to the closet near the bathroom and opened it wide. Even his clothes were gone. Not a single piece of luggage, either. She was surprised she felt so… empty. So disappointed. How had Durand managed to do all this and leave without her hearing?

Then again, she knew how: she'd been exhausted, her body pushed to its limits by Mathis Durand.

Had he even planned to say goodbye? She'd been the one to agree to one night. No more than a night. She'd never in a million years imagined he'd be so good at making her body respond to his touch, never imagined a man existed who could make her come so easily, so fully…and so many damn times in a row. Until she'd been with Durand, she hadn't even *realized* she could be multiorgasmic. She'd thought women who did that were simply faking. Now, she realized, they weren't.

But the man who'd done that, who'd lit her fire, was gone. She already felt like mourning him, and that wasn't like her. Since when did she ever let a man truly get under her skin? Sure, she'd flown halfway across the globe to humiliate Connor, but that wasn't because she truly cared about him. That was just a matter of principle, about protecting her brand. She wanted to see Durand because her body craved his touch. Because she wanted to hear his sexy voice in her ear, smell his spicy scent.

Asha walked onward, cotton sheet dragging behind her, to the dining room. She expected to see the remnants of their dinner last night, but instead, the table sported a brand-new tray with a simple breakfast of a croissant, a soft-boiled egg in a stand, and a pot of coffee next to a white cup and saucer. A single white rose sat in a vase on the tray, and

next to it, a white square box large enough to fit
a pair of shoes, tied with a red ribbon. A card sat
near it, signed by Durand. It read:

Merci beaucoup for an amazing night, chérie.
I look forward to seeing you in Berlin.

Berlin? What did he mean? She ripped off the
bloodred ribbon of the box and eagerly opened it,
feeling like she used to as a child on Christmas
morning. Inside, she saw a golden mask, and beneath that, an official invitation to the Sphinx Society's next party in Berlin in two weeks' time. Her
mind whirled and she felt her thighs warm. He'd
invited her to the next party. She'd see him again.
Maybe it wasn't just one night after all.

She studied the thick, embossed invitation, and
saw that she was, indeed, a guest. This wasn't an
offer of full membership, but an offer to the party.
She guessed she'd take what she could get, especially if it gave her an excuse to see Durand again.
Asha sat at the table and poured herself coffee, plotting about what she might wear in Berlin, mentally rearranging her schedule to accommodate a
trip to Germany. She felt a brightness in her chest.
Could she wait the two weeks to see him again? Or
would she need to see him sooner? The wheels of
her mind turned as she crossed her legs, reminded
of the delicious soreness there, remembering how

Durand had possessed her, had made sure he'd explored every millimeter of her body.

Already, she could feel the passion grow in her lower belly, the passion for him. Her want. She took a bite of the croissant, plotting about what she might be able to do to see him in the meantime. Yes, she would figure it out. Because she wasn't a patient woman. When she wanted something, she went after it.

She heard the automatic key open the lock of the main door of the suite with a telltale beep and sat up, back ramrod straight as she dropped the croissant on the plate. Asha grinned to herself, thinking that maybe Durand couldn't wait, either. Maybe he couldn't keep his vow of one night. The idea that he'd come running back to her this same day, just as eager as she, warmed her. She stood, dragging the sheet with her, but then deciding perhaps what Durand should see was her half-naked, Asha dropped the sheet to her waist as the door swung open.

And a beautiful blond French woman wearing a tight-fitting pin-striped gray suit walked in.

Shocked, Asha tugged up her sheet, but not quite in time. She'd given the woman an eyeful.

The woman seemed unfazed. "You must be Ms. Patel?" she asked, her French accent faint, just like Durand's. She seemed unperturbed, her beautiful poreless face mostly unreadable.

"Uh…yes, and who are you?" Asha tightened

her grip on the sheet beneath her armpits, her face burning with embarrassment.

The mystery woman smiled, but the smile didn't quite reach her eyes. "I am Madelyn. Mr. Durand's assistant. I am here to tell you that you are welcome to stay. Until 4 p.m., but after that…" She let her voice trail off. "I'm afraid you will no longer have access to this suite."

"Oh." Asha tried to regain some of her dignity. It was embarrassing enough getting caught half-naked by Durand's employee, a situation made more embarrassing by the fact that she seemed to be here to kick her out. Her manner was ice-cold. Did Durand intend this less than warm welcome? Asha glanced towards the bedroom, where she knew her clothes were neatly hanging in the hotel closet. "That's fine." She clutched the sheet to her chest, expecting Madelyn to leave. But she didn't. She walked further into the room. Bold wiry thing. Asha noticed her waif-like body, as opposite of her curves as one could get. The kind that fashion magazines and casting producers loved. She wondered if Durand also liked her delicate frame, sans body fat, and sans curves.

Asha watched, stunned, as Madelyn brushed past her, not caring that she was wearing nothing but a sheet, as she bustled into the room, sat down on the couch, and pulled her laptop from her case. She set the laptop on the coffee table and booted it up, even as she laid out a few pages on the glass table.

"What are you doing?" Asha asked her.

"I'm working," Madelyn said, curtly, very much a woman staking out her territory. "This is the office while we're away, and I need to send a few messages." She glanced up at Asha, stark blue eyes cold.

"You can't work in your own room?" Asha asked, her blood pressure starting to rise.

Madelyn didn't answer at first, choosing to focus on her laptop. Then, after a beat, she glanced up. "I realize this might be awkward for you, but not for me. I've worked for Mr. Durand for years, and I know his…" she gave Asha a slow sweep with her judgmental gaze "…proclivities. This isn't the first time I've worked in a hotel room with a naked woman in it."

Madelyn's words hit home in a way Asha didn't expect. They felt like a sudden blow that stole all the air from her lungs. Sure, she knew a man like Durand no doubt had lovers. A man didn't get that talented without experience. But hearing the cavalier way Madelyn talked about former conquests made her feel small. And Asha hated feeling small.

"I'm not just any woman." She wasn't, either. What they had, she knew, wasn't just like any other hookup. It had been special. She knew it in her heart. Plus, no one had the gall to talk to her like this: dismissive. Not since boarding school.

"Really?" Madelyn glanced up from her laptop. "You zink you are special?" Her accent got a little thicker now. "You zink he has not had…an exotique like you before? Believe me, he has. Many times."

"Exotique?"

"Yes, or as you say in English. Exotic, yes?"

Asha's belly burned with anger. *Exotic* was a word she hated—dismissive of her skin, of her as a person. Exotic was a backhanded compliment, the kind she'd get at those dances in boarding school, when the girls' schools and boys' schools would get together in gym. It was a word a boy would use to describe her, when he had no intention of ever letting her meet his parents. Exotic implied there was only one standard of beauty, and everything else fell into the category of foreign and strange.

"Exotic is what you call a bird. Not a person," Asha said.

Madelyn laughed, bitter, sounding almost like a woman who'd been hurt by Durand herself. Had they…slept together?

"Zhat iz not how Durand zees it." She shrugged. Asha hoped Madelyn was lying. Durand didn't seem like the kind of man who kept a tally of the sorts of bodies he'd had in his bed, treating his mattress like a color wheel that needed to be filled in. Asha knew some men like that. Men who whis-

pered, "I've never had an Indian woman before."
As if she should be flattered.

Durand wasn't like that. Was he? He'd explored
her body as if it mattered, as if it were important, as
if it was something precious. Asha felt in her bones
Madelyn was wrong. And yet…her words planted
a smidgen of doubt in the back of her mind. What
if she was wrong about Durand? What if he only
did see her as "exotique"?

"No matter," Asha said. "You're going to leave
now, so I can get dressed." She might be nearly
naked. She might be just one of another of Durand's
many one-night stands, but she'd be damned if she'd
let herself be ordered around and embarrassed by
this rude and probably jealous assistant. Nobody
treated her like that. Not those stuck-up girls at
boarding school, or anyone else. She didn't care
about the judgment. She was a woman of power
in her own right.

Madelyn glanced up but didn't move. "You are
asking me?"

"I am telling you." Asha padded to the door in
her bare feet, put her hand on the handle. "Or would
you like me to call Durand? Tell him you are bothering one of his 'exotiques'? He wouldn't be happy
about that."

The color drained from Madelyn's face. Asha
had hit a soft spot. Good.

Madelyn packed away her laptop, stiffly, and

jammed the papers in a file that she tucked under one arm. She stood on her expensive stilettos and walked towards the door. Asha swung it open for her, thinking that she hoped it hit her on the way out. As she swept by, sinking her heels angrily into the carpet as she went, Asha called, "See you in Berlin."

Madelyn froze in the hallway, her knuckles going white on the handle of her briefcase. Looked like she didn't know about the invite to Berlin. Good, Asha thought. *Point for me.* She slammed the door with a flourish, and this time, she locked the safety latch across the door frame. No model-thin assistants were going to interrupt her again. Smiling to herself, she decided to draw herself a bath in the enormous bathroom offering the clawfoot soaking tub. She had until four, and she planned to make the most of it. Maybe room service, even. She wondered if they had caviar. Or, even better, more of that very delicious and very expensive champagne. She smiled wickedly as she plotted to run up Durand's bill. Her smile grew bigger. Maybe *she* would decide when she would leave.

Maybe she would send a message to Durand. If he wanted her out, then he'd have to come and tell her himself.

Nobody bullied Asha Patel.

Nobody.

CHAPTER EIGHT

THE NEXT DAY, Durand sat in his personal gym, a sleek glass-and-chrome room above his office in Paris, and tried to focus on the bicep curls with his free weights. But all he could think about as he sat on the bench before the wall of mirrors was the night he spent with Asha Patel. The woman's body was…exquisite. There was no other word for it. Perfectly curved, perfectly molded to seem to fit his own body, and the way she'd opened up for him, like a flower in the spring. She'd held nothing back, just as he asked, and watching her find herself was…truly amazing. Even now, he felt his groin grow tight at the memory, felt the want in him blossoming. He dropped the free weight on the ground with a loud clunk, exasperated. He did everything he could to keep his mind off Asha, but no matter what, his thoughts always found her. Her and her delicious body.

Durand still couldn't believe her lack of true

sexual gratification. What man was so inept they couldn't pleasure her? She was so willing. So damn willing. All it took was a little patience, exploring the ways she herself liked to be touched, letting her show him what felt good. Women knew their bodies best and it was always wise to trust them. To listen. It was about listening to her body, understanding what she liked, and she'd come. Easily. She'd come, again and again. Her body came alive beneath his touch, and the sheer astonishment on her face had been priceless.

He'd known the second she'd climaxed the first time that her admission had been no ruse. She'd been telling the truth. Before him, she'd never truly experienced sex the way it should be: pure, bold, satisfying. Her previous lovers had been selfish and unworthy of her. He'd felt like her teacher, but more, that she'd taught him what it was like to be vulnerable, to truly need someone. He felt like he'd deflowered a virgin and because he had, part of her belonged to him.

The possessiveness took him by surprise. Never had he felt as if he should own a woman. Obviously, people could not own people, but he'd never felt a connection to someone like this. Asha was the first woman in a long while, perhaps ever, that he wanted back in is bed. He'd only just begun to teach her what pleasures they could explore together. There was so much more he wanted to show her. So much he wanted to see her experience. The idea of stopping that felt like asking him to stop breathing. He couldn't do it. Wouldn't do it. Because…why? They fit together so amazingly well. Why stop? But he knew this was a worrisome feeling. This need that was building in him, need for Asha. He prided himself on never needing anyone. Never feeling so connected to another person that that want controlled him.

He'd promised to own her for a night, but now he worried that she owned *him*.

And not just for a night.

He met his own gaze in the mirror and wondered what the hell he was doing. Falling in love? He scoffed at his own reflection. Love was for romantics. Amateurs. Men who couldn't keep their feelings in check. Durand was not one of those men. Not someone who'd fall prey to the weaknesses of the heart. He typically never ventured beyond a *cinq a sept*, simply translated, a 5 to 7 p.m., a casual relationship, like one might have to one's work. Yet, somewhere deeper, he knew Asha wasn't a *cinq a sept*. She was a flower that had opened—*for him*. He'd done that. No other man.

In fact, the idea of another man coming after him made his stomach tighten, made him feel possessive.

And that was the problem. Because he'd spent a lifetime carefully cultivating his Frenchman-who'd-sworn-off-love image, the elusive playboy who never gave his heart to any one woman. What kind of mystery society owner would he be if he married? Had a family? Part of the appeal of the Sphinx Society was being free of constraints, of living life outside the typical rules. If he married, settled down, he'd be like every other man. Besides, if he were honest with himself, love scared him. He knew exactly how love could ruin a man. Look at his father. If he'd only just kept his feelings in check, only just kept his various relationships with his mistresses strictly *cinq a sept,* he wouldn't have divorced his mother and ruined their lives. She'd died brokenhearted. Doctors said it was a coronary, but Durand knew his mother, and knew the damage love had done to her. He'd sworn never to let the emotion get to him, never to let love blind him to more important things, like wealth and reputation. Durand spent his whole life honoring history, and that included his mother's.

He shook his head at his own shirtless reflection, and the foolishness he saw there. He was not going to risk his entire empire for love. Wasn't going to risk his sanity, either, for a woman who could still be after a membership to the Sphinx Society. So why couldn't he stop thinking about her?

He stood, grabbed a folded hand towel from a nearby table, and swiped it across his face and the back of his neck. What he needed was a cold shower and something to take his mind off of Asha Patel.

A soft knock came at the door frame of his personal gym. He glanced up to see Madelyn standing there, tentative. Madelyn was hardly ever tentative. She must be delivering bad news.

"Sir? I'm sorry to bother you," she said in French, as her face grew pink. He realized it was because he was shirtless as she snuck a look at his bare chest. He stood and grabbed his T-shirt that was draped across a nearby chair. No need to give her false hope. He never would sleep with her, no matter how big her crush on him grew. He pulled the T-shirt over his head.

"Yes, Madelyn?" he asked, impatient. His gym hours should be free of interruption, but sometimes business could not wait.

The pink receded from her cheeks as she glanced down at her tablet that she held tightly. "I've got word from the Savoy."

"Yes?"

Now, Madelyn looked extremely uncomfortable. "I'm afraid…" She swallowed. "Ms. Patel is refusing to leave your suite."

At the very mention of Asha's name, Durand felt white-hot electricity shoot down his spine. Asha Patel, the woman who wouldn't leave his thoughts. Or, it seemed, his hotel room.

"What do you mean, 'refusing'?"

"She told the hotel manager that she'll only leave if she speaks to you first. She's also…" Madelyn glanced at the email on her tablet, the color deepening in her cheeks. "Sir, she's running up an impressive bill. Champagne, caviar. Spa treatments."

"How much?"

"More than $5,000, sir, mostly from ordering the Savoy's most expensive champagne bottles."

Durand frowned. What on earth was that little minx doing? Had he not satisfied her? Had he not offered an invitation to his next party? Why on earth was she acting like a jilted lover? Unless…

"Did you deliver the box with the invitation?" Durand asked, voice clipped. He observed his assistant carefully. Madelyn shifted uncomfortably on her expensive crocodile leather heels. She did not meet his gaze. She was hiding something.

"Yes," she said, voice soft. "And I relayed your message. About checkout time." She wasn't telling him the whole truth. He could feel her guilt from where he stood. He'd known her so long he could read her every expression.

"And you delivered the message…*nicely*." Durand took a step closer to his assistant. He didn't care if he was covered in sweat. She glanced up once at him, tentatively.

"Yes," she said. "But of course." She stuck her chin out, daring him to contradict her.

In that moment, he realized that Madelyn could have told Asha most anything.

"What did you tell her?" Durand demanded. His heart ticked up a notch. Madelyn's damn schoolgirl crush was getting to be a problem, Durand realized. It was becoming truly bothersome.

"What I *always* tell your women." Madelyn raised a defiant eyebrow. "We have business to conduct, no? We have the next party to plan."

Durand let out an exasperated sigh. "Asha isn't just any woman." The words were out of his mouth before he could stop them. Surprise bloomed on Madelyn's face. Surprise—and dismay. But these words were true. Asha wasn't just any woman. It was about time that he made peace with that.

"You can't be serious," Madelyn began. "She's a spoiled heir. A…"

"No more." Durand waved his hand impatiently. He was tired of Madelyn's jealousy.

"Shall I allow the Savoy to call the London Police? They will make sure she leaves." Madelyn had composed herself and now was back to being all business.

"No," Durand said, surprising himself with the ferocity in his voice. He blew out a frustrated breath and turned away from his headstrong assistant. The last thing on earth he wanted was for the police to come and take Asha. She'd never forgive him that humiliation. And, he wondered, would she even forgive him sending Madelyn to tell her to leave?

Madelyn seemed surprised. "Shall I call Ms. Patel directly, then, and relay a message?"

"No." Durand stared at his assistant. "*You* will not be relaying any more messages to Ms. Patel."

Now Madelyn seemed truly taken aback. He'd never challenged her before because, he realized, he'd never cared how Madelyn handled things. As long as they were handled. He'd given her too wide a berth these last few years. Let her get territorial, and why not? He never cared to see most women he slept with a second or third time. He'd relied on Madelyn to clean up the morning after, however she saw fit. He'd been fine with that, until now. Asha was different. Asha wasn't a woman to dismiss out of hand.

"No. You're going to book me on the next flight to London," Durand demanded. Then, he eyed his assistant. "But first, you're going to tell me, *verbatim,* everything you told Asha."

CHAPTER NINE

ASHA LAY IN a thick white cotton robe, her bare feet dangling from the white love seat in Durand's suite at the Savoy the next morning, as she dipped an oversized strawberry into her flute of bubbling champagne and took a bite. This was the kind of breakfast she could get used to: fresh fruit and off-the-charts expensive champagne. Her head fell back on the pillow, nearly dislodging the hasty bun she'd made with her tangled hair that morning. Asha knew she should think about leaving. She'd overstayed her welcome and she'd had to unplug the phone so the front desk wouldn't call. And the maids had been by five times already this morning. Soon enough, security would come knocking on her door, no doubt. And she was pretty sure this fruit from yesterday and the champagne chilling in the mini-bar was the last room service she'd get for some time. Actually, the front desk had made that clear the last time she'd called down. If she didn't offer her own method of payment, no more hospitality would be offered to her by the Savoy. She could pay, but she didn't want to. What she wanted was to teach Durand a lesson.

She told herself, of course, it wasn't that she was just licking her own wounds, nursing her pride, hurt from being told by his cold-hearted assistant she was just one more conquest among dozens, one more *exotique*. He needed to be brought down a peg or two. So did his mean-spirited, jealous assistant... what was her name? Megan? Marie? Some *M*-name.

She heard the automatic key at the suite's door, and then someone try to open it, but the safety lock was latched in place. Then, came a stern knock. It was probably Savoy management again, maybe with security this time. They'd ask her to leave, no doubt. Well, she'd damn well leave when she wanted. And not a minute before.

"Asha?" came a deep rumble of a voice she instantly recognized. Faint French accent. Durand.

She sat up, and her hand flew to her hair. She caught her reflection in the mirrored wall adjacent to the living room. She rushed to it, fluffing her hair and pinching her cheeks. She'd forgone makeup. And clothes, for that matter. She wore only the robe and had been quite comfortable for the last two days.

She swept to the suite's main door. "Durand?" she asked, tentative, as she pressed her eye to the peephole. It looked as if he were alone. No security. No hotel management. Just Durand in a sleek, expensive gray suit, no tie, crisp white shirt open at the throat, one hand behind his back, looking sexy as hell. He almost seemed to meet her gaze through the peephole, flashing a wry grin.

"Asha, my chérie. Let me in."

Her fingers found their way to the dead bolt, but then she hesitated. Durand sent his assistant to humiliate her. Now, he swept in after two days and all was forgiven? She opened the safety bolt just wide enough to open the door two inches. She craned her neck to meet Durand's gaze, just as he revealed the hand he hid behind his back. He held a single perfect red rose. She'd expected him to be angry, not contrite. The approach threw her for a minute, and she took the rose, smelling its sweet fragrance.

"May I come in?" Durand asked, but the tone of his voice made her doubt she could actually refuse him. She felt the bass of his voice in her toes. She closed the door to free the safety bolt and let the door swing free. Durand strode in, perfect dark hair combed back from his forehead, and eyed the golden room-service tray on the glass coffee table, complete with a half-empty bottle of champagne and picked-over strawberries. There was another empty tray on the dining room table with a half-eaten filet mignon, a tray filled with crackers and an empty jar of caviar.

A slow smile spread across his face. "Making
yourself comfortable, Ms. Patel?" His ice-blue eyes
met hers, and she felt a shiver down her spine.

"Are we back to formalities?" She almost felt
disappointed. Why was he so cold and distant? She
wasn't sure what she expected. Durand to rush in
and kiss her passionately? Toss off her robe and
show her all the many, many delights he'd shown
her earlier in the week? No. But maybe she'd been
hoping he would.

"I'm not sure I'd call you—how do you say it in
English? squatting?—in my hotel room, a formal-
ity." He spread his hands, his big, strong hands, and
Asha remembered what they felt like on her body.
Strong and sexy.

"No, but it's the *least* I could do since I was so
rudely left. Without a proper goodbye." She knew
she sounded like a pouting toddler, but she didn't
care.

Durand raised a dark eyebrow. "I left you a
lovely invitation. And a mask."

"And sent in your secretary to do your dirty
work." She remembered his assistant's cold manner, the way she'd delivered the news she needed to
leave. "She was *not* lovely. Not at all." Asha jabbed
a fist into her hip for emphasis. Durand studied the
neckline of her robe, which she realized was open
low enough to reveal the top curves of her breasts.

Good. Let him look. Let him remember what he left behind.

"Yes, I spoke with her." Durand frowned. "My apologies for the manner in which she delivered my message. I'm afraid I wasn't so specific about *how* she ought to deliver the news. That was my error."

Asha nodded. It was, indeed, but the things his assistant had told her still burned. "She called me... *exotique*? Do you collect women, Mr. Durand, like some men do tigers?" A small strand of hair fell across her cheek and she tucked it behind one ear. Her bun felt in danger of falling, her hair feeling heavy at the base of her neck.

Durand laughed as he walked to the white sofa and sat, crossing his long, muscular legs, his pant legs fitting them tightly. She remembered his strong limbs entangled in hers beneath the sheets of the bed. "No. Not at all. I enjoy women. Of all races and nationalities."

Asha paced in front of him as he watched her long, tanned bare legs part her fluffy white robe. "Even French blondes?" Asha stopped in front of him, the coffee table the only piece of furniture between them.

He raised an eyebrow and she felt she'd somehow given him ammunition, but she couldn't help herself. She'd seen the territorial look on his assistant's face, could almost feel the woman's jealousy.

"No." Durand didn't blink. Didn't even look away. "Not the French blonde you mean."

"She's in love with you," Asha said. She'd come to that conclusion after replaying the conversation they'd had in her mind. The secretary who seemed a little bit too territorial, a little too involved for her interest to be purely professional.

Durand didn't look surprised, either. So he knew about her feelings. Interesting.

Durand worked to keep his face neutral. "Does that bother you?"

"No," she said too quickly. Too forcefully. It even sounded to her ears like a lie. Durand stood and walked around the table, and soon was beside her. He stepped closer, so close that she smelled him, the hint of his distinctive soap, his clean skin. She found herself leaning into him, despite her better intentions.

"I think it does bother you," he said after a beat. "I think you are jealous."

"No, I'm not." She wouldn't look him in the eye. Couldn't.

Durand put his hands around her arms, squeezing her ever so gently through her sleeves. She was suddenly very much aware that she wore nothing beneath the robe, and from the way he glanced down the V of the robe's neckline, Durand was, too.

"You should be honest with me, Asha." He pulled her against him. She felt the hardness of his chest.

"Why?"

He dipped down and nuzzled her neck. She felt a shiver of desire run down the backs of her bare legs. He knew just how to touch her, just how to awaken the want deep inside her.

"Because I know you're jealous." She arched her back, pressing against him, overwhelmed with his gentle touch, with his delicious scent, with the promise of the pleasure she knew he could deliver. Suddenly, the idea of clothes, even a robe, seemed stupidly impractical. What she wanted was his hands on her bare skin.

"How?" she murmured, as he laid gentle kisses beneath her ear. Her breath caught in her throat. She yearned to taste him, to devour his mouth. He was teasing her, and it was driving her wild.

He met her gaze. "Because you are throwing a fit. Because you want my attention."

"I'm not throwing a fit." She pushed him away and crossed the room, her face feeling hot, her neck burning. But she could not escape the truth of his words.

"You are, ma chère. You are throwing a fit, no? You want my attention. And now you have it." He crossed to her, embracing her from behind. She wanted to resist, but instead, found herself leaning into him, as he gave a hard tug on the belt of her robe. Soon it fell open, revealing miles of bare skin. He cupped both breasts from behind, kneading them reverently, so that her nipples grew hard against his palms.

"Yes," she murmured, the admission slipping from her lips without her realizing it.

"You are only pretending to be angry. You are only pretending that you can resist me," he whispered in her ear. His hand slipped from her breast, skimmed down her stomach and cupped her from the front, possessive. He teased her with the soft pad of his finger, caressing her, making her swell with want. Her body responded instantly, as if she'd been made for him. She arched herself, leaning into his touch.

A squeal of pleasure escaped her.

"I offered you one night, but you want more. Isn't that so?"

"No. I—I don't," she lied. "I don't care about you."

"Another lie. I thought we agreed not to lie to one another. Not to wear masks." Durand laughed, a growl in his belly. "You very obviously care." He tightened his grip around her waist. "You want me, ma chère. You want this." His caress drove her wild with need. When she could stand it no more, she turned in his arms and kissed him, openmouthed and fierce, her anger, her desire, her jealousy, all a powerful mixture that fueled her passion, driving her to devour him. His hands slipped into her open robe, against her bare back, and he pulled her

close against him, so that she could feel his growing need. His hands drifted down, cupping her bare
bottom as she wound her hands around the back
of his neck. He tasted like everything she'd ever
wanted, everything she'd ever needed, this man
who could light a spark in her, a spark that threatened to burn her to ash. "You need me."

"I don't need anyone," she managed.

"Another lie."

Durand maneuvered her to the couch and
whirled her around once more. He took the belt of
her robe and freed it, and then covered her eyes,
tying it tightly behind her head.

"What are…"

"Trust me," he murmured in her ear, a promise.
A threat? She shivered with anticipation as she realized she could see nothing, that she was completely
in Durand's power. Exactly where she wanted to be.
He positioned her so that her hands were splayed
across the back of the couch, her legs shoulder-
width apart. Her breathing grew shallow as she
waited, listened, felt helpless and vulnerable. Durand was as a quiet as a panther, though she could
sense him in the room, prowling, his eyes on her
bare body, her exposed skin. He pinched her left
nipple, softly, making her shriek in surprise.

"What are you doing, Durand?" she cried,
shocked.

"You like throwing fits? Playing games? Then

we will play a game," he told her, this time caressing her right cheek. She whirled but could see nothing, hear nothing. She moved one hand, and his came down on hers, steading her against the couch. "Stay where you are, Asha." His voice was a command, a delicious command. Normally she hated to be bossed around, but somehow…letting Durand do it was sexy. Beyond sexy. White-hot. Her lips parted as she anticipated where he might touch her next. Her legs shook in anticipation. Being deprived of sight, she had no idea what he planned to do, and it made her slick with want.

She heard his zipper then, and thought she heard his belt hit the ground, probably with his pants, as well. Was he going to take her like this? She couldn't see. Couldn't do anything. Her palms flat as she faced the back of the couch, waiting.

His palm hit her bare bottom, a playful slap, and she squealed in shock. He'd…spanked her. Actually…spanked her. No one had ever dared. No one but Durand. He'd positioned her to do just this: hands splayed on the back of the couch, backside vulnerable. She twisted a little.

"Durand!" she cried in protest.

"Stay where you are," he demanded, righting her once more. And he gave the other cheek a slap. Playful. Not hard. Enough to let her know he was in control, enough to send white-hot desire through her veins, to set off every nerve ending in her body.

"You have been a bad girl, Asha. Playing these games. Lying to me."

"I—I did not lie," she protested, in the direction of his voice, behind her.

"You said you were not jealous of Madelyn, no? That is a lie." His breath was on her neck, and she shivered, feeling him so close behind her that his bare knee touched the back of her leg. "Admit it."

"I…" Was she going to tell this man that she was jealous? That she was jealous of Madelyn's affections, that she was jealous that she was his trusted assistant? It was all so stupid. "I'm not jealous."

He flicked her hip with his fingernail, a small sting. "You lie." He spanked her once more, harder this time, and she gave a little yelp. Then he rubbed her bare bottom with his hand, soothing the contact, as he kissed her neck. It was a possessive kiss. He grabbed the back of her blindfold, the lose tails of her robe's belt, moving her face upwards. Her heart raced.

"Tell me the truth. Are you jealous?"

"Yes," she gasped.

"Because you want me." He clutched at the tie of her blindfold.

"Yes," she managed, heart thumping hard in her chest. She couldn't see his face, the robe's thick belt stopping all but the faintest of light around the edges, and she wondered how he'd taken her admission.

"And you need me," he said, his voice deep and demanding. She could feel his thick, hard cock against her lower back. A promise of what was to come.

"Yes." Her voice sounded like a mere croak, a whispered admission of the truth. She did need him.

"Good," he murmured, moving against her back. "Because I need you, too. So very much." And then, he entered her from behind, filling her up, shocking her with the hard movement that sent her legs apart, made her whole body open for him. He sent her against the back of the couch, each of his thrusts pushing her deep into the rich upholstery, as he took her again and again, harder and deeper. She cried out, unable to stop herself, as he reached around to her front and found her swollen clit, and she nearly burst into a thousand glimmering pieces. She climaxed and so did he, two animals unable to help themselves, as they let loose two distinct cries of ecstasy.

She couldn't help but think they were made for each other, that no two people had ever been so suited for one another, so perfectly.

Instantly, Durand collapsed against her, and he removed her blindfold. He laid a dozen tender kisses on her neck, the disciplinarian gone, and in its place, a man who craved a gentle touch. He slipped off the condom he'd worn and tossed it into a nearby gilded trash can. Then he wrapped her in his arms, gently, and she went, feeling as if a mutual apology spanned between them, that the fight, such as it was, was over.

"Did I hurt you?" he asked, holding her tightly as the two walked around the edge of the couch and sank into it.

"No," she said, remembering the slap of his hand against her backside. "Though no one ever dared to spank me before," she murmured into his bare chest.

"Perhaps that is why you are so spoiled," he teased.

"I'm not spoiled," Asha cried.

"Only the very spoiled would say that," he whispered into her hair, as he pulled her tighter to him. She laughed, and buried her face into his chest, into his warmth. "I did not hurt you, did I?"

"No," she said.

"I only want to show you…the many ways sex can be," he said. "You have had such inept lovers. Such fools. There's so much you have missed."

"And you will be my teacher?"

Durand kissed her head. "If you let me, ma chère. You hold all the power."

"I do?"

"Women always do." He ran a hand gently through her hair. "You will be my undoing." His voice sounded almost pained.

"Why?"

"Because you are like no other woman on earth," he said. "Because you have crawled under my skin, made a home there."

Asha flattened her palm against his chest, feeling scared....and vindicated all at once. So she wasn't the only one who felt the connection between them, the white-hot chemistry. He felt it, too.

"So, I am not just an *exotique*?"

"No." His arm tightened. "You are much more than that. *L'appétit vient en mangeant.*"

"What does that mean?"

"*Appetite comes with eating.* It's a French saying about obsession. The more you have, the more you want."

"You're obsessed with me?" Asha laughed a little, delighted. "Does that mean you won't let me out of your sight?" Asha teased, pressing her cheek against his chest. She felt a warmth in her belly grow outward, and realized it was her own feelings for him growing.

"Maybe," Durand admitted. "I am obsessed with you, and you are obsessed with membership, is this not so?"

For Asha, their relationship was anything but transactional, and she knew that now, knew it the moment he'd taken her into his bed.

"The membership isn't what I'm after," she murmured.

Durand shifted, sitting up a bit, and Asha lifted

her head from his chest. "No?" Durand raised one eyebrow in surprise. She met his blue gaze.

"No. I want something…more."

Durand searched her eyes for a moment, and she expected him to respond in kind. But instead, he pulled her down for a kiss. His lips met hers, possessive and hungry. Yet part of her, a small part, felt like she'd revealed too much. That she'd tipped her hand. She pulled back from the kiss.

"And what about you?" she asked him, feeling the oily coating of insecurity line her stomach. Did he want her, too? Or was this a game to him? "What do you want?"

He searched her eyes for a minute. "Before you came into my life, I thought I knew. But now…" He trailed off, frowned. "I promised myself I would never fall in love."

"Why not?" Asha felt pressure in her chest, as if someone had hold of her heart and was giving it a squeeze.

"It is my image, no? The Frenchman who swore off love. But love isn't very practical. Love can be dangerous. Look at what happened to my mother… to my father… I cannot ignore that."

"But you're not your father."

"Don't we all become our parents? At some point or another?"

Asha rested her chin on his chest. "You fear you can't be faithful to a woman? Is that it?"

"I have never tried to be faithful to a woman," Durand admitted, voice seeming a bit distant. "So I do not know."

Asha felt a small sliver of hurt at his words. Would he not even want to *try* for her sake? It was the one thing she demanded from a man, any man: loyalty.

"I cannot be with a man if he won't be faithful to me." After all, she'd flown halfway across the globe to confront Connor, and they'd not even slept together yet. "It's my one absolutely unbreakable rule."

"Ah? So you *do* follow at least one rule. I thought you just liked to break them."

He was being evasive, but what did she expect? Asha felt her chest tighten even more, but she told herself she was being foolish. Silly. A schoolgirl. What did she care if Durand loved her? Loved anyone? After such a short time with this man, she was thinking they could have a future? And what future would that be, she wondered? A man who prided himself on never committing to anyone, whose assistant even told her how often he had trysts with many women. Many *exotiques*. Asha knew exactly the kind of man Durand was, one that never gave his heart to anyone. Hadn't she known that long before she'd let him into her bed? She'd been playing with fire the whole time, so why now, when he admitted he never planned to love another, should she be disappointed?

She was no fool.

Except in that moment, Asha realized, she was already falling for him. Half in love with him already. And that made her a fool.

"I believe love only ends in loss," he said, even as he stroked her hair.

"Maybe it doesn't have to," she managed.

"Why are you such an advocate for love?"

"Why are you so against it?" Asha countered. "It seems to me that maybe you're fighting a little too hard. The playboy bachelor protests a little too much."

"You think I am bluffing?"

"You certainly seem intent on letting everyone know just how much you hate love. Perhaps you're trying to challenge someone to convince you otherwise."

Durand clucked his tongue. "And you are that woman?"

"Maybe. Maybe not. I only know that I'm not the only one pretending to be something I'm not."

Now Durand laughed out loud, a big belly laugh.

"It sounds to me like you're falling in love with me. Are you falling in love with me?" he asked. In that moment, Asha could show her hand. She could be honest with him. Yet something in her held back the truth. She wouldn't give him the power of knowing he had control over her. She was used to dealing with powerful men. Her father for one, and she knew that giving them the upper hand never ended well. She'd have to keep him guessing if she ever wanted to hope to maintain power in the relationship. Because, in every relationship, there was always a dominant and a submissive. One who held the power, and one who obeyed. That had always been her experience.

"Of course not," Asha lied and then covered it with a brash laugh. Because deep in her heart she knew, she was falling for this man. Falling hard. Or was this just what happened to every woman who was truly pleasured in bed by a man? Maybe all she really wanted was his touch, the touch that felt so reverential, as if he worshipped her body from head to toe. Maybe it was that that she was falling in love with and not the man. After all, what did she really know about him? Besides, in the end, didn't all men eventually disappoint her? Didn't they all lose their ability to please?

Durand went quiet then.

"Falling in love with you would be foolish," she added. He was the man who'd sworn off love, after all, even if part of her thought it was a little bit bluster. Who could cut out love from their life? No one Asha knew.

"You think so?" he demanded, pulling away

from her, and studying her eyes. "But what if I am already falling in love with you?"

Asha told herself Durand's question was just a ploy, just a way to manipulate her or keep her off balance. And yet, as she stared at his blue eyes, so earnest, so honest, she found it hard to believe he wasn't telling the truth. And if that was the truth of his feelings, the mere idea made her giddy. She wanted this. She wanted him to be in love with her, the way she'd wanted no man to love her before. And she realized it was all because she had feelings for him. Perhaps she was already in love with him.

This would not do. How could she love a man who'd sworn never to love? If anything, her history had taught her that men couldn't be changed. Not by a woman. By themselves, maybe, but not by a woman.

"What would you say to that?" he asked her. "What would you say if I told you I loved you? That I would try to be the faithful man you need?"

"I would say that the *what if* at the beginning of the sentence means you aren't serious."

"Oh, I am serious," he teased. "Let me show you how serious," he added and pulled her close to him, pressing his lips gently against hers.

CHAPTER TEN

DURAND AND ASHA extended their stay at the Savoy far longer than was prudent for either of them, locked together in bed, forgetting all passage of time. Eventually, the two parted, as the call of planning the next party in Berlin demanded Durand's attention. Asha returned to her apartment in London, and Durand went on to Berlin, to scout out the venue, and answer Madelyn's ever more insistent demands that he come for final approval of the facilities. She wasn't wrong. The ball needed his attention.

Durand hated being apart from Asha and realized that her influence had grown to touch every aspect of his life. He wanted her more than he'd ever wanted another. Their nights apart gnawed at him, made him toss and turn through many sleepless hours. He was growing obsessed, and he had only just started to realize this might be what his father had felt when he'd left his mother. Could it be? Could he have been taken by emotions this overwhelming? Had he been too hard on his father all these years?

And yet, he'd never committed to a woman, never had a child, never left them to follow his lust or his love, or whatever emotion overwhelmed his sense. He was free to indulge in love, since he had no obligations. All he had was his own vow that he wouldn't let love rule his life.

And yet, here love was. Keeping him up at night. Making him forget his responsibilities to the Sphinx Society, soaking up every last thought in his brain. Durand had thought that he'd been the one to teach Asha about the intricacies of sexual pleasure, but she, he realized, was the one teaching *him* about love.

The days the two were apart seemed endless, but eventually, Asha flew to Berlin.

Durand waited in the Berlin Airport mid-morning for Asha to pass through customs. He'd driven there himself to pick her up, shocking Madelyn, who'd never seen him take on such a lowly duty himself, but the fact was, he needed to see Asha again and did not want to wait for the taxi to bring her to him. It had been a little more than a week, and he itched to hold her in his arms. He wanted to spend all of his time with the woman who seemed to have bewitched him. There was no other word for it. He was under her spell.

Falling in love with you would be foolish.

Her words had hurt him more than he'd like to admit. He shouldn't care that she'd said it, flippantly. After all, since when did he want a woman mooning over him? Falling in love? Wasn't that what he'd tried to avoid his whole life?

Yet Asha was different. He needed her in a way he'd never needed a woman. That unnerved him, but what worried him even more was a nagging feeling that she wasn't as serious about him as he was about her, that at the heart of things, this was just a game to her. He needed to convince her otherwise. He just wasn't sure how.

He watched as tourists poured through the customs doors, dragging their luggage behind them, glancing at the unfamiliar signs, looking for their rideshares and taxis. He grew impatient as different people walked by him, none of them the one he wanted to see. He scanned the crowd, looking for Asha's beautiful black hair, her gorgeous tan complexion, her amazing curves. They invaded his thoughts during the day and his fantasies at night. He'd only half joked about her being an obsession. Now he feared that's exactly what she'd become. He'd thought that the week they'd spent together in London would scratch the itch he'd had, and that he could move on, but instead, his want for her...hell, his need for her, just seemed to grow. He knew he was getting in too deep. Knew he was playing with fire, but he couldn't help it.

She was like no woman he'd ever met. So gorgeous, so stubborn. So deliciously responsive in bed, and he loved the idea of opening up her world, showing her what she might have missed all those years with all those selfish lovers. There was, indeed, so much the two could explore together, so many pleasures awaiting her—and him. The idea made him feel delirious. And possessive. But it was more than her body that intrigued him. It was also her mind. Her fight, her determination, they wiggled their way into his brain, told him she was more like him than he knew. When someone told him he couldn't do something, couldn't have something, that just made him want it more. That's why he'd taken the one thing his father had left him and turned it into everything. Because he wanted to show his father that he wouldn't just survive. He'd thrive. That's why he'd vowed to himself he'd never make his father's mistakes: putting love above all else.

But then came Asha. Blowing his plans apart.

He scanned the crowds walking through the doors, into the lobby of the airport. Asha had taken a commercial flight from London to Berlin. First class, of course, but as it turned out, since her father was squeezing her luxuries, he'd taken away the private jet when she'd refused to attend a company meeting. Durand wanted to know more about that. He of all people knew how tricky relationships with fathers could be.

Asha swept through the glass doors of customs looking even more stunning than he remembered. She wore a white skintight skirt and a colorful sleeveless blouse, big oversized sunglasses on top of her head. The instant he saw her, feet clad in strappy sandals as she pulled her rolling carry-on behind her, he moved quickly, his body taking over, as he swept her into his arms and kissed her. She tasted like everything he needed. Everything that had ever been missing in his life. She tasted like a purpose. His cock came to life instantly.

"I missed you," he murmured as he released her, but kept his arms around the small of her back. It felt like admitting weakness, but he did it anyway. She grinned up at him.

"Did you now?" Her lips parted and he wanted suddenly to whisk her away from this public place, hide her away in his Hotel Adlon Kempinski suite, and hibernate there until fall.

"Shall we go to my hotel?" His fingers itched to peel off her clothes, to taste her skin, to inhale her scent. He felt like an addict right then, an addict needing his fix.

She smiled. "I've never been to Berlin before, and you want to hide me away in your hotel?" Now she was playing coy. Why? He knew that she needed his touch as much as she needed his. Why pretend otherwise?

He squeezed her waist tighter, pressing her against him, so that she could feel just how much he wanted her. His groin ached with need. *Zut alors*, his whole body ached. Surely she could feel that.

"Yes," he growled. "I want to keep you in my hotel all week. Naked. Doing my bidding."

Asha laughed. "Show me Berlin first. Or I might never see it." Now he realized she had a plan of some kind. A plan he didn't like.

"You want to play tourist?" Durand felt the bitter taste of disappointment at the back of his tongue. Who cared about touring the city when he'd much rather be exploring the twists and turns of her perfect body?

"I'd at least like to eat. I skipped breakfast today."

"We could order room service." Images of him feeding her strawberries, naked, in his bed, flashed through his mind.

"Take me out first," Asha demanded, but a playful smile twitched at the corner of her pink lips. "Then, to your hotel. Something tells me we'll have plenty of time to try out room service."

Durand couldn't agree more. Once he got her into his bed, he'd not let her out again.

Asha took no pleasure in the disappointment that flickered in Durand's eyes as he took the handle of her rolling bag and led her out of the high-ceilinged sleek, modern terminal of the Berlin airport, beneath the red decorative red metal ribbon lattice hanging from the ceiling. She'd decided that she needed to try to resist heading back to his hotel room, because there, for certain, he held all the power. She knew this, knew that she'd be unable to resist his touch, since it had brought to life a need she never knew she'd ever had in her body. And then, she'd just fall deeper in love with him. Or lust. Honestly, she wasn't sure she could tell the difference anymore. She was obsessed, she knew that much. She spent every moment thinking of him, or stalking him online, or reading gossip columns about him. The man who never had a serious relationship in his life, the Frenchman who swore off love.

And that made him even more of a challenge. She hated that she wanted to convert him, like some romance novel heroine, but there she was. She liked the idea of being the one woman he couldn't resist. There still remained this stupid little flame of hope in her breast. She was the one who might be able to change him. She had no idea why she thought she could. Maybe it was the way he was looking at her now as they walked through the airport, the way he held her elbow firmly, possessively. Maybe he did this with every woman he met. Every *exotique*. Maybe they were all playthings for him. Maybe he made them all feel worshipped and adored, right up until the day he refused to return their calls. He tended to leave a trail of broken hearts in his wake. Asha wasn't about to add to that pile. She would be no one's fool.

What she needed to do was put the brakes on. Keep out of his bed for a microsecond so she could hang on to her wits. Get to know the man behind the amazing hands and mouth and cock, to decide if this was real, or just…want. It was easy to love him in bed, where his body controlled hers, where her want ran riot, but what about out of it? Maybe if she got to know the man better, he'd lose some of his power, lose some of his draw. After all, Asha knew, men, in the end, were almost always a disappointment.

No sooner had they walked out of the airport than a driver pulled up in a black Mercedes, and a well-dressed twenty-something German in a suit got out, hastily grabbed Asha's bag, and stowed it in the large trunk of the car.

"*Danke schön*," Durand told his driver, and then proceeded to give him further instructions in German. Asha had no idea what they were saying, but the man opened the back door of the Mercedes, and Durand ushered her in.

They drove through the streets of Berlin on the sunny summer morning, the blue sky partly covered in clouds. Durand reached out and took her hand, bringing it to his lips and kissing it.

"There's still time to tell him to turn around and take us to the hotel," he murmured, his voice as sexy as she remembered, tinged with that faint hint of French. She wanted to. Badly. But she needed to rein in her desires, or they'd run her life. And she couldn't afford to let that happen. She'd never willingly given over such control to anyone, and she wasn't going to do that now, with a playboy who'd vowed never to love one woman his whole life.

She was giving him too much power. She'd never intended to stay in that hotel room in London with him for a whole week, but she'd done it, without even realizing how much time had passed. Whenever he touched her, she felt powerless. That scared her. She wanted him, yes, but she wanted him on her terms.

"I am hungry, and *you* can wait. It's like you want to eat dessert first." She tugged her hand away and gave him a playful swat.

"What is wrong with that? Especially when *you* are the dessert." Durand let her hand go, moving his fingers down to her bare knee, caressing it ever so gently. She felt an electric current run right up her thighs, felt the power of his touch. He stroked the inside of her bare knee, working his finger up her thigh. She shivered. Her breath came a little quicker, a little faster, and she wondered if she'd be able to tamp down her own desire.

"You mustn't spoil your appetite," she warned him.

He gently squeezed her upper thigh. "When it comes to you, I don't know that I can ever have my fill. *Plus on a, plus on veut avoir.*"

"What does that mean?" she asked, uncertain.

"The more you have, the more you want," he whispered, leaning over and nuzzling her neck. She moaned, just a little, unable to help herself.

She pulled away, managing to fight against the rising need in her belly. She glanced at him, sharply, seeing honesty in his blue gaze. And a little bit of surprise. Maybe this wasn't just some come-on line, something he said to all the women to make them fall at his feet. Yet part of her wondered.

She leaned forward and gently straightened his tie. "Then, I'm worth waiting for," she whispered, aware that he watched her lips as she spoke, aware of how much he wanted to kiss them. He'd have to wait.

"Oui, ma chère. Worth the wait." He sat back then and folded his hands on his lap, but she saw the twitch of frustration at the corner of his lip. Good. Maybe she'd get under his skin this time. Maybe she'd be the one with the power.

She wanted to show him that they were more than just passion. They were something deeper than that.

The car slid through the crowded streets of Berlin, the sun beaming down on the gray sidewalks. Eventually, the black car pulled over and let them out. Durand took her by the hand, as they strolled along the sidewalk beneath the bright summer Berlin sun. He nodded to the left.

"That's Checkpoint Charlie," he said, nodding to the white booth situated on an island in the middle of a bustling Berlin street. Sandbags lined one edge of the booth, and a crowd of tourists stood near it, taking pictures, standing beneath an original black-and-white sign that read, "You are now leaving the American Sector."

"Wow," Asha said, recalling a little bit about the Cold War she'd learned in history in college: the Berlin wall that once separated communist East Berlin from democratic West. He held her hand as they walked. Then, he stopped her, nodding downward. "See? This is where the wall used to be." Oversized stones in the sidewalk marked the wall, labeled *Berliner Mauer 1961-1989*. Asha put her feet on either side of the cobble stones. "Wait, let me take your picture," he said, and pulled out his phone.

She smiled, feet apart, and he snapped the picture.

"Belle," he said, and pulled her to him. He kissed her on the lips, a quick peck, but a tingle ran down her spine. "You are too beautiful not to kiss," he told her as he wrapped his arm around her shoulders, pulling her to him as they walked to the restaurant, a sleek modern affair serving tapas. The host seated them in a small corner booth near the window so they could watch the tourists posing together in front of Checkpoint Charlie.

"Is this all right?" Durand asked her as she frowned at the menu, which was largely in Spanish. "It's a new restaurant in Berlin. Two Michelin stars."

"I… I don't have tapas that often," Asha admitted.

"Do you mind if I order for us?"

"No. Please." Asha folded the menu, and then proceeded to watch Durand address the waitress in Spanish. She'd never quite felt so worldly before: she about to eat tapas, in Berlin, with a Frenchman. That had to be a first. Plus, he seemed to be fluent in at least four languages.

After the waitress had taken their order and left, Asha leaned forward. "How many languages do you know?" she asked him.

"Four fluently. Seven passably." Durand shrugged. "It was part of my education. Plus, it helps to be able to speak to my society members in their native tongues." She thought of Durand's talented tongue, and realized it had more uses than just languages. Delicious uses. She pushed the thought away, though he seemed to read her mind, anyway. He glanced at her, raising an eyebrow. "Though I feel our bodies do not need words, no?"

"Now you sound like a stereotypical French-man." She laughed.

"What is wrong with that?" Durand said, and they both laughed.

"So…you learned languages…at school? Where?" She needed to get this conversation back on track.

Durand took her hand on the table, holding it possessively. "Why do you wish to know?"

"I want to know more about you." She wanted him to open up to her. To show her more than just delights in the bedroom. She wanted to know what made this mysterious man tick. He seemed to be a riot of contradictions: one minute, he was cool and aloof and in control, and the next, he was a lover who couldn't seem to get enough of her. She'd begun to understand his body very, very well, but what she wanted to explore was his mind. Maybe then, if she knew him better, she could balance her feelings, which even she knew were growing wildly out of control.

A playful smile pulled at the corners of Durand's sensual mouth. "What do you want to know?"

"For starters, if you've ever been in love."

The waitress came then with two glasses of san-gria. Asha took hers gratefully. Durand sipped at his, pensive.

"I told you before," he said, somber now, an edge to his voice, "love only ends in pain. I've spent my life avoiding it."

"Love exists, Durand, no matter how much you try to deny it."

"It killed my mother and made my father…a terrible man." Durand shrugged. "I know it exists. I just don't believe it works the way most people think it does."

"How does it work?" Asha took a sip of her ruby-red sangria, the tart, fruit-infused wine tickling her tongue.

"Most people only *think* they are in love. But, really, they are just in lust. Or in obsession. Or suffer from loneliness. Or it's just about ego. It's not love. We give love too much power these days. People believe they have no immunity. That they must suffer whatever love dictates for them. But that's not how love should be. Love is in our control."

"I disagree." Asha put down her glass and then dabbed at the edges of her mouth with her napkin. "Sometimes feelings grow bigger than you want them to grow. And that's what makes them so beautiful in the end. The fact we can't really control them. Not completely." She couldn't meet his gaze for fear he'd read the truth in her eyes. That she was in love with him. More than she'd like.

"You think you know love? Because you followed your ex-boyfriend to my party? Is that love?"

Asha laughed bitterly. "No, that is not love. I never loved Connor."

"Then what do you mean? Who do you love?" There was a challenge in the bend of his eyebrow, the slant of his mouth. It was as if he already knew exactly what she was thinking. But that was impossible. He could read her body, yes, but not her mind, she told herself. That was still hers to control.

"Do you want me to tell you that I love *you*, Durand? Is that what all your women tell you right before you lose interest in them?" Asha wasn't going to admit her feelings for this man. Not when he was so stubborn about love, about refusing to believe in the power of it, refusing to give in. She also realized that her own plan of getting to know him, trying to find his flaws so that she, herself, might lose interest, was backfiring. Durand's magnetic presence held her full attention, and all she wanted to do was crawl into the man's bed after this meal and never get out. But she could not let him know that. She could not let him know the kind of power he had over her.

If she did, she'd lose everything. She knew the kind of man Durand was. She also knew exactly the way to keep his interest. By keeping him at arm's length. A man like him knew nothing but the pursuit. A man like him would always lose interest once he caught his prey.

Durand chuckled and took a sip of his sangria.

"You worry I'll lose interest in you?"

Asha laughed. "No." She gave him a slow, deliberate smile. "I'm worried I'll lose interest in you, first. And then you'll be such a bore."

"Bore?" Durand's eyebrow rose as his blue eyes grew sharp at the insult. "You think I'll bore you?"

"Eventually, yes, *all* men bore me." She could see him stiffen. Then a slow smile spread across his face, the relish of a challenge in his eyes. She loved pushing his buttons, loved prodding him. "Eventually, even *you,* Mathis Durand, will run out of tricks."

"Not me, Asha. Not ever." His determined expression made her rethink her challenge, almost made her wonder if she'd gone too far. "You'll never be bored with me."

"Prove it," she challenged him.

CHAPTER ELEVEN

DURAND HELD ASHA'S hand tightly as they swept into the lobby of the five-star Hotel Adlon Kempinski, on the east side of Berlin, an upscale hotel built in 1905. They walked across the white marble floor and in between the plush gray seats, Asha's heart beating loudly in her ears, anticipating what would come next once they made their way upstairs into his bed. She wanted this more than she dared to admit even to herself. She glanced at the signature fountain in the center of the lobby, noting the black elephant heads midway up the fountain's tower.

"The elephant fountain was a famous gift," Durand said as they swept by it on their way to the elevators. "India's Maharaja of Patiala gave the fountain to the owner of the hotel, Lorenz Adlon, in 1930."

"Ah, you and your historical facts," Asha said.

"We all must learn history or be forced to repeat it," he said.

She squeezed his hand tightly. "What if I *like* to repeat certain histories? Like…ours?"

"That, of course, must be the exception to the rule." Durand flashed her a knowing smile as Asha admired the lines of the sculpted elephants that fanned out around the center tower of the fountain. Even in the hotels she was used to, these kinds of artifacts were rare. Durand must be rubbing off on her because she was starting to appreciate antiques.

"And do you always stay at hotels blessed by royalty? First, the King of Sweden, and now the Maharaja of Patiala?"

"Royalty is fascinating to everyone—even Americans," Durand said.

"Is it? I think we fought a revolution because we *weren't* so enamored with the institution," Asha pointed out.

Durand pressed the button of the gilded elevators, and one instantly arrived. He swept Asha in, steering her with a firm hand on her lower back. She was more than aware of the possessiveness in his touch. Her stomach rippled with nerves. She knew when she stepped into the elevator with him that once she was in his suite, she'd be unable to think, to control herself. She'd do whatever he wanted, and she'd like it. The idea of giving away her control frightened—and excited—her. No one made her feel like Durand did. No one lit up her desire, made her nerves come alive, like he did.

"Maybe you Americans regret losing the monarchy…just a little bit. Maybe that's why you are fascinated. Perhaps, even, obsessed."

"You think you know about obsession?" Asha challenged him as the elevator doors slowly closed. Durand hit the button for the penthouse, swiping his key against the sensor on the lighted pad, because not just anyone could take the elevator there.

"Yes, I do." Then, Asha leaned past him and pulled out the elevator stop button. The elevator lurched to a complete stop and the alarm sounded, which she quickly disabled with a flick of the alarm switch.

"What are you doing?" Durand cocked one eyebrow in surprise. "Do you wish to…begin foreplay here?" He spread his arms wide, and grinned.

"Maybe." She moved closer to him and ran her finger down the closed buttons of his shirt. "But first, I want you to tell me…" she glanced up at him "…what you mean to do with me?"

She pressed against him, pushing them both to the wall of the elevator, their lips were millimeters apart. She could almost taste the faint hint of sangria on his tongue. She searched his blue eyes and saw playfulness there.

"I mean to do all kinds of things to you, ma chère. Things I believe you will like." His eyes sparkled. "Things I know you will like."

She stood up on tiptoe and nibbled the bottom of

his lip. "And then?" she asked him. "Do you plan to give me that membership?"

Durand chuckled. "This is no longer about the membership, and we both know it."

He was right. She knew he was right. But she couldn't let him see how much he'd grown to mean to her. How much she was already under his spell. She needed to take back some of her power.

"If you do not plan to give me the membership, then what do you plan to do with me?" The elevator dinged and they tumbled out of it, Durand pulling her into the hallway of the hotel.

"I mean to show you many, many tricks. For many, many hours." They reached his door, and he pulled the keycard from his wallet, swiping it past the sensor. The door unlocked and they were inside, their lips meeting, locked together in a desperate dance. She ran her hand down the front of his pants, feeling him come to life beneath her fingers. Then, she pulled back as he sucked in a breath.

"What if I am the one to show *you* tricks this time? You think you are the only one with skills?"

She slipped down on her knees in the elevator. He stood stock-still, watching her with amused eyes, as she freed him from the confines of his pants. Normally, when she did this, it was simply to get something she wanted. She wanted to make Durand lose his own control, wanted to make him feel what she'd felt during that week in his hotel room.

He seemed to still believe they were casual, when she in her heart knew they were much more. Their connection was something that didn't come along very often. And she was going to prove it to him.

She stroked him, and he grew hard instantly in her hand. The carpet cut into her knees, but she didn't care. She wanted to make him moan, make him lose control, and this was the way to do it. She flicked the head of his cock with her tongue, and he tilted his head back and groaned. This time, she'd be the one in control. This time, she wouldn't be the one to succumb. She wanted to do this. Wanted to drive him wild. If she had to be on her knees, so be it. She flicked her tongue again, rolling around the tip, and then she took him—most of him—in her mouth. He cried out, unable to help himself, as she worked him, using both hands on this shaft, and her mouth and tongue around the head. She read his body silently, read his reactions, knew exactly what to do.

"*Mon dieu*," he breathed, grasping her shoulders. "You will make me come," he warned.

She freed her mouth. "That's the idea," she growled, and then she resumed her work, delighting in how she could control his body, how he was now a slave to the growing climax, how he'd have no choice but to come. She could feel it in his quivering body, how the desire was overtaking his control. But then, he pulled away.

"No, no. I cannot let you," he growled, and swept her up in his arms. He once more zipped up his fly as he hit the buttons of the elevator. The elevator began moving once more, and soon the doors opened to the penthouse. He grabbed her hand and pulled her into the hallway. A few seconds later, they were inside his rooms, an extravagant black-paneled hotel suite, complete with bedroom and dining room. The curtains were open, revealing Berlin's iconic Brandenburg Gate, the stone column structure topped with a statue of the goddess of victory pulled by four horses, the afternoon sun blazing down on it. She didn't care about the view or the lavishness of the suite. All she cared about was Durand.

He led her to the bedroom, his mouth hungry on hers. Suddenly, her plan to control his body evaporated in her mind as his tongue lashed hers, as the want in her grew to a burning need. She felt the soft bed beneath her back. Then he was on top of her, his weight delicious against her. He rolled her on top of him, and then found the zipper at the back of her skirt. Soon, it and her blouse were puddles on the floor, and she wore only lacy, sheer underwear. His fingers couldn't move fast enough, and neither could hers. Their clothes only seemed frustrating barriers to what they both wanted now.

His skin felt hot against hers as his hands roamed her bare body. Her skin came alive beneath her touch, and she moaned, even as he shed the rest of his clothes. He seemed to be ready for her as he reached into the bedside table of the hotel and withdrew a condom. She wondered how many of them he'd stashed there, and then remembered they'd gone through more than she could count in London. Would Berlin be the same? Would it be a blur of amazing sex and a growing sense of dependence on this man she knew so very little about?

But then his lips were on her neck and she forgot why she was so worried. Forgot to fear her growing feelings. All she could do was surrender to his white-hot touch, surrender to the need growing between her legs. She needed him, she realized. Needed this. He worked her body as if it was an instrument he was born to play, and as his hands kneaded her, she moaned, nearly losing herself.

He moved so that she could straddle him, and she sat up on him.

"Do you want to show me more tricks?" he asked.

She grinned wickedly. "Of course I do." She lowered herself down the length of him, taking him in, inch by inch, slowly, deliciously slowly. His blue eyes never left hers, and she could see the want in them, feel his desire grow.

Yes, want me, she thought. *Need* me.

She began moving slowly at first, rocking back

and forth, and he kept his hands on her hips, steadying her and himself.

"Do you want me?" she asked him, her voice a low purr. She kept her hands flat on his muscular chest and could feel his heart pounding as she moved her hips.

"*Oui*," he murmured, his lips parting.

"How much do you want me?"

He closed his eyes as she pulled him deeper, ever deeper, inside her. His blue eyes flicked open.

"Very much," he admitted.

"More than any other?" Now she realized it was her insecurity rising to the surface. Her jealousy. She wanted to be the only one that mattered. She was falling in love with him.

He flipped her over then, so that he had the upper hand.

"Do you want to be wanted more than any other?" he challenged. He withdrew from her, even as her knees fell open. She felt cool air against her thighs, and a disappointing emptiness. He rubbed his tip against her wetness, and she arched her back. He teased her mercilessly, when all she wanted was him inside her. *Now.* "Do you want me to want you, Asha?" he pressed. His thumb found her swollen clit, and she groaned.

"Yes," she managed, meeting his gaze. He pushed in an inch and she gasped. "More," she demanded.

"Admit that you have feelings for me," he said, moving his thumb faster.

"I don't," she lied. And he withdrew completely. This was maddening. He was driving her mad with desire, with lust, with need. She clutched at his arms. "Wait."

He pushed forward again, tip inside her, his thumb working the nerve endings in her swollen center, making her see stars. "Yes?"

"I want you…to want me," she breathed, and he pushed all the way in, touching the deepest part of her.

"I do want you, ma chère. More than I've ever wanted anyone." The admission pushed her towards the edge, and she felt her body awash in relief, and desire, and…love. "Come for me, so I can see your beautiful face."

He worked her harder, and she had no choice. A climax ripped from her, and she shouted, unable to contain the explosion of pure pleasure, as he worked his magic, and she succumbed to his spell. When she opened her eyes, he was looking at her with such reverence, as if she were a priceless work of art. Never had a man gazed upon her like that, and she feared, never would a man gaze upon her like that again.

He stroked her face gently. "Never come like that for anyone but me," he said.

"I'm worried I won't," she admitted, and he

laughed. He moved, flipping her so that he was flat against her back, and he entered her from behind.

"I want to be the best you've ever had, or will have, Asha," he promised her.

"Keep on like this and you will be," she murmured, worried that it might be true. That he would be the best sex she'd ever have, a man who vowed never to love another completely.

He worked faster, clutching her to him, squeezing her breasts in his hands as if holding on to them for support. Unbelievably, her own desire began to rise again. Would she come once more? This was insanity. She never knew her body was capable of this. But only with him. Only with this man. He nibbled her ear from behind and her logical brain completely shut off. Now was not the time to worry about the future. She felt a surge of pressure in her belly, the climax growing there. She was going to come. And so was he. They came together in perfect unison, and then Durand pulled her to him, clutching her like a raft keeping him afloat.

"I need you, Asha, like I've never needed anyone," he growled in her ear. "You are...you are making me want to love you."

"What's stopping you?" she challenged him, feeling a rush of emotion flood her.

"Do you want the membership or my love?" he asked her, nuzzling her neck.

"Maybe I want both," she told him.

"Maybe you can't have either," he murmured.

"Now you're the one who lies," she said, whipping around to face him. "You're the one not being honest with me."

"No?" Durand rolled away, and Asha sat up, fully naked. He stroked her hip and the side of her leg with one tender hand. His eyes roamed her bare body, possessive, appreciative.

"You are already in love with me," she told him. A look of surprise flickered across his face. Surprise and…fear. Had she hit on something true? She'd been teasing, but the look on his face told her maybe there was more to this than she thought. "I can read you, Mathis Durand."

"Yes, you can," he admitted to her, and he pulled her close for a kiss. She broke the contact, blinking. "But I cannot give you all that you want."

Asha pulled away from him. "You can give me what I want. And you will."

Durand laughed. "Do you always get what you want?"

"Always," she said with more confidence than she felt.

"And if I give you my heart, what will you do with it? Will you be careless like you are careless with…the other men in your life?" Durand pulled her to him, and she lay with her cheek against his chest.

"No, I would not be careless," she promised.

"Why would you give me one but not the other?"

"So this is about winning for you, is it?" Durand pressed.

"Is that what you're afraid of?" Asha asked.

"And if I asked you to be mine? Would you be mine? Are you ready to commit to me?" he asked her, rolling on top of her so they were nose to nose.

She blinked fast, her heart ticking up a notch. "What does that mean?" she asked, tentative.

"It means I want you, Asha. Only you. And I want you to be with me. And only me."

"Does this mean you love me?"

His lips parted, and for the briefest of seconds, she thought he'd admit that he did love her. Instead, he swallowed his words. "It means I cannot stand to see you with another man. Any other man," he said.

If he wasn't going to admit he loved her, then she was not going to commit to him, she decided. A wicked smile pulled at the corners of her mouth. "Well, then," she said and drew him near. "You'd better keep an eye on me. Make sure I don't wander."

Durand moved closer. "I intend on it." He glanced at her seriously.

"What makes you think you have the right to that?"

"Because it's true. You've gotten through my defenses." He sucked in a breath. "Asha, I'm powerless against you. I... I..." He paused. "I love you."

CHAPTER TWELVE

DURAND SAW THE look of surprise bloom on Asha's face and wondered if he'd gone too far. What was he even saying? He was falling *in love*? Sure, the two of them lay naked in the hotel bed, their bodies tired yet satisfied, but was this *love*? He'd sworn never to fall in love, but like so many things in life, reality had simply blindsided him. No, Asha had blindsided him. He'd never met a woman like her before, both savvy and calculating, and yet, at the same time, so innocent about so many things. He had told the truth: he was helpless to resist her. He loved her strong will, the way she fought to be included. He admired her fight, her determination not to take "no" for an answer. She was like no woman he'd ever met, and that's why he'd come to care for her. Beyond that. Come to love her. He wasn't just falling in love. He'd already hit bottom.

And she wasn't saying anything. She was staring at him, completely frozen.

"Asha?" he prodded. And then he realized that he'd gone further than she was ready to go. She wasn't ready to say it back to him. He'd overstepped and there was no walking this back. Not now. Not ever.

"I—I don't know what to say," she said, looking uncomfortable. And then he saw the hard truth: he might love her, but she wasn't sure of her own feelings. Not yet. At least, she wasn't willing to share them. He knew her body loved him. Maybe that would have to be enough for now.

"You don't have to say anything," he said quickly, to save his pride. The woman he'd declared his love for, the only woman who'd ever stolen his heart, wasn't prepared to take it.

"Besides, I thought Mathis Durand doesn't believe in love."

"That was before I met you." Durand wasn't going to lie. Not now. Her cold feet right at that instant only made him want her more. It only made him even more determined to convince her that they belonged together. They needed to be together. Now and always. "We are meant to be together, don't you see?"

"Why?"

"We are so alike, you and I. Both fighting for what's ours, it's us against the world." This was the truth of it. They were more alike than they were different.

"You sure it's *us*, not me against you?" she challenged him.

"Don't even joke about that," he growled, suddenly feeling possessive. The woman brought out a side of him that he didn't realize he had. Asha grinned, playfully, teasing him. The woman knew exactly how to push his buttons, how to make him want…more. "If you aren't going to tell me you love me, then you have to promise me you'll not be with another."

Asha blinked fast, and in that second, as he watched the emotions play out on her face, he realized she did care for him. More than she was willing to admit for now.

"You want to be exclusive?" she asked.

He thought about her reputation, of dating whomever she pleased, whenever she pleased, and understood that so much of her public persona wasn't true. "I don't want you to run off to any of your other pop stars or actors."

"You think I do that?" she asked him, eyebrow raised.

"I think that you like to make people think you do." He stroked her bare arm. "I want you, and only you, and I want you to be loyal to me."

"Or…? What will you do?"

He growled and rolled her on her back, climbing atop her so they were nose to nose. "I'll punish you." He nudged her nose with his. "And don't lie," he said, a slow smile spreading across his face. He pressed a bit harder against her. "And you *know* what happens when you lie."

"I'll be punished," she breathed.

"That's right." He pressed harder against her, as his own cock came to life again. He slid between her legs, poised and ready to enter. "So? Tell me you're going to be mine, and only mine." He nudged her and she sucked in a breath, but her eyes never left his.

"For how many nights?" A teasing smile played at the corner of her mouth.

"For as many nights as I say," he managed. And he searched her eyes, waiting for her answer.

"All right," she said at last, after she'd made him wait a ridiculously long few seconds. "But only if you promise...to punish me anyway."

"Of course, ma chère," he said, and then he entered her, hard, and she gasped, wrapping her legs around his lower back. He plunged into her depths, again and again, suddenly sure in the feeling that he'd at last found home.

Durand stood on the interior white balcony overlooking the massive ballroom in the Adlon Hotel, the crystal chandeliers hanging from the thirty-foot ceilings, as his Sphinx Society guests began to arrive and accept glasses of champagne from the elegantly dressed wait staff. This ball bore no dress code, so attendees wore all manner of colors, and the growing crowd below was ablaze in greens, reds and blues. Even some of the men traded in black tuxedo jackets for colored ones. Durand, however, wore his favorite black tuxedo jacket and white tie. He should be watching the flow of guests, making sure the gourmet hors d'oeuvres were ready to serve, but instead, he was searching the crowd for Asha. She'd left him that morning, insisting she needed salon time to ready herself for the ball. He'd hadn't seen her since early that morning, and he didn't like to be parted from her.

He wanted her by his side.

Durand played over the conversation he'd had in bed with Asha days before, worried he'd gone too far. It was damn near the closest he'd come to truly committing to one woman. He didn't believe in monogamy, and yet, he'd gone against that very core belief by asking Asha to be his. Only his. The most infuriating thing was: she hadn't given him a straight answer. *Keep an eye on her?* He wanted to scoff. She was known for discarding boyfriends and suitors faster than she could collect them. Plus, Durand wasn't entirely convinced she wasn't just playing to win, that she'd walk away from him the second she got what she wanted: this damn membership.

"Monsieur Durand?" a familiar voice behind him made him turn. He saw Madelyn, wearing a very low-cut, very form-fitting stark red dress that matched her lipstick. She had her platinum blond hair up in a French twist, and wore long, dangling diamond earrings. For most men, she'd be an absolute knockout, but he barely noticed her model-thin frame.

"Yes, Madelyn?" he asked, somewhat annoyed. He didn't want problems at the moment, didn't want to think he had a job to do. Instead, he wanted to see Asha. He wanted a real answer about whether or not she'd be faithful to him. Whether or not she'd take his ask seriously. She'd been glib about it, or diverted his attention, but he realized, tonight he needed to know.

"It looks as if we have a few members who failed to RSVP, but they are at the doors, and…"

Durand waved his hand, annoyed. "Let them in." He didn't have time for small problems like this. He needed to focus.

"Some of them have guests, and…they are former members, but not current…"

He sighed, annoyance rippling through him. "I do not care about these petty issues now." He turned and saw the stricken look on her face. He instantly felt guilty. Madelyn was a good assistant and did not deserve his bad mood.

"I am sorry, Madelyn." He reached out and took her hand. She glanced up at him, unsure. "I did not mean to snap at you."

"Are you feeling all right, sir?" she asked him, the uncertainty still in her eyes. "We usually have work meetings the week leading up to a ball, and you've been..."

"I've been engaged elsewhere," he finished. This was none of Madelyn's business, and yet, the look on her face told him she intended to make it her business. She blinked fast. He could see her struggling with the truth, with the jealousy. He'd let this crush of hers go on too long. He'd let it grow right under his nose. Maybe it had been flattering once, but now he realized that it wasn't fair to her or him to let it continue.

"I worry, monsieur, that you are becoming distracted from your work." And from her, the meaning was clear. Not that they ever had a real connection. It had all been in her head, and he was fine with letting her imagine what she would, as long as she worked hard for him. Durand realized how unfair he'd been. And now her feelings were interfering with her job, just as he feared they would.

"That is not your concern," he said.

"Isn't it?" She frowned. "I know you. I know what you're passionate about. You've spent your entire life building this society and you're going to let one woman distract you from it? Take away your focus?"

"My focus is where it needs to be."

"Is that why you invited her to the Berlin Ball? Is that why you look for *that woman* even now? When your focus should be on the other guests?"

Durand glared at Madelyn, feeling his face grow hot. "You forget yourself."

Madelyn lowered her lashes, not meeting his gaze. "My apologies for speaking out of turn, sir."

Durand wondered if the apology was sincere, and then decided he didn't care. Madelyn was a good assistant when she wasn't blinded by her feelings.

"Please don't let it happen again. You and I have a professional relationship—nothing more."

Madelyn nodded once, but still wouldn't look him in the eye.

"Do you understand that?" He took a step to her and lifted her chin with one finger. Her hurt blue eyes met his.

"Yes, I understand, sir."

"Bien. Then get back to work."

"Yes, sir. And there is a matter that needs your attention immediately. The Princess of Sweden wants an audience."

"Her suspension is still in effect," Durand said, sighing and regretting that one night in Prague two years ago. He might have gotten carried away that evening after one too many glasses of champagne. Of course, that was long before Asha.

"Yes, but she's waiting in a sitting room nearby.

She says she won't leave until she speaks directly with you. And she's threatening to call her father."

"Of course she is."

Durand let out a woeful sigh. Work, apparently, did call. He would have to find Asha later. "Fine," he said as he followed Madelyn away from the balcony and towards the sitting room.

Asha arrived in the ballroom wearing a snug, form-fitting golden backless gown, her dark hair wound up in an elaborate twist, diamond earrings hanging from her ears. After a day of spas and pampering, she felt buffed and polished from head to toe, her makeup pristine and not a hair out of place. Not that many could tell about her makeup, as half her face was covered with the golden cat-eye mask Durand had gifted her. It suited her face perfectly, however, the fit comfortable, and she wondered how he'd managed to find a mask that fit her so well. She wore gold from head to toe, and almost worried she might look too much like a walking awards statuette. Though she could tell from the sidelong glances of the men in the room that the form-fitting dress made the impression she wanted. The golden fabric of her dress draped across her lower back, held by two small straps around her shoulders. She opted for no bra and felt like she was pure liquid as she moved. One man eyed her with appreciation as she walked, a man who looked like he might even be a former president. But she didn't care.

The only person she wanted to impress was Mathis Durand. When she stepped into the elegant eggshell-colored ballroom with the crystal chandeliers and soaring ceilings, she searched the crowd for Durand, but found no sign of him.

Where was he?

She took an offered glass of champagne and worked her way through the actors, heirs and dignitaries, their identities all hidden behind gilded masks. Asha should feel glad just to be here with the official invite, smug in the knowledge that she wouldn't be kicked out. She could finally see what all the fuss was about, all the whispers and gossip. Yet all she wanted to do was find Durand.

She was getting soft. There was no other way around it. She took a sip of the expensive champagne and wondered whether she'd ever get her edge back. Durand had gotten under her skin, had become her new obsession. She could think of little else, and worried that she might never think of anything else again. Her organic makeup business almost needed to run itself this month, and she'd let at least half a dozen voice mails from her father go unanswered. All she wanted to do was focus on Durand.

Was this what love was? she thought.

Asha clutched her champagne stem as she moved

through the ball. There was something delicious about being anonymous, about moving through a roomful of powerful people without really knowing who they were, or them knowing her. The din of voices grew louder as more people packed into the room.

Where was Durand?

She flagged down a passing waiter. "*Bitte*, excuse me. *Sprechen zie English*?"

This was the extent of her German, picked up from her travels.

"Yes," the waiter replied, bowing his head.

"Do you know where Monsieur Durand might be?"

"I am sorry, Fraulein." He shook his head. "I do not know."

Asha bit her lip. "Thank you," she murmured, already turning her attention elsewhere. Where was Durand? Then, she caught a glimpse of him walking down the side steps, Madelyn leading the way. *She* wasn't wearing a mask, she noticed. She clutched a tablet to her chest as she led him away. Where was she taking him? Durand's face looked somber as he went. Society business? she wondered.

She decided to follow them. She wondered what it could be. A trespasser? A catering catastrophe? She held back a bit as she followed through the crowd, leading her to a narrow hallway near the kitchen, and a small double-doored office. She hung back as the door opened, peeking around the corner of the small hallway. She saw a striking blonde, wearing nothing but lacy underwear, reach out from the office and drag Durand in. She saw a flash of pale skin and pink nipples through the sheer lace, and then Durand was gone—inside the office. Madelyn stayed outside the door, her back to it, guarding whatever was going on inside.

Asha felt cold and then hot again as a dozen different emotions rushed through her. Anger, jealousy, hurt. Hadn't he just demanded her loyalty, her fidelity in bed? And now he was rushing into a Nordic goddess's arms? Is this what happened at all his parties? Maybe the society was nothing more than his own personal sex club. The thought made bile rise up in her throat. She'd go confront him. She'd tell him that he'd made the last mistake he'd ever make with her. She stalked up to the door, and Madelyn's eyes widened in surprise.

"Let me in," she told the assistant, who narrowed her eyes as she glanced up and down Asha's clinging gold dress.

"I'm afraid I cannot do that," Madelyn said, a triumphant look on her face. She was enjoying this. "Monsieur Durand is occupied at the moment."

"I saw," Asha said, voice clipped. "Let me in. Now."

"I warned you not to get too attached, Ms. Patel," Madelyn said, voice low and blue eyes narrowed.

"You are not the only woman using your body to try to get a membership."

Asha felt like she'd been slapped. The contempt in Madelyn's eyes cut right through her.

"That's not what I'm doing here," she countered.

"Isn't it?" Madelyn raised a knowing eyebrow, and Asha clutched one fist at her side. She wasn't prone to violence, but she had a sudden urge to shove this smug assistant.

"No, it isn't. Now, move aside."

Madelyn caught the attention of a security guard in a black jacket as he walked past the hallway. The black jacket pivoted and headed towards them. "Don't make me have Becker see you out," Madelyn said, nodding at the guard as he approached.

Asha weighed the options of making a scene and hoping Durand came out to save her and whether he'd ignore the commotion if he was too busy inside with the mostly naked blonde. As she debated, Madelyn glanced at her tablet in her hands.

"Also, you should know, Ms. Patel, that I believe Mr. Connor Henry, your former paramour, is here."

Asha glanced sharply at Madelyn. "What do you mean? Durand revoked his membership." Didn't he? That's what he told her, anyway. Had that been a lie as well?

Madelyn cocked her head to one side, a superior smile curving her mouth. "I believe he's in the ballroom now, or technically, the smoking room on the north side, if you'd like to ask him."

Asha hesitated. She knew she couldn't trust Madelyn. It was likely a trick. And yet... She glanced at the burly security guard in black, ready to do Madelyn's bidding. She had little choice but to leave. She might as well see what the hell Connor was doing here. If Durand felt so little about her, what really was the point in staying?

CHAPTER THIRTEEN

"PUT SOME CLOTHES ON, Your Highness," Durand instructed the naked Swedish princess, as she tried
to press her body against him mere steps from the
hotel ballroom. He didn't appreciate being am-
bushed in the small office off of the kitchen, and
there wasn't much room to maneuver here.

"Is that the way you treat an old friend?" Princess Lilly asked, blond eyebrow raised, as she thrust
out her impressive, gravity-defying chest. Durand
realized then that Madelyn had set him up. She'd
known about the naked princess. Had led him here
on purpose. To distract him from searching for
Asha. Were there no lengths that woman wouldn't
go? He'd thought she'd let go of her petty jealousy,
but now he realized he'd been wrong about that.

"This will not help reinstate your membership,"
Durand said.

"Come on now, I made one mistake." Princess
Lilly grabbed the lapels of his jacket.

"You tried to turn one of my events into a sex party," he said.

"That's just a little fun." She shrugged one bare shoulder.

"No. That is not what the Sphinx Society is about. If you want a sex club, form one yourself."

Princess Lilly laughed and pulled him closer. "You didn't seem to mind the sex when we had it."

Durand untangled the woman's fingers from his jacket, suddenly regretting his choice of lifestyle up until now. It all seemed so shallow, so short-sighted. He was here dealing with a woman whom he didn't care about, when the one he wanted more than anything was most likely wandering the ballroom by herself, fending off advances from other men. He was wasting his time here, just like he'd wasted much of his grown life until now. Avoiding love... Why? Because he was afraid. A coward. All he wanted to do was end this meeting as soon as possible so he could go find Asha.

In fact, he wanted to find her so badly, he thought he might have heard her voice outside the door. Or did he imagine it?

"Your suspension will be over next week, and then you can attend the year's Masquerade Ball," Durand said. This, of course, was the most sought-after invitation in the Sphinx Society, where all the guests went overboard with full costumes, outfits that made the Met Gala look...tame. "Unless you want to try to bribe me, and then I'll have no choice but to extend your probation."

Princess Lilly searched his eyes and then snatched her wrap dress from a nearby chair and pulled it around her. "I'm not trying to bribe you. I'm just being friendly." She glanced at him once more. "So, I'll be able to attend the Masquerade Ball this year?"

That's what she was really worried about, after all.

"Yes," he said and nodded. "So if that's all the business we have, I need to be on my way."

"Of course." Princess Lilly nodded her head and stepped aside. He threw open the door and nearly collided with Madelyn.

"Have you seen Asha?" Durand asked as he looked down the corridor but found it empty.

Madelyn glanced at her tablet, deliberately not making eye contact. "I believe she's searching out Connor Henry."

"What is he doing here?" Durand growled. "His membership is revoked."

"I attempted to tell you before, but…"

Durand recalled the conversation on the balcony, when he'd cut her off. She'd deliberately not led with the important news, and he'd been distracted by thoughts of Asha, and then with the Princess of Sweden. "You should have told me."

"I tried, sir." Madelyn glanced up quickly, but

then lowered her lashes. Her growing inability to separate her personal feelings from her work was becoming untenable. At a calmer moment, he'd have a very serious discussion with her about just that.

"We'll talk about this later," he said. "Where did Asha go?"

"I believe she's in the smoking room."

"Then, that's where I'm headed. We will talk about your insubordination later."

Asha saw Connor first, sitting in an oversized leather chair by the fireplace, brandy glass in another, and an unlit cigar butt in his mouth. He wore a simple black mask, and a red velvet jacket with black lapels. The small red-carpeted smoking room with the marble fireplace and the four chairs arranged in front of oak shelves lined with books seemed too small all of a sudden. Connor looked smug, his floppy brown hair was perfect, as usual, and he seemed every inch like one of the spies he played in the dozen or so movies he'd starred in. Asha glanced around for any sign of Kayli, that model he'd been dating, but found none. Had he come solo? And if so, why?

"What are you doing here?" Asha asked him, stalking right up to his chair and standing in front of him, arms crossed.

"I'm in Berlin for the premiere of *Gunshot*. And

it's good to see you too, Asha," he said, his brown eyes giving her a slow once-over, his dimple just visible in his cheek as he grinned. "You look good enough to eat."

"As if you'll ever get that chance."

"You sound a little jealous. I heard you went to the last party looking for me."

"Hardly worth finding. You'd better get out of here before Durand finds you."

Connor took the butt of the cigar out of his mouth and tucked it into the empty ashtray on the golden side table near his chair. Then, he picked up his glass of brandy and cradled it in one hand. "I'm not scared of Durand."

"So he did revoke your membership."

"I don't care if he did or not. I'm planning on enjoying myself." Connor pulled a phone from his pocket. "Selfie?" he asked as he gently put down his brandy glass next to the ashtray on the side table.

"Those aren't allowed. The first rule of the Sphinx Society is no pictures." Just as she'd finished her sentence, he clicked a photo of her.

"Give me that!" she cried, and lunged for the phone, but missed. He held it aloft, and when she got close enough, he clicked a picture of them together. "Stop that." She lunged again, but he once again kept the phone out of her reach.

"Why do you care? I've got many more pictures. Of former presidents, actresses, pop stars.

You name it. Most of them are still recognizable even beneath their masks."

"That's against the rules." Asha knew Durand wouldn't like it. Rich and powerful people didn't go to secret balls if they wanted their identities known. Durand would most certainly not like it. Not one bit.

"You can't do that," she said.

"Why not?" Connor snapped off his mask, that cocky grin plastered on his face. She noticed for the first time his nose was crooked and wondered why she'd missed the flaw before. "Why do you care?"

"Just give me that phone." She stretched forward. He held the phone to his chest.

"Take a real picture with me, and I will." Asha considered this. If she took the picture, then maybe she'd get the phone. And she could delete that one... and all the rest while she was at it.

"Fine," she managed, and she leaned in and smiled, as he clicked a selfie of the two of them together. "Okay, give the phone to me." She held out her hand.

"Give me a kiss first," he demanded.

The nerve. He was the last person on earth she wanted to kiss.

"I absolutely will n—" But Connor had grabbed her wrist and yanked her into his lap, laying a wet kiss on her mouth against her will. She struggled against him, but he held her in a vise grip, his tongue lapping at her closed mouth. How had she ever thought he was even remotely sexy? He kissed like a dead fish. Plus, he was a jerk. What he was doing was technically assault. She squirmed, but he held her fast, and as she worked to free herself, she heard a familiar voice behind her.

"Am I interrupting?" The French accent was unmistakable, and she knew even as she freed her lips from Connor's who she would find when she turned and scrambled off Connor's lap.

Durand was standing just a few feet from the chair, his face looking like he was only barely restraining his temper, his blue eyes flashing fire and retribution.

"Durand," she managed, realizing from the anger in his eyes that from his perspective on the other side of the chair, it probably looked like she wanted to be on Connor's lap. Not that she went there against her will. "This…this isn't what you think."

Durand didn't look at her. He kept his focus on Connor. "You're trespassing," Durand said, voice low and lethal. She could tell his whole body was tense, every muscle ready to spring to life.

"I'm enjoying a brandy in the smoking room of one of my favorite hotels," Connor said, crossing one leg casually over the other. "And I'm a guest here, so, no, I'm not trespassing."

A muscle at the side of Durand's jaw twitched.

"You should go, Connor," Asha warned him. "Why make a scene for your publicist? Don't you have a premiere to worry about?"

"Yes, it would be a shame if your publicity photos were marred with a black eye," Durand added dryly. But his face said he was deadly serious. Asha glanced at Connor and then back at Durand, both men frozen in some kind of primitive staring contest. Connor blinked first. Of course he would. He wasn't half the man Durand was.

"This room is getting too crowded for me, anyway." He stared at Durand. "Enjoy your *party*." He grabbed his brandy glass and then nodded at Asha. "Good to see you again, Asha. If you get lonely later, feel free to come see me in my room. I'm in 305."

Durand's nostrils flared just a bit, his eyes on fire, but he managed to keep his hands still by his sides, Asha noticed.

Durand cursed in French, beneath his breath, but Connor ignored the remark as he left the room, closing the big oak door behind him. He was just out the door when Durand exploded.

"What were you doing *kissing* that man?"

"I wasn't. I was fighting him off." She crossed her arms and turned her back to him. Durand grabbed her shoulder and turned her to face him.

"What do you mean?"

"He *forced* me into his lap. That's what. I was

trying to fight him off." She clenched her teeth. "That's more than I can say for you and the nearly naked what's-her-face."

Durand stopped then, dropping his hand from her arm. "What do you mean?"

"I *saw* you. The Nordic beauty in the expensive lingerie? Waiting for you in the office near the kitchen? You seemed to go more than willingly. And *you* were the one who talked of *me* being faithful."

"I didn't touch Princess Lilly."

"No? Not what your assistant told me."

Durand blew out a frustrated breath and turned, running both hands through his hair. "You cannot trust what she says."

Asha knew this was true. But she'd seen Durand go into that room with her own eyes.

"Why do you still keep her around? She's gone behind your back twice now, and she should've been fired ages ago."

"She's worked for me for years. It's complicated."

"Right. Maybe you have feelings for her, too." Asha snapped off her own mask and threw it on the ground. "Maybe I'm wasting my time and I should just go up and be with Connor."

Durand laughed, a growl. "You mean to make me jealous?"

"No," Asha lied, searching Durand's blue eyes, her heart hammering in her chest.

"You do." He took a step closer to her and she could smell him: the clean fresh scent of his hair pomade. He reached out and touched her wrist, and she felt the heat in the touch.

"I don't care if you're jealous."

"You lie, ma chère." He pulled her close now, her heart thumping as he pressed her body against his. "I can feel you lie. Just like I can feel your want." He pressed his hand against her bare lower back. "It's like a perfume, calling to me," he whispered in her ear.

"No," she lied again, trying to resist him, but his hands, the smell of him, his strength, they all tempted her. His hands teased her with the promise of what they could do to her if she let them.

"Admit to me that you want to make me jealous," he said, tightening his grip. He laid a gentle kiss on her bare neck, and a shiver ran down her spine.

"Why?" she asked, hoping to sound strong, but it came out a croak, a weakened plea.

"Because you care for me. Admit it." He traced her lower spine with his finger, dipping to the edge of the fabric draped against her lower back.

"Yes," she managed in a low whisper.

"Tell me that you do not care for Connor Henry. That he bores you."

She glanced up at him. "He bores me," she said truthfully, as Durand studied her eyes. In that moment, she knew he *was* jealous, that Connor had gotten to him. Interesting. It was a fact she could use later, once her senses returned, *if* they returned. Right now all she could focus on was Durand's gentle touch on her bare back.

"Tell me you will never have him in your bed. Promise me." Durand pressed against her lower back.

"Why?" she breathed, their lips close enough to touch. She glanced up at his blue eyes, ablaze with jealousy.

"Because you belong to me."

Asha laughed, though the merriment died in her throat. "And do you belong to me, as well? Or will you be fucking the next princess who offers herself up to you?"

"I do not want anyone else. I did not touch that woman. Nor do I want to touch any other woman."

"And I don't want any other man."

Then, he covered her mouth with his, and all her thoughts shattered into a million pieces. All she could think about were his lips on hers, his tongue lashing her own. How clumsy Connor had been, how unskilled. Not like Durand, who took her breath away, who made her knees weak with want. She pressed her body against him, and he clutched her closer, his hand roaming down the snug lines of her dress. His hands found the backless drape of the dress, and then they were inside her dress, against her bare bottom, cupping her, owning her.

"You are bare," he whispered, voice thick with want.

"A panty line would ruin the effect," she murmured back. Her dress was so thin and tight that she wore nothing beneath. Even the thinnest thong would show through. Plus, she realized, she'd planned for just this moment, had wanted to surprise Durand, give him a naughty little gift.

She clutched his neck, kissing him with a ferocity she didn't know she had, as he walked her backward. She went, and suddenly her back was against the smooth wall, as he lifted her knee up, pressing fully against her. He devoured her mouth and she wasn't sure where he ended and she began, all her thoughts on his talented tongue, his wet mouth. A desire, stronger than any she'd ever felt before, rose in her belly. She wanted him. No, she needed him. She needed him now.

Yet, would he break his own rules? After all, sex was not allowed at one of his parties. Absolutely against Sphinx Society rules. What would his rich and powerful members think?

Then, she heard the zip of his fly and knew he needed her as much as she needed him. He yanked on her skirt and suddenly it was at her waist, the cool air on her bare thighs. She barely registered the fact they were still in public, that anyone could open the door to the smoking room and waltz right in, seeing them as they were. But she didn't care. All she wanted was to be filled by him, now, owned by him right here in the small smoking room of this hotel. His very party guests right outside the unlocked door.

"I want you to be mine," he told her, his eyes hot with want.

"I'm yours," she managed, eyes flicking back and forth between his, just as he entered her, fully, completely, making her gasp with the shock of it. Her body accommodated him gladly, and she had no thought of anything else but him. His body, his cock, his mouth. She wanted it all, and she wanted it now. Her breath came hard as the wall beneath her back absorbed each and every one of his urgent thrusts, and she didn't care. He held her against the wall, deliciously pinned. She'd never been so reckless before, never had sex in a public place, as her heart raced with the naughtiness of it. Her climax was building in her before she could think to stop it, and as he took her, quick and hard, she found herself tumbling over the edge, into the pool of pure pleasure, biting her lip to hold back her cry. Durand came too, then, fast and hard and hot, burying his face in her neck.

The door creaked open then. "Excuse me, Monsieur Durand." Madelyn stood at the doorway, tablet in hand.

Durand withdrew quickly, zipping himself up. Asha pulled down her dress but not quickly enough. Madelyn had seen most everything, she assumed. She stared at Asha with a blank, unreadable face. A dark strand of hair fell into Asha's face and she pushed it back quickly, even as she pressed her sticky thighs together.

"What do you want, Madelyn?" Durand growled, protective, almost, as he put his body in front of Asha's.

"I'm sorry to interrupt, sir, but it's Mr. Henry. He took pictures of the guests."

"He what?" Durand adjusted his tie and scowled. "Did you call security?"

Madelyn nodded. "They've escorted him out now. But…"

"But what?" Durand's voice was annoyed, brittle.

"He sent Asha the photo. She's posted it on one of her social media accounts." Madelyn lifted her tablet and a photo of Asha and Connor came up. The one he'd taken when she'd been trying to take the camera from him. From that vantage point, it looked, of course, as if she was happy to pose with the man.

"I didn't post that," Asha said, taken aback. Somehow he had hacked her account.

"Is that you in the picture?" Durand demanded.

"Yes, but…" But she was trying to get the

camera. She was trying to help. And she'd never planned to post anything like that. Ever.

"Was this your plan all along? Did you just want to boost your own profile?" He glared at the account online. "You have already many thousands of likes."

His words felt like a cold spike through Asha's chest. How could he accuse her of that? This wasn't a ploy. This had never been a ploy.

"Were you and Connor even broken up?"

How could he ask that? Of course she didn't care about Connor Henry. How could she after being so fully possessed, fully pleasured by Mathis Durand? The two men weren't even in the same category. Plus, she wasn't in love with Connor Henry. Never had been. Why couldn't Durand see the difference?

"I am not working with Connor. How can you even think that?"

"I'm afraid I don't think that's true," Madelyn said softly, as her attention darted from Durand to Asha and back again. She swiped to another picture. "Connor just posted a new one." Madelyn showed the new picture then, one of Durand and Asha kissing, him pressing her against the wall. No nudity was present, but it was implied. The tag line beneath the photo read, "The host and his secret sex party?"

Durand cursed in French, and Asha could feel his anger, his rage.

"You planned this?" he managed, his blazing.

"No. Of course not!" How could she know that Connor would take such a picture? "I don't want that out any more than you do!" Her face grew hot. She imagined all the comments people would make, how it was probably spreading on every social media platform already.

"You were kissing him when I came in," Durand said, his suspicion clear on his face.

"He forced me. I didn't want to kiss him," Asha said, almost sputtering, feeling as if she were completely on her back foot, helpless against the onslaught of allegations, except that she knew she was innocent. She knew that as outlandish as it sounded, she'd been framed.

Durand paused, as if trying to work out whether to believe her or not. But he should automatically believe her. If they had anything like a real relationship, he shouldn't doubt her. Not like this.

"I didn't do this," she managed. "You have to believe me."

"Why? You haven't been honest with me. About your feelings. About your true aims."

"What do you mean?" Asha didn't understand.

"You played me all along. All you wanted was to increase your profile. Your followers. You never cared about me. About us."

"That's not true. It's not. You know it's not." Asha grabbed his elbow, but he shook her off, his

eyes ablaze with anger, with betrayal. He truly believed she'd plotted against him. But how could he
believe this? Did he not know her? "You can't believe this of me. I thought you loved me."

"I loved the woman I believed you were," Durand said. "I thought you were better than this. I
thought I knew you, but it turns out, you are just
like the reputation you fight so hard against. You're
just out for yourself, and no one else."

A small, triumphant little smile broke on Madelyn's face. Asha saw then that she'd lost. Whatever she thought she'd had with Durand wasn't at
all what she thought.

The insult felt like a shard of glass lodging itself
into her chest. "You can't believe that."

"We're done, Asha. *C'est fini.*"

CHAPTER FOURTEEN

A WEEK LATER, Asha sat in her father's huge office in his massive Cloud headquarters in Seattle and wondered what had happened. She'd asked a few of her contacts in the building if they'd figure out how her social media account had been hacked. She'd changed her password since, and had had no other problems, but she wondered how those pictures had managed to get there in the first place. She'd never betray Durand like that. She hadn't even *cared* about her social media presence since the two had met. She'd been too busy obsessing over Durand himself to even worry about what her follower count had managed to tick up to this week.

She stared out of her father's windowed office, to the gorgeous view of Puget Sound. A single seagull flew by, white wings outspread, and the sun glistened off the calm blue water. Her father came into his office then, his salt-and-pepper hair combed back from his forehead, wearing his company's casual wear of a logoed polo and jeans.

"Asha! What are you doing here?" He opened his arms wide, and she went into them, suddenly feeling emotion choke her.

"I wanted to see you," she said, hugging her father, leaning into the secure feeling of his strong arms around her. Even if they didn't agree on her career path, she still needed him. Her father hugged her back and then slowly released her, stepping back and studying her face.

"Does this mean you'll finally take over the company?" He looked so hopeful, but she'd have to dash his desires.

"No, Dad. I'm afraid not."

He looked disappointed for a moment, but then recovered. "I'll never get you to take over the company, will I?"

She shook her head. "No, you won't. But you'll always be my dad. And I need you." His face softened a bit.

"Come on, have a seat. Talk to me. What's wrong?"

She sank into his plush sofa near the beautiful view of the water. The rare sunshine glinted on Puget Sound.

"I fell in love. But I think it's all ruined," she admitted. She told him about Durand, about the

Sphinx Society, about the stupid pictures that some-how had been posted to her account.

"I deleted them, but they're already out there. People have copied them, reposted them else-where." She bit her lip. "I know it's going to be bad for the Sphinx Society. Already there are ru-mors that members are leaving the club."

"Simply because of a little publicity?" Her fa-ther shook his head. Her father thought there wasn't any such thing as bad publicity. That was one of the cornerstones of his business.

"It appears so."

"Have you figured out how someone got into your account? I can look into that." He took a seat opposite her, face earnest.

"I've got some of your people working on it al-ready." She shrugged one shoulder.

"You do, do you?" He shook his head. "And you say you don't want to run my company? Though you don't mind using its assets?"

"Of course not. I'm just practical. Just like you, Dad."

Father and daughter shared a smile. She reached out and took his hand, and he glanced down at hers covering his.

"I understand." He nodded and patted her hand. "I was just like you, you know. Headstrong. Stub-born. Sometimes…impossible."

"Hey!" she whipped her hand away in protest.

"*But* that's what makes us Patels who we are. I can't blame you for wanting to make something of your own. And do not worry about this Durand fellow. He'll come around."

"I'm not so sure." Asha remembered the look of betrayal on his face. The anger. She wasn't sure he'd come around at all.

"Well, you have an enemy, someone who is trying to undermine you with him." Her father studied her face. "And knowing you, I bet you already know who it is."

"Madelyn," she said, instantly. "She's his assistant. She's in love with him." Asha tapped her finger against her bottom lip, thinking. "But how did she get into my account?"

"*She* may have been the one working with Connor," her father suggested. "It's what I would do, if I were trying to discredit a rival. As for the password to your account, would he know what it was? Or, perhaps he just stole it from your phone. One of our competitors is working on such a technology. It's bringing corporate espionage to a new level."

"Really?" Asha bit her lip, thinking. If this were true, then it would all make perfect sense. Connor just wanted revenge against Durand for kicking him out, and Asha for…well, causing him to be kicked out, and losing the social status he so craved. Madelyn simply wanted Durand for himself.

With her out of the way, maybe she thought her odds would improve.

"*If* this is what happened, how do I prove it, though? How do I make Durand believe me?"

Her father leaned back in his chair, thinking. "Let me talk to some of my programmers. See what we can do."

Durand sat in his Paris office, staring at the Eiffel Tower out his window, but not really seeing it. He couldn't believe he'd been so easily played, so easily led by his emotions. Asha had played him from the start and he should've seen it. Should've anticipated it. All she'd ever wanted was to boost her own image, to gain more followers and make more money, even if it made him look like a fool. Or perhaps *because* it made him look like a fool. Maybe all this time she was just fooling him. Stringing him along. Playing to his weaknesses. He should've known better. He should've seen it coming. But he'd let his emotions blind him, and now, he was about to lose everything.

More than anything, he understood how his father must've felt. He couldn't believe he was feeling sorry for the man. Couldn't believe he'd actually take pity on him. Perhaps it was because he was about to lose the only thing his father had ever given him: the Sphinx Society, his inheritance.

And he was beginning to realize for the first

time in his life the power of love, and for the second time in his life, love seemed to be destroying everything. Maybe it would always get him in the end. Maybe it was a force he simply couldn't overcome.

All he could think about was Asha. She betrayed him. There was no other logical explanation. Even as he struggled to once again gain control of his feelings.

"Sir?" Madelyn popped her well-coiffed blond head in his office door. She'd left her hair long and loose, forgoing her usual tight updo, not that Durand cared. She could've pranced around naked in front of him and he'd barely notice. His mind was filled with Asha. Her betrayal. "Do you have a minute? We really have to find some way to control the slide. Members are suspending their memberships at a record rate."

He barely heard her. The fallout from Connor Henry's posts continued. Many of his rich and well-connected members were skittish, worried that Connor's exposing them would tarnish their reputations. Others were quitting simply because they felt he was a hypocrite, demanding that they refrain from sex during his parties while he partook all he wanted. Durand had worked hard all these years to make sure the Sphinx Society's reputation wasn't tarnished with lewdness, and now he'd single-handedly ruined it all by not being able to control his impulses, not being able to resist Asha Patel.

And it was all because he'd seen her in the lap of another man. His primal, protective instincts had taken over, blinding him to all common sense. And now he was about to lose everything. Or maybe he'd lost all that really mattered already. Asha wasn't returning his phone calls. What did it even matter if the Sphinx Society went under? Asha was all he cared about, he realized. She was all that mattered.

Madelyn was still talking, still running through messages on her tablet, but he was barely listening. He kept his eyes on the Eiffel Tower, his thoughts elsewhere.

"Monsieur? Did you hear me?" Madelyn prodded.

"What?"

Madelyn frowned. "At this rate, we'll have to call off the Masquerade Ball. Already, people are declining their invitations."

She showed him a string of texts from members, politely declining. He took the tablet from her and scrolled through them, barely reading them. She was right to be upset. The Masquerade Ball was the most prestigious invitation in the world. Declining an invitation was unthinkable even last week. Now, the idea of people turning up their noses at the world's best party was growing. Madelyn, frustrated, paced in his office, in front of his ornate an-

tique desk. Until, far back in her text history, he saw
a single number, not attached to a name. He hit it,
curious, and that's when he saw not messages, but
photos. Photos sent from Madelyn's tablet.

"What's this?" He glared at the photo, the one of
him and Asha in the study, so completely wrapped
up in their passion that they hadn't seen the pho-
tographer, hadn't bothered to notice the door had
opened. His mind worked out the puzzle before
him. The damning photo was one she'd sent. "You
took this photo."

"No! Absolutely not." Madelyn swiped the tablet from his hands, but he saw the guilt on her face.

"You did this. *You* betrayed me." Fire burned in
Durand's belly. He saw it all so clearly then: Madelyn's jealousy, her love gone wrong, and her complete irrationality about it all. How she'd cut off her
own nose to spite her face. She hadn't even cared
about what she'd do to the Sphinx Society. She'd
just been too threatened by Asha's mere presence.

Tears welled in Madelyn's eyes as she sank into
a nearby chair.

"No. I was…only trying to help."

"By sending Connor this picture? Tell me, did
you hack Asha's account? Or did he?"

"He posted the picture. He had some way of
getting into her account," Madelyn admitted. She
reached out to try to take his hands but he whisked

them away from her. The last thing he wanted was her touching him.

"You betrayed me."

"No! I was thinking of you. I was trying to free you."

"Free me?" he thundered, anger still pulsing in his veins.

"From this obsession that had taken over your life. Your good sense. You were not yourself. You told me you'd never love anyone, and so I knew you would never love me, but then *she* came and…" Tears choked Madelyn's voice.

So this was all about Madelyn's unrequited love.

"I was never going to love you, Madelyn," he said. "I thought you knew that."

"I did, and I was all right with that. As long as you never loved anyone. But…but…you love her."

"Yes, I do." The admission came instantly. Durand loved her still. And now…he realized that he'd pushed her away, accused her of betrayal, when she'd been innocent all along.

"She was too much of a distraction, Monsieur Durand. I am so sorry. Please forgive me. I…"

"No. You are not forgiven, Madelyn." He shrugged off her touch. "You are fired."

"No! Please." She clasped his elbow in desperation. He glanced at her white knuckles and all he felt was disgust. "Where will I go? Please?"

"I cannot trust you." He whipped his elbow away, glaring at her.

"But I—I love you," she managed, tears streaking down her cheeks. "I have always loved you."

"I have never loved you, Madelyn. I never will love you," Durand said coldly. "Especially now that you have destroyed all that I have built. You have sent away the only woman I have loved. Or will love."

A sob wracked Madelyn's whole body as she buried her face in her hands.

"Your services will no longer be required now or ever, Madelyn," Durand said, voice low. "I never want to lay eyes on you again."

CHAPTER FIFTEEN

DURAND STOOD IN the beautiful manicured grounds of the Le Chalet Des Iles in Paris, the venue granted to the city by Napoleon III, surrounded by Lake Inferior, and accessible only by boat. The moonlight glistened on the water, and Durand waited, watching the opposite shore for signs of life. The grounds and the chalet were bathed in beautiful twinkling white lights, and the effect was magical. It looked like something out of a fairy tale, and that was the idea. He glanced at the empty waters, feeling disappointment rise in his chest. The water was supposed to be covered with rowboats, manned by Masquerade Ball staff, an army of boats like the ones who'd ferried the twelve dancing princesses to their enchanted ball to dance the night away.

Behind him, the beautifully delicate notes of a quartet broke the silence of the night air, and Durand glanced at his watch, wondering how long he'd let them play to a nearly empty island. In the last

couple of weeks leading into the year's final and
most important gathering for the Sphinx Society,
hundreds of members had bowed out, rescinded
their RSVPs, made excuses about how they could
no longer attend. Durand knew the truth: they were
scared off by Connor's posts, worried that Asha's
social media feed had outed them. No matter how
much damage control he'd done, no matter how
many missives he'd sent explaining what had truly
happened, the tide had yet to turn. People were still
afraid to come to his party.

Durand glanced up at the waiter who stood at the
side of the lit outdoor ballroom, looking bored. He'd
put down his tray of champagne on an empty high-
top table. Durand moved towards him, and the waiter
snatched up the tray, eager to serve, and offered him
a glass. Durand took it, feeling morose, almost as if
he planned to toast the very last event of the Sphinx
Society. He glanced at his own cell phone, but found
he had no service. There was no way of knowing
if Asha had gotten his texts that morning, if she'd
gotten the message that Madelyn had been the one
to betray him and not her. He hadn't figured out exactly how she'd managed it, but he knew that Asha
wasn't to blame. But now that he'd accused her of
betraying him, now that he'd doubted her loyalty, he
wondered if she'd ever come back to him.

Love was a tricky thing, yes, but he had come to
the realization that he'd rather live a life with it than

without. He glanced back at the waitstaff, at various corners of the open, lit grounds of the chalet, and wondered if he ought to just cancel the party. He didn't need the staff of twenty to wait on him. This had been a mistake. He should've canceled the party from the start. He'd known the RSVPs were down to near nothing. But his own stubborn streak refused to allow him to do it. He still held out hope that the people would come.

Now, looking at the dark lake, absent of boats, he knew he was wrong. No one was coming. His dream, the society he'd spent his life building, was dead. And it was partly his fault. He'd built it up on a lie: that he could keep every member safe in secrecy. But no matter how many masks a person wore, eventually, the truth came out. Even if one didn't know what that truth was themselves. Asha had taught him that.

He finished the last of the expensive champagne and then thought of hurling the crystal glass into the lake, a vent for his frustration. But as he wheeled back one arm, a light bobbed in the distance. Durand stopped, midthrow, and squinted, focusing on the light. A lantern someone let go from the shore? he wondered. Then he saw what was happening: a single guest, coming to his party. He had planned for hundreds of boats to line the water, but here was just the solitary guest. He wasn't sure if he was hopeful or saddened. One guest? Who could it be?

Durand's heart thumped in his chest as he scanned the shoreline. He walked briskly to the dock, eager to meet the first guest, hoping against hope that somehow, Asha would be the one. Even as he told himself this wouldn't happen. Asha was done with him, and who could blame her? He paced on the dock, as the white rowboat slid through the water, the occupants too far away to see their faces. And even when they approached, all he could see was a golden mask, and a lady wearing gold. He strained in the darkness to see the outline of her as the boat approached. Could it be? Could he dare hope?

The lady wore a costume of a fairy in a ball gown, her clear wings stretching far behind her, the train of her golden gown flowing across the boat. Her long, nearly jet-black hair flowed down her shoulders. A fairy queen, he thought, regal and beautiful, and dangerously seductive with her low-cut gown. When the lady reached the end of the dock, the servant rowing hopped out, and helped her to shore, and as soon as she put a golden heel on the dock, Durand knew.

"Asha," he called, sweeping her into his arms.

"I thought we were *supposed* to be anonymous," she replied beneath the golden mask covering her eyes.

"I'll always know you," he said. "No mask can fool me."

"Is that so?" She pushed up her mask as Durand pulled her close. He kissed her and felt his heart thump in his chest. This woman was made for him. There simply wasn't another explanation. "I am so sorry, ma chère. You were not to blame for—" he began, but she shushed him with a soft finger on his lips.

"I know. My father's team discovered that Connor and Madelyn worked together to hack my account," she said.

"Can you forgive me for blaming you? I will earn your forgiveness. I promise you that."

"Earn it?" She arched an eyebrow. "How?"

"Spending the rest of my life bringing you pleasure, of course." He pulled her close and kissed her again, feeling his heart soar as she kissed him back, fully, pressing her body into his.

"We might never get any work done," she managed as she broke free.

"Work? What is this?" He grinned back.

"I don't blame you, Durand," Asha said, growing serious. "You were just protecting your society."

"Some good it did. You are the only guest this evening."

"Am I, now?" She glanced backward over her shoulder, and Durand followed her gaze to the opposite shore. One light came on, and then another, followed by another. Hope squeezed his chest. Those were…lanterns on boats. Many, many boats, all bringing party guests to the chalet. Soon, another lantern bobbed, and then another, as they pushed off from the opposite shore, an army of guests headed his way. He glanced down at Asha.

"You did this."

"I might have told a few of my friends that they'd be crazy to miss out on the party of the year. I hope you don't mind a few party crashers."

At this point, Durand didn't mind. Not at all. His party was saved. "None of them have invitations, eh?"

"They have one from me." She grinned. "And they're all the new up-and-comers, the new influencers, the *new* new money. They'd all love to become members if your *old* members don't care to join the society. And I bet, once they do, your old guests will come clamoring back for their spots."

"Interesting." Durand's mind turned as he thought of all the possibilities. "Maybe you're right. Maybe making it too secret was the wrong thing to do. Maybe it should be very, very public." Durand hadn't even considered the possibility before now, but it made sense, and it was the one way he could keep his society alive. "That would mean I'd change the rules."

"You make the rules. You can change them," she said.

"Change them with me," Durand said, grabbing her hand. "Be my partner."

"Partner?" Asha flipped her golden mask to the

top of her head and searched his eyes. "But I don't even have a *membership*."

"You don't need a membership when you're part owner. Will you? Please, Asha. I need you."

Asha bit her lip. "Does this mean I get a say in *everything*?"

"Fifty-fifty," Durand promised. "I want you to be my partner in business…and in life."

Asha blinked fast.

"I love you, Asha Patel." Durand clutched her soft hands, amazed how easily the words rolled off his tongue, because they were so true. He felt, for once in his life, that he was his true self with this woman. He wore no masks, and neither did she.

"I love you, too," Asha said, and his heart lit up with joy.

"I want you to be my partner in business, in life, in every possible way. Will you do me the honor of being my partner?"

"Mathis Durand, are you actually proposing to me?"

He hadn't even thought about that possibility before. Hadn't he sworn off marriage his whole life? But marriage, like love, seemed the right step. The only step.

"Will you be my wife?"

"Yes, of course, yes," Asha replied, and then threw her arms around his neck and pulled him down for a kiss.

EPILOGUE

A year later

THE GUESTS CROWDED the golden ballroom of one of Stockholm's most premiere destinations, the Grand Hotel. Each one wore a golden mask, and their reflections in the mirrored walls made it look like the two hundred or so guests were many more than that. The scene was as beautifully breathtaking as it had been a year before when Asha had first met Mathis Durand, in this very ballroom, her first introduction to the Sphinx Society.

"Are you nervous?" her father asked her as he met her at the doors of the ballroom in his black-and-white tuxedo, looking still much like himself despite the fact, he, too, had half his face covered in a golden mask.

"A little," she admitted as she fussed with her white dress. This time, she'd blend right in at the white-and-black ball. Though blending in wasn't what brides were supposed to do. "The last time I was here, I wore bright red."

"I think white suits you better. You're a beautiful bride, darling," her father said, and laid a gentle kiss on her cheek.

Asha glanced once more at her reflection in the mirrored wall. Her original designer gown offered a full train, miles of hand-stitched beadwork, and a veil that completely obscured her face through thick white tulle. She could see out, but no one could see in.

Music began from inside the ballroom. "That's our cue," her father said, and offered his arm. She took it, the butterflies anxious in her stomach. Despite a perfect year with Durand, despite her absolute confidence he was the right man for her, part of her worried that somehow, somewhere, it would all go awry. She'd never felt this lucky before, this in love, and she worried that one day she'd wake up and it would all be a dream.

She and her father stood at the doors of the ballroom, and the guests parted, standing each to the side, making an aisle straight downward. At the far end of the beautiful room stood the reverend who would marry them, and Durand himself in a black tuxedo and white mask, looking striking and dangerous, and absolutely the man for her. She sucked in a breath and walked to the beat of the string quartet. As she approached, she saw his face light up, his blue eyes glistening with joy beneath the mask. Her heart felt as if it would burst from love, and she was impatient to close the distance between them, to have her hands in his, to become his wife.

She passed all the guests, their friends and family, beneath the masks, and shook her head. The event—and the reception afterward—had been the most hyped social event of the year. Thousands of people clamored for invitations, and the Sphinx Society had never been more popular. In fact, membership had tripled in the last year, and the two of them, partners in the business, had grown. It turned out, they made as good a team in the office as they did in the bedroom.

Asha felt a little thrill of satisfaction when she thought of the year to come: the social engagements, their "wedding tour" that would bring them to cities across the world, where Sphinx Society members wished to line up and raise a glass of champagne in their honor. Their wedding had turned into the very best thing that could've happened for the elite club.

Asha took another step closer to Durand. Another two steps and they'd be there. Her father paused as they approached and kissed her hand.

"You take good care of her," he told Durand.

"But of course," Durand said. "Though it is she who has saved me."

Her father withdrew his arm from Asha's, and

Durand stood before his bride. He lifted her veil, revealing her bare face. She wore no mask. Tears welled in Durand's eyes. Tears of joy and love, and Asha felt her own eyes grow wet with emotion.

"You are the most beautiful woman in the world, ma chère," he said. "You wear no mask, and neither shall I."

He took off his own and tossed it the ground, and Asha and Durand stood facing each other, without conceit, without masks to hide behind.

"Ladies and gentleman," the reverend in the white mask began. "We are here to celebrate the marriage of Asha Patel and Mathis Durand. First, these two would like to exchange their own vows." He nodded at Durand.

"Asha, a year ago, I met you here, in this very ballroom. You were then an uninvited guest."

"As I recall, you kicked me out," Asha said, and the whole room laughed.

"You might have come without an invitation, but you made yourself at home in my heart. You made your own home there. You have done what no other woman could, and convinced me of the value of love," he said. "You are my love, my world, and my savior."

Asha felt tears choke her. Surprisingly strong emotions gripped her, and she feared she'd cry out her mascara in front of all their guests.

"I promise to love and honor you, Asha," Durand continued. "I promise to be my real self with you, and never to wear this or any other mask." He pointed to the mask on the ground. "I promise to cherish you all the days of our lives, and I will be faithful to you, and only you. I promise you this, now and always."

Asha believed him, because he had been faithful completely to her this last year, and she felt secure for the first time in a relationship with a man. She'd come to realize that relationships weren't about power at all, that true love was about surrendering power. And as soon as she'd done that, she'd realized that everything would be all right.

He took a ring from his pocket, covered in diamonds, and slipped it onto her finger. "With this ring, I claim you as my partner, my wife, my everything."

Asha swallowed back her emotions, even as the light of the ballroom glistened on her ring.

"You have shown me what it means to love, what it means to truly give myself to someone else," she said. "I have made a home in your heart, and you have made one in mine. I want to spend the rest of my years building a life together with you. Because you are the love of my life."

"And I'm yours," Durand said.

"I couldn't have said it better," the reverend said. "Now, I pronounce you husband and wife. You may kiss the bride."

"I hope so," Durand said. "Come here, ma chère. Show me how much you love me." He grinned.

"Now and always," Asha said, stood on tiptoe, and kissed him. She barely heard the cheers and applause in the room, as all she could feel were Durand's lips on hers, and their promise of the years of happiness to come.

* * * * *

MILLS & BOON MODERN IS
HAVING A MAKEOVER!

The same great stories you love,
a stylish new look!

Look out for our brand new look
COMING JUNE 2024

MILLS & BOON

afterglow BOOKS

Afterglow Books are trend-led, trope-filled books with diverse, authentic and relatable characters and a wide array of voices and representations.

Experience real world trials and tribulations, all the tropes you could possibly want (think small-town settings, fake relationships, grumpy vs sunshine, enemies to lovers).

All with a generous dose of spice in every story!

OUT NOW

Two stories published every month.
To discover more visit:
Afterglowbooks.co.uk

LET'S TALK

Romance

For exclusive extracts, competitions and special offers, find us online:

- **f** MillsandBoon
- **X** @MillsandBoon
- **◎** @MillsandBoonUK
- **♪** @MillsandBoonUK

Get in touch on 01413 063 232

MILLS & BOON

THE HEART OF ROMANCE

A ROMANCE FOR EVERY READER

MODERN

Prepare to be swept off your feet by sophisticated, sexy and seductive heroes, in some of the world's most glamourous and romantic locations, where power and passion collide.

HISTORICAL

Escape with historical heroes from time gone by. Whether your passion is for wicked Regency Rakes, muscled Vikings or rugged Highlanders, awaken the romance of the past.

MEDICAL

Set your pulse racing with dedicated, delectable doctors in the high-pressure world of medicine, where emotions run high and passion, comfort and love are the best medicine.

True Love

Celebrate true love with tender stories of heartfelt romance, from the rush of falling in love to the joy a new baby can bring, and a focus on the emotional heart of a relationship.

HEROES

The excitement of a gripping thriller, with intense romance at its heart. Resourceful, true-to-life women and strong, fearless men face danger and desire - a killer combination!

From showing up to glowing up, these characters are on the path to leading their best lives and finding romance along the way – with plenty of sizzling spice!

To see which titles are coming soon, please visit

millsandboon.co.uk/nextmonth

MILLS & BOON
HEROES
At Your Service

Experience all the excitement of a gripping thriller, with an intense romance at its heart. Resourceful, true-to-life women and strong, fearless men face danger and desire – a killer combination!

Eight Heroes stories published every month, find them all at:

millsandboon.co.uk

GET YOUR ROMANCE FIX!

Get the latest romance news, exclusive author interviews, story extracts and much more!

blog.millsandboon.co.uk